Dassos Petrou

Soho in the Dark
3rd Edition

FICTION4ALL

This book is dedicated to John Watkiss

REVIEWS

Watkins Bookshop
Leading Esoteric Bookshop in central London
A fine addition to our London Mysteries section – stories that are full of local esoteric atmospheres that haunt the West End around Soho and beyond.

Atlantis Books
Historic Esoteric Bookshop, Bloomsbury, London
Well written short stories are rather more interesting when the author knows the landscapes – urban or otherwise they are describing. Dassos Petrou has worked in London's Soho and Los Angeles for years and his comfortable familiarity with them and the people who exhibit their 'creature' side when under pressure, especially when it is their damaging, fun for only them, creature, he records in 'horrible' and clever ways. He has seen Soho loose it's tatty image by day, becoming a Boho office space for a few years and now the globally corporate anonymous place of today. But the sex and sordidness that once only came out at night to satisfy punters has grown into a very strong egregore that they still feed. Most enjoyable.

CONTENTS

Dassos Petrou

Soho in the Dark

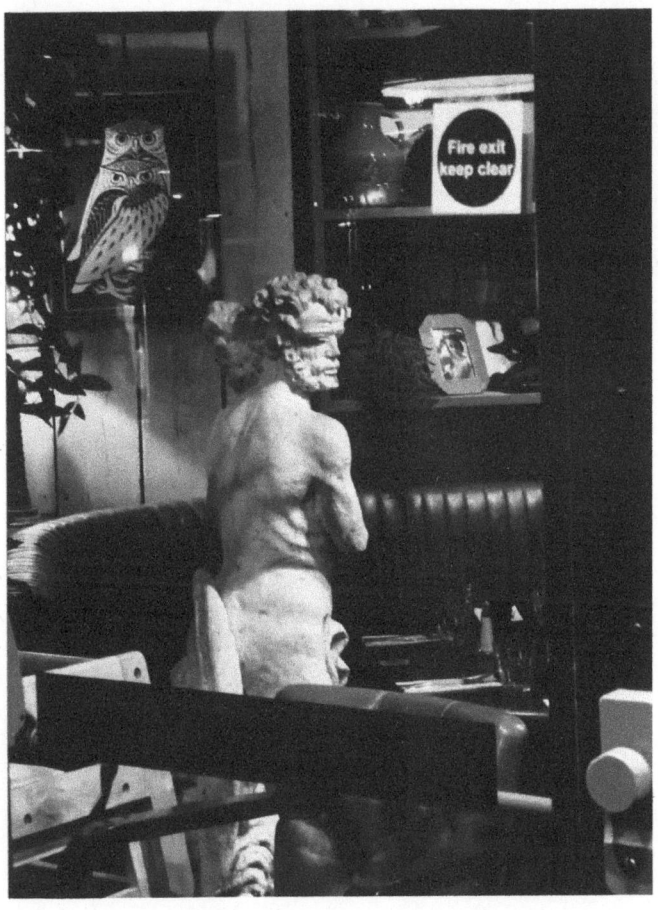

INTRODUCTION

Soho in the Dark is a eulogy to an advertising and media industry that existed in London for decades, primarily between Fitzroy Square in the north to Greek Street and Frith Street in the south, where they meet Shaftesbury Avenue. I was lucky enough to have been a part of all that in the heydays of the late 1980s up to the 2000s, by which time most of the advertising agencies had moved out to other areas such as Southwark, Clerkenwell, Shoreditch and beyond.

The title of this book refers, for the most part, to my story *The Resurrection,* although even in the tales set in LA and New York, Soho is an intrinsic feature.

The shadow of Philip K Dick falls heavily on these stories, especially with respect to his ideas on the nature of reality, his thoughts on metaphysics, and his understanding of intersecting alternative realities (the multiverse), which he constructs from his investigative readings on the advances made in quantum mechanics throughout the 20th century, as well as his interest in Gnosticism. His stories draw greatly from this fertile soil, particularly so in *The Three Stigmata of Palmer Eldrich; The Man in the High Castle; Flow my Tears, the Policeman Said; Ubik;* and *Time out of Joint* – all of which describe the consequences of metaphysical ruptures in the real world, that impact heavily on the psychology and inter-relations of his characters.

Aside from P K Dick, I have drawn on the works of many great writers of the supernatural, especially Arthur Machen, Algernon Blackwood, M R James, William Hope Hodgson and Sheriden La Fanu. I was also inspired by individual works by Shirley Jackson, William Peter Blatty, Henry James and Robert Aickman. And I cannot overstate the huge influence of Howard Philips Lovecraft, for his beautifully crafted and terrifying tales, including *From the Mountains of Madness* and *The Call of Cthulhu,* and his invaluable and unique essay, *Supernatural Horror in Literature,* which is where I first discovered Arthur Machen and Algernon Blackwood, along with many other masterful writers of strange fiction.

Last, but not least, I must include Edgar Allen Poe, who delved into the depths of the subconscious mind long before psychoanalysis came into being, to forge such powerful, dark and mysterious tales as *Ligeia, The Pit and the Pendulum* and of course *The Fall of the House of Usher*.

I hope that something of the wonder, mystery, and emotional power that I've worked hard to imbibe from these writers comes through in these stories.

ACKNOWLEDGEMENT

I would like to acknowledge the help and invaluable advice of Robert Hodgetts on all matters pertaining to Satanic ritual and invocation.

Dassos Petrou

14

THE CONNOISSEUR

Some things that should be obvious are so terrifying; you don't want to let yourself know them.

Jason Watts was an artist's artist. A genius. He owed nothing to the modern system of education, which he considered to be corrupt, pretentious and totally lacking in substance. In an era where modernist subversion and token sensationalism were the norm, Jason could draw beautifully rendered, anatomically perfect, classically inspired figures with stunningly, free-flowing finesse. It was easy to conclude he was born at least a century too late.

A highly respected figurative artist who taught him in his first year at college declared, "At the age of nineteen he can draw the human figure from his head better than I can from life!"

Even in his early teens he was driven by an obsessive nature, and from that time he spent years in an intense study of such dusty old tomes as *Constructive Anatomy by* George Bridgeman, *Anatomy for Artists* by Eugene Wolf, and *The Practice of Painting and Drawing* by Solomon J Solomon. These artist-authors were the last in their line. They understood what (for them) was the dreadful truth - Modernism was an unstoppable force that would soon suffocate traditional art, wiping out all the well-established Classical values and replacing them by a kind of anarchy. By writing down the long-established methods of their craft they hoped to preserve them, in the same way that the monks of the Pachomian monastery in Upper Egypt buried the sacred scrolls of the Nag Hammadi library after the draconian proclamation by Bishop Athanasius in 367 A.D. banning all non-canonical works.

Those (now-apocryphal) texts on the craft of drawing and painting were not written in vain because they succeeded in passing the baton. Through their teaching Jason Watts mastered the methods of long-dead Academicians, acquiring a detailed knowledge of human anatomy and perspective, and an encyclopaedic knowledge of traditional painting techniques, including scumbling, glazing and the application of mid-tones, half-tones, washes and highlights. Every specialism he needed to create the kind of art he had always loved –

beautiful, figurative, romantic painting – was part of his armoury, and he put these weapons to good use. His pictures were astonishing for their sophisticated technique and flourishes of bold embellishment. On seeing his work people were nearly always shocked to discover that, not only was the artist very much *alive*, but he was also only in his twenties.

Despite the accolades of the discerning few, Jason achieved very little success in the London galleries. He quickly discovered it was impossible to make an impression as a traditional, figurative, romantic painter in an art world hostile to those qualities. Subverting the long-entrenched principles of the Modern art world was like trying to bring down Everest with a chisel. Things had moved too far along the path of a politicized culture driven by aesthetic theory and supported by a kind of post-rationalism – leading to a preference for 'The Shock of the New'.

He kept up the good fight for a while, but in the end, he had to eat, so he wound up entering the commercial art and graphics field, where everybody he worked with understood and embraced his genius totally. Over the next few years, he created slickly rendered visuals and beautiful storyboards for ads, building up a phenomenal reputation in the process. Through that he came to the attention of the animation film industry. From there it wasn't long before he landed a three-year contract as a concept artist in Hollywood.

Leaving England to work abroad was not something he had ever geared himself up for – but the offer was too good to turn down. Life in Southern California was wonderful. But he and Rebecca had a habit of spending money like it was covered in lice. For a while, things were going incredibly well. He helped design two major features and created designs for several other productions. But when the time came for his lucrative contract to be renewed, it wasn't. So that was that. He didn't see that coming at all. It might not have been such a surprise if he'd stopped to remember how he always failed to sensor his personal views in conversation with colleagues, and even his superiors. Although he liked them all, he generally had a very low opinion of their talents. Jason never meant to upset. He was just honest. He always felt that he had full license to express himself as he pleased, for the simple reason that his astonishing talent was irreplaceable. But he was wrong, and like his great hero Michelangelo, who suffered from a similar talent for rubbing people up the wrong way, he missed out on the proper financial rewards his abilities deserved.

As if losing his job wasn't bad enough, his former employers took things to another level. They let it be known to just about every other studio that Jason Watts was more trouble than even his considerable abilities were worth. That became obvious when he started making enquiries around the different film companies to say he was available. Nearly all those approaches were cut short as soon as he mentioned his name. The two job interviews he did somehow manage to arrange were distinctly uncomfortable, because in both cases he found himself on the receiving end of cold, unsympathetic stares.

Soon it became clear, even to his limited sensitivities about such matters, that he had been blackballed. He felt shocked, humiliated and badly let down. It was so unfair. Who else could have done such original and masterful designs on those two films he'd worked on? Felix Beerbohm and Terry Swift, his art directors, were just jealous, that's all. Average talents joining together to defeat him, like ants swarming a cockroach. But there was no time to dwell on that now, not with his bank account being so dangerously low. There was no choice. He and Rebecca would have to give up their beautiful, spacious, home (with swimming pool, huge garden, and A-list neighbours) and acquire something more affordable. Rebecca was distraught, and was often seen about the house, in one corner or another, in tears. Nevertheless, Jason had to steel himself to do what was necessary, and within a couple of months, they had moved into a medium size, shabby, semi-detached house in La Crescenta, on the outer edge of Glendale. That bought them a little more time, but even then, it wasn't too long before they were struggling with bills again. Soon the only money they had left was barely enough for the price of their airline tickets home. They were now seriously considering throwing in the towel.

It was about that time when Stan Freeman rang Jason up. Stan was probably the most talented of all the artists still working at the studio. He was a big, burly, bearded Texan, who had been awe-struck by Jason's work from day one. He said he had a possible nugget to throw Jason's way, but he needed to explain a couple of things first. Jason immediately felt there was a catch, but they met up that night anyway at a smart bar in Melrose.

"So still no luck with the studios then?" asked Stan.

Jason pursed his lips and shook his head.

Stan nodded sympathetically. "Ok… well, you might find this interesting. Back before I got into the movies, I used to have an illustration agent. Nice guy, but a bit of an asshole, if you get my drift. So, this guy, Greg, he rings me up yesterday with a job. Well, you know… it would've been great if I wasn't so snowed under. But I got to thinking, it could be so perfect for my good friend Jason Watts."

Jason picked up his glass, took a sip, put it down, and wiped off the foam moustache with his sleeve. "Sounds interesting."

Stan ignored the subtly blasé nature of Jason's response. "It don't pay the kind of money you're used to. But it's not too bad."

"Pff. I can't be too fussy at the moment. Work is work"

"Damn straight, Jas. And it's not just an itty-bitty illustration. It's a goddam mural. I mean, we're talking large, fuck-off panels, they want painted in the classical-style. And wait till you hear the subject matter: stories from ancient Egypt, Rome, Greece – all that shit. Maybe nine or ten paintings – I can't remember exactly. This is a job you were born for."

Jason couldn't help feeling there was a catch. "Is it outdoor?"

"No. It's up in Gladstone Pines. Place called the Wynand Centre – sort of gallery and arts education centre for the local community. Not even a half hour from here."

"Could be good."

"I reckon."

Jason did his best, but he couldn't help looking glum. It was hard not to be after all the disappointment he'd been through since leaving the studio. Stan leaned forward and gave Jason a pat on the shoulder. Not knowing his own strength, it gave Jason a jolt.

"Hey man," he said. "Relax. There ain't nothing to worry about. Way I see it, you go and talk to the guy over at The Wynand and you'll be sitting pretty - guaranteed. You just need to hear what the fellow has to say. Remember, the devil is always in the detail."

The next morning, after a sleepless night, Jason plucked up the courage to call the number Stan had written down for him on the stained napkin. The phone rang for quite a while before it was answered by a secretary, who seemed friendly enough; jovial and worldly wise, and she was probably a grandmother. She checked through her diary and fixed up a meeting for Jason with Greg. That Friday Jason was sitting on a sofa in Greg's ninth-floor offices in Studio City. To cut to the quick, Greg joined him on an adjacent armchair and was knocked out by Jason's work samples, which he went through on the glass coffee table. He said that the work was perfect for the job spec at Wynand. But he did say that Howard, the guy who was the client, was a tough, no-nonsense fellow – although his bark was worse than his bite.

Howard Donnellon, the administrator of the Wynand Centre, had made his way up the pyramid through hard work, a no-nonsense attitude to life, a tough hide, and a strong, natural business sense. His father was a tailor in the garment industry. As a schoolboy, he made extra money working at a grocery store. Leaving school without qualifications he began selling radio aerials for cars and other electrical goods out of a truck he purchased from a neighbour. He eventually founded a general import/export wholesale company. In just a few years he had set up his first venture, manufacturing cheap sound systems using clever techniques to achieve lower production costs to undercut the competition. Manufacturing capacity was soon expanded, and he became a millionaire by his mid-twenties. Despite his lack of formal education, by his mid-thirties he had developed a very personal taste in figurative art that began to occupy him more and more. Through it he built up an impressive, if eclectic, art collection over the years, which included pieces by the French Impressionists as well as a few lesser-known works by John Singer Sargent, Édouard Manet, Joseph Sickert, Bernard Fuchs, Dean Cornwell and others. Eventually he indulged himself further in this diversion by founding the Wynand Centre.

The place didn't particularly stand out as an architectural masterpiece, being a pretty standard piece of stunted, block-like,

1980s California architecture, with a very plain white frontage. Jason drove just beyond it, parked up round the back and then walked around to the front entrance. Inside the small lobby a girl receptionist, who was far too young to wear glasses that were attached to a neck cord strap, dropped her pen as soon as he announced himself. Recovering, she stood up beaming and leaned over her desk holding out her hand. "Vanessa Hutchinson, Mr Donnellon's personal assistant.'

"Jason Watts."

Pleasure to meet you, Jason. Would you follow me please?"

They passed through two sets of glass swing doors into a modestly sized exhibition hall, with a smooth wooden floor, pristine white walls, oak panelled up to about shoulder height. A narrow, arched skylight ran the full length of the ceiling. Jason immediately knew that this would be an excellent space to create a mural.

At the far end, she led him through a wooden door into a small stuffy office.

"Please take a seat," she said. "Mr Donnellon will be along shortly."

She left the room with a friendly smile, closing the door behind her.

The room was poorly lit and slightly airless. He settled onto a 1970s, fabric-backed office chair. Between him and an oak swivel chair opposite was a large mahogany desk, with an ancient computer, four neat piles of paper, and an ink blotter next to an antique King James Bible. The window to his right had the blinds slightly open, creating striped shadows on a snarling fox's head, which was mounted to a small wooden plaque on the wall to his left. Behind the empty chair was an oak bookshelf crammed with antique hardbacks. He could make out a few of the titles from the spines, such as *Darkness Visible, Lucifer and Ahriman, The Ontological Proof of the Devil,* and *Paradise Lost.*

A gruesome but impressively executed engraving hung on the wall to his left, clearly a scene from Dante's Inferno, and probably by Gustave Doré. But he was unfamiliar with this image. He got up to get a better look at it. Some small type below the image revealed the title: *Dante and Virgil Encountering Lucifer*, from Canto XXXIV of Dante's Inferno. It also explained that the engraving was not by Dore at all, and was actually by someone called Cornelis Galle the Elder, after a drawing by Lodovico Cardi (both unfamiliar to him). Jason looked closer at the gigantic, leering, wide-eyed Devil, with three hideous faces, encased in ice, right up to his chest and gigantic bat-like wings spread out behind him. Staring madly, he ravenously devours three naked human beings, as if they were chocolate bars, and on the ice in front of him are the tiny, tiny figures of Virgil and Dante.

Jason considered how odd it was that people of extraordinary business acumen, with all their logic and hard-nosed pragmatism, were often suckers for this kind of fire-and-brimstone, superstitious mumbo jumbo.

His cousin, Rita was a typical example of that. She was an incredibly smart and very successful lawyer, ruthless in her business dealings. But she would spend thousands on things like palmistry, mediums and astrologers.

Just then a deep, gravelly voice broke his concentration.

"Ah! Jason Watts?"

Jason turned to see a fifty-ish man with military moustache, and slicked back, slightly greying hair. He walked over from the door to take Jason's hand with an extraordinarily firm grip.

"Howard Donnellon. Pleased to have you on board."

Howard gestured for Jason to take the chair he had been sitting in before and walked around to the large chair on the other side of the desk.

"Excuse my timing,' he said. "Meeting at my corporate HQ, over-ran. Had to drive back like a maniac from Orange County. Mind you, my wife says I always drive that way."

He sat down and then nudged his chair forward in a series of bumps. Satisfied with his perfect positioning, he moved a few papers around on the desk, and then rested his arms on it, and looked at Jason for what seemed an unbearably long time. Jason did his best not to look pensive. Finally, he spoke.

"Well Jason, soon as I saw those images of your work that Greg sent over, I gotta tell you…" he held out his hands with raised palms, like a statue of a saint, "They blew my mind. Couldn't help thinking of all those Renaissance greats – you know who I mean: Titian, Michelangelo, Raphael and so on."

21

Jason coughed in embarrassment. "Well, uh... thank you. It's a great honour to be associated with..."

"No really."

There followed another long silence, as HD tugged at his moustache, still looking challengingly at Jason

Jason tried to retain his humility as best he could, much as he loved compliments. His thin moustache curved down in a thin dark line to a small beard that grew below his jaw and just hugged the upward curve of his chin. It added poise, refinement and a sense of the dandy. Vincent Price would spring to mind, but he had cultivated it in honour of Velázquez. His small nose and calm intensity in his stare added to the look. His mouth was closed, thin and relaxed.

Howard gave up trying to analyse the expression. He decided to pick up where he left off.

"It's good to know that there are still people around with the ability to create beautiful art. I can't tell you what a relief that is. Too much junk is being held up as art these days. When we look around, we can see it clear as day – civilisation is becoming debased, culture distorted, roles inverted, standards eliminated, materialism and greed celebrated, and the moral tone is close to debauchery."

Jason was a bit shell-shocked by this barrage, having arrived there expecting to be quizzed about his suitability, education, qualifications and so on. He was not ready for Donnellon's personal view of the decaying values of artistic taste in the modern world, although he did his level best to hide his discomfort. Jason had his own views about all that, and he wasn't interested to hear anyone else's. Luckily, Howard was not known for his ability to empathise, so there was no danger of him picking up on Jason's disinterest.

"In the final analysis," he continued, "when a people can no longer distinguish truth and beauty from falsehood and ugliness, they are ripe for all manner of deception, oppression and enslavement.'

He took a large cigar out of a drawer and lit up from a desk lighter, taking in a deep puff before continuing. Savouring the moment, he closed his eyes, exhaled, smiled and continued.

"Tastes today are dictated by cultural vandals. And it's no accident. Not at all. It is my belief that this decay of our civilised values has been meticulously planned."

Jason coughed nervously. "By who?"

Howard answered his question in a roundabout way.

"That picture you were looking at over there," Howard pointed towards it with his chin. "Fantastic piece of work, don't you think?"

"I guess it is. At first, I thought it was by Dore, but it's not."

Howard continued, oblivious to Jason's last remark. "What it shows is the devil, let's not beat around the bush. Is that an accurate representation of him – or is it just a visual metaphor for what he represents? That stupid idea they ram down our throats of a red guy with the little horns, tail, pitchfork, you know; fire and brimstone that we all grew up as the standard version of the devil... paaah! Who knows what he really looks like?"

Jason wasn't sure if he was supposed to say anything, but Howard freed him from that necessity.

"One thing's for sure, he wouldn't stand out in a crowd, otherwise he wouldn't be able to do what he's been doing. We'd know it was him. Think about that for a moment."

Jason was starting to feel nervous. Could he be implying that the devil actually exists? It certainly seemed that way. Or was he an obsessive, and a bit of a crank?

Howard continued, "He's elevating and exalting public lewdness and vulgar anti-social behaviour to a place of respect, while vulgarising and lowering every higher moral value for the sake of convenience and personal gain."

Jason didn't have the courage to express an honest response. "Right."

"The way he's worked it, the sacred becomes a punch line. The sordid becomes a sacrament. The minister is a monster, but the sex worker has a heart of gold. He – I'm talking Satan, Lucifer, the devil, he's the one who profits from this celebration of self-contamination."

Jason was starting to wish he could wriggle out of this job, but he reminded himself of the money.

"Most people don't believe in his existence – the devil, I mean. That's fine. You may do, you may not. Me, I observe his influence everywhere."

Jason tried to look convinced.

"He's screwing around with our understanding of the world. Everything we see and feel has become warped and twisted: our loves, our freedom, everything. Especially our appreciation of all that is good, including the appreciation of beauty that we're all born with. Do you like what passes as art today? Huh? Huh?"

"Uh… not particularly."

Jason felt a bit cornered, but he wasn't being dishonest in his answer. He hated most modern art in galleries and museums. But he couldn't see why you had to attribute that to the devil, or any other supernatural entity. Jason felt that the causes for modern, imbecilic tastes were random. Maybe it was all down to the failures of the education system, today, or the impact of mass production and consumerism, and the faster pace of life. People don't have the time to think clearly and weigh things up in their heads.

"Come on, Jason. Be a bit more committed," said Howard. "These are important issues. Soon we'll all be living in a delusional fantasy world, where the devil and the dark elite who are nurturing his schemes, those 'intellectuals' who are supposedly smarter and more objective than the rest of us, rule from on high, with scientific precision and wisdom – dictating what reason is, what morality is, what beauty is. We have to call time on all that. And you're going to help us."

That really did put Jason on the spot. He couldn't help crossing his legs, interlocking his fingers around his knee, swinging his raised foot, and tensing up. Was he going to have to be a part of some kind of religious ritual, or exorcism, or something?

Howard's cigar had gone out. He lit up again and carried on where he left off, using his cigar as a gesticulating tool.

"It's my belief, Jason, that every time something truly *beautiful* is created in this world, the devil suffers a little defeat."

Jason raised an eyebrow.

"We want you to create something wonderful, an unquestionable masterpiece – a stunning mural that will glorify the magnificence of all that is great in the civilisation we inherited – and are in danger of losing."

Jason cleared his throat and said, "Well uh, it'll be an honour, sir. I'll certainly do my best."

"I'm sure you will, my boy. I'm sure you will."

Jason had an unconventional spin on the story of the rise of civilisation, so he was able to put together a remarkable sequence of images in the service of Howard Donnellon's brief. There were nine drawings in all, making a visual narrative starting from the first stirrings of conscious thought through to the rise of ancient civilisations, right up to the fall of Rome. The drawings were executed on large sheets of cartridge paper and done mostly in charcoal. The board of the Wynand Centre, were unanimous in their approval. Howard made a big, toothy grin and put his arm round him: "Jason - you just kicked Satan's ass."

Now it was time to paint the real thing.

The daily drive to the Wynand Centre was no big deal, and when he worked after 6 pm, (which he did most days); the drive back wasn't too bad either. Gladstone Pines wasn't a particularly interesting place: more of a suburb than a city. But he did appreciate the cooler climate up there and the spectacular views of the valley.

In executing this work, Jason was inspired by a whole range of artists, especially the Orientalists and Romantics, including Jacques-Louis David, William Waterhouse, Solomon J. Solomon, and John Collier. The panels were over five feet tall and eight feet wide, and the images worked mostly as diptychs.

It was towards the end of one particular day in September, while Jason was up the ladder adding a few finishing touches to the final scene, that an incident which would baffle him for the rest of his life unfolded. Anyone walking in there at the time would have seen him in his black polo neck, brand new, tight-fitting Levis, and the sharpest pair of polished black winkle-picker shoes you have ever seen. Standing below the ladder the points of his shoes peered out over the metal step he stood on, like miniature missiles aimed at the wall. He was in deep concentration. His huge forehead made more prominent by the fact that he was balding, even at his tender age. But he was receding in a very dignified and stylish way, so that he would comb his short black hair back from a sharp point.

Sally, the receptionist had already gone home and Vince, the caretaker, had taken over at the desk. Maria had already done all the cleaning and gone home. Vince was now waiting beyond the double doors at the far end at the front desk, for Jason to finish up so he could get on with his other duties.

Meanwhile, Jason was up on his ladder painting a milky glaze over the figure of Hermes, in the middle of the design, between the Gods and mortal man. At the top of the composition Zeus, Hermes, Poseidon, Aphrodite and some other Gods – all of them are looking down at the ordinary men and women below with awe and trepidation. The people below are no longer submitting to the divinity of the Gods. They're free, having evolved into intelligent, sophisticated, self-confident individuals, calmly enjoying the hard-won fruits of civilisation.

The gallery area was pleasantly quiet. Jason liked that. And no one could sneak up on you in there because the polished wooden floor was impossible to walk on without making, at the very least, a loud squeak in shoes, and a puff-puff-puff in socks. Even in bare feet you'd notice a flopping sound. Which is why he almost fell off his perch when he heard a theatrically loud cough from close by. Twisting to look down to his right he saw a medium size old man staring at him intently. The fellow looked to be (at least) in his seventies, clean-shaven, with a healthy mane of white hair drawn back from his forehead. He wore an extraordinarily wide lapelled, herringbone suit, silver and black tie and white shirt with a very thin grey stripe. Strangely there wasn't a hint of colour about him anywhere. He also held onto an antique, bejewelled walking stick, gazing at Jason with his upturned face, that was strong and owl-like, with a thin nose positioned high above the lips; and an aristocratic, domed forehead. His eyebrows were dark, well manicured, and far apart. The thin mouth was fixed with an expression of both disdain and self-satisfaction. The top half of his ears were covered by his hair, the chin was small and almond shaped, and the cheeks firm though thin. His flesh was so pale he was almost albino.

"It is a remarkable feat that you have achieved here, young man. Absolutely exquisite," he said in a pristine New England accent that sounded more English than anyone in England would today.

"Very nice of you to say," said Jason.

"It is the philosophical and historical content behind the work which impresses the most; not just in this particular scene," He gestured towards the painting Jason was now working of, showing the gods of Olympus looking down at mankind below, "but for the entire series. To me this visual narrative of yours is an open book. The images transcend even your, not inconsiderable, technical achievements, raising the aesthetic and intellectual sensibility of the whole work."

Jason wondered if this fellow was an out of work actor. Perhaps someone had hired him as a kind of prank. But who would do that?

"At the risk of sounding conceited, it verges on the tragic that there are so few individuals alive today with the requisite loftiness of mind to appreciate those sorts of qualities."

"Uh, right," said Jason, trying to work out how long this nut-job had been in there, studying him forensically while he had been peacefully unaware. The thought made him shudder. Jason hoped he'd go away, but that was looking less and less likely.

"It may interest you to know that I have met some of those people."

Jason stopped to look down. "What people?"

The fellow seemed to be indicating the Gods of Olympus with his chin. Was this some kind of joke?

"You mean them," said Jason, pointing to Zeus and Athena.

"Indeed."

Jason felt compelled to treat that affirmation with the incredulity it deserved.

"Oh, is that so?" he said, laughing out loud.

The old man thumped the end of his metal-tipped stick on the floor in a fury.

"Young man. When I tell you that I am on personal terms with these people I am making a statement of fact. Do not, I repeat, do NOT take up that tone with me again. You will come to regret it."

There was something conveyed at that moment to Jason that was in no way connected to the words the old man expressed. He was immediately aware of being in the presence of far more danger than he'd ever encountered in his life – and yet he couldn't say how he was so sure of that.

"B-b-but – they're *gods.*"

"I *know* that," said the old man.

Jason looked towards the window to see it was getting dark. He wasn't sure if he was shivering or not. There seemed to be a strange stillness over everything. Then the man's eyes gleamed as he broke the silence.

"You've definitely achieved a feeling of sublime grace with that image, particularly in the delineation of that exquisite group of naked dancers near the Acropolis."

Jason sensed that the ominous mood had dissipated. "Thank you."

"But I do have one particular concern. In the daytime scene, the dancers in front of the Parthenon, supposedly the Temple of Reason - are wild, and in a state of drunken debauchery. That seems to jar. And why are those giant figures of Aphrodite and Eros in the background of the night-time scene?

Jason shrugged. "No particular reason."

"Ha-ha-ha-ha. You are clearly playing down your knowledge of the mystery religions. Perhaps you are embarrassed or – more likely – being discrete. That is, of course, understandable. These learnings are not for the profane. Nevertheless, you have no secrets from me." He stared at Jason with a leering smile that sent a chill through his spine.

"And those other figures", the old man continued, "the ones in the night scene, they are dancing in front of the Delphic Oracle with obvious dignity and poise. That is rather odd, isn't it? Especially when you consider that they are performing in front of the temple dedicated to Dionysius – the God of wine, the passions, or rather lust and debauchery, as some would say. Have their states of mind been cooled somewhat by the presence of Apollo, the father of intellect and reason? Or am I right in my suspicions that you are knowingly depicting the supreme balance that can be achieved between the Dionysian with the Apollonian."

Jason felt naked. These were concepts he would discuss only with his closest friends, such as Alan, Geoff and maybe sometimes Debbie, and the independent filmmaker and artist, Morgan Blake. Denial wouldn't work. But he tried to play it all down. "Well, I have looked into that notion a little, yes…"

"Of course, you have my boy. And not just a little. It is obvious that you are deeply aware of these principles. Are you then, an initiate of one the higher orders?"

"Sorry?"

"The Royal Arch, or the Rosie Cross, perhaps?"

Jason shook his head. "I don't know what you mean."

"Or are you connected to one of the older bloodlines?"

Jason laughed. "I don't think you could find a more working-class family than mine."

"So then, you are a classical scholar - perhaps you studied at Oxford or Cambridge, or one of the Ivy League universities?"

Jason laughed. "You can't be serious."

The stranger seemed mildly irritated. "So how did you come to understand all of these truths?"

Jason shrugged. "I read a lot. I buy books, mostly from second hand bookshops."

"What books?"

"Lots of them. Battered old Penguin Classics even. For example... Euripides: he talks about some of this stuff in '*The Bacchae*.'"

"Stuff?"

"And in the nineteenth Century you have Nietzsche speaking about the Apollonian and the Dionysian a great deal, especially in '*The Birth of Tragedy*'. It's no big secret."

"Ah, I see. You're an autodidact."

"What's that?"

"A self-educated man."

"Is that an insult?"

"Mm. Not necessarily."

Jason was looking down at the fellow with incredulity. The man was impervious to Jason's glare. He took a business card from the inside pocket of his jacket and held it out expectantly.

"Roland Dockstader at your service," he said.

Jason thought it was a repulsive name. He was not in the least bit interested in taking the card, but was put on the spot, and felt it would have been extremely rude not to come down the ladder to collect it. Reluctantly, he wiped his hands on a dirty rag and walked down the ladder. Without even giving it a glance he put it the back pocket of his jeans. At that precise moment, the man moved impulsively forward and held out his open hand. Jason felt compelled to take it. It was like the hand of a dead man. His grasp felt cold, as if he'd just come in from a snowstorm, yet outside it was sweltering. He fought back an urge to dash out to reception and get Vince to come into the gallery to evict this madman. Then Dockstader interrupted, with more of these sweet and sticky mind games.

"You have certain qualities Mr…"

"Watts."

"Thank you. Quite honestly, your knowledge of the arcane is something of an anomaly. For an autodidact, you have raised yourself to a level reserved for, if I may say… higher individuals."

"What higher individuals?"

Roland Dockstader ignored the question. "The rituals you show in these paintings have been kept secret among the ruling elite for centuries. Take for instance the cult you depicted here," he pointed to a painting further along, "it was practiced in the Third Dynasty of Egypt. Let us give it its true name - Isis worship. Basically, the ancient, pagan, mother-worship rite and its priesthood were exclusively restricted… and its followers carefully selected."

Jason felt he had to snuff out this weirdo's flame. "Socrates had something to say about supposedly 'superior' types," he interjected. "Plato quotes him in The Apology: 'the men most in repute were all but the most foolish; and that others less esteemed were wiser and better'."

"How quaint," snarled the old man.

"The Cult of Isis", said Jason, "as far as I am aware, practiced social control, the subjugation of free will, and total exploitation of the people."

"Quite so," replied Dockstader, almost with a sense of pride. "That control model works very well. It was based on the pagan ceremonies of ancient Egypt and Rome, you know. The cult of Apollo comes from all that. You may have heard of the families of Rome who are called *the black nobility.*"

Jason leered. "Oh yes, them. They evolved over the centuries into the Venetian Black Nobility."

"Precisely. Today they're the power behind the western world."

Jason wished he'd never become involved in this discussion. He wondered if Vince would ever get up off his backside to come in and do his rounds, as he was supposed to have done half an hour ago.

"I know," replied Jason. "That's what the cult of Apollo is today. That's why I've painted it."

"Very good! Yes, the Roman republic and empire of their ancestors was controlled from Rome by the cult of Apollo, which you have depicted very well in your work. It was, of course, the chief method of fomenting debt in the Mediterranean, and it also acted as an intelligence service as well as being a cult – and was instrumental in creating other cults."

Jason nodded. He couldn't hide his understanding now. "From what I remember, in Egypt it fused with the cult of Isis and Osiris as a sort of direct imitation of the Phrygian cult of Dionysius."

"That's right," grinned Dockstader. "That was where they created the cult of Stoic irrationalism, which was based on Aristotelian Nicomachean Ethics. Your hero, Socrates was just an idealist. But Aristotle, as we all know, was a true pragmatist."

Now Jason's emotions were triggered. "Ha-ha-ha. And what kind of pragmatist was that? Not a very impressive one. He turned the growing belief that the sun - not the Earth - was really the centre of the universe on its head. He looked backwards to a time of ignorance. He proclaimed that the Earth was the centre of the universe. That makes him indirectly responsible for the death of Galileo in the 1600s."

Dockstader shrugged. "Not such a great loss."

Jason shook his head in disbelief. "You're joking, of course. In my opinion, what your 'elite' followers of Aristotle fear most is technological progress and an educated population. That would put an end to the possibility of total control of the masses by the elite."

Dockstader lowered his head slowly and lifted it to show another smile. "Which is why the methods that were used by the ancient priests of Apollo in ancient times, including the promotion of Dionysiac cults – featuring drug cultures, sexually motivated counterculture, and extremist anti-establishment fringe groups – to foment a demented rabble against progress, enlightenment and rationalism, are important."

Jason was horrified: almost speechless. "Important?"

"Please allow me to continue. There are today individuals, special people who, it must be said, regard most of mankind as less than human, which is (I hasten to add) understandable from their perspective. Indeed, one of my closest friends exhibits this quality admirably."

31

Jason frowned. "Oh? And what's so admirable about having disdain for mankind?"

"I didn't say my friend's attitude was admirable. If you listened carefully, you would have understood the point. What I expressed was the fact that she is a perfect *example* of someone who has disdain for mankind. An admirable one."

"Oh."

"Yes. A most remarkable woman, and a very dear friend, despite her few odd predilections. But then, which of us is perfect?"

"She sounds dreadful."

"Oh, no no no. She's delightfully creative and original. Charismatic to the extreme – and she has an extraordinary mind. Extraordinary. She's a very good friend. Smart and cultured, with a quick sense of humour. She's a governor of one of our finest universities on the East Coast. But despite her unquestionable intellect and political nous she can be quite irksome, although I do try to forgive some of her eccentricities."

"People are entitled to be eccentric."

"Ha. Most endearing of you to say. But I don't think you would be so defensive about her eccentricities if you knew the details. I myself despair of the peculiar urges she sometime entertains. But I do allow her some latitude because, after all is said and done, she is an inspiration."

"Well, I must get on…."

Roland talked over Jason, which irritated him, although he managed to keep his frustration in check. "Just recently, for example, she enticed two young children, a boy and a girl, to her brownstone home. How she achieved that is another story. I hesitate to describe how things developed from there."

Jason had a gut feeling whatever it was would breach the boundaries of good taste, and he wasn't wrong. Instinctively he braced himself.

"You see, my dear autodidact, soon after she procured these young people I went to visit her. I'd just been to see the marvellous Temple of Dendur, in The Sackler Wing, of the Met: built by the Roman Governor Petronius around 15 BC in Egypt and dedicated to Isis and Osiris, you know. My friend, well, she lives only a few blocks east of there. It had just stopped raining, and the sky was bright with a few long, black clouds drifting like battleships overhead. It was about six by the time I got to her brownstone dwelling. She buzzed me in, as she always does and I went right on up to her first-floor lounge, where she met me with a customary kiss on each cheek. She was dressed head to toe in Agnes B. As she went to pour me a glass of claret I sat down at the chaise longue. That's when I noticed two children, a boy of about nine, and a girl of about seven, chained by their wrists and ankles to the wall opposite."

"What? You're winding me up."

"Not at all. Well, as you can imagine, I was rather taken aback. But I was also curious about their rather luminous pink colouring. It wasn't until I went over to take a closer look that I realised their skin had been completely peeled away. The boy was groaning, and the girl was making kitten-like meows of pain."

"Oh, please." Jason lifted up the corner of his lip in a mixture of disbelief and revulsion.

"I'm stating a matter of *fact*."

"I-I-I don't… did you call the police, or what?"

"No. Of course not. She is my friend, remember?"

"Jesus." Jason's feeling of disgust was peppered with anger and frustration. The mix led to confusion. The only thought that made any sense was that he wished this person would go away. But no such luck. He was continuing the horror story.

"I did of course emphasise to Cordelia, (oops I shouldn't have named her, but I trust you are a cautious individual), I did emphasise to her that enough was enough and that her poor little victims should now be put out of their misery. However, even after a few days she had clearly not followed up on my suggestion. Quite the opposite. She went out of her way to perpetuate the situation by inserting various feeding tubes into them. She is, I'm sure you will agree, rather naughty."

"Naughty?"

Jason reacted as if he was chewing a lemon. Not only was this guy interrupting him in his work, but he was also giving him the creeps. The repulsive turn the conversation had taken was more than Jason was willing to put up with.

"Look mate," he said, reverting to his London vocab, "I really must be getting on. So, if you'll excuse me..."

The smirk vanished. "Please don't misjudge me. Of course, I do not condone her appalling behaviour, in this instance. In fact, I am repelled by it."

Those words of moral indignation were demolished by the subtle, self-satisfied smile that followed."

Jason took a moment to assess the insidiousness of this character before offering his succinct conclusion.

"Christ. You're a total nutter. There's no other way of saying it."

The smirk remained. "Not at all, my dear autodidact. Not at all."

Jason sneered; picked up the palette and brush he'd put down on his little side table and climbed back up the ladder.

But Mr Dockstader was not to be dismissed so easily. "Why be so angry? Rather you should try to see the bigger picture in everything. With your extraordinary talents, and knowledge you have the opportunity for a revaluation of all values. In the words of Robert Louis Stevenson, 'why man, do you know what life is? There are two squads of us – the lambs and the lions.' "

Jason looked down and spat out: "So what's that supposed to mean?"

"Accept what you are. The lions, my dear autodidact, are a different species from the rabble."

"Oh, I get it. You're talking about the difference between demi-gods and men."

"Indeed. And as your friend Plato declared in his Apologia, *'the demigods are the illegitimate sons of gods, whether by the nymphs or by any other mothers, of whom they are said to be the sons – what human being will ever believe that there are no gods if they are the sons of gods?'"*

"Look, you and your insane associates may see yourselves as above all men, but whatever you may believe, you're certainly not demi-gods. And ordinary are not rabble. We are all individuals, endowed with free will and consciousness."

"Oh dear – such a dismal way of thinking. Such a shame."

When he looked down again Dockstader wasn't there. In fact, there was no one in the gallery at all. But that shouldn't have been possible. Roland Dockstader couldn't have gone off without making himself heard. It's unavoidable. The room is echoey, the floor is wooden. You can hear a mouse crawl in there. Jason hadn't even heard the double doors click open, and swish back closed as they inevitable always do.

There was nothing else for it. Jason was baffled. He scurried back down the steps and went through those very swing doors to the tiny lobby. Vince was at the desk in his gleaming white shirt, with military epaulets and the ever-present red and blue plastic biro pen lids peeking out of the top pocket of his shirt. He was watching the ball game. A veteran of the Korean War, he may have been in his seventies, but he was built like a tank. He made an extraordinarily big smile by sucking his lips in, which loosened his dentures, which meant he had to stick out his tongue to push them back in place. Having completed that tricky manoeuvre, he made a little sucking noise, partly in satisfaction with the successful completion of a tricky procedure.

"How you doing Vince?"

"Good. What's up Jason? You came through those doors' kind of sudden. Everything OK?"

Jason sighed and said, "Yeah, uh sure. I just wanted to find out where that old guy went.

"What old guy?" Vince slurped up a couple of sips of coffee from his oversize mug.

"The old fella I've just been talking to in there. Is he in the bathroom, or did he just head on out, or what?"

"Sorry, Jason. You got me confused there. Who are you talking about?"

"The guy I've been talking to in there. You know… herringbone suit, full head of white hair."

"Have you been smokin' wacky-backy Jason, or what? I've had the security camera here next to the TV the whole time, and I can tell you right now, there sure as hell wasn't no one in there with you: not while I've been here."

Jason was open mouthed.

"What are you saying? I've been chatting to him for God knows how long – fifteen twenty minutes…"

"Fifteen… Jason. Listen to me. I'm watching the game, but I keep an eye on the monitor all the time, because my job's on the line, anything goes wrong. Know what I mean?"

"Sure."

"Well, there ain't no one been in the gallery but you, son."

"You sure."

"Sure as hell. Come over here."

Jason went around behind to look at the ten-inch by six-inch monitor on the cheap black swivel stand. Vince rewound the tape half an hour and then played it on fast forward. A grainy black and white picture came up, with the inevitable wobbly white bands going across the middle of the screen that come up when fast-forward comes on. The view was from the camera at the top corner of the gallery, high above the office at the far end looking down at the whole area. The huge empty wooden floor of the gallery was showing and on the far left of the screen was Jason up on his ladder painting – all by himself. There is no one else in there – at the foot of the ladder, or anywhere else. The numbers on the timer on the top left of the screen ran forward from 17.55 to 18.30. The only thing of interest was Jason coming down the ladder twice to get more paint, or to wipe his brush with a rag. At no stage was there any sign of an old man at the foot of the ladder talking to Jason.

Jason was confused. "No. That can't be right. The guy was right there all that time, until about a minute ago. So… you sure that's for today, that footage?'

Vince became a little angered. "Look, I know I'm no spring chicken, but I still have all my beans about me. Sure, it's today. Why would I have yesterday's screen playing right now?"

"But that's mad… because he was there, just now. I've been talking to him for ages."

"Jason. Listen to me, I don't rightly know if this is some kind of gag you're playing on me, but if you don't mind, I'd like to get back to the ball game."

A wave of uncertainty passed over Jason. It was the type of anticipation that comes before heavy rain, from the sense of oppressiveness and electricity in the air. Somewhere in his mind there was an idea that was totally elusive. It brushed through him, almost completely out of sight, oozing discomfort and dread, while remaining hidden in the shadows all the while. What was that? For a moment, he felt all at sea and could only stammer. He had to let go.

"Yeah… shit. Sorry Vince. I don't know what's up with me. I've obviously been over-working. Going a bit stir crazy too. I think I'll call it a day."

"You do that, son. Mighty fine job you're doing on that there mural. Looking beautiful."

"Thanks, Vince."

Jason went back into the gallery, cleaned his brushes and washed his hands. Back out in the car park he fumbled around for his car keys. When he pulled them out a little business card fell out onto the tarmac. He held it up close. It was black with shiny, gold-embossed type.

Roland Dockstader
ANTIQUARIAN
65 Prospect Street
Rhode Island 02906
Telephone: +1 401-454-5500

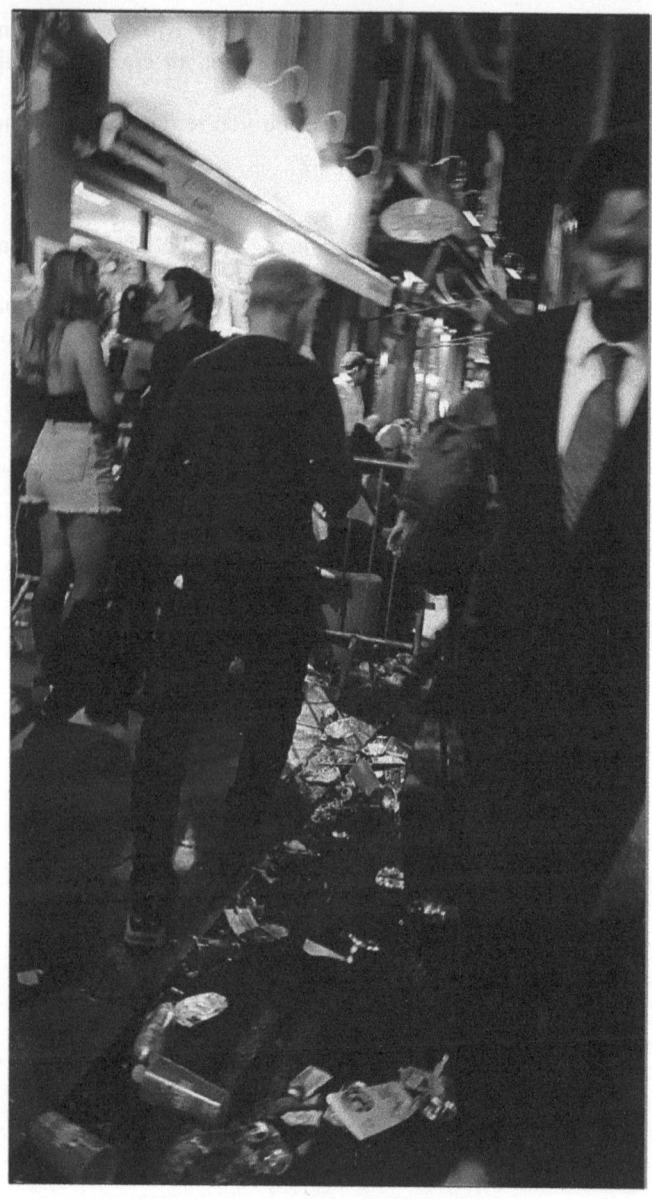

THE FORGETTING

There are sacraments of evil as well as good about us, and we live and move to my belief in an unknown world, a place where there are caves and shadows and dwellers in twilight.
Arthur Machen, The Red Hand.

There was this definite thought that there should really be nothing at all ever. That was obvious, straightforward and clear-cut. Nothing is all there is – and always will be.

Well, not anymore. Now there was *something*. It started with the blackness that shouldn't have been there. It was too much. Now it was everywhere in every direction. How did that happen? If that wasn't bad enough now there was now an awareness of the blackness too. It was so aberrant, it was perverse. There was fear happening somewhere. All of that requires thought. How was that possible? Where was it coming from? Suddenly it became undeniable.

"I'm doing it. It's coming from me."

And the change didn't stop there. The blackness was strobing, rippling – becoming unstable, tearing itself into strands, becoming brittle and then crumbling... leaving gaps. He was afraid of the spaces in between at first. They were bright. Then he became seduced by them. Now there were fascinating spaces through which the world of things started to be revealed. He embraced the change. These were staggeringly beautiful things, overwhelmingly rich with colour and shape, all of this emerging from nothingness.

Soon the blackness vanished, revealing the world of *things*. At first this was overwhelming, but then more and more 'things' became manifest. There was the wallpaper above the fireplace, which was thickly painted in a rich, matt, purple/grey. Landscape paintings were hung on the walls. Portrait photographs were propped up on the mantelpiece and to one side there were glass cabinets crammed with knick-knacks and old, hardbound books. Looking back at the shelf, there was a leaf green Art Nouveau vase filled with blood red tulips, and to the side of it a bust of a Roman Emperor. Diffused light came from a small, white polished glass sphere held up by the statue of a female nude. Above that hung a gilded, tarnished, Rococo mirror. The nearly burnt-out ashy pile of coals in the grating were covered with wriggly worm-like flecks of glowing red. In front of the fireplace a Persian rug was spread onto the polished wooden floorboards. Lying flat on that two were short metal crutches, the sort you have to put your wrists through when walking with a damaged leg or foot.

That manifestation made him worry again. Whoever those crutches belonged too must still be in the house somewhere. At the far end of the room, to his left, was a large bay window with rich velvet curtains which were not quite closed together. Through the gap, on the other side of the glass, were bare branches clawing at the moon.

Was this Crouch End?

"Where did that idea come from? I am thinking too fast. Slow down," he concluded. He breathed in. Paused. There was a definite but faint smell of stale incense. He lifted his head and discovered he was lying on a battered old, leather sofa that looked as if it had an exotic skin disease. A bristly blanket was itching his chin. He had no idea who he was, and he didn't have any inclination to worry about it. The fact was, he didn't want to be here any longer than he had to. Sitting up, he scooped the covering away from himself to find that he had been sleeping in his jeans and was wearing a sweater. This sudden desire to act was inexplicable. There were not even any flashes of visual memory. What happened last night? Was he at a party? Yes! That was it. But whose party? Why did he stay over? Did he come alone? He held onto that thought as he looked around. Were there people asleep in the shadows – behind the piano, or even under the table maybe? He thought not, though he had no clear reason to be so sure.

Upstairs maybe? Yes. He couldn't find justification for his conclusions, but that didn't stop him accepting them fully. Another thing he was sure of (without knowing why) was that he had to get out of that house immediately. In a panic, he heaved himself up and swung his feet onto the floorboards when everything in the room went out of phase. The ceiling appeared to become unstable, wobbling before spinning and then shuddering to a stop after several liquid pulses. But that wasn't all. Something was clawing away at him, scraping his insides. He arched his back and struggled to suppress a groan. A horrible burning sensation coursed through him in a wave, but the pain quickly subsided, and with its departure came fragments of memory. He recalled a girl, with short blond hair standing next to a guy in a cream-coloured Harrington jacket and blue jeans. They were both looking down at him – probably in this very room only a few hours ago. Who were they? What did it mean? Did it really matter?

He put on his boots, stood up, yawned, stretched out his arms and walked over to the slightly open door, pulling it slowly towards him. He stepped out into the hallway awkwardly, like a bad swimmer daring himself to step off the top diving board. To the far left a light was still on partially illuminating the terracotta-tiles. It was coming from a room that was probably a kitchen. He needed to have a piss, but he didn't know which of the closed doors would be the toilet. It was too risky. From somewhere up the stairs came the sound of snoring, which for some reason chilled him with worry. Turning around he crept slowly towards the oak front door, grabbing hold of the heavy chain, taking care that it didn't fall away with a clunk against the woodwork. He was lucky. No one had bothered to lock the Chubb, so he was able to click the latch down on the Yale, open the front door, and close it – all as if he were replacing the cover of an unexploded landmine before stepping out into the night.

Passing through the front gate he stopped to look at the night sky, and the cool air sharpened his thoughts. As he continued, he looked all around, studying the narrow side street, and he was struck by a moment of enlightenment: that was probably Ferme Park Road just ahead. A wave of pins and needles rushed through him, and he walked briskly towards it. He didn't know whether it was a sense of relief or elation. Turning right on what may have been Ferme Park Road he walked through a brick railway arch and arrived at a familiar parade of local shops. They must have been the ground floor of a row of dignified red-brick, three-story Victorian homes in the distant past. Now there was an off license, a newsagent, a butcher, an antique store, a launderette, and a greengrocer among them, but this street and all the other streets were empty of people.

Ahead of him the sloping roofs of tall Victorian houses concertinaed away towards the line of trees, high up on the hill around Alexandra Palace in the distance. He thought he should head in that direction, but with every step, he found it more difficult to connect his thoughts. He still couldn't recall his name, yet his deep sense of rootedness to north London more than made up for that, in that it helped to settle his rather erratic state of mind. The important thing was to head towards Wood Green. No reason really. He simply felt he should. Once he got there, he would know what to do. But unless he could remember where he lived, he could find himself walking around aimlessly the whole night long.

The thing was to try to focus. He was originally intending to walk the full length of Ferme Park Road, which ran like a spine through his life. Disconnected scenes played out: firework explosions in slow motion. Playing electric guitar as a teenager while his friend's mother brings in a tray of tea and biscuits; him again as a teenager in bed with an older woman while her husband is away: sitting upstairs on a bus with schoolmates on the way to the skating rink.

At the end of the parade, he stopped. The scene ahead had a hypnotic effect on him. Was the silence soothing or terrifying? He struggled to snap out of it. A road sign by a side street indicated a dead end. But when he looked hard it looked like there was a narrow alleyway at the side of a run down, red brick house in the corner.

He was tempted to take a closer look, but he didn't want to be diverted from his original plan, so he turned away to carry on walking up Ferme Park Road, and as he looked back in that direction, he couldn't believe what he was seeing. The road had shrunk slightly in length, and the line of trees at the top of the hill was nowhere to be seen. He looked behind in utter disbelief and things had changed there too. The road was now closed off by a row of houses that faced him, forming a cul-de-sac. Where was the railway arch, he passed through only a minute ago? How was this possible? It was as if the road was healing itself from a fresh wound. Feeling totally disorientated he turned ahead once more expecting to see the concertina of redbrick pointed roofs heading off into the distance again, only to discover that that wasn't there either. Instead of being straight the road now snaked a little and was blocked by a low flint wall just a few yards from where he stood. A thick, unkempt hedge rose from the back of it, and there was now a Romanesque church behind that. He was feeling even more entrapped than he had been in the house he'd just left.

What kind of civic planning allowed for this kind of street layout? It was madness. These changes were insidious. They had crept up on him. Ferme Park Road was never like this before.

It was becoming a strain to think clear thoughts, and there was so much strangeness going that he didn't know where to start. Nothing looked the same on second glance. What if that instability was to spread out to other places, like a cancer? The idea made him shudder. His thoughts swum around the idea of impermanence that waited for him, behind every wall, every corner, and every manicured bush. He became breathless with worry, heart pounding like it wanted to burst from his chest. Then he remembered that there may have been a narrow pathway in the shadows at the side of the house in the side street at the end of the parade of shops. It was covered with overhanging foliage. At the time, it seemed like a pointless exercise to check it out, but right now it was his only possibility of escape. Otherwise, there were nothing but dead ends in every direction.

He went back the short distance to that same side street and turned into it, walking as fast as he could, heading directly towards the corner he was thinking of. The lamplight here was weak. There was a small gap on the left of the end house there with a wooden fence at one end. He grabbed a fist full of foliage, that was mostly ivy growing from the large oak tree in the front garden and pulled it aside like a curtain. It revealed a narrow, cobbled alleyway, deep in shadow. He manoeuvred himself into it, breathing a sigh of relief. When his eyes adjusted to the darkness, he realised that it was long, and clear from that point on. Fact, walking through it was a bit of a squeeze, and he couldn't help brushing his shoulders on the wooden fence on the left and the brick wall on the right as he went. Pushing past a cluster of overhanging leaves a little further on, he made out a patch of light in the distance and felt a rush of excitement. There was a road cutting across the end of this alleyway, but beyond the tarmac and the far pavement there was only pitch black. Was it a badly lit industrial estate? If it was, he didn't fancy being around that kind of

Dassos Petrou

place at night. His imagination ran riot, and he wondered if the thick blackness might signify an abyss. Not in north London, surely? Near the other end of the alley, he made out some scattered blotches of grey, nestling inside the velvety blackness. At the very end, they resolved themselves into leaves and branches, which signified he was safe. The darkness was just a park of some sort.

Again, he had that feeling of being in a familiar place, but not quite. It certainly felt like East Heath Road, but there was something different about it. And somewhere within his entanglement of his swirling thoughts he wondered, how could an alleyway in Ferme Park Road link up to the other end of Hampstead Heath? The geography is impossible.

Across the road he saw that a stretch of grass that sloped out of the darkness up to the edge of the pavement. There were no railings to separate the road from the park. Inside the darkness the feeble streetlamps cast insipid shadows that fanned away from the nearest trees. Above them rose the upper storeys of a parade of Neo-classical, grand, Portland stone buildings of the early twentieth century, with two tiers of smaller rooftop windows inset into the long-tiled roof that extended along the whole length of the block, then a gap and to the right of that the huge, green copper dome of the Planetarium. They seemed so robust. So, imperious. He felt sure he'd be safe there. Marylebone Road was too established. Too cosmopolitan. Too dignified. That was a proper main road. It was a symbol of lost times, a return to a better world. Surely things would make sense again, wouldn't they? The geography made no sense at all but was desperate to get over there. Cutting through the park was obviously the quickest way. He could take that path (that he was pretty certain wasn't there before). It was partially lit by lamp light and probably went right through to the other side. The idea was tempting, like the sweet music of the Sirens was to Odysseus, calling him to their island, which he resisted knowing it was certain death. Gazing at the darkness beyond the visible section of the path he imagined how warped and demented things could become there. It was too risky. He would make his way around the edges of the park, until he reached the other side, even though it was a massive detour.

44

Across the road, to his right was a seemingly endless row of dignified and commanding turn-of-the-century houses, with raised front gardens and stone steps leading up to their main entrances. He felt awed by their architectural splendour but couldn't help thinking they were really nothing more than a formidable barrier funnelling him along a pre-ordained path. They seemed to be arranged like an endless line of tombs, yet they were probably full of happy, well-off families who were all sleeping peacefully and contentedly. The contrast between himself and those imagined individuals left him feeling sad, inadequate and alone. Operating in such a low gear, he couldn't think clearly enough to even recognise why that could be.

On and on he went, and it seemed like the park to his left and the row of large houses across the street would never end. However, there came a moment when he could see a Victorian mansion block rising above the dark mass of trees ahead. Despite all the unease he had been experiencing, he felt a sense of achievement mixed with relief. He started to run, head-down. In the corner of his eye someone in a dark blue Harrington jacket, khaki chords, and black Dr Martens shoes walked past going the other way. That would have been shocking if he wasn't so focused on getting to that corner. It was the first sign of another human seen since he woke up.

He stopped running to catch his breath, his mood shifting from a vague sense of anxiety and suppressed hope to one of relief. There were now railings separating the park from the street, and the road followed the eastern edge of the park. There was no question. And running across the other end of this road were the glass and steel buildings near Great Portland Street on Euston Road. He had come a long way further east than he had expected, but that was fine.

He crossed over to the Victorian mansion block, not least because he was fed up with hugging the edge of the park for so long, so. The gloomy light from the lampposts gave the large, red brick, apartment block the appearance of a stage set. Higher up the tall, bay windows loomed over balconies that stretched the whole length of the building, with ornate, cast-iron rails on the two levels below. All the front entrances were inside arched porches, ten steps above street level. As he walked alongside these buildings, things started to take on a different flavour. At the top of one of these steps ahead of him, he spotted a girl sitting in profile to him, on the low wall near a door. Again, it was pleasing to see another human being. She attracted more than his curiosity.

He soon realised as he got closer that she was young and attractive. She was gripping her right elbow with one hand and holding a cigarette from two outstretched fingers on the other. Although it was cold enough for him to need a scarf and coat, she wore only a lightweight, unbuttoned, grey, cashmere cardigan over a black Chanel dress. A cold gust of wind made her shiver. She breathed out a long plume of smoke, then gripped herself tighter, inadvertently pushing up her breasts. When he was almost level with her, he could hear muffled music coming out of the partially open front door beside her, and he couldn't help staring. In an instant, she was gazing directly at him. She seemed startled. Her eyes widened, while her eyebrows shot up and she immediately twisted round to crush her cigarette into the low brick wall. He quickly looked the other way and hurried along, hoping to avoid distressing her further. But it was no use. Behind him a girl's voice (it must have been hers) was shouting out, "Jason! Jason!"

He was worried she was calling out to a boyfriend to come out of the building and save her from him – this over inquisitive stranger – so he started to run. But it was no use. He slowed down, as a flurry of footsteps from behind came closer and he spun around, in the hope that he could think of something to diffuse the situation before he got a slap in the face. But almost as soon as he did that, a pair of soft, warm perfumed arms wrapped themselves around him. That same girl was standing on tiptoe in black ballet shoes, kissing him on the cheek. Her breasts were pushing into him, and it felt wonderful. He had no idea why this was happening. Confused and aroused he leaned back to get a better look at her face while she continued to cling to him. There was something familiar about her pale, ghostly skin, ruby red lips, shoulder length dark auburn hair. Even her large circular golden earrings.

"Well? Aren't you going to say hello, or anything?" she said.

Her, small green eyes and dark eyebrows, jangling bracelets and bangles were stirring up powerful, but fleeting images. This was the sweet and unfathomable Debbie Wright. The thing he recalled most about her was the feeling of perpetual disappointment. All she ever wanted from him was friendship. She had never invited any other kind of relationship. Among his group of friends at art school she was known as Little Deb, because there was another, taller girl called Debbie.

She said it again: "Jason?"

The smell of her last cigarette lingered. She was talking fast and breathlessly.

"Say something. What are you doing wandering around the streets this time of night?"

"I'm not really, uh…"

He pursed his lips and frowned, but she didn't wait for him to finish.

"So… do you have to be anywhere in a hurry? Please say no."

The best he could do was shrug and a smirk. It seemed to be enough. She grinned as if she'd just won big on a roulette table. This was really nice, but he couldn't suppress a feeling that something was not right about all this. Then it hit him. It had been more than twenty years since he last saw her, and yet she hadn't changed – not in the least. Down to the puppy fat and dimpled cheeks. That made no sense at all. But then an idea overwhelmed him that made no sense at all: this must be the real Debbie. Yes. Surely. He tried to work out what that meant, but her voice broke the spell.

She'd been talking and he hadn't noticed.

"And so, it's nearly over and everything, and it's only a works party. But that's OK. So… you coming in, or what?"

She raised her voice, in mild frustration, "Huh?"?

He had to say something. "Uh… so uh, what kind of party did you say it was?"

She frowned, as if struggling for the right words.

"Kind of a wrap party, I guess. Our Spring/Summer collection went out yesterday. There's a bunch of people from client side (most of them are OK, actually), the whole design team, of course, and all the buyers, sadly. And that's…"

She let go of him and put her hands to her hips, in an angry, matronly posture.

"This is so crazy." She pouted in feigned hurt. "It's been like... decades since I've seen you and you need to know what kind of party we're having before you come in and talk to me?"

Her voice seemed to be coming at him from a great distance – but it reached him. Several things that he saw and heard floated around his senses through a mist: he was like a drugged voyeur, watching events unfold on the other side of a theatrical screen.

"I-I'm sorry. I'm just... I'm not feeling right at the moment," he said. "I was going to..."

She put her finger on his lips.

"Sh. It's ok, hon. You can tell me later."

She put her arm in his and led him towards her front porch when, without warning, she let out a little scream. He had doubled up and fallen from her grasp onto his knees, like a penitent monk. She couldn't have known that his mind and body were on fire, as memories burned their way to the surface, flashing up at random into his consciousness. The pain went right through him, settling mostly from his stomach.

He remembered now. After Rebecca's death, selling the house and moving in with Alan and Jenny. They were so good. They took him in because he couldn't cope. He didn't want to be alone.

Debbie watched, worried and confused. His eyes had started to water.

"Can you hear me?" she said. "What's the matter love?"

She stepped around his back to haul him up by the armpits, struggling without success. Then she came around to face him and tried again. She managed to help him up off his knees. He sighed, dusted his trousers down, straightened up, and looked at her in embarrassment. The pain had now faded along with the memories.

"S-s-sorry about that," he stammered. "I'll be alright. Don't know what came over me."

She shook her head, smiled, and took his hand, leading him up the steps. It's not so much that he decided to go along with it all. There was just no point in resisting. That awareness elevated his spirits and refreshed him, to the point that the pain almost totally vanished. Curious.

A few moments later they entered the wide, carpeted hallway and she followed up by slamming the door behind her with her heel, giving him a squeeze around the waist. Had she ever been so affectionate to him before? He thought not, but he couldn't be sure.

Joy Division's *She's Lost Control* came from the third door along on the ground floor. The hypnotic bass vibrated through him. He wondered if there was a Byzantine ceremonial going on – maybe even a child sacrifice. Where did that idea come from? She led him inside. It was a surprisingly large living room – white walls, minimalist décor. A few fashion-conscious people (mostly in their twenties and thirties) were seated or standing around the edges of the room mingling. Only two couples were dancing. Obviously, the party was thinning out, but one person stood out like a sore thumb: a huge, bald guy, with the physique of a wrestler. He was wearing a tight-fitting suit. and sitting at the side of the table where the food had been spread. He sat with his fat legs spread wide, in a Neanderthal pose, holding a plate piled up high, and gorging a large sausage roll. His mouth was covered with crumbs. Unsurprisingly, no one made any effort to speak to him. He was obviously some kind of hired muscle, though why anyone would need security at a party like this was hard to imagine. After taking another large bite the ape caught his stare and returned it with an aggressive frown. He quickly looked away.

There were a few older women among the guests, and they nearly all wore beige, loose-fitting trousers and silk blouses. Only two couples were still dancing. Debbie was saying something. The music was so loud he couldn't make it out. She put her lips close to his ear and he could feel her warmth. She led him to a sofa and then went over to say something to the guy at the turntable. The volume came down to a tolerable level and she came back with a couple of glasses of wine and handed one over to him with a smile.

"Red any good?"

He took it gratefully. "Fine."

"I didn't recognize you straight away. You look different. Hair's going grey, and I'm not sure about those sideburns but... have you lost weight?"

He had no idea, so he considered for a moment. "Uh, maybe."

She frowned and then regained her flow.

"So, what have you been doing with yourself? It's been so long. I want you to tell me everything."

She put her glass down on the coffee table and pushed both hands onto his thigh, looking into his eyes with genuine warmth. The feeling was electric. So lovely. He tried hard to remember specific moments of his life in recent years, so he could give her the type of answer she was expecting, but it was hopeless. Still, he had to think of something.

"Well... hard to say. What about you?" It was the best he could do.

She laughed a little.

"Keeping your cards close to your chest, Jason Watts? Never mind. I'll get it all out of you later."

So, he was Jason Watts. So what? The name summarises a person who had memories he can't access. He was someone else now. In this state of mind, he was attuned to things differently. It was like a blindfold had been pulled off. Now he could see that everything was in perpetual flux. It was like riding a wave. Jason Watts? So what? You can't make a name mean anything momentous and useful when you're trying to understand an imminent reality in life. A label stops you thinking about the thing you're trying to label. Think about the thing. That's what he now understood. The more thoughtful thinking is, the more attuned to reality it becomes. Things were so much clearer. Purer, directed thinking gives you genuine meaning about what it is you're experiencing, even before it happens.

"But you haven't changed at all," he said with confidence.

"Me? Why would I?" She looked offended.

He wasn't expecting that.

"So, like I was saying," she said. "After two years in London I went over to Milan (which was great) - just as a sort of a dogsbody. Low pay, but good for the CV. It helped me get the job at Salamander when I got back. Hey, you know, I have been so lucky. I've worked on some lovely collections, and had some amazing PR in Vogue, Harpers, Marie Clare...

She stopped talking suddenly. A brown hand fell on her shoulder and stayed there firmly. It belonged to a small, middle-aged, pock-faced, man in a blue mohair suit. He was holding a large pink cocktail, with an umbrella a cherry, and a straw. He acted like he owned the place, which he probably did. A couple of underlings stood behind him, centurions with benign smiles.

"Oh hi, Shekhar," Debbie said, turning to see him. "This is my friend, Jason. We go way back. Jason, this is Shekhar, my boss."

Shekhar looked over at him, and pulled a smile you would have needed an electron microscope to notice, which he then followed up with a frown. Debbie felt embarrassed and squeezed Jason's thigh to compensate.

Much to her annoyance, Shekhar sat intrusively on the armrest next to Debbie and broke straight into work-speak. Jason understood none of it, which was obviously the intention. It had something to do with a photo-shoot that went wrong. She listened, asked a few questions and apparently reassured him. Finally, Shekhar stood up and went away, taking his followers with him.

When he was gone, she rubbed the hair on his head affectionately.

"Sorry about that. Shekhar gets very possessive of his staff. That's just how he is. He's been very good to me, apart from not giving me a pay rise in a couple of years. But that'll come."

Jason started to lose concentration again as deeply buried thoughts started to stir, but he managed to suppress them. Tears had been rolling down his cheeks. Debbie stopped to look at him in disbelief, took his face in both her hands.

"Oh Jason. What is it my love? My poor baby."

She leaned forward to push her lips into his, and they stayed that way for a while. When she pulled away, she held her face close to his.

"It's OK," she said, before kissing him again and standing up.

He felt chastened and excited by her tiny, soft green eyes. Is this where he had gone wrong in the past with Debbie, he wondered? Had he never appealed to her sexually because he was just too much of a lad, too insensitive?

"Let's go to bed", she whispered. "I live upstairs."

He smiled and she took his hand. He didn't know if he had ever been this happy before. They left the party without a single backward glance.

It was pitch black on the first-floor landing and there was a faint smell of disinfectant. Debbie flicked a switch. Some weak lighting stuttered on revealing a surprisingly large, open space. An empty area in the middle was illuminated, but the edges were left largely in shadow. To create all this space, the walls of all the apartments must have been knocked down. But how was that possible with all the strict planning regulations for these types of buildings? He had expected to see a long, narrow corridor with doors running off either side of it, as in all nineteenth century apartment blocks of this sort.

From what he could see, this large, open plan space reminded him of his old school hall, not just because of the scale, but also the parquet flooring, sash windows and oak panelled walls. In some ways, it felt a bit like a floor in Liberty. He spotted the upper part of a railing, which was part of a spiral staircase at one end, and there were dozens of clothes rails pushed alongside three of the walls. As Jason's eyes adjusted to the poor lighting, he could see that most of the rails were crammed with clothes, while others were a bit sparse. This was certainly not a living space. It was more like a warehouse than anything else. Or at best a hostel of some sort. Cardboard boxes and a few chairs were scattered all around too. But the weird thing was there were people busily at work in the shadows, moving clothes on hangers, putting away fabrics in a tall rack of wooden draws with glass fronts (the sort you get in men's clothing stores in St James. They looked like they had been doing that uninterrupted for some time. Yet how was that possible when just a few moments before the place was pitch black.

The entire wall on the extreme left of the large space was a glass partition. It was completely clear of boxes, chairs and clothes rails. Debbie led Jason over to it, and pushed at a section of it, which turned out to be a glass door. Initially it was dark in there, but she stepped on a foot switch and some dim lights faded up, they were inset as glass bowls in the ceiling. As in the other part of this floor, there were clothes rails and boxes in a haphazard arrangement. There was also a table with a reading light (turned off) a computer, and an old grey metal filing cabinet. This room (if you could call it that) felt like an office-cum-storage space in which someone had randomly deposited a double bed. Nothing about this whole setup made any sense.

"Is this your bedroom?" He asked.

She laughed. "No. It's my home."

He was quietly appalled, but he was also too eager to fulfil his imminent prospects to allow that line of thinking to persist.

He stood by the bed and watched Debbie as she walked around a stack of cardboard boxes to reach for something against the glass wall and drew down the venetian blinds across the whole glass wall, including the door. She then came back to kiss him and then let go hurriedly, to undress down to her black bra and panties. Without saying a word, he took off his coat and awkwardly started pulling off his jumper and shirt. She seemed so confident and happy, and her body was still young, her skin white, and her curves gentle as she climbed into bed and threw the duvet over herself. He followed her example of retaining a modicum of minimal modesty by keeping on his underpants.

"You coming in then?" she said as she flipped the duvet back for him.

After they had made love, she lay face down with her elbows bent, resting her head on the back of her hands. She seemed exhausted and content. He could not remember ever being this happy, and yet that wasn't saying much, because he could remember so little. He leaned up on his elbow and began to stroke her buttocks, and then he dropped back in stunned surprise. Standing behind the bed board looking down at him was the creepy, sweaty and pock-filled face of Shekhar, made even more creepy by a low light beside the bed, which lit up the roof of his eye sockets like a primordial cave. The security guy he saw earlier, chomping a pastry, was standing just behind him. Both of them were expressionless. Behind them were others, perhaps the hangers on he was with downstairs at the party. They were standing in shadow, so he couldn't be sure. He gasped in astonishment. How long had they all been there? Were they watching the whole time he and Debbie were making love? He felt humiliated and confused. But despite the embarrassment he jumped out of the bed naked, seething with anger and frustration. Rapidly hauling up his clothes and shoes from the floor, he scampered past the hateful voyeurs, stumbling over a stray chair leg as he went, yelling obscenities all the while.

Eventually he fumbled around and found a featureless white door at the back that opened into a tiny bathroom. It smelled of mould. There was a shower, a cracked sink, a nearly used-up bar of green soap, and a toilet. A dirty grey towel hung on a metal rail. He slammed the door shut, closed the lid on the toilet, sat down and got dressed. He didn't bother to wash.

When he finally came out Shekhar and his crew were foraging around some cardboard boxes and clothes rails, completely oblivious to him. He was still shaking from an adrenaline rush, but he opted to just get out of there. He didn't want any trouble. Debbie was still lying face down on the bed crying. He went over to take one last look at her flawless, milky skin. There was a large mole on the bottom of the left shoulder blade. Despite the scene that he had caused when he saw Shekhar and his cronies staring at them both, he felt that there was something else that was not right. This was not a normal reaction. She was so totally devastated, it was insane. There must be something happening here that he didn't understand. Each time she sobbed, her body shook. She was so helplessly emotional that she hadn't pulled the duvet over herself. It was barely covering the back of her thighs. Was she having a nervous breakdown? Her soft, reddish-brown hair completely obscured her face. He considered talking to her, to find out more – but his greater need was to get out of that place. He turned away, not even bothering to cover her naked body, storming out of the glass enclosure, tramping through the length of the shadowy warehouse to head down the stairs.

When he had almost reached the last step, a large figure came out of the shadows to block his way. It was the fat security guy. Up this close he stank of old sweat. The way he stood it was now obvious he was knock-kneed. Not even his expensive made-to-measure suit could hide that. His dark hair was slicked back, and his eyebrows were thick. He looked down, as if to admire his own black patent leather shoes, and his double chin spilled over his tight collar. Then his dead eyes came up into a fixed, cold, dark stare as he spoke through gritted teeth. He had a deep, gravely cockney accent.

"Where'd you fink you're going?"

His anger made him brave. "None of your fucking business."

The fat man grabbed him by the collar and dragged him down the last few steps to hold him up close. His face was now only a centimetre away. He was more or less growling now and spraying spittle while he spoke.

"Mr. Skekhar doesn't like anyone upsetting his people. You made Debbie very unhappy. Know what I'm saying?"

Jason shook himself away from the fat man's grip. "Me? You must be joking. It's you and your boss that did that. Staring at us while we were in bed. What was that all about? Fucking pervs."

There was no warning for what was about to come. The fat man sniffed and looked to one side, as if distracted, raising his right hand to wipe his nose with the back of his wrist. Suddenly he swung back and landed a powerful punch into Jason's face. As he began to topple back onto the stairs, the fat man grabbed his jacket and followed up with an uppercut into his stomach. Jason doubled up. There was an unbearable burning and clawing inside him. Then the fat man opened the front door and pushed Jason out, down the steps, then slammed the door closed behind him.

Jason fell face flat onto the pavement, blood flowing down his chin from his nose and mouth.

Alan and Jenny rushed down the stairs when they heard a thump from their bedroom. The smell of stale incense was stronger than ever now in the lounge. He was face down, spread out partly on the Persian carpet and partly on the wooden floor, close to the sofa. He'd obviously tried to leave the house, but didn't even manage to make it to his crutches. Most likely, he didn't even remember that he needed them.

Alan went to call for an ambulance, but they both knew it was already too late. Jenny sat on the sofa and burst into tears. Alan put the phone down and went over to comfort her.

"We did all we could, Jen. We couldn't watch over him 24/7."

Jenny sniffed and said, "The mixture of opiates they prescribed for his pain didn't mix with the high doses of cannabis he insisted on taking, thinking it would cure his cancer. He just had to go for an alternative cure, didn't he. Modern medicine wasn't to be trusted. Stupid, stupid, stupid."

They heard the ambulance pull up. Alan got up and went out of the lounge to pull off the chain and unlock the Chubb. There were two paramedics standing there, both big guys. They came straight in. One of them kneeled and held Jason's wrist, then looked up at his colleague and shook his head.

They carried him to the ambulance and invited Jenny and Alan to go along. In the ambulance Jenny had a phone call from an old friend, Rosie. She had called with sad news about an old college friend, Debbie Wright.

"What about her?" asked Jenny.

"She died in a car crash on the Archway Road on Tuesday."

"Christ. We're all dropping like flies."

She told Alan the news when she hung up.

"Shit. I remember her. Didn't she go out with Jason for a while?" he asked.

"No', she said emphatically. "But they were very close."

UNDYING TALENT

Through the huge bay window, the sun hung low over the turquoise sea, flooding the room with clean blue light. In the middle of the large, almost empty room, a slim, naked girl with long red hair stood very still, not even ten feet from where he sat. She had been like that for over an hour, making quick glances at the clock above the door every now and again, before turning her head back into position. One arm was raised above her head and the other rested on the back of a battered old wooden chair, where a piece of purple velvet was draped, spilling onto the wooden floor, where it gathered into complex folds.

He was one of five students sitting around her. Two of them were drawing on easels and the other three sat with drawing boards on their laps. The rest of the class had given up and gone back to the main building. These were the hard-core life drawers, but not all of them were any good.

When it hit six o'clock the girl dropped her arm to her side and shook her hands, to allow the blood to flow while she walked over to the wooden screen in the corner, where she would get dressed. Everybody seemed relieved it was over, but there was also a collective sense of achievement.

Imogen, who sat in front of the window and was almost silhouetted from Alan's point of view, theatrically leaned back over her chair, and stretched out her arms in a long, balletic yawn, like a cat seeking to be stroked. At that same moment Dick and Phil, who had been sitting to the left of her, put down their boards and wandered over to check out Alan's drawing. He sat with his drawing board propped up on his knees, while pretending to evaluate his final drawing, knowing perfectly well that it was good. The line-work was bold and confidently executed, the figure correctly proportioned, and there was none of that clumsy foreshortening and incorrect anatomy you get in most students' work. Without question, this drawing was mature – and full of weight and grace. And that was why Dick and Phil had so much praise for it when they came over.

Rosie Tushingham, who noticed this outpouring, wanted to know what all the fuss was about, so she got up and strutted over, pushing through Dick and Phil as if they were nothing more than curtains, to get a good look at it.

"Oh… that's so gorgeous," she said.

Alan was surprised more by the softness and warmth of her breath than her voice.

"Cheers Rosie."

"My drawing was rubbish today," she said, as she straightened up. I don't know what's wrong with me."

Alan twisted round to face her. No. There was nothing wrong with Rosie. Like all the boys, He couldn't help being attracted by her all-black outfits, Nico-Velvet-Underground-period-look, and her luscious, long, blonde hair.

"Come on Rosie. We all get bad days," he said, even though he long ago concluded her drawing ability was limited. She pursed her lips to one side, and frowned, still looking at the drawing and perhaps also weighing up weather Alan was being genuine or not. Even Imogen came over to get a good look, sidling up next to Rosie. By this time Phil and Dick had gone back to pack up their equipment.

"Oh. That is so perfect," she said with a pained expression, as if the drawing was discharging bolts of electricity. "You've captured her stance beautifully."

Alan's thick black rockabilly quiff wobbled as he turned around to look at her.

His eyes were deeply inset and in shadow, while his skin looked even paler than usual in the cool sunlight.

"Cheers Imogen."

Suddenly a deep, sonorous voice exploded Alan's aura of stardom,

"Ah! Is it already six?" it boomed. This was Raymond Jacques, the drawing tutor. He breezed into the room with his red silk scarf hung loosely around his neck, and his battered leather flying jacket left open at the front. He sat on a tall stool, slightly behind Alan, taking a tin of tobacco from his jacket while studying Alan's drawing. Imogen and Rosie took this as a sign to pack away their equipment. Raymond commanded great respect. His knowledge of anatomy was staggering. He could draw the muscles and bones of the figure you may have been struggling with in your drawing, and explain the mechanics of it all with great knowledge and ability. None of the other tutors could do anything of the sort.

He would say things like: "The foot is attached to the tibia - like that… and it articulates at the base. It's actually a lever. The fibula comes in on the outside and hinges to it here, like this." Then he'd draw another picture. "OK. Now, the gastrocnemius muscle attaches from behind the knee at the top and pulls the heel up at the back, while the muscles that attach to the base of the fibula at the front come down and splay out to attach to the front of the foot, like so. They are the ones that lift it up."

The students would bathe in the warm glow of his knowledge. He was the only graphics tutor who knew what he was talking about when it came to drawing the figure, which gave him an air of superiority, sophistication and quiet calm. But at that moment that last quality was absent. If anything, he was exuding despair – even sadness.

"That's a nicely resolved figure, Alan," he said, while dangling a pinch of tobacco over the Rizla paper. Raymond was Belgian, but something about his deep voice and foreign accent hinted towards the Slavic. He rolled the tobacco in the paper; using both hands then lifted it up to lick the sticky edge, before mumbling something.

Alan wasn't sure he'd heard right.

"What's that, Raymond?"

"I said we may as well all give up," he said, as he lit his thin roll up using an ancient, battered brass Ronson.

That was what Alan thought he'd heard. What did it mean? Raymond took a seemingly endless drag and breathed out a plume of smoke. Everyone waited with bated breath for further clarification, as he brushed a fleck of tobacco from his lower lip. But all he said was, "I've never seen anything like it."

Something about all this was really dispiriting. Raymond had left the conversation hanging. Alan almost didn't want to enquire further, but he felt obliged to.

"Never seen anything like what, Raymond?"

"That kid Jason Watts - he's made us all look like scribblers."

"I don't understand."

Scribblers: that was a word he hadn't heard since primary school. Was Raymond implying that the life drawing that was pinned to his board was in that category too – a scribble? He was certainly looking at it when he said that word.

"I'm a bit confused. Who did you say?"

Raymond shook his head almost imperceptibly and took a deep puff of his cigarette.

"Jason Watts. First-year student. I'm telling you... listen. In front of me he drew me a male nude, with the arms outstretched and a slight twist, weight on one leg. It was like watching a Renaissance master at work."

Imogen, who had been stuffing her layout pad into her bag at the other end of the room, looked up and responded.

"Jason Watts? He's a bit weird, but his work is like, just so amazing. He can draw *anything*."

Alan looked from her to Raymond and back again in utter confusion. Raymond raised his eyebrows and shrugged, in defeat more than affirmation.

"It's true," he added. "I've just come back from doing the course assessments for Year 1. Most of that year is pretty average. He's way ahead of everybody. I don't just mean the first years, I mean second years, third years and, let's be honest, the tutors too"

Alan felt like the camera was on him in one of those Hitchcock shots where you zoom out while you move in, creating a kind of vertigo sensation. He couldn't speak. In blank amazement, he watched Raymond shaking his head and staring into infinity as he continued:

"He can draw any pose from his head - better than I can from life. And he's just nineteen. Nineteen."

Alan looked again at his own drawing, the one that everyone had been drooling over a few moments ago. Now it just looked sad and inadequate. "Jesus," he muttered.

Raymond shrugged and took out his Ronson again from his top pocket to re-ignite his half-smoked roll up, then lifted it delicately from his lips to let out another plume of smoke, before closing his mouth and turning down the corners of his lips in painful contemplation. It was difficult to know how to challenge Raymond's defeatism.

"Could it be some kind of trick?"

Raymond coughed, before he replied. "Ha. Well, if it is, I'd like to learn it."

Alan winced and asked, "What's his name again?"

"Jason Watts."

"Hm."

Alan and Jenny lived in a first-floor flat, in the middle of a row of small Regency houses, between the grounds of an eighteenth-century church and the hospital. His live-in girlfriend, Jenny, was staying with a friend in London, which was a shame. He could've done with her being around, because he had left the life class feeling totally deflated. What a miserable situation to be in. To find yourself usurped by a first year. How was it possible? It didn't seem right. How could anyone be that good? Yes, some people are fortunate enough to be born with a huge reservoir of innate talent, but even then, they have to put in ridiculous hours of hard work and sacrifice to be anywhere near as good as the level of drawing ability Raymond was describing. People who are that obsessive tend to have under-developed persónalities. It's like those boring maths geniuses, with their slave-driver parents. The effort involved in becoming so much better than everybody else leaves them devoid of personality. Probably this Jason Watts character is just like that: boring, arrogant, quiet, and a bit shifty. Yeah. And another thing... these brilliant, ambitious types also like to keep their cards close to their chest, to cultivate a kind of fake, cold, reserve. They want to appear as if their phenomenal abilities come naturally to them, but really, they're just swats. An image of a slightly older, taller and skinnier version of the Milky Bar Kid, wearing gold, wireframe specs rose to the front of his mind. Alan was sure that he wasn't far from the truth. But right now, he needed to focus on tea.

Alan put the previous night's spaghetti Bolognese on the stove. Then he took a beer from the fridge and sat down by the coffee table and picked up a book on the work of Augustus John that was lying around. He opened it out to a double page spread showing a drawing of a nude girl that had been created with sweeping, sensitive outlines and rapid, pencil strokes for tone. She is face down, legs slightly bent, levering her upper body up with her elbow so that her left breast hangs down, sensually touching the blanket beneath her. It was a staggeringly beautiful and skilful piece of work, mixing knowledge, talent, subtly refined technique and experience with expression and sensitivity. How does anyone get to become that good? John was on a level very few artists had ever reached, when it came to figure drawing. Henry Tonks, his teacher at The Slade (and a great draughtsman in his own right) thought John had reached the same stratospheric standards as the Renaissance masters, Leonardo and Michelangelo – and he wasn't exaggerating.

In fact, Augustus John was good enough to get into the Slade by the time he was just seventeen. Even before he graduated, he was recognised as one of the greatest draughtsmen of his generation. Probably the third-year students at the Slade, who were in their twenties, would have been looking at the drawings of the teenage John and wondering why they bothered - rather like Raymond reacted to Jason Watts, and most likely he would too.

Jenny called after a while. He listened to her talking about the great photographs she'd taken in the north London dress factory, of all these sad, poorly paid and over-worked women. He told her about how much time he'd spent on his thesis, and how it was developing slowly. But he didn't say anything about the genius in the first year whose ability had caused such anxiety and despair to himself – and even Raymond Jacques.

That night Alan had trouble getting to sleep. Try as he might to find reasons to disregard what Raymond had said he couldn't ignore the fact that Raymond was never flippant about anything. His tendency was to find fault. He was even a little critical of a Rembrandt drawing once. So, when he said he was overcome by the brilliance of Jason Watts, he must have meant it. There was no point in denying that, so he was left with the solace of despair. But as he pondered the issue a little more he was overcome by curiosity. What were those incredible drawings like, the ones that had made such a powerful impression on Raymond? A kind of fatalism overcame him, and he sensed it could be a life-changing experience to find out, though he had no idea why he thought that.

In the morning, after brewing up a strong coffee and munching on some toast, he left the flat in his favourite red and black plaid shirt, his US-made Levis 501s and a pair of black DMs. This was his cool rockabilly persona. It was like wearing a suit of armour. Ten minutes later he came down the hill to the side of the long, slightly bowed glass and steel, Bauhaus-inspired art school building, which was bathed in shadow. He entered the foyer and walked purposefully up the main stairs, taking two steps at a time, not even stopping on the mezzanine to buy a layout pad and pencils from the college shop. Reaching the first floor landing he turned left, moving away from the stairwell to push through the plain, grey double doors leading to First Year Graphics. On the left of the corridor was a row of small admin offices. Opposite them were two very large rooms. One was First-Year Design, but the nearest one was the illustration studio. The door was open. He plucked up the courage to go in and approach the nearest person, who happened to be a skinny boy sitting at the desk in his cubbyhole (all students had their own desk, which was walled in from the desks either side). This particular lad sported a thick mop of blond hair, that made him look like a young Andy Warhol, which was probably intentional. Being completely engrossed in a dog-eared paperback, he didn't notice Alan. Alan coughed loudly. This caught his attention.

"Hi. Any idea where I can find Jason Watts?"

The kid looked up at Alan over his transparent frame specs and blinked.

"Huh? Yeah… yeah! Sorry. He's on the other side, just before you get to the desks near the windows."

"Near the windows?"

He closed the book up decisively (a Penguin edition of Sartre's, The Age of Reason) and stood up, as if having been sparked to life.

"Hold on I'll show you."

Alan followed him along a meandering route, among a narrow maze of desks. They came to a booth where a pretty girl with a neat brown bob sat on the desk swinging her legs. A tall, dark-haired lad in a gleaming white shirt, black drainpipe trousers and carefully polished black Oxford shoes chatted to her while pinning up some drawings. Alan noticed they were obviously photocopies of Augustus John's work, although he wasn't familiar with any of them.

The kid went up to the white-shirted lad and tapped him on the shoulder.

"Jason. Someone to see you."

With that he zipped off to finish his book. Jason stopped what he was doing and twisted around.

Alan held out his hand. "Hi."

Jason shook it firmly. "Hi."

Alan White. Good to meet you. I've heard a lot about you."

Jason laughed and said, "Doesn't sound good."

"Oh no. It was all very positive. It's not very often that Raymond Jacques praises anyone's work."

The girl exchanged a confused look with Jason.

"Better get my art history done," she said, totally ignoring Alan.

"Sure. See you lunchtime, Deb," he called as she left.

"So, uh… what can I do for you?"

Jason fixed Alan with his hazel green eyes, not so much in an unfriendly manner, as a deep curiosity. Alan had spent hours working out what he would say, and he tried to follow that script.

"I just wanted to introduce myself and, if you don't mind that is, get a look at some of your work. That's if you have the time."

"Sure. Are you an illustrator?" he asked.

"Third year," said Alan.

"Oh, right."

Alan studied his face for any signs of concern or evasiveness, but the opposite was true. Jason seemed to be delighted by the request. He was nothing like Alan had expected. There was no reserve, no coolness. In fact, the opposite was true. He seemed to be a genuinely warm and friendly soul.

As Jason opened the draws in the plan chest, Alan pointed to the drawings he had pinned up on the wall.

"I see you're a fan of Augustus John."

Jason was looking down at the time. "What?"

"I was looking at a book of his work last night," said Alan. "I thought I knew all his work, but I've never seen those ones before."

Jason got up looking confused. "Which ones?"

"Those."

"Where?"

"There."

He laughed a little. "Oh no. They're not Augustus John's. They're mine."

Alan was sure he misheard.

"Sorry?"

"He is a big influence, for sure, Augustus John, I mean. But I did those."

"You?"

Alan thought he hadn't heard properly. He was certain there was some confusion. "No. I mean those drawings on the wall there."

Jason nodded politely. "Yes. They're mine."

It was just like a custard-pie-in-the-face moment from a Laurel and Hardy film. Had he ever felt this stupid? Words swirled around in his head, but they wouldn't slow down enough to coalesce into sentences. He didn't know how long it took for him to say, "You uh... wow! That is incredible."

Jason Watts could have laughed out loud and humiliated him, but he simply waited for the truth to sink in so that he could show Alan some other work.

Alan felt as if he was in the presence of a deity. Over the next ten minutes Jason showed Alan a fantastic selection of drawings, including anatomical studies, pencil portraits (many showing people he had seen hanging around the college bar and several of the girl who was talking to Jason when he arrived). All of it looked as if it was executed by Augustus John. In the portraits, the eyes and lips were full of life and expression. Like John, he used fluid outlines, along with clean, parallel, diagonal pencil strokes for shadow. Alan was convinced that if he was still alive, even Augustus John would have believed he did them. They talked for another twenty minutes or so, before Alan had to depart for his art-history review. They got on very well, and Jason was pleased to have someone who could half draw really appreciating his work. They agreed to meet up at the Wheatsheaf when Jason returned from Paris, which is where the first years were going for a few days.

When he got back home that evening Alan was buzzing. He was also confused. There was no denying the incredible quality of the work Jason Watts had shown him, as well as the extraordinary facility he possessed. It was stratospheric. Frightening: and because of it, Alan's confidence in his own ability had been badly dented, probably beyond repair. There was no way on earth he could ever reach that level. Yes, he could improve a few notches, better than most mortals, but whatever he did, however hard he tried, he would always be looking up at Jason Watts. How could it be that a nineteen-year-old kid could draw in the exact style of a great master? Alan's wounded ego prompted him to suspect there must be something amiss about it. He rummaged around every corner of his mind to cobble together an acceptable diagnosis, but it was a hopeless exercise. What does it take to be that good? Was there a sinister secret behind Jason Watts' abilities? Could it really be some kind of trick, as he'd expressed to Raymond?

The first thing he noticed when he got home again was that a few more days of dieting had made a visible difference to Jenny's silhouette, which saddened him a little. He liked her puppy fat. She looked up when she heard him enter and squinted a smile that emphasised her tiny roman nose. She was pouring herself a glass of wine in the lounge. He walked around the table to kiss her on the lips. She showed him the bottle, and he nodded so she filled another glass and handed it to him. He raised it in gratitude and took a slurp. Her blonde, spiked-up, hair was now brown at the roots.

"Alan?" she pouted.

"Mm."

"I've just spent ages scraping that horrible, sticky charcoal sediment off the bottom of the saucepan."

He sucked in his lips and nodded. "Mm."

"Are you going to enlighten me?"

"Yeah, well, you know…that's not my fault."

"Excuse me?"

"When we were chatting on the phone last night you were just, you know… too interesting, so I forgot all about the saucepan."

"Oh, I see. So, it's my fault?"

"Looks that way."

She shook her head in mock despair. "I am going to kick you where it hurts."

She stood up. "We're having Bolognese again. Do you want to make some salad?"

While he chopped up the lettuce, Jenny stood by the stove, stirring the saucepan. She stopped to taste the sauce with the long wooden spoon, nodded, and then looked over at Alan.

"Fancy going over to the Feathers?"

"Why not?" He shrugged.

"Alan! You don't sound particularly enthusiastic. We don't have to go, you know. What's put you in this weird mood, have I done something wrong?"

"No! It's just, you know... shit, now I know how Raphael felt when he saw Michelangelo's Sistine Chapel for the first time."

"What do you mean? How did he feel?"

"He fainted."

"You're going bonkers. You haven't seen me for a couple of days and you're rabbiting on about Raphael and Michelangelo like I give a shit. I was expecting a bit more of a warm welcome. Are you having a fling?

"No! No way. I just, you know. I'm a bit shell-shocked – and depressed."

"Huh?"

"Do you know someone called Jason Watts?"

"Should I?"

Alan explained how Raymond came in at the end of the life class looking shell-shocked, talking about this first year that was so good that "we" (he was including himself in this statement) should all give up.

"Really? Raymond said that there's a kid in first year who's better than him? No. He was probably just being facetious."

"It's true. I had to check it out for myself – so I did. I wouldn't believe it if I hadn't seen it with my own eyes. I found the kid, and his work looks exactly, and I mean exactly, like Augustus John's."

She frowned. "What are you on?"

"I'm not kidding. You should've been there. I watched him drawing this incredible figure from his head. No word of a lie – the drawing he did looked more like an Augustus John than Augustus John could've done."

"So, let me get this straight, he does copies of Augustus John?"

"No. You're not listening to me. He draws like Augustus John. That's his style. It comes natural to him. It's what he does... they're proper, beautiful, original drawings."

Jenny seemed to be staring into space. He realised that her thoughts must have moved on a couple of stages. She nodded to herself then looked hard at Alan.

"When did Augustus John die?"

"Sorry?"

"Roughly, I mean. When did Augustus John die?"

A strange, almost devious look came over Jenny as she half-squinted with one eye and raised the eyebrow of the other. It made Alan feel nervous whenever she did that.

"Well, he was already an art student in the 1890s so..." he started counting his fingers, then he dropped his hands. "It's unlikely he died any later than the 1940s or 50s."

"You're not sure?"

He shrugged.

"A few months ago," she said, "I saw this documentary about a kid in Ireland (maybe he was four or five). The thing is, ever since he could talk, he was describing his past life as a grown man. He said he was a fisherman living on Mull, an island off the west coast of Scotland, hundreds of miles away from where the kid lived with his mum and dad, which was in county Cork. He would say that he died in a fishing accident. It sounds mad – but no one could explain how he was able to describe the island of Mull and its geography. He could name the family members from his past life too."

"Sounds a bit fanciful to me."

"Shut up a minute."

Alan leaned back in surprise. Jenny continued.

"His mother took him to psychologists and other experts and stuff to work out what this was all about. In the end, she saved up and they went to Mull by plane. When they arrived, he was able to show her around the place. They even found the house where he said he lived - and it was just like he had described it – even the surroundings matched."

"Blimey. So, when was this programme on?"

"Maybe August."

"Right."

"If that kind of stuff is possible – and what they showed is very convincing - then this Jason Watts character might actually be a reincarnation of Augustus John."

Alan was left gawping in stunned silence.

But she wasn't done yet. "Didn't you say Raymond told you Jason Watts was nineteen?"

"Mm."

"So, if he's nineteen he was probably born in, let me see…" She splayed out her fingers and started counting, bending each finger in sequence. Satisfied, she lowered her hands and nodded.

"1961. Right. Now you've got nearly a whole fucking shelf of books on Augustus John. Pick one out and look up when Augustus John died."

Alan winced. He had always been so disparaging about anything to do with the supernatural. Whenever she mentioned star signs, or the emotional energy left over by the dead being visible to sensitive people' (presumably like herself), he would wind her up, implying she was over-exercising her considerable imagination. Anyway, he was pretty sure that John could not have died any later than the mid-1950s.

"Alright, alright. Don't get your knickers in a twist." Reluctantly he went over to the bookshelf running his fingers along the spines before pulling out a pale-yellow hardback. It was a biography of Augustus John by Michael Holroyd. He was never really interested in Augustus John the man, just the work. Despite being a genius, as a human being John left a lot to be desired. Alan opened it up to the last chapter and within seconds he looked up, visibly shaken. "Jesus."

"Give it here."

Jenny snatched the book, ran her finger down the page, stopped at a particular sentence and laughed.

"Ha! 31st October 1961. What did I tell you?"

It would be hypocritical of him to admit it, but Jenny's reasoning could explain everything.

Half an hour later Alan and Jenny were sitting in an oak-panelled corner of the Prince of Wales Feathers, watching the regulars, drinking, chatting, cheering and groaning as the darts team (predictably) lost to a team from the other side of town. The cigarette smoke seemed particularly irritating, though it really wasn't any more intense than usual. Jenny was genuinely interested in the darts, so

Alan was free to concentrate on his own despair. He considered again how he'd been so far ahead of everyone... and now there was Jason Watts, who had come along and pulled the rug out on him. The extent of this kid's talent was obscene - *unnatural*. That's why he was now weighing up this crazy explanation that Jason could be a reincarnation of Augustus John. The thing is, if Jenny was right it would relieve some of his misery, because it would mean Jason Watts was effectively a kind of passive cheat – in that he'd just inherited his ability from a dead artist. But his long-held scepticism wouldn't completely go away. It's surely the case that if you were reincarnated you would retain the personality and characteristics of your previous life - otherwise you're effectively someone else. But Jason Watts was nothing like Augustus John, despite their drawing styles being so alike. John was a thoroughly unpleasant human being: arrogant, selfish and bullish, while Jason was easy-going, and just a very chilled out sort of guy.

When the darts were over Jenny was not in the least bit interested in any discussion of Jason Watts.

"Listen," she said. "I'm not going to say this again. If Jason was born after October 31st, 1961, then we might be onto something. But if he was born before that day, then there's no way he's a reincarnation of Augustus John. You can't be reincarnated into a person who's already born, can you?"

But Alan wouldn't let go, and she became bored, which was why she turned away to join in other people's conversations. He was left alone with his battered old penguin edition of 'Against Nature'.

About an hour later it was last orders, and Alan looked up to discover that Jenny was getting floppy. Having mingled with people standing at the bar she came back and sat next to him again. He put the book back in his jacket pocket and told her he was looking forward to getting back, putting the kettle on and watching the late-night horror film on ITV. But things didn't quite turn out that way, because as soon as they closed the front door she lunged towards him, lifting his sweater and pushing him up against the hallway wall and thrusting her tongue down his throat. She then pulled away and quickly opened the door leading to the stairs to their apartment and dragged him into the bedroom, where she pulled off his jeans, tugged off his jumper, and spread herself over him.

When it was over, she dropped beside him, and fell almost immediately into a deep, open-mouthed sleep. He lay there for a while, allowing the quiet glow of his orgasm to percolate, before carefully getting off the bed to wash. When he came out of the bathroom, he didn't feel like going to bed yet, so he went into the lounge to watch whatever was left of *Frankenstein Must Be Destroyed*. Peter Cushing in his mad scientist's laboratory was sawing off part of the cranium of a corpse, after which he took out the deceased's brain and replaced it with a living one. Then he put the cranium back, like a lid, leaving a gooey red line at the join, and started up some machinery. Slowly the corpse was re-animated. Usually Alan would enjoy these far-fetched, surge-of-electricity-powered-moments in Hammer Horror films, with their over-the-top dramatic music, cheesy acting and low lighting. But he couldn't focus properly because he was thinking about Jason Watts again. It certainly wasn't outrageous to put him on the same level as the Renaissance masters, as Henry Tonks had said about Augustus John. This line of thinking interrupted his ability to enjoy the film. In frustration he lunged at the remote, switched the TV off, and went over to the kitchen to make himself a hot chocolate. Finally, he came back and sank into the sofa, rested the mug on the coffee table, and while waiting for it to cool down, he fell asleep.

It was early evening in the graveyard, and it was getting dark fast. The bleak setting was overgrown with nettles. Orange and brown, crusty leaves scattered around the patches of grass and mud. He was standing under the dark mute trees, gazing at the partly shattered, ivy-covered, grey headstone and the words: 'Augustus John, 1878-1961' engraved onto its partly shattered surface. The soil in front of the headstone seemed to soften and shift, as if a molehill were forming. Then a frantically clawing hand pushed out, enlarging the hole and the reanimated corpse of Augustus John emerged in full. He was wearing a shabby raincoat, like the tramp on the cover of the Jethro Tull album, Aqualung. At first his head was in deep shadow, but as he looked up his bloodshot eyes and ragged beard, encrusted with earth, came into view in the moonlight. He gave a leery grin, and his rotting flesh cracked, crumbling away from his face, which made his lips rip open from the nose to the chin. It was a horrible sight. Alan was terrified. He tried to run, but it was like moving through a pool of viscous fluid, and Augusts John's living corpse came closer and closer, stumbling towards him inexorably, arms outstretched.

Alan woke up with a startled groan, just as the festering fingers were about to grasp him at the shoulders. He could hear faint snoring from Jenny in the other room. His heart was beating fast, and he knew he'd have trouble getting back to sleep, so he poured himself a brandy.

The next morning (Saturday) they were in the old town, where Jenny was trying out different outfits in the Oxfam shop. While she was doing that, Alan was hanging around outside. It was clear this was not going to be a quick sale, if indeed she did end up buy anything. To kill time, he walked along the road a bit and came to a shoe shop which had a nice pair of maroon DMs on display. Sadly, they were just out of his price range. Wondering slightly further afield he came to a weird shop that featured a human skull, black candles, a knife with strange carvings, a crystal ball on a plinth, and a ceramic statuette of a hand with lifelines drawn in across the palm and fingers. There was also a set of tarot cards and a large tome, which was opened out to a spread showing a range of strange alchemical symbols. The shop was called Bell and Candle, and he'd never noticed it before. He studied the artefacts with contempt, and then it struck him. Surely, they'd have some information on reincarnation in there.

At that moment he felt a tap on the shoulder. It was Jenny. Luckily, she was too distracted to notice what kind of shop window he'd just been looking at.

"I've just seen Imogen in Oxfam. She's trying something on in there right now. I said we could go for a coffee. Wanna come?"

As Alan wasn't feeling sociable this was a good opportunity for him to get away. "Uh, you know what?" he said. "I'm all coffeed out. I had, like, three cups before we left home. I'll just wander around the second-hand bookshops for a bit. You go ahead and I'll catch up with you both a bit later."

Jenny went off merrily to join her friend and Alan sneaked into the Bell and Candle once she was out of view. Once his eyes adjusted to the lack of natural light, he looked around the small, higgledy-piggledy interior. It smelled of incense. At a cluttered bookshelf to the right stood a frail looking, white-haired old man in a black suit, which must have been at least two sizes too big for him. He was thumbing through a massive tome with some difficulty. There was another bookshelf, filled with more valuable looking antique texts, covering much of the back wall. A small, homely looking lady in her sixties and a younger woman were sitting at a desk just in front of that, intently looking over a ledger. The older woman had obviously dyed black hair and wore a heavy, beaded necklace over a colourful patterned dress. She reminded Alan of Mrs. Tiggywinkle, from the Tales of Beatrix Potter. The other, probably in her thirties, was in a white blouse and pale green cardigan.

Alan went over to them and coughed.

"Uh, sorry to interrupt you," he said. "I'm uh, I'm trying to find out about uh, reincarnation."

He waited for an interval while they bickered in a low whisper about some numbers. Then the older woman looked up, holding him in steady focus and eventually spoke, with more than a hint of irritation.

"Reincarnation?"

"Uh yes. That's right."

The younger woman stopped writing so she could look at Alan too.

He hadn't felt this uncomfortable since he was summoned to the deputy headmaster's office for failing to deliver his French homework for the second week running.

"What is it you want to know about reincarnation?" said the older woman.

"Uh... you know, general information, like how it comes about and what it all means - that sort of thing."

"That sort of thing?"

"Well, whatever you can tell me."

"Mm. Tell me now; would I be right in saying that you've never been interested in the subject before?"

"Uh... no."

"And is this sudden interest in reincarnation in relation to a certain individual, a well-known person perhaps?"

"Well… yes."

"I see. And just for the sake of avoiding us having to beat around the bush, shall we say that this someone could be, for example, Augustus John?"

There was a pregnant pause before a shiver ran down his back and he thought the room was floating on rough seas. A thousand thoughts tumbled over each other in his head, becoming knotted up and wisp-like before fading altogether. How the hell...? All he had asked for was some general information about reincarnation. There was no mention of Augustus John. He stared at the women speechless, then took a step back and stumbled, knocking a bronze candelabrum off the table.

"Do be careful!" shouted the older lady. "We wouldn't want to have to ask you to pay damages."

He was feeling totally overawed and confused by now.

"S-s-sorry," he stammered, kneeling to pick up the candelabra to replace on the table it had rested.

"How did you know?" he said finally.

"Know what? You're not making much sense."

His mind raced. Had Jenny gone into this shop and spoken to these women already? No, impossible. He'd been with her the whole morning.

"About my interest in Augustus John, in relation to reincarnation."

Then the older woman said, "What a ridiculous question. It was obvious."

Alan was stunned into silence. This whole experience was making him feel very uncomfortable. Both the women laughed uncontrollably. He wished he'd never even stepped into this blasted store.

Meanwhile, the other customer who had been looking at the heavy book, shook his head angrily, put the book he'd been studying back on the shelf, and walked out in a huff. With him gone Alan relaxed visibly.

"Could I trouble you for a glass of water? I'm, feeling a bit dizzy."

"Bella." Said the older woman. And the younger woman immediately got up and went through a door at the back of the shop.

The older lady held out her hand. "I'm Cornelia, and you are…?"

"Alan", he said, taking her hand.

The younger woman came back with a glass.

"And this is my daughter, Bella."

Alan took the drink. She had something of the librarian about her, with her dark hair tied back in a tight bun, and the wire frame glasses.

"Pleased to meet you," said Bella, also shaking his hand.

Alan smiled, and Bella sat back into her chair.

"Good. Now, where were we?" said Cornelia.

Alan coughed and became alert again. "Augustus John… and I really don't understand how you could possibly have known that…"

Cornelia interrupted him, as her fat fingers began twisting the lid back onto her fountain pen.

"Goodness," she said, exasperated. "Do stick to the facts! You wanted to know about reincarnation or, as we call it, the doctrine of cyclic existence."

Alan shook his head and forced out the words. "I'm sorry if it irritates you for me to ask, and I don't mean to be rude, but it really is quite baffling, and I would very much like to stop you there before moving on. Now please - how did you know it was Augustus John who was integral to my inquiry?"

Cornelia folded her arms, sighed and looked up at the ceiling.

"The fact is," she said, "you just look as if you're interested in Augustus John. Doesn't he Bella?"

Alan could not have been more frustrated and perplexed. "What?"

"Yes. It's quite obvious," added her daughter.

These two witches were running rings around him, and he didn't have his wits about him to respond. He shook his head, took a deep breath and shrugged in submission.

"Whatever."

With that Cornelia gave him her full attention.

75

"Now, back to the main point. We're not short of books on reincarnation. Bella, show Alan what we have will you?"

Bella stood up and led him. over to the shelf where the man who was in earlier had been rummaging. From the lower shelves, she pulled out a large, dusty looking tome and handed it up to him. Alan took it and opened it out to the index. As he flicked through the pages, Bella took out a bright orange, glossy paperback and stood up to flick though until she found a particular passage.

"Look. You can see here," she said. "It really is very succinct: 'The Monad, the Divine Spark, the Ego – whose individuality remains the same throughout the whole course of reincarnation – is truly a denizen of the three higher worlds, the spiritual, the intuitional, and the higher mental, but in order to further its growth and the widening of its experience and knowledge, it is necessary that it should descend into the worlds of denser matter, the lower mental, the actual and the physical, and take back with it to the higher worlds what it has learned in these. Since it is impossible to progress far during one manifestation, it must return again and again to the lower worlds,' and so on."

He had no idea what she was talking about, but he tried to look impressed. He took that book from Bella too, handing the other one back to her.

"Feel free to buy that, if you wish," said Cornelia. "How much is it darling?"

"Nine pounds," replied Bella.

"There you go. You'll probably find it very enlightening. However, I strongly suspect you are not being as open with us as you should be?"

Alan stopped reading and regarded her as her podgy fingers fiddled menacingly with her necklace.

"I'm sorry," he said.

She gave a knowing smile. "Clearly, Augustus John is the spirit in transition, that is of interest, but who is the suspected receptacle?"

A cold tremor ran through him. She was like a burglar burrowing into his innermost thoughts.

He gave a shrug. "There's this kid," he said. "Well... he's nineteen and his drawings are inseparable from Augustus John's. I mean, *exactly.* The thing is… Augustus John died in 1961, and this kid was born that same year. You see where I'm going with this?"

"Yes. That could be an appropriate explanation, if he was born after the time of John's death – preferably at the exact time of his death."

Bella interrupted at that point. "Mama. The coincidence of dates may be interesting, but it's not the only possible explanation."

Cornelia's eyes widened and she turned to face her daughter with a look of utter disdain.

"What are you harping on about, Bella? If this young fellow was born soon after, or at precisely the same hour that Augustus John died, it would be exceedingly difficult to ignore the possibility of him being a reincarnation of the former."

Bella closed her eyes and lowered her head slowly in submission.

"Now!" Cornelia said, filling the sudden silence with a smile of smug satisfaction, turning her attention back to Alan "I should like to hear the symptoms first, and any deductions will fall out of that."

"Symptoms?"

"The manifestations that make you think this is a case of reincarnation."

Alan shrugged again. "Well, that's pretty much it really."

"You're sure that he doesn't just procure these wonderful drawings elsewhere and bring them in, as homework, so to speak?" Have you witnessed him in the act of creating these wonderful images?

"Yes, I have! He did four or five of them, right in front of me."

"Interesting, but still… to my knowledge, reincarnation is not known to automatically confer the previous abilities and skills of the deceased into the new life."

Bella nodded in agreement, as Cornelia continued.

"I see."

Bella interrupted again.

"The question is whether this young man could be a passive recipient of Augustus John's soul, or if he has advance knowledge of magic and occult practices that enable him to channel Augustus John's soul?"

Alan was baffled, and Cornelia bashed the table with the palm of her hand in fury.

"Don't be so ridiculous!"

"I'm sorry. I don't understand…"

Bella wriggled her prodigious bottom into the chair so she could get more comfortable.

"Bella is suggesting that the young man in question may be a seriously powerful adept of the dark arts."

"Magic?"

"Precisely. That would be beyond anything you could imagine. He's only a young man, as you say. One would need decades of knowledge, built up through endless reading and practice – as well as secret initiations. No. It's a ridiculous notion?"

Alan nodded blankly.

Bella interrupted, obviously intending to clarify things. "There are different types of channelling: intentional, spontaneous, classic (of a particular entity), open (inspired speaking from an unknown source), sleep and dream, clairaudient and clairvoyant."

"Christ," said Alan, almost in a whisper, not least because most of this was just gobbledygook to him.

But then Cornelia confused him even further by raising her arms in despair and scowled at her daughter.

"Bella, please. If I need your elucidation, I shall ask for it."

Bella submitted and Cornelia addressed Alan directly again.

"Now, where was I?"

Alan had no idea, and Bella was in no mood to be helpful, so Cornelia had to find the thread for herself. "Ah, yes. Channelling.

"Generally, a channeller will go into a trance, which manifests itself in different ways. Sometimes they go rigid, into a type of catalepsy."

"That's definitely not what happens with Jason. When he does these drawings, he's totally relaxed. No way is he anything like catatonic."

"There are some channellers who are able to open their eyes during the process and walk around and behave quite normally – and so on."

"Do you mean for hours?"

"No, no, no, not at all. It would take an extraordinarily powerful mystic, someone with decades of experience, someone who has achieved the magisterial status of wizard, having built up a monumental store of knowledge of the occult arts to join with a consciousness from the other side to achieve that."

This was all beginning to sound rather fanciful to Alan, as it was completely off target. He was pretty sure that Jason had no interest in the occult whatsoever.

"But first things first," said Cornelia. "You will need to find the date and the hour when this young man was born. Everything follows from that."

But Alan couldn't help noticing that Bella, who was behind Cornelia, was shaking her head, in silent (and hidden) disagreement with her mother. Alan wondered what she was thinking. He concluded that their ramblings were either unintelligible or sheer nonsense. They also managed to make him feel uncomfortable in their presence – so he thanked them for their time, made his excuses and left.

By the time he emerged from Bell and Candle, the street had become considerably busier. The daylight hurt his eyes. He stopped to rub them. What should he do now? Jenny and Imogen could be anywhere: having coffee, checking out shoes and clothes, looking around the Saturday market, or perhaps going through the record boxes at Rooster. He didn't know where to start looking, so he gave up and went to see a lunchtime screening of *American Werewolf in London* at the main cinema on the seafront.

Jenny called out to him as soon as she heard him coming up the stairs. He found her stretched out in the bath using her big toe to block a dripping tap.

He went in and kissed her on the lips then leaned against the wall in preparation for whatever underwhelming news she was going to give him.

"Guess what?" she said, with a mischievous look on her face."

He folded his arms. "Tell me."

"Chloe called up Imogen this morning."

"Mm."

"She wanted to find out what she could bring her back from Paris. You know, being nice to her big sister. Imogen said she'd love a white shirt from Agnes B (as if you'd be interested)."

"Alan shrugged."

"And then…" she added, "She asked her when Jason Watts was born."

Alan perked up. "And?"

"Imogen remembered his birthday drinks at the King and Queen this year."

"When?"

"In July. It was his nineteenth."

"Shit. Augustus John died in October. That's a few months early."

"Yep. So, he was born when Augustus John was still alive."

She looked up to see his reaction, and he was desperate not to have one.

"Yeah, well… that reincarnation business was always a bit far-fetched."

Jenny, who had sunk lower and lower into the water, suddenly rose up a little.

"Look at you trying to sound like the cool sceptic! You totally believed me when I said about reincarnation!"

"I wouldn't go that far."

"Pf. Anyway that's not all. Chloe said something else – probably just as interesting."

"I bet."

Jason Watts is into magic."

He stared open mouthed as Jenny started splashing away at the bubbles in her usual carefree way, clearing bubble free zones on the surface of the water

"She said he's totally obsessed."

"H-how does she know that?"

"That's all I know. Chloe had to get off the phone after that, because the tutors were rounding everyone up for their visit to the Louvre."

He moved his shoulder away from the wall, blinking hard frantically as his thoughts ran wild. How could he have been so wrong in his initial assessment of Jason Watts? In the time, he was speaking to Jason, he didn't see any sign of the reserve and cunning that you'd expect from someone who dabbled in magic, like that guy who was the head of the Church of Satan, who was supposed to have had Marilyn Monroe under his spell. What was his name? Oh yes… Anton LaVey."

Jenny was getting bored at this point.

"Right," she said. "I need to wash my hair. So, if you don't want to risk getting soaked…"

Alan went into the lounge and stood looking out of the window, facing the street below and the hospital beyond, seeing cars parking, people walking to and fro, perceiving nothing, trying to let it all sink in. He tried to remember the precise words Cornelia had used:

"It would take an extraordinarily powerful mystic, someone who has achieved the status of wizard – or Magus; someone with a monumental store of knowledge of magic – and beyond that – a considerable predisposition of soul, to join with a consciousness from the other side in order to achieve the results that you describe."

He pulled out a stick of tough liquorice he'd bought in town and started chewing.

What do experts in magic do exactly? Cast spells. He had read about Aleister Crowley who had a reputation for being a supreme master of magic. There were many rumours about what he got up to, perhaps unsubstantiated. But it was said he performed weird rituals, using rhythmic chanting and bizarre spells. He organised and took part in ceremonial orgies and animal sacrifices. Rumours are that he was driven out of Italy for sacrificing babies. How could Jason Watts, who grew up in an ordinary terraced house in north London, have done that sort of thing? Where would he do it? Did his dad have an unused garage, or something? He tried to imagine Jason in a black hooded gown in a candlelit room, with hieroglyphic charts on the walls, and skulls, skeletons, and antique globes and strange measuring instruments all around, while a large cauldron made of dark pewter bubbling away, creating a foul smell. Maybe there would be glass tubes and beakers brewing up colourful elixirs and strange potions. If Alan became too inquisitive, would he be able to cast a curse on Alan, giving him some kind of disease, or even sending him

81

mad? Despite Imogen's information, it all seemed totally preposterous.

The next afternoon the first years were back from Paris, and Alan was hoping Jason hadn't forgotten their arrangement for that night. All day Jenny was covering the floor with her photographs and drawings to prepare for a presentation on Tuesday. In fact, that's what she was still doing when Alan was about to leave.

"You going to get legless?" she asked after he kissed her goodbye.

"Not so as you'd notice," he said.

For days, he'd been agonising over what it was all about, Jason's supposed interest in magic. He still wasn't a hundred percent convinced it was true. It sounded crazy. How would anyone get into that sort of thing? But if there was something in it maybe it would explain the Augustus John business. Tonight, was his chance of finding out, but he had no idea how he would bring the subject up. If he was lucky, it would fall out of the conversation naturally.

It was cold and the wind was coming straight off the sea and hitting him full-face. The pub faced the seafront, though the only entrance was on a side street. When he arrived under the portico, he stopped to consider whether he should just forget the whole business and go home. In defiance of what he considered to be his cowardly predisposition; he grabbed the brass handle and pulled the heavy oak door open; to discover he was using more strength than was required. A wave of warm air washed over him, leaving him surprisingly invigorated as he walked in.

Despite the big crowd at the bar, he managed to get served quite fast before heading into the main bar. The sun dropped just below the slate grey sea through the huge front window, leaving a dull yellow glow in its wake, and the large ceiling fan and wicker seats gave the place the feeling of a colonial clubhouse in India. Alan looked around and saw Jason sitting at a table in the corner with a bunch of people. Alan went over there and stood drinking on his own for a moment, but it wasn't long before Jason called him over to their table, standing up and reaching over to give Alan a good, firm handshake. Around the table were Debbie, Ryan, Sophie, Emily, Geoff and Ali. Debbie was the girl who had been sitting on Jason's desk the day he met Jason in the first studio. Jason introduced him to them all and then asked Geoff and Ali to shift over a bit so that Alan could squeeze in.

"Alan's a third year," said Jason to the ensemble. Ryan, a tall, lanky, good looking blonde Aryan type said, "Hey Alan. Maybe you can tell us what you think. Most of us here believe Jason is a killer and he should definitely be arrested."

Alan was stunned. "Killer?" He couldn't suppress a look of utter astonishment, which he quickly tried to disguise as irony. Unpleasant thoughts flashed into his brain and made him hesitate before taking the next step.

"Ha! Perfect. Who is he supposed to have killed?"

He waited in silence for what was to come.

"It was only a cat," said Debbie protectively.

Alan feigned indifference, but he could feel his heart beating a little quicker and a sudden chilliness in his back. He imagined a wooden glade at night, where Jason is standing poised knife in hand, under a gibbous moon, wearing a ceremonial robe, by a stone alter on which the cat is to be sacrificed. Alan forced the image out of his mind to calm his racing thoughts.

"What colour was the cat?" he asked.

Jason and his friends looked at each other bemused.

"What's that got to do with anything?" said Ali.

Jason came to Alan's rescue. "That's OK, he said. "It was Tabby."

Alan was relieved. "Oh." This wasn't connected to a ritualistic murder then. That was a relief. "So, what happened?" said Alan.

"Murder", said Ryan. "That's what happened."

"Oh, shut up!" said Debbie.

Emily sniggered.

"Look. I didn't mean to kill the fucking cat," said Jason. "Where we lived in Finsbury Park, our house backed onto this wasteland behind the school playground that was at the end of the garden next door. Sometimes, when me and my cousins played in the garden, our ball would go over there, and we'd, you know, we'd have to climb over this low wall to get it. Now we had two cats, Streaky and Tiger who were terrorised by this bruiser with one ear. I used to see him clawing at my cats and often chasing them in our back garden. Well, one afternoon I went into that wasteland with my little cousin Dean and while we were there, we came across this scruffy, bullying beast. I happened to have my granddad's pitchfork with me,

Ryan interrupted. "Oh right, so your intentions were non-violent."

Ryan, Sophie, Emily, Geoff and Ali all laughed. Debbie shook her head disapprovingly.

"It's not what you think," said Jason. "I only wanted to scare the bruiser by slamming the pitchfork into the ground near him, but he was unlucky he leapt right over to where I was thrusting it. The prongs went right through him and got stuck in the hard soil."

"Uh! This is getting worse. I'm calling the RSPCA said Ryan jokingly," as Geoff and Ali doubled up with laughter

"Oh, shut up," said Debbie.

"I didn't mean it. Honestly." Dean was distraught, poor kid. How old was he?"

"I dunno. Maybe about eight?"

"Great influence you are."

"Like I said! It wasn't part of the plan."

More sniggering.

"Sure... so, what did you do after that?"

"I put my foot on the dead cat and pushed it off the pitchfork. I tried to wipe the blood off on some grass."

"Eee-yuk!"

Alan listened to all this in bewilderment. He was beginning to be ashamed of his suspicions and a change gradually began to take shape in his thoughts.

"We went back over the wall into our garden, and I put the pitchfork back in the shed. After that we went into the kitchen, and I drew batman and Superman for Dean until my aunt came to pick him up. We didn't tell my mum or grandparents anything."

Jason's pals continued to rib him about the incident, except for Debbie, who seemed annoyed with them all. Eventually the subject ran out of steam and was overtaken by hunger. Only Jason decided he wasn't going to go along to Samson's, a trendy burger restaurant not too far away. Even Debbie deigned to leave Jason's side to join them. Ryan and Ali even invited Alan to come, in the hope that Jason would join them, but Jason stood firm. He was going to the Market Diner later for sausage egg and chips, he said, and he had been looking forward to it the whole time they were in France. When they had the table to themselves Alan took the opportunity to get back to a more meaningful subject.

"I must tell you after I came over to see you and your work, it had a major impact on me. I can't get over the way you draw..."

Jason took a sip of his beer, and his eyebrows lifted a fraction into his noticeably large forehead, which gave him a look not too dissimilar to a young Jack Nicholson.

Alan waited for a modest return, but there was no response. It was as if to say, "Yes. I know I'm good. You're quite right."

This left Alan a little lost for words, so he tried to fill the uncomfortable silence.

"What I was wondering was, how did you set out to draw the way you do. I mean, the knowledge and sophistication in your work must have come from somewhere."

"You sound like my mum. She used to look at my drawings and say, 'you didn't come from me. You came through me'."

"I can understand that."

Jason let out a loud burp. Then he stood up with his empty glass. "Fancy another?"

"Uh... Thanks."

Alan handed his glass to Jason, who went off to the bar. It was a few minutes before he came back with the beers and two packets of cheese and onion crisps, which he threw on the table. "Feast to your heart's content."

"Cheers," said Alan, as Jason squeezed around to get back to his seat in the corner.

"To get back to your question, I was a pretty sickly kid. I missed a lot of school. Mum used to buy me comics when I was in bed, you know, the American sort: Batman, Superman, Tarzan and stuff like that. I used to sit up in bed and copy the figures, resting my pad on the tea tray. I filled in a lot of sketchbooks like that. But I didn't learn as much as I would have liked. One day I went into the library and started rummaging and found these books on anatomy for artists. They looked promising. I took them home and forced myself to draw from them. I bought an action man and started drawing him in various poses, trying to do the same pose a few times until I could draw it without the doll being there. Then I got a small plastic model skeleton and learned all the names for the bones, and after a year I started on the muscles. It helped a lot. But I still wasn't getting it. It was like that for a few years. And then I had the dream."

"What dream?"

Jason took a good long glug of beer and thumped the glass (not too hard) on the table for emphasis. "The dream that changed everything."

"Now I'm curious."

Jason took another sip of his beer and frowned, as if what he was about to relate somehow pained him. Alan couldn't help noticing he was getting through his pint fast. Neither of them spoke for what seemed an uncomfortable long time, and then Jason took another sip before breaking the silence.

"When my nan died," he said, while wiping the foam off his upper lip. "I had this dream."

"How old were you?"

"Thirteen. I'm not sure if it was the day after the funeral, or maybe a day or two after that. In the dream, I remember I'm back at the funeral, but it feels different. I'm not sure that the people there are my family, but they could be. We're all standing around the coffin… it feels like something is about to happen, and I'm kind of gearing myself up for it, but I don't know what it will be. Suddenly the lid opens slowly on its own. No one has touched it. Everybody stands back, but I go forward and lean over to look inside. Nan's body isn't in there. Instead, all these beautiful geometric shapes start floating out. They're semi-transparent, and in amazing pastel colours: glowing triangles, squares, circles, as well as cubes, cylinders, cones and spheres. A fountain of shapes – so perfect. I am stunned by the beauty of it all: mesmerised. When I woke up, I felt this irresistible urge to grab my pad and start drawing. And what flowed out of my pen at that moment was absolutely the type of drawing that I had been struggling to create for years. It was a wonderful, wonderful feeling. The figures came out just right. All that stuff I was practicing and trying to learn, it suddenly came together - like magic."

There was that word again, thought Alan. Time to take advantage of the moment. "Magic? Oh yeah. I hear you're very interested in magic."

"Love it," replied Jason without flinching.

An involuntary shiver ran through Alan, dissolving the delicacy and wonder of the story he had just heard. He resolved to meet Jason's eye as he spoke.

"So, uh, how did you get into magic? I mean - you don't seem like the sort of person who would be interested in that kind of thing."

Jason seemed utterly and genuinely perplexed. "Why not?"

"Well, I dunno. I mean... What's it all about?"

Jason chuckled, which made Alan even more nervous.

"I'll show you?"

Alan looked on as Jason rummaged around in his jacket pocket for a minute and pulled out a red silk handkerchief which he dangled near Alan's face. "Now watch closely," said Jason as he closed his left hand into a fist and, pushed the red handkerchief deep into his now tightened red fist with the fingers of his right hand, until it was all in there. Alan took a big sip from his glass, feeling a bit bored. Meanwhile, Jason blew onto his clenched fist and opened it out to reveal... the handkerchief was not there anymore. It had vanished.

Jason grinned and said mischievously, "See? Magic."

Alan burst into laughter, spraying beer in all directions. He struggled to stop himself laughing, leaned forward so his head hit the table. People started staring and Jason worried that Alan might be having a seizure. Finally, the cacophony subsided, and Alan sat up, wiping the tears from his eyes.

"You all right, mate?" said Jason.

"Sorry," he said, in a slight falsetto voice. Then he caught his breath. "I just can't tell you how funny that was.

Neither of them knew it, but this moment was the start of a friendship that would last a lifetime.

Postscript

A week later Alan was walking home from the station, having gone up to meet a few old school friends. It was after six, so most of the shops in the Old Town were closed, but the lights were still on in the Bell and Candle. Curious, he crossed over to peek through the glass and saw Bella standing by the large shelves with a small pile of

87

books under her arm. She was wearing another mohair jumper. This one was lemon yellow and much more tight fitting. Also, she looked completely different with her long, black hair loose, covering her shoulders and glistening from the lighted candles distributed all around the shop.

He pushed the door in and stepped forward, so the jingly jangly things tinkled like wind chimes. She twisted around to look at him and he was immediately surprised by her hourglass figure.

"Oh. It's you," she said.

The place smelled strongly of incense. He looked all around for Cornelia.

"I wasn't sure you'd be open," he said. "Is Cornelia around?"

"Mother has gone to Glasgow to hear a lecture at the Theosophical Society. Not my cup of tea."

"Have you come back to buy that book?" she enquired.

"Er, I'm still thinking about that. But... I wanted to say thank you. You were very helpful the other day, you and your mother, I mean."

She sucked in her lips and raised her eyebrows.

"Look," he said, as he tried to find some courage. "Can I ask you a couple more things about, you know, the guy we were talking about?"

He was pleased he managed to get that out, but he wasn't sure how to continue.

"You mean your outrageously talented friend?" she said.

"Mm hm."

"I thought we'd exhausted that subject."

Everything she said seemed to be a challenge.

"Well yes, but there's been a development, which kind of changes things and I would really be grateful if I could just get your take on it."

She seemed to go cross-eyed for a few seconds. Then she suddenly sparked into life and marched over to the table, took off her glasses and placed the books down so she could open a draw to pull out a set of keys, which she held up and jangled with an impish expression.

"I was just about to close up," she said.

"Oh, right. I'll get along then."

He was halfway towards turning around to leave, when he heard her say," "Fancy a splif?"

He turned to face her again.

"Sorry?"

"What's the matter. Don't you smoke?"

"I do but..."

"Give me a minute."

She walked past him to lock the front door, pull the bolts, and then turn the closed sign around. Then she dragged down the blind over the glass door.

"Right. This way."

In a state of utter confusion, he followed her through a door at the back, which opened into a narrow room, which featured a sink and work top on the left, with a kettle, a cassette player, and a sofa.

"No need to stand," she said.

Taking his cue, he sat at one end of the sofa, wondering if he was making a big mistake. Bella, meanwhile, rifled through a shoebox full of tapes.

"What do you want to hear?" she said. "John Martyn? The Cure? Mozart?"

"You got Solid Air there?" He asked.

She rummaged a bit more. "Mm-hm." She slotted in the tape and pushed the button in hard, so that the soothing vocals and hypnotic baseline came up.

"Tea?" She said, still standing.

"No thanks," he replied.

"Fine."

She sat down at the other end of the sofa and opened the lid of a battered old tin of Golden Virginia on her lap. Then she took out the cigarette papers, flattening one out.

"So, you're not into theosophy?" said Alan, as she took a large pinch of the dried, crumbled green leaves, forming the mass into a worm shape along the opened out, King Size Rizla.

"Not really," she replied. "Obviously mother and I share an interest in matters metaphysical and spiritual, hence the shop. But we tend to approach everything from a diametrically opposite standpoint.

That irks her somewhat, as does any challenge to her way of thinking, which I'm sure you noticed."

He laughed. "What can I say? But why do you let her talk to you like that?"

She gave him a sideways glance, and a corner of her mouth turned up.

He hadn't stopped to censor himself before speaking. It just seemed to come out. He began to wish he'd kept his trap shut. She put the joint to her lips, put a lighter flame to it, and took a long deep breath, till she was sucking in a centimetre of glowing red at the tip. Then she took it away from her mouth to let out a plume of smoke and said, "Because I love her."

He found the floodgates to his courage open.

"Yeah. But still..."

She took another small puff and spoke as if resisting a cough at first.

"I was at university in London studying philosophy," she said. "It was all going so well. I had a flat in Camden, and I really loved London. I found the course work fascinating at first, but when it started to get political things fell apart for me."

"Political?"

"Compulsory cultural Marxism?"

"Oh. So, you're right wing?"

She squinted in frustration. "No! Not at all. Just not into Marx, or semiotics, or linguistic theory. One of the tutors in particular - and some of the students - had it in for me. Like you, just then, they thought I was a Conservative, and the psychological bullying that followed was relentless. I was ostracised and had all sorts of vile, juvenile things done to me. I won't go into details, because it still pains me to remember. Anyway, the long and the short of it is... I buckled. I had a breakdown."

"What does that mean?"

"I was a gibbering wreck sitting in bed, staring into space, with hot tears streaming down my face. I didn't eat for days. I wasn't even answering the phone. Mum drove up, and asked the landlord to let her in. She came in and cleared my room out, pushed me into the car and took me home. She was so worried, and she was wonderful. Truly.

She hired someone to look after the shop while she nursed me back to health. I've been with her ever since."

She handed him the roach and he took a puff, which caused him to immediately struggle to hold off a coughing fit as he said, "Christ. When did all that happen?"

"Let me think now... yes. It was eleven years ago."

Recovering somewhat, he said cautiously.

"Surely, it's time for you to go your own way now?"

She said nothing as he gave her back the roach, which she put it into an ashtray, then stood up to lift off her yellow mohair jumper, to reveal the pale, flawless skin of her stomach. She reached back to unclip her white bra. He was transfixed, feeling a mixture of astonishment and pleasure. Instantly he knew what to do. He was, at that moment, like an actor who had almost forgotten his lines when he stood up to wrap his arms around her. He kissed her cheek and then her lips, before bending down to kiss each breast softly. She breathed heavily and pulled him over to the sofa. Half an hour later they were lying down. She was playing with his hair as he lay back, contented and perplexed."

"Where did that come from?" he said.

"The moment," she replied, with a smirk. He admired her confidence and her impulsiveness. But he guessed these were qualities she couldn't switch on at will.

"Am I allowed to ask you about my friend now?"

"Feel free," she said, leaning over to take the roach out of the ashtray to light it again.

"He has no interest in the occult, alchemy, spirituality – whatever you want to call it," said Alan. "His only interest in magic is in illusion – tricks. Not the occult, or supernatural, or dark arts."

She laughed. "That is so funny."

"I know. And the other thing is - he was born two months before Augustus John died. So, no way is he a reincarnation of him."

"Don't be so stupid. That's like adding two and two and making five. Time is not as simple as you think. Thought is dynamic and it can actually accomplish material results. It can even act at a distance - not just in terms of proximity, but also of time. So, the thoughts of others can be accessed. Time is not linear."

"What do you mean?"

"It can split into different branches - like the Northern Line does after Camden Town."

"What are you talking about?"

Quantum theory describes it like this: systems interact with each other, outcomes split into alternative versions, and they're all real. There are superimposed worlds passing in and out of existence, along a parallel timeline, and some of us are in the process of moving toward greater, rather than lesser, interconnection with these paths.

"Now you've lost me."

She smiled.

He told her then about how Jason told him about this wonderful dream where he is at a funeral and the coffin lid is opened before it is lowered into the ground and out of it float these beautiful, colourful, light shapes: triangles, squares, circles, rectangles, cubes, cylinders, spheres... he is awed and fascinated by them. He said he remembered that dream perfectly when he woke, and from that day he was able to draw the way he does now. He was thirteen.

She nodded seriously and stared at the ceiling. "He was chosen."

"By who?"

She got up and started to put on her bra while she said, "I think you'd better go now."

A little later Alan was walking home, trying to put everything into order in his head. Having sex with a woman over thirty, accepting there was a glass ceiling to his creative potential, and coming to terms with the truth about what is real and what isn't. It seems we can't understand what's really going on through experience alone. There are many layers. He got the idea that there was a definite order to it all, but only in an intuitive way. On a conscious level, he just didn't get it. Much like Jason's genius.

THE RESURRECTION

The week before the day of the lecture had been a blur of rain and mist. The venue was a quietly dignified building on the southeast corner of Regents Park, with rows of Ionic columns and three stories of tall, narrow windows. Sadly, since its heyday, in the Regency period, it had fallen into some disrepair and was now a sort of temporary arts centre, and was scheduled for conversion into luxury apartments, but there was no sign of that happening any time soon. The lecture theatre was situated on the ground floor and was an original feature of the building. High ceilinged, light and spacious, it was laid out like a small, indoor, Greek Amphitheatre. Alan thought it was just the sort of place where medical students of the nineteenth century would have sat to watch autopsies being performed by leading surgeons of the day. However, on this afternoon the only thing being dissected was the subject of Divine Proportion. Alan's interest in the topic was connected to his love of classical and neo-classical architecture, but he also wanted to be able to apply its principles in the composition of his drawings and paintings. Having sat down at one of the upper benches facing the lectern, he rummaged around in his rucksack, so as he could take notes. Ultimately though, he decided against that. After all, it wasn't as if he was going to be tested or anything.

Finally, the speaker came in wearing a loose-fitting, grey flannel suit and carrying a battered brown leather briefcase. His unkempt mop of curly blond hair gave him an air of relaxed warmth and intelligence, which was pleasantly reassuring. Having removed a glasses case from his jacket pocket, he withdrew a pair of gold frame wire spectacles, and put them on very delicately, with the little finger of each hand protruding prominently. Then he sighed and stepped up onto the lectern, gripping it with both hands, before looking around the room and coughing loudly. It had the desired effect, because the chattering from the benches came to an abrupt halt.

"Good evening, and a warm welcome to you all," he said, with a smile. "My name is Harold Cohen, and I am a professor of Renaissance studies in the department of European History at London University."

His voice had the soothing qualities you'd expect to hear in a country sermon. It reminded Alan of the TV actor, Derek Nimmo.

"What we are going to talk about here today," he continued, "Is Divine Proportion, which will help us see how objects of beauty can be appreciated through geometry. We will be looking at the 'Golden Section' of the Greeks, and showing how it is not just a means of creating art and architecture, because it also describes how nature takes shape, from the smallest seashell to the furthest galaxy."

This was a good start, thought Alan. And for a few minutes at least, he was able to follow the flow. But when an element of mathematics entered the mix, Alan's thinking became undisciplined, particularly when the speaker said,

"There are many points where you could cut a piece of string, and every one of them would give you a different ratio for the length of the small piece of string to the large piece."

Alan waited to see if he could latch back into the flow again but instead found himself looking blankly around the room. It was no good. His consciousness was sinking into a sickly sweet, deep miasma and there was nothing he could do about it.

When Dr Cohen came to say, "This is where the ratio of both is 1.618 to 1, or, as we shall henceforth refer to it, Phi becomes significant," he tried once more to follow the flow, by focusing hard on the speaker, watching him speak, seeing his lips move. It was no good. He could no longer make out words, just low, hollow sounds, as if he was underwater.

The game was up. His focus was drifting further and further, and he found himself looking absent-mindedly at the people sitting in the rows behind the speaker, while a dreadful sense of anticipation took slow possession of him, and he became somehow conscious of a sort of displacement, an uncomfortable awakening that was baring down on him by unknown means, leaving him nervous and perplexed by its inevitability. Soon those people's faces began to lose their sharpness, as they began bobbling like waves, and that was when one of them came inexplicably into sharp focus separating itself totally from the others. This particular face happened to be looking down. The forehead was large, and around the mouth was a suave musketeer-type moustache and goatee beard, and on the cheeks, were well-groomed, knife-sharp sideburns, reaching right down to a pronounced set of jowls. It seemed like he had been staring blankly at this person for several minutes, when he then became hypnotised by his grass green corduroy jacket. He struggled to recall where he'd seen it before when he had an insight that struck him like a bucket of iced water, washing away his waking dream and leaving a shocking realisation, followed by utter confusion. There was no question. This person was Jason Watts. But Jason Watts was dead.

It was nearly two years ago that the cancer beat him. In just two or three months this tall, dignified man of fifty-three was devoured inside out by the disease. In the end, he looked like a tiny, pathetic, shrivelled-up octogenarian. In his last two years, Alan and Jenny had put him and Rowena, (his girlfriend after Rebecca died) in their spare room. This was during the period following Jason being forced into bankruptcy by his creditors, and they lost the flat. After a while it got to the point where Rowena couldn't look after him anymore, even with Jenny's help, so they had to arrange for Jason to go into a hospice after that. Alan recalled that strange moment in those last few days when he was sitting with Rowena by Jason's bed in the hospice, talking about the funeral arrangements. Jason had fallen into a deep coma and the doctors said he could expire at any moment. But something extraordinary happened. Jason suddenly sprang up, into a sitting position, and looked directly at Alan.

"Oh Alan. Hi!" he said, as if he'd just been woken up by the alarm.

Almost immediately after that awakening, he fell back into the deep sleep, from which he never emerged.

Alan gave the eulogy at the funeral, and then watched as Joy Division's, 'Walk in Silence' played while Jason's coffin slid slowly behind the curtains, on its journey to incineration.

So how could Jason be here now, alive, fit and well, taking notes at a lecture! This was no ghost or vague spiritual entity that would dissolve way like autumn mist. It was the firm, solid, physical Jason – and he was just as much a part of the audience as everyone else.

Alan knew he would have been terrified if he was on his own, and he was genuinely scared for a second or two, until everything began to coalesce in his mind. Having all these other people around at the same time was powerful reassurance, a sort of paperless safety certificate. Still, the question remained, how was it possible for Jason to be here now, fit, healthy, solid, breathing? He had to know. A fiery urge welled up in Alan to talk to Jason, to ask him about absolutely everything – immediately. Fuck it! This was no time to be self-conscious. He stood up, oblivious of the consequences, and stomped down the steps and across the floor of the theatre, past the speaker (who smiled benignly at him) and shot up the aisle of the tiered rows of seats opposite, to squeeze past the people seated at the end of Jason's bench (who weren't pleased). One of them, a bearded fellow in his forties (who looked like he was all set to go hiking in the Welsh mountains after the talk), gave him a filthy look. Jason, meanwhile, was blissfully unaware of all this activity, focusing completely on whatever it was he was writing. Alan went right up to where he sat and tapped him on the shoulder. Dreamily Jason turned around, looked up and smiled, before beaming into a wide-eyed look of recognition.

"Alan how are you?" he said. It was so ridiculously casual. It was as if Jason had returned from a week's holiday in Margate, instead of having risen from the dead. Alan dispensed with formalities. "Jason... We need to talk. Can you come for a walk?"

Jason pouted, went wide-eyed, then shrugged and stood up to put his notebook and pen in his pocket to follow Alan out, squeezing past the thoroughly discomposed people at the end again. Alan didn't much care; although he did stop and turn around to face the speaker when they reached the door, to say, "Look... I'm really very sorry about all this, but we..." He searched around for a reasonable statement that would qualify such an interruption, but could only come up with, "we haven't seen each other for years."

The professor seemed to sympathise, nodding and smiling when he said, "Obviously your friendship must be of divine proportions."

That caused a ripple of restrained laughter, so that even Alan smiled.

They went out on the park side of the building, taking the few steps down to the pavement that was strewn all over with orange and yellow leaves, like tickets to a rained-out concert.

"Jason. You know you died, right?"

Jason simply nodded with a mild shrug. A million thoughts ran through Alan's brain, and none of them amounted to anything that would correspond to an appropriate response. His heart was beating

fast, he was a little scared, but he knew he had to try to stay calm –
even though it was superficially so.

"OK. Listen," said Alan. "When we get across that fucking road
we can talk properly."

"Sure."

The sky was milk white, bestowing a soft and nearly shadow-
less light on Euston Road. There wasn't the typical roar of traffic,
because there simply weren't as many vehicles as usual, which was
odd for a road which was virtually a motorway running across the
northern edge of central London. It was almost empty of pedestrians.
Alan wondered if this was a public holiday that he wasn't aware of.
But then he remembered there weren't any public holidays in
October. They crossed over to Great Portland Street Station, and he
tried to make sense of it all, without success. Soon they came up to a
car showroom not far from Warren Street Station, where they turned
right, and for some reason the atmosphere was more conducive to
conversation. On entering the realm of Fitzroy Square, a universe
away from Euston Road, Alan felt he had license to ask the pile of
questions he had been holding back.

"OK. Now tell me... Jesus, what the fuck is going on? You died.
Ok, just give me a sec... I mean, after death, did you experience,
heaven, angels or what? It's crazy, you being here now... resurrected.
Christ. There can't be many people who get resurrected."

"No, there aren't," replied Jason slowly, following it with that
barely suppressed impish grin, the type he would have pulled just
before he was about to wind you up, or perform one of his magic
tricks. "I mean... did you talk to God?"

Alan was expecting at least a little reticence, but the response
was immediate and confident.

"Yes. And we understood each other."

He couldn't believe his ears.

"You what?"

"That's all I can say about that."

What a show of monumental arrogance! But what if this
response was not quite as egotistical as it seemed? Although Jason
did have a propensity for arrogance. But it could be that he simply
understood (correctly or otherwise) that somehow his return made
him one of a select group, like an angel or something. Alan felt that

97

there might have been just a hint of pain and reluctance in his blasé response. There was a sort of rapid squint, which might mean he was somewhat embarrassed about his apparent divinity – as if it was an encumbrance. Of course, this was all pure speculation, but Alan suspected that Jason genuinely wanted to talk to him about how it was that this completely incomprehensible turn of events had come about - but he was clearly anxious about doing that. Alan decided to give him a little nudge.

"What's it all about Jason? I mean... what the fuck?"

Jason pinched his nose.

All around Fitzroy Square the leaves were falling like rain.

"Give me a second," said Jason. "I'm trying to work it out. To be honest, I only know bits, and it's tough getting my head round any of it."

Alan couldn't miss the pained look in Jason's eyes. Obviously, he had to temper his exuberance if he didn't want to aggravate whatever it was that was troubling Jason, because clearly something was.

The Telecom Tower loomed high to the right, like a monstrous hypodermic syringe. Before long they were walking past the offices of Solomon & Obadiah. The building was huge, stretching east to Whitfield Street and south to Tottenham Street. Although he was badly paid during his time as an art-director there, working mostly on British Airways and Fosters, Alan still had a soft spot for the place. He couldn't resist looking through the huge plate glass window, to see if there was anyone he knew in there. Strangely, it seemed devoid of life. There seemed to be only the one receptionist on duty, which was unusual. He could make out a cleaner working close to the waiting area, but there was no one seated. And where were all those account people working late, and hanging out on the sofas? The whole of Charlotte Street seemed empty of life and Alan's mood was now sufficiently impressionable to see the whole neighbourhood darkened by an ominous shadow. That may be why he was struck by a tidal wave of fear when Jason gripped him by the arm. He reacted as if he was being clawed by a reanimated corpse, which wasn't that far from the truth. However, he recovered quickly, and luckily Jason didn't notice. Jason was almost meditating now, as if trying to build up some inner strength. It seemed to work, as he soon built up to a look of resolve in his eyes.

"These memories, if you can call them that – they're a bit all over the place. I'm not sure how much sense I'll make."

"OK. Whatever you can say. Take your time," said Alan.

Jason turned to Alan, resting the knuckle of his forefinger on his chin, which is something he always did when he was working out a difficult problem.

"Everything was black. There wasn't anything else. That's the best way I can describe it. Then it kind of dissolved away and I found I was in your living room, sleeping on the sofa. It was the middle of the night, just after a party, I think."

"What? But you were in the hospice when, like… you know, when you died."

"I know, but I'm telling you what happened."

Despite being totally confused, Alan thought it best not to interrupt any further.

"Go on."

"At the time, I didn't know where I was. I just realise now, on reflection. My mind was a blank slate. I didn't even know who I was. I was desperate to get out of the house before anyone saw me, and I didn't even know why. And that's where it gets hazy again. I remember walking into the night, and somehow, I end up in bed with Debbie."

"Whoa. You skipped a couple of stages there. You did what?"

"I was making love to Debbie."

"Making… wait. Which Debbie? Not Debbie Wright, the girl who was trying to get into your trousers the whole time we were at college?"

"What?"

"Never mind. Look, you do know that Debbie Wright was in a fatal car crash, around the same week you died, don't you?"

Jason frowned and raised his upper lip on one side, in a show of disgust, and said, "Alan. Why do you always do this? What the fuck has that got to do with anything? Why are you bringing up peripherals? This is really doing my head in trying to remember everything that happened. I'm not *meant* to remember. Everything that I drag out of my memory makes me feel like my head is in a fucking microwave. I've got a proper migraine now – and I never,

ever used to get those…"

"Last time you were alive…"

Jason fired a dirty look at Alan.

"Look, I'm sorry…"

Alan was stunned and humbled by this tirade. It would have been totally unconstructive to deliver a riposte, even if he had one. The main thing was he didn't want to cause Jason any more suffering than he was already going through. But he did want to know what the hell was going on. This wasn't simply a reincarnation of Jason, or some kind of ghostly apparition. This was a solid, living, breathing, animated material resurrection with a totally brand, spanking new fully restored human body. Christ, even in those old Hammer Horror films, the mad scientist needed fresh bodies to re-animate, because when decomposition set in, it was too late. All that was left of Jason's body after he died was a pile of ash. Where would you start putting him back together again after that?

"Jas. I'm really sorry," he said. "I'll shut up and let you explain everything in your own way."

Jason shook his head and sighed, like a schoolteacher despairing of a naughty child. Alan took that as a sign that the tension was now diffused.

The dull clouds allowed a frugal light to seep through their dirty cotton wool mass, down to the almost deserted pavements and near-empty office buildings of Charlotte St. It was easy to believe that the shadow of death was looming large over London. Then, out of nowhere, Jason said,

"But this was the real Debbie," puncturing Alan's melancholy reverie. "Huh?"

"She wasn't all sad and worn out by a breakdown and anorexia and all that, which we were all hearing about her over the years. I didn't think too much about it then, but she looked the same as she did at college."

"You mean the same age?"

"Yes."

"So… she couldn't have been real."

"No. I think she was. It just depends on your definition of 'real'."

Alan thought about that as they crossed Goodge Street, pulling a quizzical expression and saying nothing, preferring not to risk antagonising Jason again. However, by the time they were passing the Charlotte Street Hotel the silence between them was becoming painful. He had to say *something*, and just as he was about to, Jason beat him to it.

"She was crying," he said, "and it was because of me. I can't remember what I did though. All I know is that I had to get out of there, and I charged down those stairs to the front door."

"So, you have no idea what happened that led to you wanting to leave like that?"

"No. But I do remember walking along the pavement afterwards and then... everything went black."

"Again?"

"Something happened. This time the blackness seemed to hang around for ages. I was in this massive tunnel, and I couldn't see the end of it for ages, it was so dark. I just knew I had to keep walking. And then I saw a point of light ahead, and I don't know how far I had to go, but after a while the light got a little brighter, slowly becoming like a sun – almost unbearably intense – and I ended up walking right through it: it kind of swallowed me up and it felt invigorating and cool. Slowly it faded, and the dark tunnel wasn't there anymore. My eyes slowly recovered from the intense brightness, and I was looking down at luscious woods, with vines, and plantations of olives that stretched along a river. On one side was a range of snow-capped mountains, with their summits covered by clouds, which thinned out to reveal the gigantic, jagged peaks beyond..."

Jason stopped talking and became dreamy and distracted. Pinching the bridge of his nose he frowned, as if in pain, before he was able to continue.

"OK, so uh... yeah – the mountains above the clouds would become lost again when the mists thickened for a while, and sometimes blue sky would peak through in places."

Alan felt he had to say something.

"Sounds awesome."

"It was. There were these soft green pastures and woods below that sort of clung to the skirts of the mountains, and I could see flocks of birds and herds of sheep. To the other side, in the distance, huge plains were becoming lost in the mist. Behind me was a gorgeous, deep blue sea."

"So, it's like one of those typical near-death experiences you read about."

"Except this *was* death, remember?"

"Oh yeah. Sorry."

"One thing that confuses me now, but I didn't see anything odd about it then, those mountains were bloody miles away, but I could see the individual flowers growing on their slopes really clearly."

Alan perked up on hearing that. He'd read a couple of books on remote viewing that suggested something to him.

"Interesting. Could it be something to do with a kind of four-dimensional consciousness?"

Jason turned to Alan with heavy eyes. "No idea what you're talking about Al."

Alan scratched his head and tried to explain. "I read about these guys who were sort of psychic spies, in the USA, back in the seventies. They say they could set their minds free to see things that were many miles away, while their bodies were left behind in a darkened room. They're in a dream state; they can see in four dimensions. It's called remote viewing. To reach that state of mind they need to access what they call theta and delta waves.

It's like meditation, I guess. Some of them have written about it. One remote viewer who worked for the intelligence agencies said it was a divine gift. Speaking of the divine, did you say you had a conversation with God?"

"What? Did I say that?"

"Yes, you did."

Jason shook his head. He looked heavy-eyed and fatigued, as if he'd just woken up with a horrendous hangover. "Look, can we give it a rest for a minute?" he said. "Let's talk about something else. I'm feeling a bit groggy. I could do with sitting down somewhere."

"OK. OK. I'm sorry. Just – you know, take it easy."

Alan was starting to think that if Jason had been suddenly resurrected, maybe he also had some place where he was living now. If that was true, it would show that there was some divine force pulling a lot of strings., re-shaping reality. To test that hypothesis, he put his hand to his mouth and coughed and tried to sound as matter of fact as he could. "Where do you live now?"

"Camberwell," said Jason, rubbing his eyes.

"Camberwell? But you've never lived in Camberwell."

"Well, I do now."

As they walked past the post sorting office in Rathbone Place Alan became struck by something that made no sense.

"Alan. Back in the lecture theatre I saw that guy Kevin Sharpe, the sculptor guy who had the studio next to yours."

"Oh yeah. He was there."

"But he didn't seem bothered about you being there."

"No. He was cool. I chatted to him on the way in."

"But... that's crazy. I mean - he was at your funeral. He *knew* you died."

"Well, he's obviously forgotten."

"How could he forget?"

"No idea. Why don't you ask him?"

"Maybe I will, if I see him again. Not that I'm too keen on the guy. His work is terrible. Absolutely talentless."

"Yeah. I don't like what he does either. But he's good company in the pub. Drinks like a fish."

"And what about Steve Ormsley, who used to play guitar with you. I saw him sitting right near you. He was at the funeral too. I saw him crying like a baby. He should've been totally traumatised by you being there – alive and well."

"Well, he was pretty relaxed when we had a jam in his studio last night."

"What? Didn't he even wonder how the hell you came back from the dead?"

"Never asked."

"This is insane. So, they were both totally cool about your resurrection?"

"Nope. They probably don't know I was ever dead."

"Christ. Maybe I'm the only person who does remember."

"Could be."

Alan had to consider that for a moment. Was it possible that some divine entity had somehow constituted a completely new life for Jason, to make his resurrection fit in with everything again? That would involve some major tinkering. Of course, for that sort of intervention to work it would mean everyone who was part of Jason's life would need to have their memories wiped. As they crossed Oxford Street it occurred to Alan, that amnesia wouldn't be enough. There would have to be major physical changes to everyone whose life had been in any way connected to Jason. The idea was unsettling. Alan felt a sudden urge to call Jenny. Of course, he wouldn't tell her anything about Jason being here now – *alive* – over the phone. She'd have a seizure. Or, most likely, think he was losing it."

That instant Jason stumbled sideways into Alan, almost knocking them both over. They were just entering Soho Square at that point. Fortunately, Alan reacted fast enough to keep them both upright, taking a firm hold of Jason and ushering him over to the nearest bench.

"Whoa. Take it easy there, fella."

Jason looked pale and dazed as they both sat down. He wiped his brow with the back of his hand.

"Just give me a second. Feeling a bit queasy."

"Sure. You just take it easy. I'm going to give Jenny a ring, see what she's up to. Won't be a minute."

Jason sighed and looked down between his legs, as if he'd just run a marathon. Then he wiped his brow, which was covered in sweat despite the coolness of the day.

"Sure," Jason nodded. "You go ahead."

Just behind them on Carlisle St a small crowd of media types had built up outside the Guinness bar. Meanwhile, near their bench, in the square, a Goth girl dressed in black stopped and waited for her boyfriend to light a cigarette.

Alan got his phone out, punched in Jen's number, and held the handset to his ear. All he could hear was a screeching, high-pitch, tone. What did that mean? He tried again, with the same result. Maybe her phone was damaged somehow. He would try the landline.

This time the phone rang as normal, but there was no reply, although he waited for quite a while. That was strange. She had a big deadline on an illustration job she was working on for the Radio Times, so she wouldn't normally go anywhere in that situation, and was probably ensconced in her studio upstairs listening to Radio 4. Perhaps she was struggling, and didn't have time to answer the phone. But she could rarely resist taking a phone call, in any circumstances. He fought back an urge to go home right away, but when he saw Jason resting his elbows on his knees, with his head in his hands, in apparent pain, he put that on hold.

A forty-something man in dark glasses, black leather trousers, and a mop of bleached blonde hair was walking a white Airedale, heading towards the hut in the middle of the square.

"Uh, Jason?" said Alan.

"Jason sat up, looking at Alan with tired eyes.

"This bag is a bit of a pain. I'm going to drop it off at Capricorn Films. It's only down the road. You OK to move on?

Jason nodded.

They went out of the square towards Dean Street, passing through the throng outside the Guinness bar, and every step they took Alan could see that Jason was becoming visibly more and more lethargic. They carried on, along the narrow alleyway where Private Eye Magazine was based, which was just around the corner from one of their favourite lunchtime venues, the faithful old Star Café. But this was no time to think of food. Turning into the road with the Old Hat Factory they headed towards Wardour Street. It was getting dark now, even though it wasn't that late. Confused, Alan looked up to see a massive cloud spreading itself across the sky, a black duvet moving in slow motion.

Soon they entered a small alleyway leading into a square courtyard, just off D'arblay Street. In Georgian times these four-story buildings would've been housing for many families, but now they were functioning as offices and studios for the media industry, although some of the lofts had been converted into apartments, for those occasions when the director would find he was working too late to go home, or whenever a comfortable bed would come in handy. In the left-hand corner, the ground floor had a modern frontage, with the word 'CAPRICORN' emblazoned on the glass frontage, in foot tall, bold, sans serif type. Alan led Jason over there, pushed the buzzer by the door and waited. After a crackle a high, pitch male voice came through the intercom.

"Hi."

Alan leaned closer to it, "Oh hi. I'm a friend of Rosie's."

There was no reply. Simply the prolonged farting sound that indicated the catch was now released. They entered a reception area with a bare brick-walled interior, wooden floorboards, and a long, polish steel curved desk, with a thick, beech wood top, and a couple of plate glass shelves on raised plinths at each end, on one of these was propped a large computer screen. Behind the desk sat a pale, young lad with ginger hair, wearing thick, black framed glasses. As soon as he set eyes on Alan he nodded.

"Hi. Oh... I remember you. Alan West, isn't it? You've done a few voice-overs, here."

"Just a few." That was a major understatement. He must've made two-dozen commercials here over the years, for various agencies.

"I just wondered... is Rosie around?"

"Sure. She's around the back getting drinks together for Studio 4, but I'm sure she'll have time to chat. Do you mind signing in?"

"Sure."

The lad pushed a large open pad with a pen attached to it on a piece of red string. Alan took the pen.

"Great. Thanks," said the lad, turning the pad around so he could do the honours. "Go right on through. You know the way."

Jason followed as Alan walked over to the double doors on the right. They went through into the narrow hallway, where framed gold and silver discs were mounted along the whole length. Jason asked Alan if he knew where the toilets were.

"I'm bursting," he said.

Alan pointed to a small alcove to the right and told him to meet him in the room at the end. Jason nodded and hurried off in that direction.

Edit suites 1, 2 and 3 were bunched together on one side and 4 was on the right. It had a red light outside it, to indicate that a recording was in progress. Ahead the kitchen door was slightly ajar. When Alan got there, he pushed it in gently, and there was the unmistakable profile of Rosie Tushingham, with her blonde, pixie-style hair, tight three-quarter length jeans and black ballet slippers. She was trying to find a space for a pot of tea on a tray, which already had several cups and saucers on it, and a plate of chocolate biscuits. That done she lifted the tray. Having looked up she stood open mouthed and immediately put it down again.

"Alan!"

She rushed over to give him a big hug. He couldn't help noticing how she had filled out beautifully over the years.

"What are you doing here?" she was still holding his elbows as she spoke.

He held up his rucksack.

"Can I leave this with you and pick it up in the morning?" he asked.

She took it from him and shook her head.

"Is that it? That's a terrible excuse for coming over to see me."

He shrugged nonchalantly.

"Well, I had to think of something."

"You look a bit tired," she said. "Is everything alright?"

"I was..."

There was the sound of footsteps in the hallway. Instantly Rosie's eyes widened, along with her mouth. She looked as if she was going to say something, but it turned into a little, high-pitched yelp as she collapsed with a thud onto the floor, where she lay twisted, between the kitchen and the hallway by the open door.

"Shit."

Alan immediately realised that the sight of Jason approaching must have given her the shock of her life. Why didn't he think? How stupid could he be? Rosie had known Jason even longer than he had. She was there at Jason's funeral with her husband, Derek. They gave Alan and Jenny a lift to the crematorium and sat next to them at the service. Fuck. He should have considered all that before bringing Jason in there. Why didn't he do that? Maybe he was confused by the fact that some of those people at the lecture who would have known Jason had died didn't react at all to him being there alive – sitting among them all. They had their studios on the same floor as him and they knew him very well, but they reacted as if everything was normal, Jason sitting in there among them, very much alive. This was all becoming totally incomprehensible. Some people knew, some had no idea. But the issue now was Rosie. He crouched down beside her. "Is Rosie OK?" said Jason.

Alan looked up to see him staring at her with a look of concern.

"What do you think?" said Alan.

Jason looked as if he didn't know what to do with himself, as Alan tried to shift Rosie into a slightly more comfortable position, inadvertently he lifted her T-shirt and felt the warm, soft flesh on her back. He rubbed it, in the hope that massaging would help her somehow.

A runner who heard the commotion came out and asked what was going on. Alan stood up. A big guy in a black polo-neck sweater rushed out of studio 4. He had no shoes on. "What the fuck happened here?" he asked.

More people came out from other rooms, including the red headed guy in glasses who was at the reception desk. This was all getting a bit too weird now.

"Did you see what happened?" the bearded guy said accusingly to Alan.

He was trying to work out how to explain that seeing Jason was probably the prime cause of Rosie collapsing, because the sight of him, living and breathing did not compute at all. God knows how they would react to that explanation. Best to obfuscate.

"It's crazy," he said. "She uh, she just came out of the room to say hello and I don't know what came over her. She just dropped. Could it be her blood pressure or something?"

No one said anything for a few seconds. The bearded guy just shrugged.

"Shall I call for a doctor?" said the ginger guy. Everyone ignored him.

The guy in the black polo neck came over and checked her pulse. More people were rushing out of various rooms to see what was going on. It dawned on Alan that the best thing for him and Jason to do right now was to take full advantage of the chaos and make a swift exit. He tugged Jason's sleeve, and they walked back along the hallway discreetly, taking a turn into the alcove where the toilets were. Alan remembered there was another door there opening into the room where staff stored their bicycles. Alan tried it. Fortunately, it wasn't locked. They went in and navigated the obstacle course that was caused by the pile of bikes, reaching the fire door. Alan pushed the bar, and Alan was relieved to be out in the courtyard again, although Jason was still anxious. "Was that all because of me?" said Jason. Alan simply looked sideways at him. Jason winced. Alan immediately felt sorry for Jason because of the confusion and guilt he must have been going through. It seemed unfair, because it wasn't his fault, he found himself back in this world - alive again. Somehow it had happened, and there would of course be all sorts of repercussions from that. Reality seemed to be in a mess. If Alan wasn't careful, he would lose his grip. He had to keep his composure.

"OK. Look. Let's get away from here," he said, putting his arm around Jason's shoulder. "I just need to walk for a bit and get my head around what the fuck is going on here."

That wasn't going to be easy.

Was everything that had happened since he went to the lecture just a figment of his imagination? There were many reasons to justify being distressed, especially given that, for nearly an hour, he had been walking and talking with someone who had been dead for over two years. But Jason hadn't been plonked back into the world just like that. The way things were now, it was as if his death never happened. Whatever tinkering had been done – it had not been done only in the present. The main change must have been made to the past. There's no question – things have been shifted going back at least two years. That's how long Jason said he was living in Camberwell. Crazy as it sounds, what it means is that the previous segment of time which everyone had gone through has now been re-edited, so that they have all had different lives since then.

If that's what's happened, he reasoned, then it's like we're all nothing more than fucking chess pieces, and some omniscient, supernatural chess player has dropped the whole game he was playing on the floor and decided to try to put everything back like it was before, only some of the pieces are in the wrong places now. It's a mess. If it had been done properly then Alan wouldn't be able to remember how things were before – most importantly, that Jason had died. Neither would Rosie. But as soon as she saw Jason walking towards her, she was a scared shitless. That's why she fainted. So, she knows what he knows. But then there's Kevin Sharpe and Steve Ormsley: they were both in tears at the funeral. Their whole memory of Jason's death has been wiped from their minds.

What chaos had been caused because of all these changes? The metaphysical tweaking done to accommodate Jason's re-insertion into reality must now affect everyone whose lives intersected with Jason. Were he and Jenny together even in this version of reality? She didn't answer the phone, did she? The only way to know for sure was to go home. He didn't even want to be with Jason now. If anything, he wanted to get as far away from him as possible. He wished he'd never gone to that sodding lecture. This Resurrection, if that's what it is, has clearly cast a shadow over everything.

And then he suddenly wondered, why was it so dark this early? It was about four o'clock when they went into Capricorn. They couldn't have been in there more than ten, fifteen minutes, max. He looked at his watch and stumbled. "Shit!"

"What?" said Jason.

"What time do you make it?"

"Jason looked at his watch, then gave Alan a look of bewilderment. "That can't be right. Eight twenty-five."

"No!" Alan fumbled in his pocket for his phone.

"Christ. What's going on? We've jumped ahead four hours."

"Is that my fault too?"

They were turning into Lexington Street now,

"Look, Jason. No offence, but I need to go home now. I'm worried about everything. It's hard to explain, but I just want to go and find Jenny... just to see she's there. I'll get the Piccadilly Line to Finsbury Park."

Jason thought about that for a bit and shrugged.

"Sure. I understand. I'll walk that way and get the number 12 to Camberwell."

"Fine."

They turned out of Lexington Street into Brewer Street, and it happened again. Just before they reached Lower James Street a tall, slim, dark haired young man in a North Face jacket stopped in his tracks, right in front of Jason and Alan. He had a look of wide-eyed horror, as he said under his breath, "No..." before collapsing like a demolition job onto the pavement, hitting his head hard on the curb with a crack. There was blood. Jason rushed over to the prostate young man and knelt beside him. "Robert!"

"Do you know this lad?" asked Alan.

"He's my son."

Alan stood open mouthed. "Your what? I didn't know you had a son."

"Alan says," of course I do, and you're his fucking godfather!"

"But you never had a son!"

110

"What are you talking about, Alan?"

Alan glared at the miserable scene, with Jason and the prostrate young man that was his son, before shaking his head slowly, feeling no empathy whatsoever.

"I'm off," he said, without even stopping to look back as he hurried south along Brewer Street. There came to him a brooding apprehension that there definitely had been a seismic shift in reality - a catastrophic, and all-embracing, emotionally devastating disaster. Jason had been Alan's closest friend. He was an inspiration in every way, and he loved him for everything he'd done for him and everyone else. But his resurrection – because that's what it was – had been totally destabilising. Everything in this world had become uncertain and unreliable. Nothing made sense anymore. He even worried that autumn would give way to spring.

His mind was running on overdrive as he turned into Swallow Street and walked under the white arch/bridge to the station entrance at the end of Glasshouse Street. Jenny was the priority now. He needed to know she was OK.

The people rushing in and out of the station all seemed to have pale and worried faces, reflecting his own state of mind. It compounded his anxieties. His heart was pumping, and his head was spinning. He hurried through the barriers and to calm down, he stood on one side of the escalator until he arrived at the bottom, trying to ignore the stressed-out folk rushing down on his left.

The train carriage was crowded so he had to stand all the way to Kings Cross. But it didn't matter. He was pre-occupied with how he to tell Jen about Jason to dwell on the woman's rucksack that was digging into his back, and the odour of the sweat stained armpits of the guy standing next to him.

At Finsbury Park, there was a W3 bus ready to leave when he came out of the back entrance to the station. He managed jump on just as the driver was closing the doors. In two minutes, it stopped at the start of the seemingly endless, canyon of large, redbrick Victorian houses on Ferme Park Road.

Stepping out of the bus and back into the night, he walked along the parade of small shops. Ahead the rooftops and leafless trees were silhouetted against the iridescent, moonlit sky, mottled here and there by dark, drifting clouds.

Outside the local Londis a girl in a white cycle helmet was fixing a metal mesh basket full of groceries to her bike. She turned towards him as he passed, and her face caught the strong yellow light from the shop window. There was something about it that disturbed him. Maybe it was much older than he thought, or too expressionless to make him feel easy or comfortable. Picking up his pace, he crossed over, and walked a little further in the same direction, and then turned left just before the brick railway arches.

The first thing he noticed outside the house was that the hedge was ragged and overgrown, and the hydrangeas were dry and sagging. In fact, the whole front garden looked shabby. That was weird, because when he left home it was trim and neat. At least the upstairs light was still on. A feeling of trepidation overwhelmed him. For a while he stood poised, with keys in hand, at the front door, building up the courage to enter. For some reason, he decided to knock first. While he waited, he glanced nervously over at the neighbouring house. As he expected, the nosey old lady was there watching, behind the slightly lifted curtain.

"What the hell does she do all day?" he wondered.

He knocked again and again, but his rapping resulted in no reaction whatsoever. There was nothing else for it. He tried the key, and the door opened. He stepped in and turned on the hall lights. His bicycle was leaning against the wall, though Jenny would never allow that. Bikes had to go in the shed. Looking ahead he saw that the stair carpet looked grubby, and the kitchen door was open. But the lounge was his first port of call. In the prevailing gloom, he couldn't make out the outline of the glass cabinets that Jenny's grandmother left her. Turning on the dimmer switch he discovered why that was: they weren't there. Maybe Jenny had moved them. The table, sofa and several wooden chairs, and of course the immense fireplace with the antique clock on the mantel were still there, but there was a stack of books piled awkwardly against the wall. What was that all about? Jennies framed pictures and furniture were gone too and the bay windows were filthy. Jenny would never let them get into that state. Only his paintings and photos were on the walls. The room felt characterless. None of this was reassuring. He left the lounge and clambered up the stairs, two steps at a time, going straight into the bedroom. The door was left ajar, and the bed hadn't been made. Inside it felt chaotic - like a student flat. On opening the wardrobe, he found only his own clothes. None of Jenny's jeans, dresses, or coats were there. He couldn't help breathing deeply as he opened the top draw of the chest, where she kept her underwear. Inside there were only his underpants and t-shirts, all of them un-ironed and unfolded. The world just got darker. He tried to compose himself, as he sat down at the side of the bed, but all he could do was tremble. Tears were streaming down his cheeks. He fell back into the pillow, physically and mentally exhausted, and somehow sleep came.

In the morning, he was woken up by a hand shaking his shoulder. He looked up with bleary eyes, trying to get a focus on the face looking down at him. It was Jenny! Her pale blonde hair was dripping wet. It was a little shorter than when he'd last seen her. But she looked great. She smiled and her little piggy eyes lit up, her cheeks swelled, and her tongue pushed up hard against her front teeth. Did she know exactly how sexy that was? Was this a dream, or was yesterday a nightmare?

"What time did you come to bed last night?" she asked. "You look terrible."

He sprung out of the bed and lifted her off the floor with a massive bear hug. She had the big white towel wrapped around her body.

"Easy Tiger. You'll have a hernia. What have you been taking?"

Alan dropped Jenny on the bed and laughed so hysterically that she began to worry for his sanity.

"Are you OK?"

He had to reach for a tissue from the sideboard to wipe his eyes before he spoke.

"Jenny, you have no idea. How can I say it? I had a bad dream last night that Jason was alive again, and it was... it was so distressing. Horrible."

Jenny pouted and squinted at the same time. "Horrible? I thought he was your friend."

"Sure, he was my friend. But... forget about it."

She shook her head, reproachfully. "Sounds boring. Now put me down. I need to make the coffee."

He lowered her gently.

"Where did you go last night?" she asked. "I mean, Christ, you were out from lunchtime, right through to God knows what time, I went to sleep about eleven."

He tried to remember what had happened the day before, but it was all quite hazy. Events were dissolving rapidly from his memory.

A few weeks later Alan was working on a campaign at McCann Erickson, and he was running late on his way back from a long lunch with an old friend in a Thai restaurant on the Tottenham Court Road. He almost ran through Bedford Square, and across Gower Street, then through Keppel Street, towards Senate House. Alan loved that building, with all its art-deco features and its tall white Portland stone edifice. It was like a stunted version of the Empire State Building. He often used it as a shortcut to and from Russell Square. On entering the grand marble hall, he saw a strange figure in a baggy grey suit coming down the opposite entrance towards him. He looked fortyish, skinny and gangly, with a frizzy head of hair that reminded him of Bamber Gascoigne. He was carrying a battered old brown leather suitcase, and as he came closer to Alan he stopped, causing Alan to wonder why.

"I remember you," he said to Alan.

Alan thought it was some kind of joke. "Sorry?"

"You're the fellow who briefly interrupted my lecture a few weeks ago to collect your friend and leave rather hurriedly."

He was smiling as he spoke, and seemed perfectly sincere, as well as being very confident in his recollection of events. That's why Alan felt it was a case of mistaken identity.

"Sorry, but I really don't recall that at all. You must be mistaken."

"No really. I never forget a face. You said you hadn't seen this fellow – your friend – for years." Continued the guy, undeterred. "Though you did apologise, which I fully appreciated at the time, despite the interruption of proceedings. So... was it a spectacular reunion? Was it worth missing out on the rest of the lecture?"

"Lecture? What lecture?"

THE INFERNO

Gary Beecham was dead, and Alan was totally mystified. How did it happen? He was supposed to have had a heart attack, at least that's what the obituary said in the press. Yet he was only in his early forties, at most. And there was no history of any kind of heart condition. You hear about these kinds of things happening in spy versus spy situations in the news, where they have some advanced, hi-tech means of inducing heart attacks that are untraceable, even by the most experienced pathologist. But Gary had no political or intelligence affiliations or connections whatsoever. He was just an animator. He drew cartoons, for fuck's sake. But the disturbing idea Alan wanted to get out of his head was that Gary's death was the result of some kind of curse, hex or voodoo; that it was some kind of inexplicably weird scheme that was meticulously executed by strange means. Alan had always been a natural sceptic, yet he found himself seriously considering if the supernatural may have been involved in some way, though he had no real evidence to think that. How did that vague suspicion come about?

After spending a year in Paris, Alan and Jenny moved to New York. They had a wonderful time there. Alan was working for a production company, while Jenny found work for an events magazine. With the help of friends who had been living there for nearly five years, they found a spacious and beautifully furnished apartment on the first floor of a former Victorian sewing machine factory in Brooklyn Heights. The owners were antique dealers, currently on sabbatical in Florence, and they weren't due back for two years. When Alan's contract was up eighteen months later, Alan and Jenny were sad to leave, but they were starting to feel a little homesick. It was coming up to Christmas when they left, and the snow had been falling so heavily in Brooklyn that the cars on the street below lined up like sacred mounds.

London, as they expected, was grey and wet, and the skies over Kentish Town Road seemed to be perpetually dark. However, it was good to be back, and thanks to their New York earnings they were now able to pay off all their debts (mostly accrued in Paris). They even had a good sum left over which they set aside in case of an emergency. But, as it happened, that emergency came around sooner than they expected, because Alan couldn't get any work. It became clear that the main obstacle to employment for Alan was the fact that London's animation studios had become incredibly cliquey, and he'd simply been away too long. Six months after they returned home, he hadn't even managed to find a single day's work, so it was no surprise when their savings were all used up. Yes, Jenny did get the odd bit of illustration work, but their overdraft facility was still nearly stretched to the limit, and they were getting behind on their mortgage. These were worrying times. Neither Alan nor Jenny's family could help them out.

That's why they had to thank God for Alan's best friend, Jason. He lent Alan some money and made it clear that he was in no rush to get it back. He also put the word out to various studios that he knew a great layout and storyboard artist who was available. And while that message was percolating, Jason also had an idea of how he would go about getting Alan to work alongside him. This was at Jago Productions, the hot shop in the London animation scene. Jago was set up by Gary Beecham, an animation director from New York who had been living and working in London for nearly ten years. They had built up a fabulous reputation for creating a whole string of stylish animated commercials and for their beautiful and entertaining, animation shorts, which picked up awards all over the world. Their achievements had eventually attracted attention from Dino Guinizelli, the famous Hollywood director behind the Vietnam classic *Two Days to Saigon*, and the Mafia feature *Capo dei Capi*. Their work had made such an impression on him that he chose Jago as the production company for his first animated feature – *Dante's Inferno*.

Gary Beecham was a talented animator, and a fine draughtsman too, and as Arthur Conan Doyle once said, since "Mediocrity knows nothing higher than itself; but talent instantly recognizes genius", and that's why he hired Jason to help design the project.

Jason was producing some stunning work. Gary loved everything he did, so he was sure he'd built up enough brownie points to get Alan in there. When Gary Beecham came back from Montreal, Jason waited for an optimum moment to ask. But the result was not what he hoped for. Gary said he knew and respected Alan and his work, but he didn't feel it was right to make any changes to the personnel at Jago. Jason let Gary know the bad news the next day.

The following Tuesday Alan spent the morning hawking his work around the visualising studios in Soho, in the hope that he would be appreciated in that side of the creative industry. But as he found with the animation companies, even though the people loved his work and they were very impressed by his experience, business was slow, and they couldn't take on any more artists. Alan was starting to think that he posed a threat to some of the senior creatives in these London companies. Whatever the reason, week after week of disappointment was taking its toll.

The last studio he went to was Snapper Art. He left there feeling useless and miserable. Within seconds of him stepping out onto the pavement in Cleveland Street, it began to rain. He ran to Goodge Street Station like a demon. From an ever-present old stallholder there, whose face he knew, he bought a cheap, fold-up brolly. Then, instead of making use of it, he decided to go into the underground station. He got on a southbound train to Embankment, where he switched over to the District Line. The whole time he was thinking about whether they should go abroad again, but neither he, nor Jenny would want to do that.

At South Kensington, he walked along the long tunnel leading to the Science Museum. When he had climbed the steps leading up to Exhibition Road it had already stopped raining, the sun was out, and there was a patch of blue sky over the trees in Hyde Park. He walked the short distance to the Royal College of Art. The RCA library subscribed to all the trade journals and possessed an amazing collection of books on art & design, film, illustration and much more. It was an excellent place for him to dry out too. He spent some time going through D&AD annuals, especially the advertising awards pages. Then he started scouring the back pages of various media publications.

By half past three he was on his way home, again via the underground. Coming off the escalator at Camden Town he discovered it was raining again. He thought about getting the bus to Prince of Wales Road, but he had his fold-up brolly in his rucksack. When he reached that part of Kentish Town Road going over the

Regents Canal, the rain became torrential, and a powerful gust of wind turned his flimsy umbrella inside out. In a fit of rage, he threw the spineless appendage into the canal. It took a fair bit of self-restraint now for him not to do the same with his portfolio.

Rain was dripping from his nose, hair and his coat. Jenny looked up from her drawing board and rushed to the airing cupboard to grab him a fresh towel.

"Been for a swim, have we?" she said, when she threw it over to him. She was clearly in a good mood.

"Something like that," he said as he started drying his hair with the towel.

She sat back at her desk and carried on with her painting of an Edwardian waitress serving a young couple in an oak panelled room.

"Just had another wasted morning," he said. "Carting that folder around. I even went to the RCA to check out the magazines."

"Oh, right," she said. There followed a moment of silence, before she felt emboldened to ask," Did you look in Creative Review? I've just found something interesting for you."

He finished scrubbing his head and hung the towel over the back of a chair, on which he then sat down.

"I looked in the latest edition," he replied. "There was bugger-all there… far as I could see."

She stopped painting and grabbed a magazine from the small table to her right, where she kept her brushes and paints and walked over to hand it to him.

"Oh yeah? Well, take a look at that."

She opened it out to the back pages, and she had ringed one of the small square ads with a red magic marker. Alan put on his glasses to take a closer look. He shook his head in disappointment.

"Yeah. I saw this," he said. "It's for a manufacturing company in Yorkshire. What are they doing advertising in Creative review? It says they're looking for film technicians. Jen - I'm not a fucking film technician."

Jenny sighed. "Just stop and think for a minute, Al. How the fuck would they know what a film technician is? They're a manufacturing company in Yorkshire. They've probably never made a fucking film in their lives, and they wouldn't know where to start.

But they obviously need to for some reason. With your experience in storyboarding, animation, working with special effects people, cameramen, actors, technicians, and sitting in on script meetings and edits you could do it."

"But I'm just me. I'm not a studio."

"Yes. But you know plenty of people. You could even set up a little company."

Alan shook his head. "Jen. Listen. Even if you're right, we don't live anywhere near Yorkshire. How would I get to work every day?"

Jenny shook her head in disappointment, like his old head of maths used to.

"What's come over you, all of a sudden? Yeah, okay. Like… you've had a hard time looking for work and getting lots of rejections. But that shouldn't mess your brain up. Look."

She went over and grabbed the magazine from him and pointed to the ad again. "There's hardly any description there. Who knows? Maybe they don't need you to go up there to do the job. Maybe you can work here, then send the work in the post. Do me a favour love. It's not even half past four yet. Give this number a call. What've you got to lose?" She gave the magazine back to him.

Confused, he looked at it again. Jenny came over, hugged him to give him a big, long kiss, so that he began to have other things on his mind.

"Uh-uh!" she said. "Phone first."

A voice came up that sounded like it belonged to a middle-aged woman sitting at a 1950s-telephone switchboard.

"Baskin Industries, how can I help?"

"Uh… Hi. I've just seen your ad in Creative Review, saying that you're looking for someone with expertise in film making and I wondered if the position was still vacant?"

"Oh that. To be quite honest with you, we haven't had any enquiries at all. Are *you* a film technician?"

Alan avoided answering the question directly, but he did explain his background in media and animation.

After a couple of minutes of listening to Alan, she said, "I think the best thing is for you is to talk to Mr Marshall. Let me see if I can get him for you."

He heard her shout through a muffled receiver: "Harry, my love. Can you nip down and see if you can tell Mr Marshall there's a call for him?"

Alan felt as if he was in the middle of an Ealing comedy. It took over a minute before her voice came up again.

"Sorry about that, love. You still there?"

"Uh, yes. I'm here."

"Lovely. We've located Mr Marshall for you. Putting you through now."

There were a few clicks, and the odd crackle before he heard a gravelly male voice, with a thick Yorkshire accent say, "Alan White?"

Alan had to think about that for a second. "Uh, yeah that's me."

"Andrew Marshall. Good of you to get in touch. Sorry about the delay. Just been on the factory floor sorting out an order. I might be the chairman, but I still have to get my hands dirty from time to time."

Alan pictured a small, man in a waistcoat, with a military moustache on the other end of the line: a kind of modern equivalent of the benevolent mill owners of the mid-nineteenth century.

"So, Brenda tells me you've had a lot of experience in film, is that right?"

"Uh, yes. That's right."

"Very good, very good. Tell me more."

Alan was prepared for everything, except a direct and positive response. It was an effort to suppress his excitement and stay focused. He described his educational qualifications, his degree in visual communication and his experience in animation and film, all of which impressed Andrew Marshall.

To reciprocate, Andrew Marshall told Alan that in the early days of home computing, Baskin developed their own version of the Sinclair ZX80, which was a success. Since then, they've moved more and more into computing – including computer software. Now they're looking to get involved in computer games, which they see is the logical next step forward in a burgeoning market. The problem is that they have no experience in creating the moving visuals, and they don't know where to start. And that's where Alan may be able to help. He explained that the company is based in Scarborough, which is 250 miles away from London, but the work can be developed off-site. He asked if Alan could come up next week to meet with him and the rest of the board at Baskin Industries. Alan agreed, without hesitation.

Alan put the phone down, clenched his fists and shouted, "Yes!"

Jenny looked at him in semi-disgust, as he charged around the table to swoop her up. He asked her how she was so sure that the small ad in Creative Review was going to be so such a winner.

"It just stood out for me," she said.

He looked incredulous. "Come on! I mean, there's absolutely nothing about it that could stand out," he responded. "It's just... completely utterly ignorable."

Jenny shook her head from side-to-side, and raised her eyebrows, as if surrendering to the inevitable. "Well, if you must know,' she said, "it was because of the dream I had."

"What dream?"

"About us being back at college."

"Tell me more."

"Yeah. It could have been the end of a three-week project or something, where we all had to do a book cover for Wuthering Heights. Along with the whole illustration group, we've had to put our work up on the wall. Then Geoff and Andrew and some other tutors (I think) are doing the crit. I remember you put up this drawing of a Yorkshire terrier, and everyone loves it."

"Ha-ha-ha-ha. That's a bit mad."

"But think about it for a minute. Where is Wuthering Heights set?"

Alan thinks for a second, before saying, "the Yorkshire Moors."

"That's right. And the dog was, wait for it... a Yorkshire terrier."

"Ah. That explains Yorkshire. But still..."

"And what did we used to call those gatherings, you know, when the tutors would assess all our work in front of us on Fridays?"

"They were creative reviews..." suddenly the penny dropped, and he nodded.

"Oh, I see."

The receptionist told Alan that Jason had gone out for a coffee with 'Dino', but he wouldn't be long. It suddenly struck Alan that she could only be referring to Dino Guinizelli. It was incredible to think how his old buddy from art school was hobnobbing with one of the biggest names in Hollywood, who also happened to be one of his favourite directors, up there with Hitchcock and Orson Wells. Just at that point Alan heard a voice in a distinct New York accent from behind him.

"Alan White, isn't it?"

He turned around to see a relaxed, smart casual guy in his late thirties or early forties, with loose dark wavy hair, white shirt with open collar, unbuttoned navy jacket and brand new Levis – hands in pockets. It took a moment before he realised this was Gary Beecham, Jason's boss and the owner of Jago Productions. This is the guy who told Jason he didn't want Alan in there, so Alan wasn't feeling sociable. He worked with him before, but without too much contact. Alan felt then that he was hard to work out, but he was always charming and friendly.

"Oh, hi Gary. Good to see you again. It's been a while."

"*The Silver Salamander* wasn't it?" said Gary. "Seems like a lifetime ago."

Alan nodded. "A lot of talented people did some great work on that picture. I just wish the studio had let Richard finish it!"

"Yeah. Jesus. Then I think… yeah, that's right. You were at Crossbow Pictures on that short directed by Harvey. He was there at the same time as me?"

"Yeah. But I met you before that at Jason's life class."

"Yeah. I remember you did some neat life drawings. So how are things with you right now?"

"I got back from New York in January. I was working for a visualising studio out there. Hard work, but I learned a lot. Been quiet since then, but I may have found something that could turn everything around for me."

"Sounds good. Any place I'd know?"

"Doubt it. It's a software/tech manufacturing company up in Yorkshire. They need a lot of help setting up a games division. I'm going to go up and talk to them next week."

"Wow. Sounds great. How the hell did you get a connection like that up there?"

"Saw it in an ad."

"An ad?"

"Yeah. In Creative Review, of all places."

"Wow. I never would've thought there'd be anything like that in the back pages of "Creative Review."

"Not sure what they'll need exactly, but they seem keen to talk to me about drawing, storyboards, character design, concepts – who knows what else?"

Gary nodded in deep thought.

"Well done. Hope it works out for you. You deserve a bit of luck."

"Cheers."

At that moment Gary was summoned by a producer to come in on a phone call.

"Sorry Alan. I need to take this call. Uh… why don't you go over and wait at Jason's desk. You can check out what he's been up to. He won't be too long. Good to see you again. Take care."

"Cheers Gary."

Gary held out his hand to Alan, who shook it, and with that Gary was away into a conference room.

Alan walked over to the corner of the room that Gary had indicated. Despite Alan's familiarity with Jason's work, these paintings still acted as a shock to the system for Alan. There was such distinct focus to all the elements, and everything was so perfectly proportioned, yet vigorously executed; every character totally brimming with energy and life, every expression executed with perfection. This wasn't just Jason's vision of hell, it was an eruption of seething suffering and malice, torture and torment, a cacophony of unrest and upheaval beheld by two observers, who may appear undaunted, but there is a suggestion of suppressed horror tightly coiled up that is ready to spring at the slightest pressure. This wasn't a product of fantasy or romanticism, it was an outpouring, an expression. And it wasn't an attempt to slavishly depict a fantasy. It was a depiction of a place – and that place happened to be hell. The blasphemous creatures that soared and leered at the tortured souls below were so believable you would think they were painted from life.

Jason was uncompromising in his desire to convey the haunting and stunningly real images in his mind's eye. His deep understanding of human anatomy, and profound knowledge of divine principles, including scared geometry, allowed him to create a composite reality of evil, that was a truly gruesome physiology of the demonic. With these images Jason stirred up smouldering sensations of strangeness from the primordial regions and shadowy ancestral memories buried in the subconscious mind. Jason had shown us the rush of ecstasy that a lizard-skinned demon is experiencing from the pain of the naked individuals immersed in the burning hot, treacle-like liquid below. His leathery wings are outstretched, as his minions hover nearby in wait, and his lascivious, red tongue protrudes obscenely through his glistening fangs.

"What do you think?" said a voice from behind.

Alan turned to see Jason hands plunged into his black jean pockets. A slight paunch was beginning to show over his belt, but he looked smart in a brand new, smart, two-tone, viridian green jacket with a silky beige shirt. Since he and Jenny were abroad, Jason's hairline had receded dramatically, making his high forehead seem even more pronounced. The top of his head now featured a sharp triangle of thin, wispy strands protruding from the mass of dark brown hair at the back. Angular, well-groomed sideburns divided his face vertically.

"Oh, Jas. Yeah. Fuck me, all that work it's brilliant. Beautiful stuff. What is it?"

"That, Alan my boy, is the eighth circle of hell.

Seems a bit sadistic though, what those geezers in the black goo are being put through."

"They're being totally burned and blistered every second they're in it. And get this. If they stick out of it too far, then those flying demons with the leathery wings a hovering around, ready to tear them to shreds. Nice, eh?"

"What exactly did they ever do to deserve that?"

"They committed fraud when they were alive."

"Fraud? Is that it? Seems a bit excessive if you ask me, boiling people for all of eternity and ripping them to shreds, just for ripping few people off."

"Nah. Fuck 'em. Fancy a beer then?"

"Let's go."

Jason kept his black trilby hat on in the pub, while Alan explained about his call to the Yorkshire company, and how it could lead to big things. Jason wasn't really listening. Something was bothering him. The best thing was to let him come out with it in his own time. Sure enough, when they sat in the Greek restaurant eating their main meal the formerly hidden thoughts were flowing freely. The trigger was when Alan asked him about his job.

"So how you getting on. It must be amazing working on an animated version of Dante's Inferno?"

He puckered his lips dismissively and shrugged. "Ah, it's OK."

Alan couldn't believe the blasé nature of his reply.

"What are you saying? This is a dream project. You're working for one of the top directors in Hollywood. How is that just 'OK?'"

Jason frowned forming a long, deep vertical furrow.

"You don't know him," said Jason. "I'm telling you... he's really frustrating. Keeps changing his mind about *everything*. I give him exactly what he wants, he almost orgasms over it. Then the next day it's, 'Hey Jason. I was just thinking how we could do that a little different.'

"But that's not an unusual thing for a director to do."

Jason sighed. "I'm having to do loads of versions of the same scene, over and over again. Even though I followed the fucking script – to the letter."

"Does he give you a reason for the changes?"

"Yesterday it was because his wife had a good idea."

"What?"

"Alan. You know me. I don't like to re-do anything."

Alan was speechless. He couldn't quite believe that Jason could throw away the opportunity of a lifetime, through a quirk about hating re-dos and his frustration with one of the greatest living movie directors. Alan could sense Jason's concern, and it pleased him, in a mildly sadistic sort of way.

He pulled that firm-set, calm, self-satisfied, and knowing smile, which was enhanced by the intense stare of his pale blue eyes, and broad jaw and decided to twist the screw a little more. "Do you know what he blurted out to me the other day?"

"Surprise me," said Alan.

He said: 'Jason. You're right. I don't know what I want. But I do know what I don't want.'

Jason leaned back pushing his hands against the edge of the table, as if a plate of bad eggs had been put in front of him.

"How can you expect me to work with someone like that?"

Images of a Kamikaze pilot performing his last heroic act came to Alan's mind.

"Uh… OK. So, what did you say to him?"

"I said 'Dean, how the fuck did you ever get to make *Capo dei Capi* with an attitude like that?"

"Shit. How did he react to that?"

He went quiet, and then he burst out laughing. Then he said he liked me for being so straight with him.

Alan could see that this gesture might have not been as conciliatory as Jason believed it was.

"Does Gary know you said that?"

"Sure, he does. He was right there when I said it, wasn't he?"

"What did he say?"

"Nothing."

"Nothing?"

"No."

Alan was getting increasingly excited about the meeting with Andrew Marshall in Yorkshire. On the morning before he was due to travel up there, he had intended on taking a walk along the Grand Union canal to Kings Cross from Camden Town, to pick up his train ticket, but when he walked out of the house he found it was too hot and humid, so he decided to wait until later. He decided to play the guitar instead, and while doing that he could hear Jenny answering the phone downstairs. In less than a minute, she was yelling from the bottom of the stairs.

"Alan. It's for you!"

He put his guitar down and went over to pick up the receiver that was on his side of the bed. A woman with a strong Northern accent said, "Hello. Is that Alan White?"

"Yes."

In a very matter-of-fact way she uttered, "Brenda Sidebottom, Andrew Marshall's secretary." I wanted to let you know that the meeting scheduled between you and Andrew tomorrow has been cancelled."

"Oh?" Alan supposed that Andrew must have double booked. "OK. So, when would it be convenient for us to re-schedule?"

"That won't be necessary," she said.

Alan had spoken to her four or five times, and she had always been warm, friendly. Now her tone was assertive, cool and matter of fact.

"Sorry, butI don't know what you mean."

"We wouldn't want you to waste any time and money to travel here unnecessarily."

"But…" Alan was lost for words. He tried to work out what could have led to this snub. Nothing sprang to mind. Baskin surely couldn't have found someone else from their ad in Creative Review, could they? He wondered if they'd thrown out the whole idea of setting up a computer games section. But that was unlikely, especially after all the time and research Andrew said they'd put into it. And even if they had made such a reversal surely, he at least deserved a chance to have a conversation with Andrew Marshall.

The cold fish voice became even colder. "Mr Marshall is busy. Thank you for your time. Goodbye."

And with that she hung up.

He stayed sitting on the bed in disbelief, slowly coming to terms with the finality of it all, feeling it. That was the end of his dream of launching a new chapter in his career. He thought about all the hope his forthcoming trip to Yorkshire held for him. The prospect raised him up in the morning to plan, to forge new ideas, to work out where he could rent some space when things evolved beyond the capacity of a virtual studio to handle. This was the vision that enchanted him as he lay down at night. It was the one idea that seduced him, the rose-tinted window between him and the world. And now it was gone.

Jenny was even more surprised than Alan when she heard. Had she read the dream wrong? Impossible. Still, the important thing was to console Alan, because this stupid phone call had left him feeling very low.

He went on long walks on his own most days, from the flat to Highgate and then Hampstead, and then back along Chalk Farm Road, stopping for the odd coffee or pint along the way. Sometimes he went to Muswell Hill and then trudged along the abandoned railway line to Finsbury Park. He wrote a lot in his diary a lot too. All of this helped him channel his initial despair.

After much soul-searching and reflection, he found himself recalling the time he was working in the visualising studio in New York. He was always curious about those various advertising people who used to breeze in and out of the studio to brief him and the other artists on how they wanted their scripts drawn up. They were generally smart and confident in themselves, much more so than the artists he was working with in the studio. They were interesting, quick-thinking and confident, they also had a bit more style about them too. However, most of the scripts they brought in were often cheesy, and uninspiring. Even the ones that were meant to be funny were usually just corny. There were exceptions, but in nearly every case he knew himself well enough to believe he could do better. Maybe he should have a stab at getting a job in advertising. After that, Alan started investigating and he found out from a friend who was already in the business about something called the D&AD (Design and Art Direction) Course, in which he would learn how to become an advertising creative over three months. He signed up, and it was hard work, and very intense. He and the other students were to learn the ropes from some of the most well-respected figures in the industry. Those twelve weeks released his creativity and enthusiasm in ways he had never experienced before. He soon became the star pupil from that class, and at the end of it all, he was hired by J Walter Thompson, a very prestigious agency. He would, however, be starting at the bottom as a junior art-director, so the salary was low, and he and Jenny would continue to struggle financially. But luckily, within a few months, he was headhunted by another big agency, and his salary was almost trebled. Life was good. He and Jenny were now hoping to buy a large house they had found in Crouch End, although someone was trying to gazump them, which was proving to be stressful.

By then, Jason had set up his own visualising and storyboard company, which was backed by a print entrepreneur, who set him up with premises in Great Marlborough Street. Jason recruited at trusted team of artists and reps and named the business Hey Presto Studios.

Now that Alan was an advertising art-director, he could pass a fair bit of work Jason's way. Jason would usually come over to the agency where Alan Worked, in Charlotte Street to get briefed by Alan and his copywriter, or send his rep. Occasionally, Alan would head over to Jason's studio in Great Marlborough Street to talk him through what was required. They were based on the first floor of a 1950s redbrick building, in a small white boxroom at the back of a large design and print studio, which belonged to Jason's backer.

On one occasion Alan went through, knocked on the door of Hey Presto, and entered. It was the sort of space where W H Smith would store all their unsold books if they had a shop on the ground floor. There were two large, metal-frame portrait windows that faced onto the back yards between Poland Street and Carnaby Street. A fire escape ran down along one of them. Two of the windowpanes were open, but the room still reeked of magic markers. Hundreds of them were clustered on desktops, alongside lightboxes and layout pads. Jason was sitting on a tall stall, playing guitar by his drawing board, a black polo neck, black drainpipe trousers, and ultra-pointed Churches winkle-picker shoes. Dave, Geoff and Mick had obviously all gone home. Jason saw Alan and gave a broad smile. He stopped strumming and leaned his guitar against the wall.

"Hey Al. You want to do this here, or in the pub?"

Alan took his rucksack off and rested it on a chair.

"I dunno. I reckon it's better if I spread all the bits out on your workbench. We can get a drink in later."

"Sure."

Alan started getting bits of paper out of his bag as Jason picked up one of the scripts. "Oh, this'll interest you," he said. "I bumped into Gary last Friday."

Alan shrugged. "Which Gary?"

You know, Gary Beecham – my old boss at Jago. He's moving his studio over to San Francisco."

Alan didn't much care. "OK. Why's that?"

"He's had a bit of good luck; picked up a project for Warner Brothers. It's kind of an animated version of "The Day the Earth Stood Still", set in the fifties and everything, like the original."

"Uh-huh."

"I was having a fry-up in Juliet's, and he came in and sat at my table. We chatted a bit and I ended up back with him to Jago. They've been designing this new computer game."

"Oh, right."

"They're working on this cereal ad too. But their main bread and butter, since they lost Inferno, is the computer game job. It's for some tech company. I asked him how the fuck he managed to get connected with a business in Yorkshire. He said he felt a bit bad, but he heard about it from a freelancer who thought he had the job in the bag."

Now Alan pricked his ears up and stopped rummaging as Jason continued.

"But, unluckily for that freelancer, Gary rang the company up and got in there first. Business is business, I guess."

"Fuck!"

"What's the matter?"

"I don't believe it."

Jason looked blankly at Alan.

"That fucking freelancer was *me.*"

"Huh?"

"I found that work in Creative Review, in an ad – or rather Jenny did, while you were still working on Inferno. The CEO in Yorkshire was keen to meet me after I told him about my experience in animation at Disney, Universal, BBC and all that. I was gearing up to go up to Scarborough, and then they cancelled on me, for no reason. I was gutted, and I had nothing else at the time."

Jason said nothing in reply.

Alan continued, regardless. "I told him about it when I went to meet you for lunch one day. He made out he was concerned about me being out of work, and coaxed information out of me when I said I found something interesting. Sounding all sympathetic. He must've gone off to make a sly phone call to steal my client the minute he walked into his office."

Jason still said nothing. His face was blank. It was impossible to read what he was thinking. It didn't look like he was sympathising. Maybe it was disbelief, or even utter confusion. He may have found it hard to believe Alan was that 'freelancer'. But Alan had no doubts.

He found himself plunged back into that familiar morass of moodiness that came from that betrayal. Growing up in the tough, West London streets, he and his pals had a harsh code for dealing with injustice. Art college and working in the media business had bred those rough edges out of him. Part of him wanted to waltz right over to Jago, and smack Gary Beecham in the face. But Beecham was an internationally renowned animator, and Alan was still a nobody. The story would get about, and Alan's name would become mud. Although he no longer worked in animation, the advertising industry intersected with animation in many ways. It could damage his career. But he felt not taking some kind of revenge was like failure. In time, those feelings simmered down.

Alan had risen from junior to middleweight status in the creative department in less than a year. What's more, he and his copywriter had even won a prestigious award for one of their alcohol campaigns. It was at that ceremony, during the post presentation meal, that Alan bit into an excessively chewy steak, and broke off an expensively fitted crown at the back of his mouth.

Alan and Jenny kept the same dentist they had when they were students, which made having their teeth fixed a bit of a chore, involving a hundred-and-twenty-mile round trip to the seaside. So, he left work at midday and took the train from Victoria and made it to his dentist by 2.30. The treatment didn't take too long.

By the time he stepped out of the dental practice on the east side of town, thin cloud cover had muted the sunlight, and a cool breeze was coming in off the sea. It was gorgeous.

He decided to walk to the station instead of getting the bus. He took the back streets, behind the law courts and his old college, and crossed the main London Road to meander through the old town. This was the time of year when the foreign language students prowled the street in packs, outnumbering the locals. It made the streets seem remarkably busy for a Tuesday. He stopped in at a second-hand bookshop, where he rummaged around and picked up a battered old paperback of Camus' Myth of Sisyphus for a quid. Pleased with his purchase, he went further along for a short distance before deciding to walk back a bit and check out what was happening at the Bell and Candle. What he discovered was that they had finally changed their window display. It now featured an antique, white enamel Ouija board, surrounded by five small ceramic skulls, a large, illustrated astrology book, a nine-prong candelabra, and an ornately framed image of a pentagram. These items were placed onto the ends of two long pieces of purple velvet curtain fabric. In the V-shaped gap, between the draperies he could see Cornelia and her daughter Bella sitting together at their table. Cornelia was taking a payment from a customer, while Bella was typing. He decided to go in to say a quick hello.

The customer was just preparing to go as Cornelia said, "Oh yes. It's so typical of a dead parent to keep hounding you. I wouldn't worry. I'm always being pestered by my dead father, and I find myself having to give him a good telling off. Anyway, lovely to see you again as always. Take care."

As the customer was heading out past Alan, Cornelia spotted Alan entering. She put her hands on her hips in a matronly manner, that reminded him so much of Mrs Tiggywinkle.

"Well, I never! Look who it is Bella."

Bella stopped typing immediately, looked up open mouthed. "Alan!"

Cornelia tilted her head to one side and beckoned him over, like a policeman conducting traffic. He gave her a hug and a kiss on each cheek. Bella, meanwhile, merely smiled and said, "How have you been?"

"Very good, thanks. Keeping busy. I've just been to the dentist. Broken tooth."

"Oh, you poor thing," said Cornelia. "Is your mouth numb?"

"No, no. It was a dead tooth. I had a root canal done on that tooth years ago. The dentist just put in a temporary filling, and I'm going to have to come back to have a crown fitted in a few weeks."

"Oh. So... Alan. Tell us, what exciting things have been happening in your film career then?"

"You mean animation?"

"Yes."

"Well, since we got back from New York I've not worked in animation. I 'm in advertising now. And I'm no longer freelance – I'm safely ensconce din a full-time job."

"Oh. Why did you change careers like that?"

"Well, it's a long story, but I was hawking my wares trying to get work from animation studios in London, but there were no takers. I was out of work for over six months, and it was getting a bit scary. We could've lost the flat."

Cornelia was listening with genuine concern. "Oh dear. I'm sorry to hear that."

"The straw that broke the camel's back was when I found what I thought was a great opportunity that would not only get me back into animation again, but it was also going to be a fantastic source of work. I would be able to set up my own animation studio."

"That sounds wonderful. So, what happened?"

"Someone stole the work from me.

"What?" Cornelia shook her head in disbelief.

"Was it someone you trusted," asked Bella.

"Well, yeah, I guess it was," shrugged Alan. "But I was naïve. Maybe I should've been more careful. You know I... I just didn't believe anyone could do that to a fellow creative, especially when they already had a successful business."

"Oh dear," said Cornelia. "Was it a big company that did that to you?"

"Not huge."

"Would I have heard of them?"

"Unlikely."

"Try me."

"Jago Productions."

"Quite right. No idea. And was it their CEO who did the foul deed?"

"Haha. You make it sound Shakespearean. I'm not exactly sure if he is their CEO. He's certainly their animation director."

"Oh. Famous, is he?

"Only in the business – within the London animation scene. Maybe in New York too. You won't know of him."

"Try me."

"Name is Gary... Gary Beecham."

"You're right. I've never heard of him. Anyway, you're probably in a rush to get the train back to London, but will you have time for a cup of tea with us?"

Alan looked at his watch. "Well, I was going to get the ten-past-four…"

"Oh, come on." Said Cornelia. "We haven't seen you for, what… three years? You can't just rush off now."

He shrugged, in complete surrender. "OK."

"Milk, no sugar?"

"Perfect."

"Good." Cornelia weaved her way around to the back room, and Bella leaned over to make sure her mother had gone in. When she was satisfied Cornelia was quite out of sight, she stood up and walked over to Alan purposefully. Her black hair was now shoulder length. She was wearing a black polo neck sweater and cream slacks. When she came closer, Alan was expecting a peck on the cheek, but she pushed her breasts into him, grabbed the back of his neck with one hand, and thrust her tongue into his mouth. When she pulled back a little a strand of saliva stretched away with her.

"It's good to see you again, Alan," she said.

She was back at her seat before Cornelia came out with the tea tray. At that point Alan was glad he was wearing a long coat, because he needed something to hide the bulge in his tropusers.

The rest of the conversation was about his current job, which he explained was full-time, and that he was really enjoying creating ads for Martini, Coke and other big products. His pay has already matched what he had been earning in animation, and he and Jenny no longer have any worry about losing the flat. In fact, they were hoping to buy a house in north London, near Crouch End. It needed a bit of work, but it had a big garden and lots of room. Cornelia said that that was great news. But they both see Alan's pained expression."

"You look worried. Is it up in the air about your house?" asked Bella.

Alan's eyes widened, and he raised his brows. "Well… we've put in an offer, but the estate agent says there's this well-off couple in their thirties who are also chasing it. We're anxiously waiting to hear back. We'll need some luck, but it's looking dicey."

Cornelia put her hands on her hips again, as if she meant business. "Ok. Leave it to us."

"Pardon?"

Bella interrupted. "Mama and I will help you."

"Uh, really? And how exactly will you do that?"

Cornelia gave him a stern look. "We'll perform an incantation."

Alan shook his head. "You're having me on?"

"Not at all. I'm deadly serious. We'll make a fire with wood, and sprinkle incense into a bronze chalice, while we walk around it and chant."

Alan knew they meant well, and he didn't want to insult them both by looking too incredulous. "Well, uh… that's very thoughtful of you both," he said.

"Not at all," smiled Cornelia, as she gave him a big hug. "It's our pleasure."

It was too late to go back to work by the time he got back to London.

A few weeks later, Jason came into the agency to get a re-brief on a job his studio had done for Martin, Alan's boss. Jason, Dave and Geoff drew up a storyboard for an alcohol campaign and it wasn't quite what Martin was looking for. Martin insisted that Jason come in to take the debrief himself, and not to send his rep. Jason was not happy about that. He hated being made to change his work, and he didn't like formal meetings.

Alan waited until Jason came out of Martin's office and then took him for lunch at Italia Uno. They got in before the lunchtime rush, and Alan treated him to a ciabatta sandwich with salami, sun dried tomatoes, mozzarella, with the usual dab of Felice's, secret basil, lemon and garlic sauce. After a few bites Jason's grim expression softened. Alan waited for that to happen to ask about how his works drink had gone.

Jason perked up a bit more, "Oh, it was a good laugh. Geoff, Dave and Mick were all there. Richard turned up, and I took Rebecca along too. I did a few of my tricks. Picked up a few new ones from the magic shop under Charring Cross Station.

"Sounds good," said Alan.

"Richard had a bit of shocking news though."

"Really?"

"Yeah. Get this… Gary Beecham is dead."

Alan stopped chewing and coughed. He spluttered out, "What?"

"He's dead. Massive heart attack. He only just set up that studio in the states, you know – to work on that feature - and then that happens."

Alan's pulse quickened.

"Fuck. Did he like… did he have a history of heart trouble, or what?"

"No, he didn't. Nothing like that. He was sitting at home watching TV and that was it."

"Shit." An alarm went off at the back of Alan's mind, and he couldn't quite work out why he was feeling so guilty.

The time came for Alan to head off to the dentist again for his new crown to be fitted. As before, no anaesthetic was needed. And he walked towards the station again, through the old town, this time more purposefully, and popped into the Bell & Candle. Both Cornelia and Bella were there. When the formalities and greetings were over, he told them that he and Jenny had moved into the house they were after, and the couple who tried to gazump them had found somewhere else near Stoke Newington. Then, half-jokingly, he thanked them both for whatever they did to make that possible.

"Oh, it was our pleasure," said Cornelia, in all earnestness.

Bella just smiled and said, as if half distracted by some paperwork on the table, "By the way, whatever happened to that fellow who defrauded you of all that work?"

The blood ran from Alan's face.

"Since you ask. He uh, oh him. Well, actually it's very sad. I heard the other week that he had massive stroke."

Just at that moment Bella sniggered, and Cornelia nudged her.

"Uh, did he recover alright?"

"No. He's dead."

Bella snorted again and it turned into a coughing fit. Alan thought Cornelia was suppressing a smile. Alan strongly suspected they were toying with him.

"Bella! You're spreading your germs around the shop. Go and get yourself a glass of water!"

Bella excused herself and did just that.

"I'm sorry Alan," said Cornelia. "She's not been feeling herself today. A touch of flu I think."

After Alan left the shop, he took a few steps along the street, before deciding to sneak back and peak through the shop window. What he saw through the velvet fabric was disquieting. Cornelia and Bella were laughing so much they had to hug each other. It was as if he could hear their cackling through the plate glass. The colour drained from his face.

What had those witches been up to?

Dassos Petrou

THE SUCCUBUS

Chapter 1

It was the second time he had worked in New York. The first occasion was a couple of years before the children came along. Back then he was working as an illustrator in a storyboard studio, which was dissatisfying but it was an experience that whetted his appetite to make the switch, to become an advertising art-director. In the studio, he was working from mostly unexciting, poorly written scripts, most of which weren't particular good ideas, (most of them were terrible). He felt that (given half the chance) he could do much better. That's why, on his return to London, he signed up for a specialist course in advertising, became the star of the class, and was hired by a big London agency. He quickly
built a solid reputation and moved on to a much more fashionable agency, within a few years he became a golden boy there too. Then the time cam when the CCO needed him to transfer to the New York office to work on an account that needed some resuscitation. It happened so fast that he had to travel without Jenny and the kids, living in a hotel for three months, then moving to a fantastic apartment in Brooklyn. The family would be joining him before Christmas. What could go wrong?

When he met Juliette Doyle, she was working at Seraphim Sound, on West Broadway. What happened was that Gary, Alan's copywriter, accidentally slammed the door into her as she was carrying a tray of drinks into the studio they were recording in. The hot coffee and tea went flying. She was a bit shaken up. Alan held the door open for her and asked if she was OK. She said she would be fine and ran off almost in tears to return with a plastic bowl full of hot, soapy water. She crouched down to clean up the mess, and Alan noticed her long, dark auburn hair, tied in a tight bun at the nape of her neck. He found himself making small talk. She said she was a drama student at Juilliard and was only scheduled to be at Seraphim for two weeks. When she had just finished clearing up the spillage, Gary came back in.

Two hours later, they were listening to the final edit, when Larry, the client, announced that he wasn't happy. Gary, Alan and Sally looked at each other nervously.

Sally asked him what the problem was.

He said he hated the actress doing voice-over. (Luckily, she couldn't hear him, because, at that moment, the intercom was turned off in the recording booth). Sally reminded Larry the ad was due to be aired the next morning, so the audio had to be delivered to the various radio stations in the next two hours. There was no time to book another actress. Larry didn't care. Gary had his face in his hands.

Alan bit his lower lip. He had an idea.

"Listen," he said. "We can fix this. It's going to be OK. There's another actress here. We should give her a go. What's the worst that can happen?"

Sally thanked Aurelia Quinn, the actress whose voice Larry disliked, and told her she was done. Meanwhile, Alan went along the hallway to the main kitchen and saw Juliette preparing drinks. He tapped her on the shoulder, and she turned around surprised when he told her to stop what she was doing and to come into Studio 4 straight away to do a sound test.

"I can't," she said. "I have to take these to Studio 2 straight away."

"They can wait."

He led Juliette back to Studio 4 and ushered her into the recording booth.

It couldn't have gone better. Larry, the (up to now) monstrously difficult and obstructive client, thought she was great. The ad was recorded in double-quick time and Juliette was so delighted about having earned a ton of money for less than an hour's work, that she wanted to thank Alan personally. She snuck out of the booth and rushed straight over to him. When Sally had finished going through Gary and Alan's next schedule she pounced, in her own demur, but rather emphatic way.

He listened politely.

"Uh, Alan. I wanted to say thank you and, uh… just an idea… (cough) I know you must be very busy and everything… but some amazing musicians from Juilliard I know, well they're playing tonight at a place in East Village. I mean, they are *so* cool. Be great if you could come along. Well, I at least owe you a drink. What do you think?"

Juliette arrived just as the band was covering Round Midnight. She stopped near the door to make small talk with the staff, with whom she was obviously very familiar. She eventually caught Alan's eye with the sweetest of smiles, and made her excuses to her friends, before gracefully negotiating the closely packed tables on her way over to him. She took off her fake fur jacket to reveal a black Chanel-style sleeveless dress. Her hair was loose, silky and flowing and her legs were bare, despite the chill in the air.

"Well!" she said, holding out her smooth white hand. "He half stood up to take her hand and kiss her on the cheek. A plane gold bracelet clung to her arm, and she wore a black leather watchstrap loosely against the base of her thumb. A silver cross, dangled over the table from her neck when she leaned forward to get comfortable in her seat.

"I see you're a celebrity in these parts," he said.

She laughed a little. "Oh, I used to work here," she said. "Bernardo is so lovely."

"You mean the guy at the door?" asked Alan.

She didn't answer, as she was twisting around to hang her bag from the back of her chair.

"What do you think of the band?" she asked. "Aren't they brilliant?"

"Impressive. They've been playing some sophisticated tunes in a remarkably mature way," he said.

Her mischievous smile made him melt. "You said that like you were sixty or something."

He feigned disapproval. "How do you know I'm not?" he said.

She frowned, and her pixie-like features screwed up. "Are you cold?" she asked, not waiting for a reply. "I should've told Bernardo to turn up the heating."

Alan studied her long eyelashes, and transparent brown eyes as she casually glanced around the room. Something had obviously grabbed her attention.

"There's Janice and Simon, she said. "I won't chat to them now, though."

Alan had no idea who Janice and Simon were.

"I hope he doesn't bring up his boring journalism course again." She seemed to be talking for her own pleasure. Stream of consciousness. Nothing mattered. It was like being in flux.

The musicians were picking up their instruments again for the second set. Alan examined her profile against the spotlight falling on the small stage: her button nose and thin upper lip, the chin, faintly pointed. There were smiles and nods being aimed at her from all directions. She was in her element.

Alan summoned the waitress and ordered a bottle of Chateauneuf, while they looked at the menus. Juliette recommended the onion soup and said that the steak frites was to die for.

The whole time, he didn't mention he was married with kids, and she didn't ask.

Later he would look back and ask himself how he had ever allowed things to get so far. But he was totally under her spell. Any thoughts that even threatened to intrude on any feelings of affection and tenderness evaporated at the very sight of her.

After the first set, two of the band strolled over to Juliette and Alan's table. She sipped her wine and her eyes lit up.

"Hey!" She stood up to greet them both with a kiss on each cheek.

"So, what'd you think, Jules," asked Dan, a smart-casual, swarthy, square-jawed, slim boy, with a slicked-back mane of black hair.

"C'mon. You know how much I love you guys. You were amazing."

"Jules, you're always exaggerating." said Mike, shaking his head and turning to Alan, as if for confirmation.

"No, it's true." said Alan, "and this is coming from a big Miles Davis fan."

"Hey," interjected Dan, as if in a moment of revelation. You the advertising guy who gave Jules the radio gig?"

"Guilty, as charged."

"Cool."

"We're gonna go get some beers," said Mike. "But listen, if you ever need any cool music for a TV ad, or radio thing... whatever, we're your boys."

He pulled a business card from his shirt pocket and handed it to Alan, who took it respectfully.

As Alan and Mike headed off to the bar, Juliette touched the back of Alan's hand, which was resting on the table. "It would do them so much good if you could do that."

Alan smiled and said nothing.

"How are you finding it here?" she asked, taking her hand away.

"You mean the restaurant – or New York?" he said.

She gave an ironic smirk. "What do you think?"

"This isn't my first visit, you know. I've been coming over to New York since I was a student – (and do I need to say?) – that was a long time ago."

"How long?"

"I'm not saying. Are you originally from New York?"

"Not exactly, but not too far away. I moved over when I started at Juilliard's. I grew up in a small town in Connecticut called Groombridge, about an hour's drive from here."

"Was it like *Happy Days*?"

"Boring as hell. And it gets worse. I went to a Catholic School. So, lots of guilt, punishment and repression."

"Ouch. Any brothers and sisters?"

"No. But I nearly had a sister."

"Nearly?"

"I was one of twins, but my sister didn't make it. Not that I remember anything about her. She died a few months after we were born."

"Oh. That's sad."

She shrugged. "I didn't know about that until I was about seven. I often think about what it would've been like to have a twin sister. You know, hanging out, and sharing clothes and make up and stuff. Maybe even boyfriends! Only joking. Anyway. Mum said it was cot death. And we wouldn't have been identical."

She took a sip of wine and caught him looking at her just a little too forensically over the glass. He reddened.

"I'm sorry," he said. "I couldn't help thinking how much you remind me of someone."

"Who?"

"Well, it's not anyone I actually know, or even knew. Just a person in a portrait by one of my favourite artists - John Singer Sargent. You are so much like her, or at least like the way he painted her. I think it was done in the mid-1880s, when he was in Boston. She was a society girl."

"Ooh. Now you've got me interested. Who's is this person?"

"Someone called Mrs Charles E. Inches."

She squinted. "Eeow! Inches? Sounds like she should have kept her maiden name."

"Ha-ha-ha. Yes. That had a much nicer ring to it - Louise Pommeroy."

She nodded in approval. "Oh, I like that."

"She was just twenty-two when she married, and like a lot of marriages at the time, her husband was a lot older than her. But he was a highly respected general practitioner (doctor, in our language) rolling in money and, more importantly, he was stinking rich. He probably could have married any woman he wanted to. And I have to say he made a brilliant choice; she was absolutely beautiful."

He realised how much he had just revealed, but it was too late. She looked at him pointedly, while appearing to resist a smile. "Oh."

"I uh... you know, Sargent was very taken with her looks. He painted her face with great sensitivity, care and detail. But for her arms and her red velvet dress he used thicker, bolder brushstrokes. Some critics say this girl, Louise Pommeroy, was typical of those fragile, beautiful and strong-willed heroines you often get in Henry James stories. And you know what? She may even have been a model for the heroine in *Turn of the Screw*."

"Ah! Now, I know that story very well. I didn't read it, but I saw an excellent play over at the rep in East Village. If I remember rightly, it's about a young governess, who's haunted by two dead, sinister, servants, and a couple of weird, precocious kids. Very creepy. Do you know that much about *everyone* Sargent painted?"

She swallowed a small mouthful of food and there was a mischievous glint in her eye.

Alan coughed, and some of his wine sprayed onto the white tablecloth. A few spots got onto the collar of his white shirt. He started dabbing at it with the corner of his napkin.

"Uh, no. I can't say I do."

143

Satisfied, she leaned back.

"So, when did you first discover all that about... what was her name again?"

"Louise. Louise Pommeroy. It was just the other day."

She smiled knowingly.

After desert, the waitress came back to clear the dishes and ask if they would like to order coffee. Juliette beat Alan to the answer.

"Could you give us five minutes, Josie?"

"Sure," said the waitress. As the waitress departed with the dirty dishes Juliette leaned forwards and said in a conspiratorial whisper:

"The coffee here is a bit hit-and-miss."

"Oh?"

"Well. Depends on who's making it. Tonight, it's Maurice – and excuse my English, he's crap. The good news is I have some lovely Columbian coffee at my place. It's just over on Park Slope. Oh... wait! I left home in a bit of a hurry, so I didn't get a chance to clear up and it is a bit cramped. What's your place like?"

They didn't speak as the cab headed over Brooklyn Bridge, while overhead the dark clouds twisted and stretched into interesting shapes. Alan made out a camel, a watering can and a map of Europe.

The driver pulled up on corner of Boerum and Court. Under the green awning Alan fumbled around in his pockets and opened the heavy door.

They went up the short flight of narrow stairs one flight and he opened the apartment door, taking her coat when he entered.

She looked around approvingly. "Nice place."

"Put on some music if you like," he said.

"What've you got?"

"Lots of stuff. Everything from Charlie Parker, through to the Thirteenth Floor Elevators, The Cure – and some dub reggae too."

"Hmm." She didn't sound impressed.

By the time he came into the lounge with the coffee tray, she'd put on Joni Mitchell's *Blue,* and seemed to be more than a little distressed, turning her head from wall to wall as if she was lost in a maze that had no exit.

"What's the matter?" he said.

She shook her head and looked at him, like a child who had lost her toy.

"All these photographs…" were the only words she could muster.

"Photographs?"

"Of your children and – it must be your partner?

"My wife. Jenny."

Juliette picked up a small, framed photo from the mantlepiece and held it out at arm's length, then bought it up really close to her face. "She's very pretty."

Alan pretended he hadn't heard that as he put the tray down onto the small table.

She put the picture back and walked around the coffee table to sit next to him.

"So, uh… what do your mum and dad do?" he said, handing her small the milk jug.

"No thanks," she said, touching his hand to stop him pouring. I take it black."

"Sugar?"

"No."

She took a sip, coughed nervously, raising her hand to her mouth.

"My dad owns a construction company. Mom was a district judge, but she also does a lot of work for children's charities and the local community, that kind of thing… mostly through the local business association. Dad's involved in that a bit too."

"Right." He didn't let on, but that made him feel inferior. His mother worked in a shop, and his dad was a barber. Luckily, she didn't ask.

"What's your star sign?" she said suddenly.

That stumped him. "Are you into all that?"

"Does it offend you?

"No. Not at all."

"Then I'd like to know."

He shrugged. "My birthday is January 6th. What does that make me?"

She curled one corner of her lip up and shook her head in mock despair.

"Oh dear."

"What do you mean?"

"Capricorn. Let me think… you're rigorous in the way you do things, and you move ahead in a very systematic manner, with rules and systems. What else? Oh, you're determined and always aim to turn plans into action and enjoy leading others with your matter-of-fact personality and pragmatism."

"That's completely wrong," laughed Alan. "I'm a mess when it comes to organisation."

She looked at him for a moment and then stared at her knees, rubbing them self-consciously.

"I saw you in action at the recording studio. The way you sorted out everything without any stress. The rest of your team; Sally and your partner… what's his name?"

"Gary."

"Yes. Him too. They were all blind-sided by the client. Not you. You're a Capricorn all right."

Normally, he had nothing but disdain for the subject of astrology. However, he had no desire to shatter the atmosphere of sensitivity and revelation that was building up, so he went with the flow.

"When's your birthday?" he asked.

"June 21st."

"So, you're a…"

"Gemini. Well, I'm on the cusp actually. That makes me flighty and disorganised, and I focus on too many things at the same time." She spoke hurriedly, and with enthusiasm, as she continued to rub her knees.

"Oh, how terrible," he said in mock-disapproval.

"Hey!" She nudged him playfully. Geminis are great - totally adaptable. You don't know how lucky you are, having a Gemini for company. We accept people for what they are, and we're probably the most sociable star sign of all." She looked a bit lost then – as if she'd run out of things to say.

They both smiled, and then turned away from each other, embarrassed by this unexpected gap in their conversation. She eventually thought of something to say.

"Gary doesn't like me, does he?"

"What?" Alan leaned back, wide-eyed with surprise. "Where'd you get that from?"

"C'mon, he was giving me the evils the whole time I was in the studio."

"Ah… You just caught him at a bad time. When you get to know him, he's like a big teddy bear."

She squinted. "Don't forget. He was the one who pushed the door into me while I was carrying the tray."

"That's not fair. He didn't even know you were there. I'll tell you something right now… he loves the job you did on the V/O."

"Really?" She turned to Alan, pouting and frowning at the same time.

"Sure."

She stopped to think about that for a minute, looked over at the sound system, and then she turned back to him.

"Did he know we were meeting tonight?"

"Why should he?"

"Do you always answer a question with another question?"

Alan shrugged, and she looked away. This time the silence was longer and deeper. They had run out of things to say, and the discomfort was growing by the second. He could have come up with random small talk, but something told him that was inappropriate. She gazed blankly at the opposite wall. Clusters of half-formed ideas whirled around in his head. He studied her elegant, gently tapering neck, her calm face and her thick eyebrows for clues. What if she was just waiting? What if it wasn't right to say anything at all? Without thinking he touched the side of her face with his thumb and forefinger, slowly turning it towards his. He saw a sleepy, sad and submissive look. He leaned forwards and his lips touched hers. Their tongues rolled around each other in a sweet, wet frenzy. Their teeth clashed. A wave of electricity ran through him. They gazed at each other knowingly, and stood up to undress themselves quietly, as if it was the most serious task imaginable, and words would shatter everything. Her skin was pale and flawless, and her breasts small and firm, with dark, clearly defined nipples. She was supple and disarming. He had fallen under a spell, and the wonderful part was that, even at the time, he didn't want to resist. Something inside him was turning away from the deeper things he had always valued. She lay back diagonally across the sofa, her head resting on the corner of the hand rest, where it met the back of the sofa, and her legs stretched.

"Let's go into the bedroom," he said.

"I can't." she moaned.

"It would be much more comfortable."

She looked scared. "It's your wife's bed."

"She's never even been here."

"But…"

Soon she was crying softly. Then she shuddered, making a baby noise and her nails bit deep into his upper arm. When it was over, she stroked his face, and a tear travelled down her cheek. "Hold me," she said.

He lay down beside her, in what little room there was on that sofa, stroking her like a cat. They stayed there, saying nothing. He noticed her toenails were painted a rich, glossy black as she twisted around to face him, open mouthed and needy, like a hungry baby. They kissed, twisting into each other. She gazed up to the ceiling, breathing hard and moving her head from side to side. Tears flooded down her cheeks. She seemed startled and at that moment things went out of focus for him as another face started to resolve itself and it became superimposed over hers, vibrating erratically, while forming a faint double image. This other face was slightly harsher, yet still beautiful, though with a more serious expression. He thought perhaps it was a flashback – the type of thing that can happen after taking LSD, but he'd never dropped any, though he had taken magic mushrooms as a student, which apparently has the same sort of effect. Perhaps he'd had more wine than he realised

He started to withdraw, partly through fear and confusion, but she whispered, "No."

Soon after they fell asleep. He awoke a little later, got out of bed quietly, lifted her up into his arms (she was surprisingly light) and carried her over to the double bed and got in with her.

At dawn, he was woken by a squealing sound, which he associated with a child being hurt. Juliette had been rolling around in her sleep, eyes shut tight and looking pained. He could see she was in a sweat. He touched her forehead and realised that she was running a temperature. She kept repeating something, quietly at first. Eventually he made out it was the name Vanessa. Who was Vanessa?

In the morning, she left for work before he did, because they expected her in early at Seraphim Sound. He was still eating toast and drinking coffee for a while, thinking about her and wondering if he'd just given himself a major complication in his life. Jenny had arranged for the house in London to be rented out, and in just three months she and the boys would be moving in here in the new apartment. They had already organised a school and nursery – everything was set. What the fuck was he going to do?

Dassos Petrou

Chapter 2

Alan had to make a decision – and that's exactly what he did. He decided not to decide, so he was free to carry on regardless. He took Juliette with him to Martha's Vineyard one weekend, even fielding a few interrogative phone calls from Jenny while they were there. Another time he and Juliette went to dinner at Windows on the World, in the World Trade Centre. They would spend a couple of nights together at her place some weeks, and other times she would do the same at his. Most Fridays they would do lunch. One Saturday they saw La Traviata at the Met. They even did that cheesy thing and took a horse and carriage around Central Park a few times. It was like an advent calendar with a time bomb on the last day. What finally shattered the illusion was an impromptu visit from a friend, Jason Watts.

Jason was in transit, on his way back to London from Los Angeles, and Alan was really pleased to hear his voice. They arranged a long lunch at his favourite Irish bar the next day, throughout which Jason wore his brown trilby hat, with its little partridge feather in the brim. (Alan suspected it was to cover up his fast-balding cranium.) Over a pie and mash, and a couple of pints of Guinness, Jason insisted on discussing the philosophical merits of Plato and Socrates over the "dark, nihilistic, free-for-all" of Sartre and Camus (who Jason had never read). Jason then pulled out an A4 portfolio from his bag to show Alan some of the incredible work he'd created for, *The Adventures of Randolph Carter,* an animated feature. He followed that up with some family snaps, showing the spacious, colonial style house in LA he and Rebecca had settled into, with its huge swimming pool and incredible views of the city below.

Alan was pleased that Jason appeared to be thriving, not just because he worked so hard, but also because he was an unbelievable talent. He only hoped, for Jason's sake, that he didn't revert to his kamikaze-like propensity for throwing it all away by opening his big mouth and saying precisely the wrong things.

After he'd bought another round of drinks, Alan couldn't help putting on his mischievous grin and telling Jason about the little fling he was having with this gorgeous young girl, who was just twenty-four. Jason's reaction was not at all what Alan expected. He slammed

150

his jug of Guinness on the table, his huge forehead furrowed, and his eyes stared straight at him in terrifying and unadulterated fury, Alan was more than a little startled.

"What the fuck are you playing at?"

"Well, I..." Alan was too stunned to make a cohesive reply, just stammering an explanation of sorts, about how he could easily keep Juliette in the shadows when Jenny and the boys were here.

"I know how you operate, said Jason, raising one corner of his mouth into a sneer. "You're such a big kid. You just think with your dick whenever you meet a bird that gives you a smile. You were like that at college. Remember what happened with that girl Erica, when you were seeing Jan? How many years ago was that? Haven't you grown up yet?"

Alan was clearly taken aback. He wasn't expecting anything like this from Jason.

"Yeah, but that was then, and this is now. Jas, this is nothing like what happened with Erica. I've got all this under control."

Jason shook his head and looked up at the ceiling. "I can't believe you. You're putting the future of your children and your life with Jenny on the line for a... for a.... what is she? A fucking actress, only just out of her teenage years."

"I told you; she's twenty-four."

Jason leaned forward and banged his head on the table. Then he looked up and said,

"You're an idiot."

That night Alan found it impossible to sleep. Finally, he concluded that Jason was right. Things had slipped away from him. It was just too awful to have to admit that even talking to Jenny was becoming a chore. That's not good. He was painfully aware how wrong that was, but he couldn't stop himself feeling that way. It took all his composure just to hide his sense of detachment. When the phone rang, he felt a horrible sense of dread and discomfort. He became resentful about even having to talk to the boys. He couldn't help himself. But afterwards that feeling of disdain would go away, to be replaced by a dark cloud of energy-sapping guilt. The result was that he was drifting away from his family, and sinking into a sweet, and sticky miasma of his own making. Just at that moment the dark flow of his thoughts was interrupted by a loud dull thud on the windowpane. He pulled on his dressing gown and raised the blinds. A thick covering of snow was everywhere, burying every parked car in sight. A group of boys, obviously on their way to school, were wading through it all just below, and they were in the middle of a massive snowball fight.

Later that day at work he struggled with the dark mood that was eating away at him, hoping that no one would notice. But he wasn't doing a very good job of hiding it. Some didn't care, but others (especially those who had to brief him, or work with him on existing projects) became visibly irritated by his gloominess. Gary was away, handling a photoshoot in South Africa, so at least he wasn't around to see him in this state. However, he had just enough self-control to take in briefings (up to a point), and to communicate with people to start the job. But that wasn't enough. He was hired to blow people away with his ideas – and that required total, one hundred percent focus and dedication. Things could get rocky. Something had to change.

Chapter 3

A twenty-something mother in expensive designer ski gear was pulling her toddler along the sidewalk as he entered Washington Square Park. The kid was wrapped up warm in a long, tweed coat, woolly hat and scarf. The black, antique lampposts, and snow-covered branches created the vibe of a Victorian Christmas card. An ice-cold wind rubbed against his cheeks like steel wool. Near the fountain a woman let her Alsatian loose, as she brushed away some snow from the wooden bench with her bright pink mittens and then parked her track-suited bottom on the exposed wood. Further along a middle-aged dad in a military style grey coat picked up an armful of snow that he'd rolled into a large ball and carried it over to a similar sized lump his young son had built up on the ground. Alan started to worry about whether he had the courage to do what he had to do.

The green wooden frontage of Cafe Reggio always felt like a warm invitation from a much-loved friend, but not today. Dots of snow drifted down as he entered its small, dark, baroque interior. A rush of warm air greeted him. He looked around to see that his usual table, next to the ancient chrome espresso machine was free. Dangling light fittings spread a feeble glow over the marble-topped tables, wooden benches and metal-backed chairs. Sitting at a table by the main window was a student with a Jimi Hendrix-style hairdo. The guy was concentrating deeply while he scribbled notes into a small, spiral-bound pad. Behind him was a little old lady in a thick headscarf, leaning her elbows on the table while chewing a sandwich with apparent difficulty. The stage was set.

Juliette came in hurriedly, encumbered by a large Gucci carrier bag, dusting flecks of snow from her heavy black jacket. As she sat down, she seemed slightly taken aback by the brevity of his kiss.

"Been here long?" she asked, removing her white Russian hat and gloves.

"Not really," he said.

Her hair was in a bun and as she shook her head a strand came loose and hung against the side of her forehead.

"Don't get me wrong," she said. "I love Bergdorf Goodman, but some of those floors are literally ghost towns. It took me fifteen minutes to track down some assistance."

She reached for his glass of water and took a sip. Her long, dark eyelashes flickered, as she looked at him over the rim of the glass.

"Are you OK?" she asked, as she put the glass back down.

"He squinted, as if in pain, and scratched his forehead. Why wouldn't I be?"

"I don't know… you look a bit sallow."

"Sallow?"

The waitress came over to hand out some menus.

"We're not really eating," said Juliette. "I'll just have a dry cappuccino and a Portuguese tart."

Alan ordered another Americano. Then the waitress trotted off and Juliette pulled out a little box that was beautifully wrapped in black paper with silver polka dots.

"For you," she said.

He studied it with undue concern (that she didn't notice), rotating it slowly in his right hand, as if it might be a bomb.

"Oh."

"Go ahead. Open it up."

She watched eagerly as he peeled back the wrapping paper to reveal a white cardboard box. He lifted the lid and slowly pulled out a snow-globe, incorporating a New York skyline, set on a black Bakelite stand.

"Nice."

"It's antique," she informed him. "Fifties, I think."

"Right."

He shook it and put it on the table, and they watched the tiny flakes swirl around it in a spiral. He wanted to break the spell, so he looked up, with an unmistakable look of sadness.

"As if we haven't had enough snow this the last few days," he said.

She frowned. "'Thank you' would be nice," she said.

"Uh, yeah. Sorry. Thank you."

She was biting her lower lip. "Well, do you like it?"

"Why wouldn't I? It's really sweet."

"I spent ages choosing it, from this darling little place in Tribeca."

He rested the globe next to his cup, and she looked at him quizzically. She was beginning to sense his mood.

"Jules. What are we going to do?" he said.

"Um… maybe we could go to the galleries in SoHo."

"That's not what I mean."

"I know what you mean. You're going to go on about the age difference again."

"No, not that. Look, we've been burying our head in the sand bit? Jenny and the boys will be here soon and…"

The waitress arrived at that point with her coffee and cake. When she departed Juliette brushed something from her shoulder.

"You know what that means."

"Alan. I'm not trying to take you away from your family. That was never my intention. We've been through this."

"I know. I know," he replied. "But I've been thinking about things and… we've got to get real about all this, it won't work."

"What won't?" All this time she left her coffee and tart untouched. "What are you talking about? Where's all this coming from?"

"We can't duck and dive now. Jenny is no fool. She can sense when my mind is elsewhere, even over the phone. Imagine when she's here."

A hot tear grew in her eye and rolled down her cheek slowly, like a glass bead. Her lips quivered.

"I can't..."

He couldn't remember ever having been so cruel. He tried to summon the state of mind he turned on for client meetings.

He couldn't help reaching out and squeezing her hand.

"Jules. Don't... it makes it worse for both of us. We knew this time would come. You've got so much ahead of you. You're getting offers from everywhere… Broadway, TV…"

She wiped her eyes with a napkin.

"Stop patronizing me."

She closed her eyes, as if in prayer, and then opened them again – focusing through him now. Outside the snow was falling heavily. It was hard to see the terrace of houses across the road.

She cried passively and noiselessly.

He fought back the compulsion to hold her in his arms.

"Why are you doing this to me?"

"I… I'm doing it to both of us."

She sniffed and leaned over to pick up her bags, then stood up without looking at him.

"I have to go."

He watched her leave and looked back to see the guy with the Hendrix hairstyle and the old lady in the headscarf trying to avoid his gaze. Shaking his head, he pulled out a few bills from his wallet and threw them on the table.

Chapter 4

"Are you well?" asked the little Jewish lady who lived a few doors further along his floor as she was leaving the building. "You look so pale."

She studied his face with almost motherly concern. She had passed him on the stairs and then stopped on the step below to look back up at him.

"Oh, er... not too bad, thank you Mrs Spielman," said Alan, turning back to face her. "Just finished work. Tough day. I'll be raring to go again, after I have a cup of tea."

She watched him go up, shrugged and turned to continue her way down.

At his apartment door he fumbled and dropped the keys on the floor. His fingers were like sticks of ice. He picked the keys up and had another couple of goes at the lock, eventually managing to get the door open. When he took off his damp shoes, he found he was almost sliding along the wooden floor in his socks. He went over to pull the blinds down on all five sash windows and then made himself a pastrami sandwich on rye, without losing a single finger, which was quite an achievement, considering the state he was in.

To calm down he poured himself a JD with ice and sat in the large armchair in front of the TV. Even the Star Trek Original Series episode that came on failed to cheer him up, not least because it featured a female android with long dark hair (who had fallen in love with Captain Kirk). She reminded him too much of Juliette.

He switched it off. The bits of pastrami stuck between his teeth were becoming annoying. In a huff, he went to the bathroom to brush his teeth, when he was startled by a warm breath brushing against his cheek and a woman's voice whispering in his ear, "Alan!"

He twisted around, swallowing toothpaste while coughing and spluttering. There was no one there.

There was a sense of warm, scented air. Maybe it was a lingering odour from the many times Jules had stayed over, some kind of after-shower cosmetic. She always has a bag full of lotions, potions and sprays. But this fragrance wasn't one he was familiar with. Not that he was an expert. It could be a perfume used by the previous tenant, after all, he hadn't been living there that long.

Somebody told him that some smells like cigarette smoke or spicy cooking can be absorbed into wallpaper. But there was no wallpaper in the bathroom. It was completely tiled over. Hmm. Perhaps... the grout between the tiles soaks up smells, or maybe the blinds or shower curtain.

Baffled, he went back to armchair and knocked a whole glass of JD back in one go, enjoying the sweet burning sensation at the back of his throat. He poured another glass and took a sip. It was probably just nonsense, the sweet smell, the smoke that never was. He couldn't deny he was kind of, tinged with fear. And now he understood why. It really felt like there was a woman in there with him, in the bathroom – even though he couldn't see her. Maybe he was going mad. That's what stress at work can do to you. Or was it what just happened with Jules?

That night, he took his battered old paperback version of The Age of Reason to bed with him, but he found himself reading the same paragraph again and again. Surrendering to the inevitable, he turned the lights out and fell asleep almost and immediately sunk into a dream.

He is outside the office on Park Avenue. It's daytime, but for some reason it's dark. A storm is brewing. He is waiting for Jenny. The buildings are not in their proper places. He can't work out why. There are no people and cars. He has a deep feeling that something terrible is about to play out and there's nothing he can do to stop it. Why isn't Jenny here yet? There are thick, time-lapse, dark clouds, twisting and flowing above, obscuring the day, merging into a blanket of darkness. A bright scar, opens between them, flooding the top stories of the buildings opposite with light, but at street level all is cold, dark shadow.

Behind him, over the entrance to the tall glass building, are the words *Sam Hayne House*, not Goulding Graham and Puller son (GGP), as it should be. There are people there now, walking along – oblivious to him and each other. Where did they come from? They all have curious red spots on their faces. 'Is it measles?"

It's going to happen now. He knows it and he is afraid. An old couple come towards him. As they lean close to his face they fill him with horror. The old man is a leering, and heavy-set. His thin wife is lascivious, pulling an evil grin. Their lips salivate and they have a look of wide-eyed lust as they start up a chant:

"The yellow truck is coming. The yellow truck is coming."

Others join in, encircling him and the rhythm of this chanting becomes fearful, hypnotic. He can feel his heart pump faster and faster. It's unbearable. He closes his eyes tight, hoping they'll all go away, and the chants are replaced by a low humming. It builds slowly, changing from the sound of an electricity generator to the noise of a large truck approaching… becoming louder.

Suddenly it stops and he opens his eyes to see the street is now empty again.

Then a slowed down car horn starts, followed by a low, rumbling sound. He wishes Jenny would hurry. The rumbling gets louder, causing all of Park Avenue to shudder. There seems to be no source for the sound. Confused and anxious he attempts to go back into the building through the revolving door, but it won't turn. Meanwhile, the sound of the engine is now a defining roar. Turning behind he sees a huge yellow truck is closing in and he finds he can't move.

He woke up in a cold sweat, shaking. The digital clock said 2.35. He couldn't help wondering if he was going mad.

Chapter 5

Alan was having a hard time finding creative solutions. Gary didn't stress about it at first, because as long as one of them is delivering the goods, there's no worry. People have off days. Trouble is this was turning into an off-week, then an off fortnight, and it was now approaching an off-month.

Gary was coming up with the lion's share of the ideas, and when the creative balance tips this far, it's the stuff that leads to break-ups. To add to the burden, Gary was also carrying the can when it came to fighting all the battles needed to sell the ideas within the agency, and to the clients.

At one presentation to the Chrysler account team, Alan found himself sinking into a soft, foggy, sweet oblivion. Everything seemed to be happening behind a wall of glass for him. Gary, who had no idea what his partner was going through, was presenting the TV script to the account team. The idea and the script eres clever, witty, and edgy (thanks to Gary). The problem was the Chrysler account team were the most boring, risk-averse bozos in the agency. Their unwritten mantra was 'safe ideas make for easier client presentations.' Not the way to make great, unforgettable, award-winning ads".

This was why Gary really needed his partner to step in and say something, to help him to sell the idea. But from the corner of his eye, he could see the vacant expression on Alan's face, and at that point he realised he was on his own.

While Gary was struggling to salvage the Chrysler script, Alan was becoming fascinated with Gary's lips. He remembered a goldfish that he had won in a funfair on Hampstead Heath when he was a small boy. The guy gave it to him in a clear plastic bag and he held it up against the bright blue summer sky and gazed at it in fascination. Gulp, gulp, gulp it went – just like Gary.

Soon Gary was immersed in a fierce argument with Paul, Brendan, Christine and Elaine and it became obvious that Alan was making no effort to back him up, so Gary gave him a discreet kick under the table. As a result, Alan's eyes flickered into life. The room came back into focus for him, and he was instantly able to register the alarm in Gary's face and hear all the voices that were raised in anger at Gary. The trouble was, he couldn't attach any meaning to it all. Words were not attached to meanings. The relevance of the situation was washing over his head. And so the boring account time got their way, and the idea was dead.

The minute they were back in their office, Gary exploded.

"What the fuck is the matter with you?"

Alan had to admit, he didn't know. He just didn't feel right. Gary simply glared at him before slamming the desk and storming out of the office. Stunned, Alan tried to spark himself into action, but the lethargy was too overwhelming when he stood up and then he was struck by a sudden rush of vertigo, dropping down into the chair, feeling useless, knowing that Gary could well be on the way to Steve's office to demand a new art-director. And who knows? Steve might even agree. If that happened the most likely outcome would be that Alan would find himself out of a job. What then? The three month's severance pay he'd get wouldn't even cover the money he'd laid out to secure a nursery place for Simon as well as signing an eighteen-month contract for the apartment. He'd be with all those payment obligations if he was fired. Anyway, maybe he was jumping to conclusions, thinking the worst. Gary may have just nipped round to O'Reilly's Bar, to let off steam with some liquid refreshment. Perhaps he should go over there to find him. He tried to get up again and failed.

When he did eventually succeed in stringing a few thoughts together, he concluded that although ending the relationship with Jules was hard for them both, surely it wasn't the cause of the psychological and physical collapse he was currently experiencing. Yes, it immediately followed the relationship ending, in terms of timing, but that was probably just coincidence. So, what was the cause? Could it be a virus, or a genetic disorder? Maybe even just stress.

Alan was talking to Dr Hardcastle, who was recommended by Mrs Spielman. He listened to Alan with an expression of deep concern while stroking his goatee beard, after which he recommended Alan should take some time off work – at least a few weeks – and wrote a prescription for anti-depressants. He decided to ignore the advice and threw the prescription in the nearest trashcan when he left the surgery.

Over the next few days Gary's frostiness began to thaw, although it was probably down to necessity and the passage of time than anything Alan was doing to redeem himself.

That Friday he was in the office early, trying to come up with ideas for a product that was a kind of lazy person's cheese on toast. His concentration was broken by Gary pushing the door open violently, but in good humour.

"You still awake?" he shouted.

Gary seemed to have recovered his high spirits, which was a relief. They sat down together and threw around some ideas. It was as if the preceding tension between them had never existed. Again, Alan's contribution that morning was simply to listen to Gary, with minimal interjections, and there were certain moments when he could feel himself slipping, but he made an excuse about having a weak bladder and rushed out to splash some cold water on his face. Those kinds of emergency measures worked for a while, but he knew he was on shaky ground, and he couldn't expect to keep this crisis at bay forever – unless it went away by itself.

When he was back home, he sat down to dinner and gazed at the photo of Jenny and the boys in Regents Park the previous summer, on one of their Saturday morning strolls. Jenny was sitting on a bench with her arms around the boys. Simon had been crying a few moments before, because Jack had bitten a huge chunk out of his choc-ice.

Alan finished eating and went over to pour himself a drink and then sat down and grabbed the remote. The screen showed nothing but grey static. Again, he was sinking into a heavy drowsiness. Unconsciously, he dropped the remote to the floor, as every object in the room started to go out of phase. Meanwhile, he found himself thinking deeply of Juliette. Her thin, tapering neck. Her long eyelashes. The way she sighed when she saw a painting she liked. How she always shed a few tears after sex… and then the phone rang. He didn't answer, instead he waited for the answerphone to kick in. It was Jenny.

"Hey Al. I'm happy with the nursery we've found for Simon, but I just wanted to have a quick chat with you about the school we've chosen for Jack. Give me a call if you don't get back too late. Bye. Love you."

Being in no frame of mind to discuss mundane issues, he continued to sit there lifelessly, for a little longer, hoping to build up the energy, eventually standing up with an effort, to stumble into the bathroom to take an ice-cold shower.

After recovering some composure, he intended to read in bed but found himself going over the same paragraph again and again. Giving up, he turned out the lights.

Soon he began to slowly drift towards sleep, though he was never too far from wakefulness. He thought he heard a breathy sigh coming from the corner of the room at one moment, so he opened his eyes and out of the velvety darkness he noticed a faint greenish glow coming from outside the door, which was slightly ajar. This soft light began to spill more and more into the room, like a slow, tide on a sandy beach. Then he noticed that the ceiling was throbbing, almost like a membrane. Suddenly he couldn't move. A sense of cloudy anticipation welled up inside him. A hidden and undefined change was happening, in the room and in him. Peering deeper and deeper into the velvety darkness, near the large wardrobe, there was a whisp of luminous, green smoke, growing and slowly morphing into a long lozenge shape, before evolving into the form of a lithe and slim woman. Her long dark hair fell onto her shoulders and breasts, while the white light from her eyes seemed to pierce him. He was tingling with terror yet he couldn't move a limb. She looked at him with affection, like a mother adoring her sleeping baby and tilted her head to one side, shuddering in and out of phase with the room. His fear was battling with his sense of incandescent lust. The room became ice cold, and his breath came in clouds of vapour. As she stepped closer to him, she had the grace, poise and elegance of Aphrodite emerging from the sea. His pulse raced. His heartbeat was so fast and hard, he thought it would explode. In a liquid motion, she was visibly pulsing as she moved towards him. When she reached the end of the bed, she stopped and smiled, lowering her knee onto the mattress, and began crawling on all fours, like a lynx stalking its prey. He wanted to scream. Licking her upper lips, she leaned onto him and her breasts teasingly fell on his chest. A shock of electricity, passed from her skin into his body. Her eyes fixed upon his with a look of curious intent, as a soft and silky fire ignited every part of him. His breathing came faster and faster, and he waited for the inevitable. But it never came. In an explosion of horror and unfulfilled passion, she was gone.

The only thing he understood clearly at that precise moment was that something in him had swiftly and inexplicably changed.

Chapter 6

Resisting a feverish yearning to go back to sleep, he went into the kitchen and brewed up a huge jug of strong coffee. He drew back the blinds to see there was no moon or stars. Then he went back and sat on a stool in the kitchen to watch the sky slowly turn from black to pale grey Soon the heavy atmosphere he was experiencing lifted and his numbing fatigue faded away.

Was it a coincidence that this nocturnal psychedelic weirdness was happening while he was experiencing a sort of mini nervous breakdown? Who could he talk to about this. Ironically, Jenny was interested in the supernatural, but obviously he couldn't talk to her about it. Then it struck him: what about Cornelia and Bella? Ever since he wondered into their occult bookshop in the seaside town where he was a student, they had taken an interest in him, and in some ways, he had with them. It was about seven in the morning in New York, but in England it was coming up to midday. He could call them right now.

Cornelia answered. She was delighted to hear from him.

"Well hello stranger. We were talking about you this morning, Bella and I: how is life in America?"

Alan was relieved to hear her voice. "Good. How are things with you and Bella?"

"We're fine, although a heavy, cold mist has rolled in from the sea, and it looks like a steamy shower out there right now. Not good for trade."

"Oh dear. Sorry to hear that."

"So, what's all this about strange, disturbing visitations?"

Alan was startled. "But... I didn't say anything about... you're doing it again. How did you know?"

Cornelia sounded disappointed with him.

"Alan, I'm not doing anything. You probably mentioned it at the start of this conversation."

"No, I didn't..."

"Will you get on with it and tell us what the problem is. We haven't got all day."

It was pointless to argue any further. He went on to describe the weirdness he had been experiencing: how he was losing his grip at work and he also described the visitation of the naked girl glowing out of the darkness in his room and his effective paralysis throughout.

Alan realised that Cornelia must have put the conversation on speaker, because suddenly Bella said: "Hmm, interesting. Does she remind you, even just a little bit, of anyone you know?"

"Oh… hi Bella," he said.

"Does she?"

"Uh, sorry. He had to think about that. "Hm. No. Not really."

"Are you sure about that? Think about it."

"Well, maybe just a little…"

I had this thing going on with a girl… a young actress. But that's all over now. Jenny and the boys are coming soon, so I had to nip all that in the bud."

Cornelia let out a Eureka groan.

"It sounds to me like you should be getting some serious help."

"What kind of help? What exactly do you think is wrong with me?"

"There's nothing wrong with you, *per se*. But you are in a dangerous predicament that cannot be allowed to continue unabated. You need proper assistance."

Alan was speechless. He wondered if they were being over-cautious.

Bella, Cornelia's daughter, broke the silence.

"We know who you should talk to over there. He's an old friend of ours; he's knowledgeable, honest and incredibly gifted. You need to see see him as soon as possible. He lives just along Central Park. We have his address somewhere."

"But who is he? What's his background? Is he some kind of shrink?"

"No, no, no. He is certainly not a psychiatrist, or psychoanalyst, or anything of the kind," said Cornelia. He is an expert in paranormal phenomena. We invited him to lecture here at the Conway Hall a few years ago. He was quite brilliant. It was a sell-out.

"So, you're sure about that?"

"I couldn't be more certain. Robert is a very serious man. The CIA would never hire a crank, would they?"

"CIA?"

"Indeed. He was with the Agency for a time. Before that he was special forces. The man's a war hero."

"You're not giving me much confidence. What war?"

"Vietnam. He graduated from West Point and went straight out here. Also majored in Classics, as well as being a prolific author. Highly respected. And his wife, Isobel, is lovely."

"Oh yes," said Bella, to add emphasis, "I thought she was wonderful company. Talented artist too."

"What's his name, again?" he asked.

"We didn't say. But it's Robert Stringfield."

"Right." Alan sounded nervous.

He overheard Cornelia giving Bella some instructions.

"I think we've still got that book on demonic possession by Robert, haven't we?"

"Oh yes. Let me see if I can find it."

"Demonic possession?"

Chapter 7

Alan found Gary working hard at his keyboard in the morning, in a newly pressed, white shirt, and sporting a brand-new haircut. Tracy, the art buyer, was right behind him carrying a portfolio. Alan turned around to keep the door open for her.

"Hi Tracy," he said.

"Hey guys. Guess what?" she said. "The illustration samples have arrived."

Gary looked up. "About friggin' time!"

"Wash your mouth out, Cummings. Let's see them," said Alan, taking off his coat.

Tracy laid the large portfolio on the desk, and Alan sat down to go through all the delicate pen and wash studies. Gary was too busy typing to look. His concentration was interrupted by three rapid knocks on the glass. It was Gordon, in his black and white check short sleeve shirt and clipboard. He came in uninvited and looked over Alan's shoulder at the illustrations.

Tracey looked peeved. "Gordon. Whatever it is, can you leave it till later? I need these guys to approve an illustrator."

"Not until they explain why the Boston Mutual ad in the Times went out with the wrong phone number."

"What the fuck? That's not possible," said Gary, breaking off from his typing.

"I was the last one to sign it off. The phone number was spot on when it left my desk. No one else touched it."

Alan coughed nervously and mumbled, "Well, uh... I think I had one more look at it after you did, Gary."

Gary stared at him accusingly. There was a deathly silence for a few seconds.

"Run that by me again."

Tracy gave them both a frown.

"I called the artwork back to uh... fix something. What might have happened, you know, because of the lack of time, I might have rushed things and inadvertently used an earlier version as a template for my changes. It's a... possibility. I guess."

"Inadvertently?" Gary looked up at the ceiling, his arms raised, as if he was summoning a deity. "Let me get this straight," he said, flopping his arms back onto the desk. "You called back artwork which had final sign-off, to make changes and then you sent it out again – without telling me, or anyone else?"

Alan shrugged meekly. "Like I said, there was no time..."

Gary dropped his head in his arms, which were now folded on the desk. "I don't fucking believe this."

"Yeah well..." Gordon interrupted. "I do. The agency is coughing up for print costs. Thirty-five-grand, at the last count."

Gary looked up now, and his face became flush. Then he stood up and walked purposefully around the desk to, opened the glass door, and steer Gordon out. Gordon didn't offer much resistance. He'd already made his point.

Tracy left the illustrator's portfolio on the desk. "I'll come back later when you've made your selection," she said as she left. "I'm meeting a photographer in five minutes."

When she was gone, Gary sat down, dangling his arms at his side, as if he'd lost the use of them. Alan said nothing. There was nothing he could say. He had screwed up badly and cost the agency a considerable sum of money. Never in his career had he done anything like it. His mind was not working properly, that was becoming clearer by the day. He wanted to get away, to be out on his own. His self-respect had plummeted.

Then Gary suddenly lightened the mood. "Gordon's a jerk," he said suddenly, as he leaned forward and rested his elbows on the table.

"Uh, well yes... I suppose he is," said Alan, relieved.

"But you have to admit, he has a point."

Alan found himself looking through the window, as a distant airplane moved slowly left to right, between two skyscrapers.

Alan looked down at the desk, shook his head and sighed. "I wanted to make a tweak on the face of the girl in the photo. Her complexion seemed a little bit...you know, bright. That's all."

Gary made a little chuckle, in despair.

Something inside Alan snapped. "Fuck it. I made a mistake, OK? I'm human. People fuck up sometimes."

Gary gave him a cold, hard stare. "The day I go into a zombie state in a briefing and make a fuck-up those costs the agency top dollar, you can get on your high horse. Right now, in case you didn't know it, you're the guy with pie on his face. If I was you, I'd shut the fuck up."

They were getting louder. People were looking in as they walked past.

"You know what?" Alan said. "Before I came here, I lost count of just how many people warned me off of working with you."

Gary's mouth froze open, before he said, "Oh yeah?"

Alan nodded, "Yeah."

"I'd like to know who the fuck they were."

"I'm not naming names, but the words 'liability', and 'unstable' were used more than once."

Gary stood up and his face was beetroot red as he punched a framed movie poster of Apocalypse Now, on the wall. The glass cracked, and the soft skin under his little finger ripped open like a purse. Blood splashed onto his new shirt and also dripped freely onto their shared desk. Gary studied the wound as if it was a rare and beautiful bird.

Alan stood up immediately.

"Stay there," he said. And then he rushed over to find Jackie. She stopped tapping away on her keyboard and looked up. "What's up?"

"Someone said you were the official First Aider on this floor?"

"And?"

"It's Gary."

She shook her head, like a disappointed primary school teacher.

She took out a metal box and Alan followed her back to the office. She picked up Gary's hand and said, it's going to need stitches. That was Alan's queue to go and get the coffees.

He came back with a cardboard tray of drinks. "OK for me to come in?" he asked.

Jackie looked round. "We're all done here," she said, giving Alan a stern look as she took out one of the paper cups and left. Alan put one of the cups in front of Gary.

Gary leaned back with a pensive expression and showed Alan his newly stitched hand.

"See what you made me do?"

Soho in the Dark

Chapter 8

A few days later Gary and Alan were working on the finishing touches for a car poster campaign when Alan's desk phone rang. It was Jackie, the creative director's secretary, putting on her curt, serious voice.

"Alan?"

Alan suspected he was going to get a dressing down for the screw-up on the print job. "Hi Jax. Everything OK?"

"Can you get over here straight away? Steve wants to talk to you."

"You mean me – or me and Gary?"

"Just you."

Jackie's desk was just outside Steve's office, allowing her to serve as passport control to the creative director. She told Alan to wait at the door, and tapped on the glass wall. Steve looked over and nodded. "Go right on in," she said.

Steve, with his dark hair and thick, long Rudyard Kipling Moustache, was bent down facing the desk, writing elegantly with his stubby Mont Blanc pen. Alan sat down on the seat opposite, studying the various awards on the shelves behind, waiting for Steve to acknowledge his existence. Steve looked up eventually, with a disarming hang dog expression. That look could mean anything from, I'm going to give you a raise, to can you make a few changes to this script, to get out of here, you're fired. He uses it in meetings with account people, biding his time with supreme calm, leaving them in suspense. On this occasion there was just a hint of warmth in his eyes.

"How's everything?" said Steve.

"Pretty good I think," replied Alan.

There was an extended silence while Steve put the lid on his pen and his lower lip came forward. He put the pen down on the blotter and threaded his fingers together and leaned back into his seat to give Alan an intense stare. "Your name's been coming up a lot lately."

Alan cleared his throat nervously. "Oh?"

"A few people were concerned about you, more or less dozing off in a briefing."

171

Alan leaned forward. "Steve, let me explain…"

Steve didn't want to hear. "And then there's the question of a press ad that ended up costing the agency $55,000 to put right."

Alan squeezed his temple between his thumb and third finger and continued to listen, hoping the axe would fall fast so he could just go.

"Now, I know you've been going through a stressful time. I make it my business to be aware of things like that."

Alan nodded reluctantly.

Steve then broke the flow of the conversation to walk over to window and pull up the blinds. It was still snowing, forming a net curtain between them and the towers on the other side of Madison Avenue.

"I won't probe. I don't have the time or the inclination," he said, coming back to take his seat. "All I want is for you to be at your best. That's not because I'm a nice guy. I'm a pragmatist. We have major pitches coming up and I'm thinking of putting you on some of them. They're not happening for a few weeks."

He stopped to drink his glass of Perrier.

"That's why I want you to recharge your batteries: take some time out when your family get here from England."

He put his hands in his pockets, pulled out a set of keys and threw them on the table.

Alan was confused.

"I have this house upstate. Place called Cold Spring. It's on the Hudson, maybe sixty miles north. I don't know if you've ever seen the Hudson Valley, but it really is beautiful."

He pointed to the keys with his chin.

"Pick 'em up."

Alan reached forward and did as he was told.

"You'll like it there," said Steve, basking in his own benevolence. "So, will your family. It's very pretty in the snow."

Alan couldn't help sighing with relief.

"And when you come back, I want to see the Alan White I hired."

Gary wasn't in the office, so he grabbed his coat and went to lunch. In reception, he saw Jay and Pete coming into the building through the revolving doors. They seemed pleased with themselves. They said they had just recorded a couple of scripts at Seraphim, with the actress Alan had discovered.

"You mean, Juliette," said Alan.

"Yeah, that's her."

"She's really good Al," said Pete. "Went like a dream."

"We were going to ask her if she wanted some lunch, but her boyfriend showed up near the end of the edit, to whisk her away."

All that steely resolve he had built up to break off with her was starting to fracture. He tried to appear indifferent, but inside he was burning.

"Oh, that's a shame. What was he like?" he asked, trying to sound blasé.

"Blonde, tall guy," said Jay. "Uptown type. About her age."

"Yeah. Maybe a little older," said Pete.

Alan had a good idea who it might be. He had a sinking feeling.

"Oh right. Never met him".

Alan didn't feel like taking the subway, so he hailed a cab. When they got to the end of Brooklyn Bridge, he told the driver to stop, because he had a strong urge to walk. He found there was thick, slippery ice packed hard beneath the soft, snow when he got down the steps. He trod carefully, knowing his expensive, industrial, big-brand boots were not reliable in these conditions.

A pencil thin cloud drifted behind the glass towers of Wall Street across the river. A seagull circled over a barge, climbing higher, in consecutive spirals. He walked on and turned left to Montague Street, by the play area, which he used to walk with Juliette on weekends. How could she have found someone else so soon?

Later he was pouring himself a drink in the apartment, when there was a knock at the door. It was Mrs Spielman. She had a small FedEx package in her hands.

"I was coming in from the doctors earlier and this man asked me if I knew you, so he let me sign for this."

"That's perfect Mrs Spielman. Thank you."

"She tried to look either side of him, "So when are your family coming?"

Alan had to think about that. "Uh… Next week. Thanks again, Mrs Spielman."

He closed the door and sat down by the coffee table, and took a sip of his beer, before opening the package. It was from England, from the Bell and Candle. Inside was the book Cornelia had spoken about, 'A Study in Demoniality'. He opened the first page, and a plain business card fell out, with the author's name.

Robert Stringfield
Apartment 9F
800 Fifth Av
New York 10065

There was also a phone number. They hadn't included a letter, but there was a note from Bella on the inside cover.

"To Alan, with love. Cornelia and Bella x"

Just then the phone rang. It was Jenny. He didn't feel up to speaking to her right then, so he waited for her voice to come up on the answerphone:

"Hi darling. You must be out – or still at work. Give me a call if you get home in time. The boys are so excited. We're all packed and ready now. Love you. Bye."

Alan started rummaging through the pages of this odd book that Cordelia and Bella had sent him, flicking through diagrams of pentagrams, and wood engravings of witches and demons when the phone rang again. This time it was Bella's voice coming over the answerphone.

"Hi Alan. Bella here. Did you get the book alright? I'm…"

This time Alan reacted fast, jumping up immediately to pick up the receiver.

"Bella! Hi! Yes, I got it. Thanks so much for sending it. I was just browsing through it. Quite unsavoury subject matter."

"And that's because you have a quite unsavoury problem."

"Hm. Anyway, so how are you?"

"I'm alone in the shop this afternoon. I wish you were here! Mama has gone to have tea with a friend at The Grand."

"Oh."

"You need to read the first twenty pages and arrange to see Robert. You'll get on very well with him and Isobel. She's delightful. When I was at school she came over with Robert. She was recovering from intensive radiotherapy treatment at the time, but she was always smiling. She had a lovely red scarf around her head to cover up the hair loss. I gather she's fine now. She's an artist, like you."

"I'm not really an artist…"

"Listen, I must be quick, some customers have just come in. This is important. "Read those pages. Make that call to Robert. Do it soon – it's important. Robert is expecting to hear from you."

"I have to go. Bye."

What did she mean? he wondered. Why did she sound so concerned?

Chapter 9

The Chinese take away arrived when he was coming out of the shower. He quickly grabbed a towel and went to the door, paid the guy, dried off, got dressed and sat down at the dining table, listening to Chet Baker. He ripped open the thin, white plastic bag of prawn crackers, and lined up the foil containers of egg fried rice, vegetable spring rolls, crispy shredded beef with chilli, and stir-fried vegetables onto a tray, picking up a knife and fork from the kitchen, and sitting down at the dining table with a glass of St Emilion, and listening to Bill Evans' *Sunday at the Village Vanguard.*

The apartment felt less oppressive now.

Having eaten his fill, he pushed the tray up the table and picked up his new book, "*A Study in Demoniality*' by Robert Stringfield.

It opened with a general history:

A succubus is a female sexual demon: a paranormal entity, with a history going back thousands of years. In recorded history and myth, the succubus has had many ways to creep up and seduce her victims, usually during sleep. Some men have described these experiences as pleasurable. Others have experienced malignant overtones, and an undeniable sense of evil. Some victims may suffer enormously after experiencing full sex with a female demonic entity. The experience can lead to a decline in physical and mental health, impotence, - and sometimes death.

In his principal work Antiquarum Lectionum, a fifteenth century Venetian writer, Cœlius Rhodiginus, described how a young man called Menippus Lycius, was having a sexual relationship with a woman who begged him to marry her. At this wedding, there happened to be a philosopher, and this man guessed the woman was actually a sexual demon. When he told Menippus of his suspicion she began screaming hysterically and vanished into thin air.

Alan shuddered, and skipped over to a section about, Ludovico Maria Sinistrari, a seventeenth century author. It said that Sinistrari was an advisor to the Supreme Sacred Congregation of the Roman and the Universal Inquisition in Rome. He was also an expert exorcist, as well as an authority on demonology and he also advised in investigations of people who had been accused of sexual relations with demons.

He said that when a female sexual demon has sexual relations with a man, there is always an ulterior motive – usually to give birth to a half-demon. Sinistrari also believed that satanic cults and covens are the means by which a demon is summoned, through collective prayers to an evil deity and sacrifice.

They must promise the Devil sacrifices and offerings, or a homicidal act of sorcery. In exchange, the demon declares she will fulfil their material desires in this world and make them happy after their death. But for a demon to be able to appear a dead host is needed.

Apparently, the cult has to subject themselves completely to the demon's will, to pray to her, to do her every whim, to follow only the will of the demon to enjoy material wealth and riches in abundance.

In the hands of the Devil, they vow obedience and subjection; they pay him homage and vassalage... to observe none of the divine precepts, to do no good work, but to obey the Demon alone and, to attend diligently the nightly conventicles.

The coven/cabal are then expected to do all they can to bring others to partake in sexual liaisons with the demon. They promise to strive with all their power, for the enlistment of other males and females in the service of the Demon.

The demon, or Succubus, can also have sex with a man who is in no way connected to an evil religious cult, sect or coven. She is then just a passionate lover, with only one desire: the carnal possession of one she loves (the victim). There are examples of this in history.

Alan threw the book down in a mixture of horror and disbelief. Cornelia and Bella would have known that the content of this book would worry him, but they obviously wanted to help, in their own way. Perhaps the problems he'd been experiencing were related to a succubus manifestation. For Cornelia and Bella, it was a certainty. However, he couldn't help feeling they had jumped to that conclusion without foundation. Undeterred, he skipped a few pages to discover another intriguing section:

The French nineteenth century novelist and art critic Joris-Karl Huysmans became obsessed with the occult in his later writings, some of which were considered blasphemous. This is particularly so in his novel 'La Bas', which deals primarily with Satanism in France, during the 15th century, and in the France of his day. But later Huysmans turned away from his interest with the occult, turning to full-blown Catholicism. The interesting thing is that in the early stages of his conversion, he went through a "powerful and singular experience". This happened in 1892, when he was staying at a monastery called La Trappe.

Robert Baldick, his biographer, describes the experience:

Again and again, he awoke from some dreadful nightmare, trembling with fear and convinced that he had just been visited by just such a succubus as he had described in his study of Satanism. As he later explained in En Route, these were no ordinary nightmares.

It was not at all that involuntary and commonplace act, that vision which is blotted out just at the moment when the sleeper clasps an amorous form in a passionate embrace. It happened as in nature, differing only in degree; it was long and complete, accompanied by every prelude, every detail, every sensation, and the orgasm occurred with a singularly painful acuteness, an incredible spasm.

Stringfield then states quite clearly:

From that moment on, Huysmans totally lost his drive. His character completely changed, and he became sexually impotent.

Alan's face turned white.

Chapter 10

On Alan's last week before his enforced holiday upstate, he and Gary were given the brief that every team dreaded. The task was to create a new campaign, across all media, for a huge disinfectant brand. The job was worth millions of dollars to the agency, but it was a creative black hole. The client had no idea what they were doing or what they wanted, although they were happy to pay for all the man-hours that were going into it. The agency didn't mind, one bit, because the job was a big, fat cash cow. But it was also depressing, especially for creative people who wanted to do exciting work that was worthwhile. On that Monday, when Alan told Gary he was taking the afternoon off to pick up a few things for the boys, Gary said he didn't blame him.

"Sure. No worries. I might take the morning off tomorrow," he gave Alan a wink, "to see the dentist."

Alan laughed.

What Gary didn't know was that Alan was going off to meet Robert Stringfield.

The snow was still falling hard as he walked along Fifth Avenue, along the east side of Central Park. Despite wearing a thick ski jumper, black puffa jacket, beige, brush cotton pants, long-johns, Timberland boots and a thick, black woolly hat, he was bitterly cold since he was facing a strong headwind. He arrived at the address Cornelia gave him. It was a high-end, 1970s apartment building on the corner of 61st Street. The entrance featured a huge metal awning, and it was manned by a stocky, short, middle-aged, suntanned doorman, in a long, thick black pea coat, with matching flat cap, that looked like he could have been a driver for a sheik. The doorman opened the glass door for Alan. On entering, the lobby immediately had the feel of a Mausoleum, with its enormous, grey, granite walls. He was greeted inside by another doorman – a small, much younger guy, with jet-black hair and a black uniform, minus the coat and flat cap, who sat behind a long, slab of dark stone reading the sports pages. Alan gave his name and asked for Robert Stringfield. The man stood up and nodded deferentially. "Of course, sir. Come this way."

He escorted Alan to the elevator, located behind the large ornate, cast-iron grill, the sort you get outside the grounds of stately homes.

On the tenth floor Alan took off his gloves and stepped into a spacious granite hallway. A tall, well-built figure in a well cut, single-breasted suit was waiting there for him to the left of the elevator. It was hard to tell if this fellow was blonde or if his hair was going white. He reminded Alan of Lee Marvin. Despite being so relaxed, and welcoming, there was something about those steel grey eyes that told Alan he was looking into the face of a killer.

"Robert Stringfield," he said in a deep, gravelly voice, smiling as he held out his hand.

"Thanks for taking the time to see me," said Alan.

"My pleasure. Any friend of Cornelia's is a friend of mine."

Robert asked Alan if he wouldn't mind leaving his slush-covered boots in the hallway and then helped him off with his snow-flecked pea coat. A small, white-haired woman drifted out from a small room on the left, that seemed to be some kind of art studio. Alan thought she looked to be in her seventies, and yet she dressed young, in fitted blue jeans and a loose woollen ski sweater. She reminded Alan of Katherine Hepburn in her later years: high cheekbones, flashing eyes and a very dignified posture. "Alan, isn't it?"

"That's me."

She wiped blue paint from her fingers with a heavily stained rag as she spoke.

"Cornelia and Bella said so many nice things about you."

Alan laughed. "Don't believe a word of it."

She jogged him playfully with her elbow, as if she'd known him for years.

Behind her shoulder he saw a small, framed photo of her with a red silk scarf wrapped around her head. "That's you, isn't it?" he said. "Bella was telling me about that scarf."

"Oh that. Yes, I wore that for nearly a year after the treatment, when we went to England. Robert was presenting a talk in Bloomsbury somewhere, that Bell & Candle were sponsoring, along with a few other occult bookshops and publishers. We. were staying in Cornelia's lovely cottage in Hertfordshire. Bella was still a schoolgirl at the time. Such a lovely, sensitive and intelligent child. And I absolutely adore Cornelia. They work so well together. So, what will you have - coffee, tea? Being an Englishman, you'll want Assam or Earl Grey, surely?"

"Oh no. Coffee please. Black. No sugar. Dark as the night.

Robert led him into the main lounge, which was really an extension of the front hall. The apartment was spacious and modern with a series of large windows at the far end facing Central Park. Below the traffic had ground to a standstill. A big, black, cloud was expanding slowly from Harlem and would inevitably smother the sky. Snow was still falling, but more slowly now.

"Incoming guys!"

They both turned around to see Isobel coming down the two steps with a tray of drinks.

"Here we go. Coffee blacker than a coal miner's T-shirt, a pot of breakfast tea for his lordship, and home-made ginger cookies."

"Oh, ginger biscuits – my favourite." said Alan.

"Good. But I'd hurry up and tuck into them before Robert pigs out on them."

She set the tray down on the coffee table and hurried back to her painting. Robert sat on a green leather armchair at one side of the table, and directed Alan to a black leather sofa opposite.

"So, you've been reading my book on demonology," he said. "What do you think?"

Alan almost spat out a mouthful of coffee.

"Kfff. Excuse me. It's not the sort of subject matter I would normally read, you understand, but I... you know. Of course, I'm impressed with the quality of the writing and the research."

Robert shrugged. "Thank you."

Alan continued, still retaining a hint of nervousness. "And, I must be honest here, the passages that focus on Huysmans, the French symbolist writer, did strike a chord. But is it all true, I mean, did he really go through all of that, you know... when he was in that monastery, and what happened after all that?"

Robert leaned back into his seat, spread his fingers into a makeshift comb, and then pushed them through his thick head of white hair.

"I confess, Alan, that I have been made aware that the supernatural is a subject you've only recently started to acquaint yourself with, albeit with some reluctance."

He nodded, with some embarrassment. "Well, you're not wrong there."

"No need to feel ashamed. Joris Karl Huysmans was a complex personality – effectively a mixture of the mundane and risqué. And there's no question about it, he was entranced, set upon, and seduced by a succubus, which climaxed (excuse the unintended pun) in an orgasm, for both him – and the demon. The whole thing is well documented."

Alan took a sip of coffee and almost missed the saucer in putting the cup down.

Robert continued.

"So, while Huysmans was a remarkably drab and uninteresting fellow, in one respect, being a civil servant all his life. Then again, he also mixed with a select bunch of revolutionary, decadent, artists, poets and painters: Symbolists. People like Flaubert, Mallarme, Verlaine and Rimbaud – dabbling in all sorts of dark stuff and strange quirks that I won't go into. The irony is, that he was also starting to edge away from all that, drifting more and more towards the Catholic Church."

"I gather. But did the impact of that supernatural sexual experience effectively leave him – there's no other way of saying it – castrated?"

"Castrated? Come on. That's like using a surface to air missile to shoot a rabbit. What happened was he underwent a complete personality change and became sexually impotent."

Alan sat back and sighed, then rubbed his eyes. Robert leaned forward and dipped a biscuit in his tea, taking a bite, and speaking while he was eating.

"The succubus is a demon."

He stopped to take a sip of coffee to moisten his mouth and then swallow. There was a kind of breathlessness in his measured tone when he continued. "She's neither corporeal nor imaginary. She lies waiting and hiding. Though dead, she is amazingly alive. You feel her touching you. She takes from you. She enriches herself. And when she leaves, you are less than you were before. That is the general view of many scribes who have studied the subject over the centuries, since ancient Greece and beyond."

Neither of them said anything for a while, then Alan became distracted by a painting on the wall behind Robert. It looked like a genuine Egon Schiele. To the side of that, and just below, was a small sculpture on a plinth that looked like the work of the Futurist, Umberto Boccioni. Surely not.

"More coffee?" said Robert.

"Oh, not for me thanks. I'm fine for now. But can I just ask you, is it true, you worked for the CIA?"

Robert laughed. "Guilty."

"Sorry."

"No. Nothing to apologise for. I was part of team carrying out specialist work – a very hush-hush project in collaboration with the Stanford Research Institute in parapsychology. And you know what? Isobel was there too, that's where we met. But we weren't doing the same kind of work."

"Oh, I see. Both of you… Am I allowed to ask exactly what the nature of this work was?"

Robert knitted his fingers together again and then pushed them out causing the bones to crack in sequence.

"Well, to be quite blunt, in involved sitting in a darkened room in a basement in Langley and making observations."

"Observations" I don't get it?"

"That's all it was."

"So, you didn't do anything sinister or unethical."

He laughed. "Isobel and I didn't. But there were a bunch of guys in the StarChild set-up who kept themselves pretty much to themselves. We had an idea that they were up to some black project stuff."

"What was that about?"

"I got to know one of them. I learned enough from him to know the work he was doing was sending him over the edge, bigtime. He couldn't come to terms with what they made him do, but I am not at liberty to say any more about that."

Alan cleared his throat.

"So, what kind of observations did you make in that basement? Am I at least allowed to ask you about that?"

Robert thought for a moment, took out a cigarette, lit it and blew out a plume of smoke.

"In the late 70s," he said, "we identified a Soviet Typhoon-class submarine that was under construction, before any of our field agents or military knew it even existed."

"What? You did all that by sitting in a basement in Virginia?"

Robert continued, "During the SADF pullout from Angola some nuclear weapons ended up in the hands of fanatical, right-wing Afrikaners in the South African Defense Force. We found their exact location in Zululand, and they were eventually recovered safely."

Alan looked baffled.

"I… this is hard to get my head around. So, the CIA was investing in an ESP-paranormal type-thing, for want of a better description?"

"That's about the size of it."

"And it worked?"

"Sure did."

Alan had to think about all that for a minute. Eventually Robert put his cigarette out in the ashtray and said with dignified finality.

"That's quite enough about me. Now tell me about these visions and emotional stresses you've been having. That's why you're here, isn't it?"

Alan told Stringfield about his night of broken sleep, and the manifestation of a naked woman in the darkness, followed by more broken sleep, and her appearance the room, permeated by a strange, penumbral, green glow. He described how he was paralysed throughout the whole episode, as she crawled towards him on the bed, naked, poised over him, lowering her body onto his heaving chest. he described his horror at that moment, and his desire.

Robert listened passively, occasionally pouring himself some more tea. When Alan was done, Robert simply nodded.

The day was fading fast leaving a soft, vaguely inadequate, melancholy blue glow in the room. Robert stood up and went over to the window. The lights were coming up in the buildings on the other side of the park. Alan watched him, this big powerful enigmatic figure. Robert took the drawstring, obviously considering lowering the blinds, and then he changed his mind and returned to his armchair.

"So, Alan. Why do you think all this is happening to you? Don't answer straight away. Just think about it."

Alan's eyes were moistening, despite his best efforts. He wiped them with his sleeve. "I have no idea," he said.

"Did you have any unusual, slightly disturbing experiences? It could be a sudden oppressive mood clouding your thoughts, or a sequence of dreams?"

Alan interrupted him. "Yes. There was a particular dream. Alan described the nightmare, which began with him waiting outside the agency, and although it was day, everything was in deep shadow. There was a sense of sinister and malignant intent, oppressiveness and evil. The aggressive crowds on the streets, and then the coming of the yellow truck – the rumbling, getting louder and the strange, leering couple with red spotted faces, like measles, and all those people with red, spotted faces too.

"Describe this strange couple."

"They're in their late fifties to mid-sixties, I think. She's sort of skinny, with glasses and curly, light-coloured hair. He's medium height, but stocky and balding at the front, with a big leering smile. Horrible."

"Any idea who they might be?" said Robert.

"I've wracked my mind to try and work that out for myself. I can't connect them with anyone."

"I need you to let me know if you come across any signs of these characters. It could be very important."

"Sure. I can do that."

"I'd also like to ask you, have any of the other residents in your apartment building said anything about hauntings, or strange things going on?"

"No, nothing. I'm on speaking terms with a couple of people on my floor, an old lady and a middle-aged woman whose husband works during the day. No one has mentioned anything like that to me."

"Do you have any information about the owners of your apartment?"

"No. I don't even know their names. We got the flat through a realty company and the contract is through them. The realty guy told me in passing that one of the owners is an antique restorer. He's on a three-year sabbatical in Italy with his boyfriend, who I think works in the fashion industry. That's all I know."

Isobel came out of her studio after a while to ask if the guys wanted to drink anything a bit stronger. Alan said a glass of bourbon with ice would go down nicely. Robert opted for a brandy.

Alan felt emotionally drained; he was also more relaxed now. The sky had darkened, and a few rogue snowflakes were blowing around, while more lights had come on in the buildings across the park, so that the view looked like a typical nighttime skyline across the dark expanse of park

When she returned with the drinks Alan asked her about the painting. "Oh yes, it's an original Egon Schiele. It was passed on to me from my grandmother in Austria."

Alan drew back a bit, wide-eyed in amazement.

"Unbelievable. I'm lost for words. I've loved the work of Egon Schiele since I was an art student. I went especially with a friend of mine to the Leopold Museum in Vienna to see the collection of his work there. Incredible."

Alan took a sip of his drink, then pointed to a plinth in the corner. "But what about that sculpture just there? Is it a real..."

"Boccioni. Yes."

Alan took a deep breath. "Christ."

"Alan, as you so obviously appreciate figurative art, I have a little show coming up in SoHo. Would you like to come along to the opening?"

Alan perked up. "That would be great. Is it a one-man show?"

"No. It will be a one *woman* show."

Alan laughed.

The mental effort Alan exerced to supress his many doubts about the credibility of the analysis of his experience, plus the onset of the fatigue that regularly came upon him these days, led Alan to make a move. He stood up and thanked Robert for his time and apologised for having to leave. Robert said he completely understood, but he did have just one more question.

"I gather you're going upstate with your family for a few weeks."

"Yes. We're staying in the Hudson Valley in a property owned by my boss. Apparently, it's very nice up there. Cold Spring."

"Oh, yes, I know it. Across the river from where I graduated at West Point. We go there quite a bit ourselves in the summer. Beautiful countryside. I'm sure you'll all enjoy it. And, while you're there, would you mind if Isobel and I had a chance to look around your apartment?"

"Uh... sure, why not? Are you thinking of renting in Brooklyn?"

Robert laughed. "No, no. We're quite happy here. It's just that, well, I don't want to say too much, but there may be some residual causes to your troubles laying semi-dormant there that helped to somehow became manifest – disembodied spirits of low level, or anomalous disturbances arising in connection with a particular place or person."

"Really?" Alan's long-held cynicism about anything to do with the supernatural returned, but he kept these views in check, if only for the sake of politeness.

"It's a possibility," replied Robert.

"You mean like a sort of poltergeist-type thing?"

"Well, you could think of it that way. Can you arrange for a set of keys to be sent over with your address..."

Alan shrugged. "I don't see why not. But are you sure it's worth the trouble."

"I'll let you know after I've been there."

187

Chapter 11

Alan's biggest worry was that his sexual demon, could return – when Jenny was with him, and God knows how that would turn out. Cornelia and Bella told him not to worry and assured him that Robert would deal with the situation. Alan wasn't totally convinced, but there weren't any other options on offer. He also felt that the line of questioning Robert subjected him to made little sense. And as far Robert and Isobel looking around the apartment while he and the family were away, well, there was no harm in it, but he couldn't see the point. On the other hand, Robert Stringfield couldn't be a complete crank. The CIA, for all their dark schemes, do not hire cranks. So, he sent the keys over to Stringfield via courier, as requested.

Now he had to focus on the poster concepts he and Gary were working on for the disinfectant client. They did have an idea that could work quite well – and it would probably sell a lot of products, but because it was so clever and original it would be a hard sell-in to the client. It would probably be rejected out of hand. For that reason, they needed to come up with a couple more routes, just to be on the safe side

He came into the office, set down his coffee, and as he was taking out his pad and pens from his bag, the book on Demoniality dropped out. Gary grabbed it, with a look of surprise.

"Demoniality? I didn't know you were into this shit. The occult isn't your bag."

Alan snatched the book away from him.

"What's it to you?"

"A lot. I interviewed him a few years back, when I was working at the Village Voice. That's one of the books they gave me for research. Powerful stuff, and very scary... if it's true."

"Interviewed who?"

"Robert Stringfield, the author. The guy whose name is on the cover, if you haven't noticed.

Alan sat down and scratched his head, in embarrassment. I know who he is. I met him yesterday.

"You're a man of many surprises..."

Alan tried to focus the conversation away from the supernatural.

"So, when did you work for the Voice? I didn't know you were that far left."

"Easy tiger. You know me better than that. I did it for the money. Kept my head down and avoided any discussion of politics."

"I guess you would."

"I wasn't out of university that long at the time, and they asked me to do this filler piece about hauntings in SoHo. They pointed me in the direction of this Stringfield guy, because he's an authority on anything supernatural. He turned out to be a very decent guy. Very bright. Hard as nails too. We ended up having a few beers. His wife, Isobel, she's a lovely lady. Comes from one of the older banking families. They live in this amazing pad over on the Upper East Side."

"So, you don't think he's a crank?"

"Christ no. He's deadly serious. But why are you reading that book? And why the hell did you meet him?"

Alan put his face in his hands and then looked straight at Gary.

"I can't tell you right now. But all this shit I've been going through... some friends say he might be able to help."

"Really?"

Chapter 12

Getting out of bed was a struggle. His eyes were full of sleep. When he opened them, things were out of focus at first. He slowly got out of bed and drew back the curtains. It wasn't snowing anymore, and the sun was out. Jenny and the boys would be at the airport in a couple of hours. Before making coffee, he decided to shave. When he was nearly done, he leaned forward to get a closer look at the last bits of shaving foam on his face to tackle, and a woman's face flashed up next to his in the mirror. She had a sad expression, her big brown eyes peering through strands of dark brown hair. He straightened up quickly and found that he'd nicked his chin. A line of blood was mixed in with the shaving cream, and some of it dropped onto his white dressing gown. He turned around furiously, but there was no one there.

At JFK Arrivals Alan had a Band Aid on his chin and a pain in his neck. The previous last night's heavy snowfall had delayed all incoming flights, so he found himself staring at the main airport monitor for a while, and it became clear that no new information was filtering through, so he went to one of the restaurants and took the opportunity to sit down and have a full breakfast, with endless refills of coffee.

He was in no mood for all this uncertainty and waiting, not after the sleepless night he'd had. Still, at least it was demon free.

Speaking of demons, he was reassured that Gary respected the work of Robert Stringfield. He was more confident now that Robert might actually be able to help him out avoid more sightings of his sexual demon, and maybe his sex life will be saved. But who for?

He thought of Juliette again, cooking breakfast with an apron thrown over her bra and panties, and then he tried to banish the thought. Jason was right. Jenny and the boys were his life. Messing around with a pretty undergraduate was not the way forward. Just then there was an announcement: BA flight 714 was due to land at 20.36. Thank fuck for that.

Soon people started to flow out of arrivals. A small man in a brown suit was followed by his wife and three kids, dragging their cases behind them. Just then there was a tug at his elbow, and he realised that Jack was standing there in his duffel coat, ski jumper and yellow wellington boots. He was holding up a piece of paper with wax crayon scrawls on it and his nose was running.

Alan crouched down, took the drawing, kissed his eldest son and lifted him up. Jenny and Simon walked towards him among the throng emerging from immigration. Her short blonde, pixie-cut hair was brushed to one side, which emphasised the soft curves and beauty of her face. She was pushing a luggage trolley and holding Simon in her left arm who was wearing his superman pyjamas under his blue coat and hugging his mummy koala bear-style while sucking his thumb.

As she came close, he kissed her and said,

"Hi Jen. Gosh. You look tired."

She gave him a soft, warm smile that filled him to the ears with guilt.

"You've lost weight," she replied. "What happened to your love of the great American breakfast?"

"No, that hasn't gone away. It's just the stresses and strains of the advertising business chipping away at my belly."

She raised her eyebrows knowingly.

"Talking of stresses and strains, you should try travelling with these two on a plane for eight hours. I think everyone in business class will be asking for a refund. Here, can you take this one too?"

"If you can just grab hold of this," he said. Handing her the drawing. She let go of the trolley and took the sheet of paper, then leaned forward so he could scoop Simon off her back with his free arm. Now he was carrying both the boys.

Her three-quarter length, grey herringbone coat was open, revealing a grey green fine-weave sweater, tan-coloured, slim-fit jeans and brown Chelsea boots.

Shall we pick up some coffee and drinks or something?" he said.

"I'm shattered," she sighed. "First thing I need to do is get some sleep. Can you handle the boys for a couple of hours when we get to the apartment?"

"I guess so, but don't they need some sleep too?"

"Oh, they're much too excited for that. Maybe later." She smiled. "I really have missed you... but I hope you're not going to snore tonight."

"I'll do my best to try not to breath."

She shook her head and gave him a sideways look. "Hey, guess what? Dorothy and Ralph next door are selling up and moving to Highgate. He's just had the most ridiculous pay rise."

Alan tutted. "Why didn't I ever get into banking?"

"Because you're crap at maths."

Jenny pointed to the Band-Aid on his chin. "What've you done to your face?"

"Uh... well, you know, I was in such a hurry to get ready..."

"Oh. So, it's my fault, is it?" she joked."

"Isn't everything?"

"They were both laughing now.

"Hey Dad," said Jack, as they headed towards exit doors. "You should've seen this great big robot. He could fly into space, and he blew up like this," he held out his arms, "POOOOOM!"

Alan looked at Jenny for enlightenment.

He saw "The Iron Giant" on the plane," she said, "but he actual..."

"YEEEE-OWWW!" yelled Alan.

Simon was pushing his finger onto the sticking plaster on Alan's chin. "What the fuck?"

"Language," said Jenny, as Simon burst into tears, and started to take deep breaths between each cry, attracting the attention of nearly everyone in Arrivals. Jenny snatched Simon from him.

"Alan! What's the matter with you?"

"It hurts," he said, lowering Jack to the floor. Jack became quiet and confused as she ushered him to her side. A pear-shaped Mexican man and his tall wife looked at him accusingly.

"Look,' said Alan, in his defence, showing her a dab of blood on his finger, after having touched the offending plaster. "It's starting to bleed again..."

"Can we go home now?" she hissed. "I'm not enjoying being the centre of attention."

Alan pushed the trolley while Jenny carried Simon, with Jack walking alongside her.

Once they were through the sliding doors they stopped, so Jenny could take the pushchair off the trolley and set it up for Simon. It seemed like an eternity before they reached the car park. Jenny got into the back of the Chrysler, with Simon and Jack, who she strapped into the kiddie seats. They set off without anyone saying a word. Alan felt more like a taxi driver than a dad.

The insipid sun was losing its battle with the stern winter sky. The widely spaced out and battered warehouses of Queens didn't exactly soften the mood. Jenny told Simon not to be upset with daddy, because he was just a bit tired.

"He really does love you."

Simon sniffed, in reply.

Alan could see Simon trying to hide a smile. Jack finally perked up and asked if he could plug his DS in when they got home.

It was almost dark, when they pulled up outside the apartment building, and Simon was just starting to perk up. Jack was brimming with energy too, because of the excitement of seeing their new home. When Jenny went to the bathroom, Alan took the boys into the lounge and put on a video of *One Hundred and One Dalmatians,* then they all sat down to watch it. Within quarter of an hour Simon was asleep, and Jack was dropping off, but fighting it. Bleary eyed, Jenny got up to take them both to their brand-new bedroom.

Alan was heating up a saucepan of milk to make him and Jen a hot chocolate, when he was surprised by two arms wrapping themselves around him.

"Hey, relax," said Jenny. "It's only little ol' me." He turned around to kiss her.

The kitchen spotlights highlighted her doe eyes. She kissed him softly, and then again – longer and harder. When she pulled back, she looked at him longingly and said,

There was a brief pause.

"Jen. I'm sorry for getting mad at Simon in the airport."

She closed her eyes, as if not wanting to even think about it.

"Let's forget the hot drink." Her voice was soft and deep.

They lay on top of the duvet, and he stroked her goose pimpled, milk white skin while they chatted. He missed her more than he realised.

"You've done well to find this place," she said. "It's clean and classic and... you know, it still has a sort of modern feel about it too. If your job works out, maybe we should stay here."

"Those guys who own the place are moving back in two years. Remember?"

She screwed up her face. "Shame. I think I could really get to like it here."

"Let's see how things pan out at the agency. I mean, you never know what's around the corner."

Leaning on her elbows, she hauled herself up a little, and sucked in her lips before saying,

"Alan, is there something you're not telling me? Because if you've got any doubts about job security now, what the hell are me and the boys doing here?"

"No, no. Nothing like that. It's just that... you know, bosses come, bosses go, jobs change, opportunities arise... Look at Nick."

Nick was his old copywriter in London. Alan continued. "He went off to Hong Kong as a head of Copy, ostensibly for a year, but ended up being headhunted by TBWA Paris. He's Creative Director there now. Living in a plush apartment in the 16th Arrondissement and earning a fortune."

"Why doesn't that happen to you?"

"Well, it sort of is, isn't it? Look. We're in New York. And you don't get to be creative director overnight. Cut me some slack, Jen."

She considered that for a moment, while Alan thought her nipples were each like flying saucers parked on snow-covered hills.

Jenny was up bright and early. The first thing she did was to check if the boys were still asleep, which they were. Then she went for a shower, and when she came out Alan sat up and admired her beautifully varnished, red toenails as she towelled herself.

"I'll get breakfast together," she said. "What do you fancy?"

"Maybe just some toast and a grapefruit. I can make the coffee, if you like."

"OK. I'll go and get the boys up. I don't want them over-sleeping."

Jenny had just put on her kimono when the door opened slowly and Simon walked in his oversize pyjamas, dragging his teddy bear and sucking his thumb, which he pulled out just to say, "I'm hungry."

"Hi honey!" said Jenny, whisking him up. "Mummy is just going to make you some breakfast."

He scratched his nose and pulled his thumb and said with a very earnest expression. "Soldiers." Then the thumb went back.

"Great." She turned to Alan. "Do we have any eggs?"

"Yup. Fresh bread too."

Jenny sat him down on the bed next to Alan. "You stay and have cuddles with daddy, and I'll bring you in when your egg and toast is ready."

"OK."

When she left the room, he gave Alan a furtive glance with his big blue eyes, pulled his thumb out and said, "Daddy? Who was that shiny green lady in my bedroom last night?"

Chapter 13

"You are such a clever boy, and when we get to Cold Spring, daddy's going to buy you a big ice cream, with a chocolate flake and lots of raspberry syrup. How does that sound."

"Yeah!" said Simon, all wide eyed.

"Now, can you tell daddy what this lady was wearing – the one you saw last night? Or… maybe she wasn't wearing anything at all?"

Simon leaned back and gave him a look of complete disapproval.

"Don't be silly daddy. Of course, she was wearing clothes."

"Oh yes. What was I thinking?" He tried to hide his relief.

Alan wiped Simon's eyes and asked him to blow his nose in a tissue he handed him. He did that and then handed it back to his dad absent-mindedly and went back to sucking his thumb. But very quickly he withdrew it.

"Clever boy," said Alan. "What happened next?"

He shook his head. "Nothing."

"Right. What did Jack say about this lady?"

"Nothing. He was asleep."

"Oh yes," said Alan ruffling Simon's hair affectionately.

"Can daddy ask just one more thing?"

"Can I have a really, really big ice cream?"

"Of course."

Simon nodded, with a pretend sadness.

"Could you move?"

"What do you mean daddy?"

"Like… could you move around?"

"That's silly daddy. 'Course I could. I sat up and watched her, didn't I?"

Alan picked him up and kissed him on the forehead.

"Listen sweetheart. I don't think we should tell mummy about all this. She might think it was a burglar or something, and then she'd really start worrying. We don't want that, do we?"

He looked to one side for a moment then faced his dad again.

"Are there lady burgule-lars?" he asked with a look of profound concern.

"Uh, could be."

"Oh."

"Maybe the lady you saw lives along the hallway, and she got a bit lost."

"Uh-huh."

"Anyway, let's just keep this to ourselves, shall we?"

Simon nodded thoughtfully.

Alan was now desperate to find out what this demon's appearance to Simon could mean (if she was a demon). Clearly, she was not natural, not if she was green and glowing, like the time when she appeared to him. Which obviously makes her supernatural. He had to call Robert Stringfield to let him know what happened, but not with Jenny around. When he took Simon into the lounge Jenny was laying out the plates and cutlery. He put the boy into his new highchair, next to Jack.

"I'm going to nip out to get a newspaper and some French bread," he said.

"OK. But be quick - the bacon's nearly done."

"Sure!"

The cold air sharpened his thoughts. He took a couple of deep breaths, and sighed, watching the vapour leave his mouth. There was a call phone in the Italian coffee bar, next to the bookshop on Court. He made his way there and dialled Robert's number. What he couldn't know was that Robert and Isobel were not home: they were walking downtown for brunch, before heading over to Alan and Jenny's Brooklyn apartment after he and the family were on their way to Cold Spring. The phone went straight to answerphone. He didn't leave a message. It He wondered if Cornelia and Bella might be able to help. He dialled them at the Bell and Candle, and Bella answered.

"Listen, things are bad," he said. "I have to be quick. Jenny doesn't know I'm calling. I'm using a café phone."

"Are you calling to tell me you love me?"

"Bella, please. This is serious."

"OK. Tell me."

"I don't know how to put this but – that demon, or whatever it is – the succubus, she appeared to Simon, my youngest son, last night, in the boys' bedroom. Simon is a smart kid. He described her pretty well. He said he was sitting up and looking at her for a while. She was green and glowing, but she wasn't naked."

"Shit. He must have the second sight, like you, if he can see her."

"Gifted? What kind of a gift is that?"

"Never mind. She is harmless to him. There's nothing he can do for her. She must have just been curious."

"Are you sure?"

"Honestly Alan, I can't emphasis this enough. Robert will get to the heart of your problem. By the time you get back to your apartment, there will be no demon or succubus to terrorise you."

Alan desperately wanted to believe Bella, but he couldn't see how she could be so certain.

Arriving home he found that Jenny and the boys were already having breakfast.

"What took you so long?" she asked.

"There was a queue in the bakery," he said.

By eleven o'clock the kids were strapped in the back of the car, and Alan had put all their luggage in the boot. They left before midday, and it took a good half hour just to get across the water and out of Manhattan.

He felt tired from lack of sleep, but a little later, as they were driving through Westchester, he thought how good it felt to be in the countryside, and it perked him up considerably. The sky was pale blue grey, except for a glowing patch of yellow to the right. On one narrow stretch of road the ploughs hadn't done their work, so Alan couldn't do more than twenty. At one point they had to stop because Simon was getting restless. So, Jenny got into the back next to him with his head resting on her arm, while she read him *The Tiger Who Came to Tea*. Jack, meanwhile, was engrossed with his Gameboy.

When they finally arrived at Steve's house in Cold Spring, Alan had to park on the road, because Steve's driveway was knee deep in snow. Jenny thought the place looked sweet. It was a white clapperboard small family house, surrounded by snow-covered pine trees and many other trees that shed their leaves weeks ago. The other houses were obscured by foliage and set back, so you could only see the gables. Alan started to unload the car, while Jenny got the boys out.

Although they were only about fifty or sixty miles from Manhattan, he felt safe here, from you know who. He dreaded having to go back to the Brooklyn apartment, which was obviously haunted. If he could convince Jenny of some reason for them to move, his worries would be solved, but then he remembered, no they wouldn't he's signed an eighteen-month contract. Just then he felt a playful kick behind the knee.

"What are you waiting for, Christmas?"

It was Jenny. She was standing beside him with the boys at the front door.

"Sorry love," he said, putting the bags down and fumbling for the front door keys.

As soon as they entered the place his mood brightened. Jenny took to it immediately too. Considering Steve was an unreconstructed modernist, he was surprised by just how traditional the style of the layout and furnishings was. And it let in plenty of natural light, especially in the hallway and lounge. Jack ran into the lounge and flung himself onto the Red Indian rug by the hearth. Within seconds Simon jumped onto him, and they were rolling around like pigs in mud.

The ground floor had a sort of captain's cabin feel about it, with pale green, wood slat walls, a white wooden ceiling, brown cross beams and narrow and white painted floorboards. Jenny went to the still wrestling boys, shaking her head in mock despair. Alan raised his eyebrows and then pointed upstairs with his chin.

He carried the bags up to the pink, main bedroom room, where he discovered there was a complex antique counterpane covering the bed. On the walls were framed collections of pressed wildflowers, along with a black and white print of a nineteenth century whaling vessel. The bedside cabinet was home to a dozen or so embossed hardcover books by Nathaniel Hawthorne and Ralph Waldo Emerson. There was obviously a side to Steve he never knew.

He opened one of the cases and was startled by a tap on the window. He turned around to see a branch beating against the glass. The wind must've been stronger than he thought. He went to take a better look at the view across the Hudson Valley. The luminous sky shone through the ice-coated, bare branches, making them collectively glow, like a giant spider's web. Through a gap between the firs, he could see the long line of rocky, snow-covered hills on the other side of the frozen river, when something caught his attention. A tiny, dark figure was walking slowly on the ice. Because the window glass was ancient, and uneven in thickness, there was some rippling and distortion, so he wasn't sure if he was looking at a fleck of dirt on the glass. Then he realised that there was something, or someone, walking on the ice. That was a very dangerous thing to do. The ice was not very thick and it was quite liable to crack with the weight of a person. Perhaps it was a fox, he thought. Whatever it was, it stopped, becoming a smudge on a wintery scene, before dissolving away. Almost immediately he had an overwhelming foreboding: a sudden fogginess clouded his every thought, and when he tried to focus, he was left with nothing but worry and confusion. A dark mood was about to set in, that was interrupted by Jenny's voice.

"Are you done here?" she said.

He turned to find her at the door holding a grumpy Simon, with Jack standing expectantly at her side.

"These two fellas need to expend some energy."

"Sorry hon, I was miles away," said Alan.

"Daddy," said Jack. "We don't want no ice cream now. It's too cold."

"That's very sensible, Jack. We'll go out into town and sit down somewhere to have a nice hot chocolate with marshmallows. How does that sound?"

They both yelled together, "Yaaaay!"

Walking along the riverside, they soon came to a Victorian gazebo. To the right of it, a part of the pathway branched off inland, slipping underneath the railway track, towards Main Street, which is where they headed. It was a quirky small stretch of road made up of two rows of charming small-town stores, with wooden verandas and brass door handles. They visited a well-stocked, no nonsense general goods store that sold Levis 501s at an excellent price. There was even a shop that had nothing but Scottish goods, including tartan scarves and ties, Highland Whiskies of various varieties and prices, and of course haggis. A little further on was an 'English' shop that sold Marmite, marmalade, pale ale, Toby jugs, union jack mugs, and Lipton's Tea.

"Liptons? I don't know anyone in England that drinks Lipton's Tea," said Jenny.

They also went into a cosy tearoom for hot chocolate. It was run by a friendly, East European couple in their thirties. There were five tables, all of them covered with charming, gingham waxed tablecloths.

The rest of the day went by uneventfully. They went back to the house, had a rest, and then Alan started rummaging around in Steve's shed where, among the tools and pots he found a toboggan. The boys were excited when they saw it. He had his work cut out for him then, because he ended up dragging the boys around in it for the next hour in the back garden. It was twilight by the time they went back inside. Jenny fed the kids and then Alan washed them and put their pyjamas on. When they were tucked up in bed and fast asleep Alan put on his coat and went out onto the veranda. There was virtually no street lighting, and the grouping of fir trees in front of the place was now just a mass of darkness. Jenny put on her woolly hat, jacket and scarf to join him.

There were far more stars out than they'd ever seen before, and lower down in the sky was a gibbous moon. He felt this was an excellent opportunity to broach the subject he'd been thinking about all day.

"Oh, it's beautiful," she said.

"It certainly beats Kentish Town."

The crescent moon cast enough light to turn her eyes into luminous pools and highlight the dimples in her cheeks.

"So, what do you think of the Brooklyn apartment?"

"I love it," she said.

"Don't you feel it's, you know, a bit awkward in shape. You know, with the bedrooms and kitchen all attached directly into that great big lounge like limpets. It seems, well, kind of disconcerting to me."

"Limpets? Where are you going with this? We looked at a dozen places and that was easily the best, maybe not the most affordable, but not the most expensive either. And it's such a great location, with two subways close by, some great shops, you can go running along the river to the Brooklyn Bridge. I think we're very lucky to have it."

"I'm not so sure."

Her eyes widened, and she opened her mouth a fraction. "Are you crazy?"

"Seriously. Something about it is putting me into a weird frame of mind, and it's affecting my work."

"What? How? What are you smoking these days?"

"Well… I don't know how to say this, but I think our apartment might be haunted."

"Jesus. Haunted by what? Have you actually seen or heard anything strange?"

He didn't want to lie, but he also didn't want to worry her, so he had no option.

"Not really. It's just a sort of… feeling."

"Alan. I don't want to hear any more nonsense like that. There's no way we could think of leaving that beautiful apartment. It's perfect for us. And anyway, we can't afford the financial penalties for breaking the lease."

"Yeah, I was thinking about that too. But maybe with a good lawyer, who knows? Maybe there are ways around that issue…" he said hesitantly.

"Alan, please! That's enough of that. Now, do you want to go in and eat, or what? I'm hungry."

He was completely in the hands of Robert Stringfield now.

Chapter 14

McDuff's is an old-style drinking and eating joint on the ground floor of a five-story brick building downtown that has survived the advance of the designer brands that have been invading SoHo. The plain black exterior is straight out of a Hopper painting, and so is the inside, with its mustard embossed wallpaper, black painted columns, and the fleur-de-lis tiled floor. The place features the same type of red chequered tablecloths they used during prohibition. George McDuff ran the place from the time he retired from baseball in the early nineteen-twenties right up to the early eighties. His grandson Liam was in charge now. Liam was built like a tank but was really just a big softy.

Robert and Isobel were sitting down at one of the tables by the wall, which like all the other walls, was surrounded by framed photographs of the greatest baseball hitters of the twentieth century. Isobel seemed to be staring into space before she finally piped up.

"What the hell am I doing here? Jacob Schulz is having puppies because I haven't delivered enough work, and the opening is only days away. I should be in my studio painting, for Christ's sake. If my show goes wrong, you're gonna get it in the neck, Springfield."

Robert softly banged both his palms on the table and leaned back, waiting for her full attention before he spoke.

"Listen, Izzy. It's no big deal. I need you for just this one thing. We'll eat here, digest and then make our way across the river to Brooklyn, do our thing and get a cab home. Easy-peasy."

Isobel watched him with deep reservation, uttering only, "Hm".

They sat together quietly for a while, before Isobel said, "Strange that Bella should bother to tell Alan about my recovery from cancer, don't you think?"

Robert shrugged. "Not really. That's how you were when she first saw you, at their house out in the country. She was only a kid then, but she absolutely adored you."

Isobel nodded. "And I her, though she was a strange child. There was something sad about her, I couldn't help but be motherly."

The waitress came to ask if they were ready. They ordered brunch and went back to their discussion.

"What I'm wondering is, where does a succubus come from?" asked Isobel.

"Good question. A Succubus doesn't just come out of thin air. She has to be summoned: usually by more than one person - a cabal or a coven, maybe. It involves blasphemous oaths and sacrifices."

"How does that work?"

"The existing texts say that on certain unholy Sabbaths, witches can summon a Succubus for their sexual gratification – and for the power they offer to any individual that the Succubus will serve. That's when they make sacrifices and offerings to the devil."

"Ugh! What kind of sacrifices?"

"Blood sacrifices. A woman, a child maybe."

"Ugh. Disgusting."

"If we were to find out who was behind it all - we could undo what they've done."

"But why choose Alan as the victim?"

"Hard to say. Maybe he was in the wrong place at the right time."

There was a trio of Wall Street-types at the table next to them who had been laughing like hyenas. Now one of them was kicking up a fuss with a waitress because they were dissatisfied with their sausages. Robert was going to say something, but Isobel kicked him.

"The Demon has to be summoned by a sacrifice, but after she is summoned, she can choose to uh… copulate with men or women without any need for sacrifices, just because it desires the carnal possession of a certain man or woman."

"You mean it depends on whether it (or she) has the hots them?"

He nodded. "That's what it comes down to."

"You know what?" she said. "I was kind of curious about that series of dreams you said he described to you. You know that couple with the measles?"

"He didn't say they had measles. He said they had red spots on their faces."

"Yeah, yeah. The thing is, what does it all mean?"

"I think those dreams are connected to the demon's appearance. I want to find out who that old couple are, or at least who they represent."

Isobel had a steely look in her eye.

"Stringfield, I'm going to play devil's advocate here, if you'll pardon the irony. Could it be maybe that there is no demon haunting Alan at all, and he's just losing it?"

Robert had to think about that for a few seconds, and then he shrugged, "You know me, Izzy. I like to play safe. Like these fellas here, I'm like hedging my bets."

One of the bankers looked over when Robert said that. Robert ignored him.

Just then their food arrived. They waited for the waitress to set everything down, including the drinks, and then Robert continued, after supping a bit of his beer.

"Psychologists talk about something called the 'Old Hag phenomenon'. That's when people imagine that some weird creature is visiting them in bed. This thing usually ends up sitting on their chest, making it impossible to move or speak. Some people describe it as a terrifyingly ugly, old woman with demonic or supernatural powers."

"Oh. Is that common?" asked Isobel.

"Not especially," said Robert,

"It's a kind of sleep paralysis, caused by the mind not being fully awake. It can happen when you're hovering between a dream-state and waking. Funnily enough, it's more or less the perfect condition for RV. Some people who've been through that think they're being visited by aliens."

"So, Alan could be nuts?"

"I'm not dismissing that possibility. The important thing to remember is that the Succubus – or whatever you want to call it - did not appear to Alan till he moved into his new apartment. I need to find out as much as I can about that place."

"And what about his apartment, I mean his current landlords? What if they have something to do with all this? Who knows, they could be the leaders of some satanic cult, or whatever."

"Let's not get ahead of ourselves."

"You could make a call to Mitch to do some checking? He could get you some answers, using the company database. "

Dassos Petrou

"No. I don't want to get anyone at Langley involved in this. Those days are gone. Whatever I need to know, I'll find out for myself."

"You are one stubborn son-of-a-bitch."

Soho in the Dark

Chapter 15

When Alan, Jenny and the boys were arriving at Steve's house in Cold Spring in their car, Robert and Isobel were outside the main doors of Alan's apartment building, under the green marquee. The Victorian condo started life as a factory for Singer sewing machines, close to the subway station at Bergen. It was located in a narrow, residential, tree-lined street, just along from a characterful fire station. The red brick walls of the sides of the building took up half the block.

Robert used the keys Alan gave him, opened the front and they entered the lobby. Isobel followed him up the narrow stairs to the first floor. An old lady was coming out of a door at the far end of the hallway. She didn't seem interested in their presence.

Robert unlocked the apartment door and felt a little iciness at the nape of his neck when it opened straight into the lounge. The room was about the size of a school hall. An eerie glow squeezed through the bottom of the blinds that made the place look like a museum after hours. He groped for the light switch and hit it. White walls and minimalist modern furniture flooded into view. The floor was wooden and polished, covered by only one comparatively small rectangular rug, between the black leather designer sofa and the TV.

In one corner was a desk stacked with a row of marker pens standing on their ends, at the side of a layout pad. White shelves crammed with books filled a large expanse of the wall facing the windows. Robert glimpsed at some of the titles. They must've been Alan's because they were mostly relating to mass communication, artists monographs, and design theory, along with some advertising annuals, classic novels by Poe, Lovecraft, Sartre, Camus and Dickens, and a few American crime writers like Hammett and Chandler. On the wall there was a framed poster of an Edward Hopper Exhibition Isobel had visited in London, in the 80s.

In the main bedroom everything was white, apart from the wooden floor, an antique wardrobe, glass vase of purple freesias and a photo of the family on the dressing table. On entering Robert sensed the feint residue of an intangible miasma, although he wasn't properly geared to sense the presence of supernatural activity – but Isobel was. In fact, her internal Geiger counter went off the scale. She looked stunned. Robert had seen her like this a dozen times during the Cold War, helping to prevent parapsychological assassinations. This was different. She had a pallid look which he hadn't seen in her since the cancer was eating her up. He thought she would faint, and he quickly took her arm. She shook herself free of his hold and took a couple more steps into the room.

"It's OK", she said in a low whisper, as if she was in slight pain.

Heading towards a corner she turned around to stare at the window directly above the double bed, where the blind was still lowered. Her face developed an expression of bitter anguish, and she sank slowly into a kind of trance. For about a minute she was motionless. Robert looked on as she started to sway gently where she stood. Her hands brushed down her side to her thighs, like an exotic dancer then she hugged herself and writhed around, again as if she was suffering. He'd seen her hoovering up supernatural essences many times, but nothing like this. Her hands moved around each breast, in slow orbits, and then eventually slid across them and back down again and she looked like she was going to burst into tears any moment, but instead her eyes widened, giving her a startled appearance and with the caution of a tightrope walker she walked towards the bed. Again, she seemed to be fighting some inner pain when she stopped at the foot of the bed and fell slowly face-forward into the mattress, crying hysterically and beating at the mattress with her fists. Robert stood there helpless, knowing that he should not interfere, for fear of losing the thread she was connecting to, which could be vital to their investigation. The longer she was able to remain in this state, the more she would learn. When she stopped quivering, and it was clear that the experience had passed he went over to sit with her on the bed. He hugged her and said, "What is it, Izzy?"

She rolled her head so she could face him, glaring at him with utter fury and almost spat her words out.

"What the fuck am I even doing here? You are such a bastard. Did you know that was going to happen? What am I, your bloodhound?"

"What?"

"Don't give me that, or I'll give you such a thump, Stringfield." She always looked so cute when she was angry.

He got up and left her sitting there, as he walked over to the corner, where she began taking everything in, and then turned to speak to her.

"Honey. I had no idea. I brought you here hoping you could maybe pick up some sort of sign, you know... of this demon. Obviously, we got a lot more than we bargained for."

"You mean I did," she said.

She sat at the edge of the bed looking at her knees. There was a silence that lasted for maybe twenty seconds, but it seemed like an age.

She lifted her head and glanced at him wearily.

"Get me a glass of water," she said.

He fiddled with some spotlights, which came up softly in the kitchen to reveal white tiles to shoulder height all around and a top of the range coffee machine on the grey work surface. He found a bottle of mineral water in the baby blue Smeg fridge, poured some into a glass, and went back into the bedroom. She reached for it dreamily, took a slow sip and sighed.

"You want to maybe take a lie-down before we look around some more?" he said.

She looked up at him while her chin rested on her chest to say, "And what is it that makes you think I can get much of a rest on this bed?"

Robert sighed. "Sorry. Stupid question."

He waited until she was ready. Slowly she started to describe what she had perceived.

"This essence is very intense, emotional – not just passionate, but sad?"

"Sad?"

"Yes, sad too. A bunch of mixed-up emotions. And it's definitely a she."

"So, Alan was on the level."

"The feeling I get is of wallowing in a deep, black pit of endless misery, occasionally broken up by powerful lust, from which there is no escape."

"Wow. And... is there a clue as to what this mix of emotions are directed towards?"

"I get the words 'This man that must be loved.' That's all."

"Hmm. OK. That's good, Izzy. Take it easy now and we'll head back when you're ready."

She drank up the rest of the water, handed him back the glass, and walked out of the room. He went to pay a much-needed visit to the bathroom and then went into the small bedroom. A Spiderman duvet covered one of the beds and on the other was a giant image of the Incredible Hulk. Alphabet charts and a large Star Wars poster were blue tacked to the wall. There was a plastic crate full of toy trucks and robots and another full of cuddly toys.

She turned to face him and said, "She was in here too."

"This time all I'm getting from the ethereal residue is curiosity and sadness."

"From the succubus or the kids?"

"Her, stupid."

"What the hell would a Succubus be doing appearing to the kids?"

Isobel shrugged. "Can we go now?"

Robert remembered Alan saying that his landlords had stored away a few of their things in a wall cupboard near the front door. Robert tried the handle, and it didn't give.

"What are you doing?" said Isobel.

"I just need to take a quick look in here," he said.

She closed the front door, turned around and looked at him with a frown. "Didn't Alan give you the key to that room?"

"No. He doesn't have one."

"Listen Stringfield, don't overstep boundaries. You're not working for the agency now."

"I feel responsible, Izzy. Those kids… Who knows what could happen? I need to do this…"

He pulled a standard issue lock-pick out of his pocket.

"Oh, for Christ's sake…" She scowled as he crouched down to poke around inside the keyhole.

After a short while there, footsteps getting further down the hallway getting louder. They stopped directly outside the front door to the apartment; neither Isobel nor Robert said a word. Robert was halfway through releasing the fourth lever on the lock, when there was a click. Immediately there were a series of loud knocks on the door. Isobel shook her head and quietly opened the door, just enough for anyone outside to see her standing against the wall by the entrance, and no further. She put on her singing voice, "Hello?"

It was an older woman, and she seemed to be nervous.

"Oh, hi," she stammered. "Is Alan still here with his family? We thought they'd gone upstate."

"Yes. They have. But Alan asked us to pick up a couple of things he needs to finish off a project. His office has asked him to work on a project while he's on vacation." Isobel then did her pantomime look of despair.

"Oh, that's so unfair."

"Isn't it?"

"So, will you be staying with them?"

"No. We have a place in Poughkeepsie, so we're just going to be passing through Cold Spring. Probably have a bite to eat with Alan, Jenny and the boys… and then we'll just move on."

That seemed to diffuse any tension.

"Well lovely to meet you," said Isobel.

After the woman left, Robert managed to pick the lock. He stood up and opened the door. The cupboard was much deeper that he'd expected. It was mostly piled with boxes of books. Robert lifted a couple and opened them up. There were a lot of heavy, well-produced art, architecture and design books and quite a few antique texts too. One of them, the *Lives of the Most Excellent Painters, Sculptors, and Architects* had a green cloth cover, and title and author in gold, embossed letters. Isobel said it was one of the most important books on the Renaissance, originally written in Latin by a contemporary and friend of Michelangelo. In the same box was another 19th century English first edition of *The Civilisation of the Renaissance in Italy* by Jacob Burckhardt. The book underneath that was a yellow tome. Isobel knew next to nothing about that, but Robert did. It was Cornelius Agrippa's *De Occulta Philosophia Libra Tres*. He only had schoolboy Latin, but he was totally familiar with the English translation of this work. In the same box were other titles, such as Robert Fludd's *Utriusque Cosmi Historia*, *The Most Holy Trinosophia* – attributed to Count of Saint Germain, *The Autobiography of Benvenuto Cellini*, and *Steganographia* by Johannes Trithemius.

211

Robert stood up, sucked in his lips, and shook his head.

"You know what?" he said to Isobel. "There's a good chance that the people who summoned that demon are the guys who own these books."

"Really? Aren't you just jumping to conclusions? The other books are Renaissance texts. Maybe these guys are just interested in the philosophical writings of the time."

"From where I'm sitting, you'd have to be a really dedicated scholar of mysticism, alchemy and dark magic to own these texts. They're practically instruction manuals on occult philosophy, going back hundreds of years. Some of them even refer to the summoning of demons. Izzy, I'm not kidding, we have to check these guys out.

Chapter 16

Before making coffee, Alan went into the bathroom. His eyes were encrusted with sleep, and he badly needed a pee. Afterwards, he rested his palms on the edge of the sink and leaned close to the mirror to look at his still half-closed eyes. He ran the cold tap, leaned down, and splashed some water onto his face. He wiped his face and looked in the mirror and let out a scream. His face was now covered in blood-red gore, some of which was dripping from his nose and his chin. There were bits of entrail coagulating around the plughole, partially blocking the sink. He around as the bathroom went out of focus and found that he was losing his sense of balance. He found himself stumbling back, almost falling into the bath. Jenny pulled open the door in utter confusion. He tried to say something, but no words came. Looking into the mirror again his face was now clean. What's more, there was no sign of any gore in the sink. Thinking on the hoof, he mumbled something about the water being too hot. Jenny gave him a cold stare and walked away without saying a word.

After that he toweled his face and went to sit on the edge of the bed, trying to convince himself it was all just a hallucination, brought on by lack sleep, since he'd been tormented with doubts and fears about the demon, tossing and turning all night.

The sky was a pale turquoise. There had been a fresh snowfall overnight and the hills across the frozen river were no longer in mist, so the dark rocks jutting out of the snow were in sharp outline. So, after breakfast they decided to go for another walk along the riverside. They let boys run on ahead. Jenny was discussing their itinerary for the next few days with Alan, who nodded blankly and found that his thoughts were drifting off onto other things, including what Robert had been saying about demons and, most worryingly, the danger of impotence if the demon were to get its way with him. And now there were signs that she was not rooted in the Brooklyn apartment, and that she had transferred her presence here in Cold Spring. He felt that it was probably her that he observed on the ice in the bathroom mirror when they first arrived at Steve's house. Jenny saw that he looked glazed and distant. She suspected there were pressures at work he was not ready to talk to her about yet. She'd observed this phenomenon before, back in London. He liked to let stresses work there way through before expressing them, although this seemed like a much more extreme version of that.

She put her arm through his as they walked. A couple of times she opened her mouth, and the words didn't come. Finally, she built up the courage. "I didn't want to say anything, but. I've never really seen you like this before. I was hoping you'd relax and settle back into yourself. I mean, you've been acting strange since we arrived at the airport, and what was all that shouting in the bathroom this morning?"

He was on the verge of telling her the truth about the demon, in the hope that she would understand, but Jenny suddenly interrupted him.

"Oh, for Christ's sake." She ran off ahead. Something was up. Simon was face down in the snow. Jack was standing and pointing nervously at him.

"Did you trip him up Jack?" said Jenny, angrily.

"I... I didn't do anything mum, honest."

"Come here, baby boy." Jenny lifted Simon up, he was red faced and blubbering. She dusted the snow off his cheeks.

Alan arrived on the scene as Simon calmed down a little, resting his chin on his mum's shoulder.

"What happened, Si?" he said.

"Did you just fall over?" asked Jenny.

He quickly stopped crying to sniff and then nod shakily.

"Jack didn't push you, did he?"

He shook his head and closed his eyes, then opened then again. She put him down and wiped his eyes. "Right! Now will you try to be a bit more careful?"

"Uh-huh."

She turned to Jack. "And will you try not to go so fast, because you know he'll try to keep up with you, and his little legs can't do that."

Jack nodded.

"Now go easy."

They let the boys walk ahead again.

"Look. I'm sorry love," said Alan. "I've been a bit stressed with work and everything..."

"Is that why Steve let us have the cottage for the week?"

"Well, if you have to know..."

"Is your job under threat?"

"No. Nothing like that."

She gave him a sideways look. "Tell me the truth."

"Honestly," he said. "Things will be fine. Steve wouldn't lend me the house if he thought I wasn't worth it. I haven't been myself and he sensed something was up and he wanted to help. It's a big deal leaving London and coming here to start all over. I'm just starting to feel the pressure, that's all. I've won too much business for GGPNY to even think of kicking me out."

She said nothing, but she wasn't entirely convinced.

They eventually came to the part of the riverside near the town centre, by the pagoda where a few families were milling about. The boys wanted to build a snowman near the old black canon. Alan organized the construction while Jenny went over to the giant Christmas tree, close to the gazebo, from where she took a video of Alan and the boys at work on their snowman, capturing the beautiful winter scene along the Hudson valley.

Meanwhile Alan helped Jack and Simon roll a huge ball of snow, which became the base of their snowman. Then the boys rolled another ball of snow, which Alan lifted onto the first one. Alan then rolled another ball for the snowman's head. Alan then placed the head onto the body of the snowman and watched the boys smooth it all down, when he felt a touch on the shoulder. He turned to see a hand resting there briefly and heard a soft, low woman's voice.

"Excuse me," she said, "You're not from around here, are you?"

He turned to see a girl in her early twenties."

"Sadly not," he replied.

Despite the oversize round sunglasses, there was something quite dignified about her. She wore a black Russian fur hat, black three-quarter length double breasted coat, with a brown fur collar, black narrow hose trousers and brown boots. He studied her smooth, ivory skin, high forehead and the delicate shape of her nose, and was mesmerized by her blood red lips as she spoke.

"I'm sorry to be a nuisance, but I am a bit lost."

He wasn't listening. "Pardon?"

"I was just wondering if you might know where the cemetery is?"

He was vainly trying to work out what it was that made him feel so curious about her. It wasn't simply her looks. Perhaps it was because she was slightly anachronistic.

"No, I don't. But that's the Hudson House Hotel over there," he said, pointing to the large, quaint gray clapperboard building behind her. "I'm sure someone in there will be able to help you."

Alan could see in the distance that the boys were now collecting stones and talking to some other children, who were building a less successful snowman nearby.

Alan went back to the snowman. "Well done chaps," he said, holding out his hands to be filled by a pile of stones. "But we only need two for the eyes, and one for the nose.

"But the rest can be buttons," said Jack.

"Good idea!" said Alan.

"And he can have my scarf too," said Simon.

"No. Mummy would not approve of you giving him that. Come on, let's add the finishing touches."

He looked back to see if the girl with the Russian hat was walking towards the hotel, but she was nowhere to be seen. Dressed the way she was in such a wintery scene; she would have stood out like a silhouette.

Jenny then came over to join them, having finished filming. She suggested they go into town for a hot drink and then head back to the house. Maybe the boys could do some tobogganing.

"Yay!" They both said in unison.

They were exhausted by the time they got back. In fact, Alan had to carry Simon all the way home. The tobogganing would have to wait for another day. Jenny made Simon have something to eat before putting him to bed. Jack stayed up for a bit longer, and then Alan eventually put him to bed, reading him another chapter from the recently published *Harry Potter and the Philosopher's Stone.*

When Jack had finally dropped off to sleep, Alan came back down to the lounge, where Jenny was struggling to connect her video camera to the back of the TV. Alan said if she made the tea, he would sort out all the wiring.

Just as Jenny was coming back in with the tea tray, Alan had it working, so they sat back on the sofa to watch. The first thing that came up was some shaky camera work of Simon and Jack playing shots in goal in their back garden in London. Then came a short sequence from the school nativity, where Jack was playing Joseph. After that they watched a slow panorama of the Hudson valley, ending up on Jack and Simon rolling a big ball of snow, followed by a shaky zoom-in when Alan comes into frame, while he's picking up a huge ball of snow to place onto the body of the snowman. Then the camera follows the boys as they ran off to the bushes further back to dig up some stones. As Alan watched, he could see himself in the distance, a small figure wrapped up warm in a dark pea coat and woolly hat. But something was wrong.

"Hold that!" he shouted, as he snatched the remote from Jenny.

Jenny was quite perturbed, "Hey!"

"Sorry love. Just need to see this again."

She nudged him on the shoulder, as he pushed rewind and then play, rewind and then play, over and over again.

"I... I don't understand," he said.

"What is it?"

Alan stared at the screen in disbelief. He could see himself turning away from the snowman to point out the hotel. But the girl he had been talking to was not there. He was having a conversation with thin air.

Alan told Jenny that he needed to get some beers in from the off-license, and before she had any time to reply, he was out of the house. He ran to a call box, a few hundred yards along the path and dialed Robert's number.

Robert Answered. He was in quite an ebullient mood, and didn't leave Alan much time to speak at first.

"Ah, Alan. Good to hear from you. Well, we checked out your apartment thoroughly, and our conclusion is that whatever may have caused your predicament is no longer there. There are only residual traces. But your landlords may be worth investigating further."

"That's good to know," said Alan dismissively. "Look, something important has happened."

There was silence on the line for a few seconds.

"Like what?"

"She's appeared here."

"Who?"

"Who. The demon."

"You mean where you are now, in in Cold Spring?"

"Yes. Am I in danger?"

"Did anyone else see her?"

"No. But I felt her touch on my shoulder. I heard her voice. I spoke to her. I *saw* her. And yet she wasn't there in a video my wife took while I was talking to her. It looks like I'm talking to no one. How is that possible?"

"A succubus can be very selective about who they can appear to?"

"I'm honoured."

"OK. Now listen. Keep me in touch of any developments. It's going to be OK I promise you."

Back in his Central Park East apartment Robert put the phone down and immediately turned to Isobel,

"Izzy. Get everything ready in the spare room. I need to do some RV."

"Now?"

Chapter 17

Normal, everyday thinking is disjointed and hyperactive, being made up of numerous disconnected objectives, perceptions and ideas, strung together by unifying imperatives. It must be that way – to reflect reality – and that's how waking consciousness works normally. On an electroencephalogram (EEG) this shows up as a harsh and scraggy line of peaks and troughs: condensed because of the tiny amount of time each of those peaks and troughs registers. We call this saw-toothed consciousness, beta wave thinking. This is as far as you can be from the state of mind that is required to do what Robert was taught to do by his controllers at Project StarChild, in Virginia: namely remote viewing.

Alpha wave consciousness is a more relaxed way of thinking, showing up as a slightly stretched out version of the beta wave on the EEG, still having the look of a mountain range, but less compressed, and with slightly reduced peaks and troughs. Nevertheless, the remote viewer needs to pass through this phase to reach a calmer state of consciousness, akin to pre-consciousness. This is the type of thinking that heightens the imagination, and the capacity to visualise, recollect, learn and perceive. It's also a bridge to the lower frequencies of the subconscious mind. But it's still not suitable for RV. You need to go even deeper to find a smoother, much more stretched out wave, one that looks like soft, rolling hills on an EEG. This state of consciousness can only be achieved for a short amount of time, typically in the moments when you drift off to sleep or wake slowly from a deep sleep. This is theta consciousness. Your mind's most deep-seated programs are at this level. In the theta state you experience vivid images, and garner a higher level of inspiration, creativity and insight. These brain waves are indicators of deep meditation and light sleep, including the REM (or dream) state. To perform RV, you absolutely need to be in the theta state – and to stay there for some time. That takes some doing.

It was about ten at night. The blinds were pulled down and the lights were low. They were in the spare room, which is basically Robert's office. It had a few bookshelves, some computer equipment, and an EEG monitor, which was to be connected to Robert, who was seated at the table. Isobel came over to put the headband on him, slightly messing up his mane of white hair. He squinted and gave her a look of annoyance. As he had requested, Isobel put on a Pink Floyd CD and selected the track, *Careful with That Axe Eugene,* which had always helped him relax, paving the journey to the required state of consciousness. She left him alone for about a quarter of an hour after that, before returning quietly to sit opposite him.

"How are we doing?" she said. But she could already see Robert was transitioning nicely through to the alpha state, according to the monitor.

"I'm... good," he said, in a mellow tenor voice.

Isobel then got up to dim the lights a little more. Then she sat down again to face him, passing him a sheet of paper and a pen. She read out some numbers and he copied them down one by one. "Forty-three... seven... eight... three... three. OK?"

"OK."

"Eleven... two... five... zero... zero."

Unusually for Robert, with his chiselled, square-jawed, warrior's face, the hard steel grey eyes became calm and dreamy. Isobel passed him a pencil, which he calmly took, and began to draw a rectangle. Inside the rectangle he drew three rows of squares. This was his subconscious response to the numbers – or coordinates. In Langley they used to call this an ideogram. It facilitated his link to the deep subconscious. After a short while, he put the pencil down and looked at what he'd drawn.

"OK," said Isobel. "Have you started counting?"

He nodded sleepily. She turned to look at the monitor showing a beautifully, smooth theta wave. He was ready. His head dropped forward, closed his eyes, and his eyelids started to flicker, almost as in REM sleep.

"Falling, falling, falling," he said softly.

"OK", said Isobel."

He nodded, and then there was a long silence.

"I see snow."

Chapter 18

Jenny went to bed earlier than usual, while Alan stayed in the lounge and opened a bottle of JD, polishing off half of it by the time he got into bed. By then Jenny was in a deep sleep. After he turned off the light, he found it impossible to relax. And then it was impossible to deny that the temperature was falling, even though the heating was full on. He knew what this meant – she was about to appear again.

There's no other way to describe it, he was terrified. His breathing became heavy, and his head throbbed. A series of gloomy, shapeless ideas weighed him down, and if he tried to reflect on them, they vanished. It was impossible to string together thoughts – there were just too many of them. When ideas did begin to form, their meaning was sinister, and sleep was further than ever. In an effort to distract himself he crept out of bed and walked over to the window, drawing back the curtain just enough to see that it was snowing heavily. He stood there watching for a while, but it the cold was intensifying, and his breath was coming out in strands of vapour. He had to get under the covers again to warm up, but he was shivering so hard his teeth were chattering.

The clock ticked loudly, as his thoughts ran away with themselves, and he lacked the strength to resist the inevitable as all the unwelcome thoughts flooded in, eventually emotionally and physically draining him. Slowly he sank into another dream.

He is five years old, in his old primary school London. The other children play around him. He savours the freedom and lack of responsibility. The children are not there now. The atmosphere shifts and he is alone, surrounded by four ridiculously tall, Victorian brick walls. A teacher's whistle blows, and a deep shadow grows towards him from the wall opposite, moving like a pool of dark blood. He can't move, and everything goes black.

"Where's mum," he says.

But he knows she's far away.

There's an echo of a woman's voice singing a lullaby. He listens to the words.

Dassos Petrou

There's a long line of mourners driving down our little street
Their fancy cars are such a sight to see
They're all of your rich friends who you knew in the city
And now they finally brought you back to me

The words mean nothing to him.

He hears it being sung repeatedly. He wants it to stop. The strange words disturb him.

He woke, almost crying.

A faint light came into the bedroom from the hallway through the door, which he was slightly ajar. He tried to sit up and found that he had pins and needles in his arm. He was shivering too. Jenny was still fast asleep, breathing deeply and facing away from him. He whispered her name. She didn't move. The duvet was pulled up high. He tried to wake her by touching her shoulder. "Jen?" he said.

But she didn't respond, so he levered her gently towards him.

A rush of blood pounded his temples, and he screamed. His heart was beating madly. Instead of Jenny he saw a half-living, festering corpse next to him in the bed. It had long strands of lank hair, crawling with lice, and the face was a hideous, grinning skull with bloodshot, glassy, bulging eyes. There were patches of putrefying flesh and muscle, clinging to yellow, slime-covered bone. He drew away from it in disgust, and then it started to move. In a fear-driven frenzy, he gripped the thing around the throat - tighter and tighter he squeezed with all his might, with both hands. His face and hands were sprayed with its spittle as the half-dead thing squeaked and hissed in its struggle to break free. Then a blinding light filled the room and his brain swam. Suddenly he lost all sense of reason and grew deadly sick. His vision failed and he involuntarily loosened his grip as his eyes adjusted to the light. What he saw at first was that the bedroom door was now fully open, and Simon and Jack were both standing at the foot of the bed. Both were crying. He wondered what was wrong.

He looked to his side, where the living cadaver had been and saw Jenny, coughing, crying and spluttering. Her neck had a bright pink bruise around it and her face was puffed and pale. She rolled her head to the edge of the bed and started to vomit.

He stood up and the room started to spin, and he had to hold tight onto the bedpost to avoid fainting. He didn't know how long he was in that state. The sound of Jenny coughing and puking up seemed somehow muffled and distant. He tried to slow his breathing and as he relaxed his senses slowly returned to normal.

Jack and Simon were around Jenny's side of the bed. He got out of bed and walked over there to try and comfort her, but when he reached over to touch her head, she hissed at him, and twisted away from his reach, causing her to fall awkwardly to the floor.

"I hate you!" she whispered, while trying to shout. "Don't touch me. Get out. Get out!"

Jack was crying profusely. "Leave mummy alone daddy! Go away."

Simon was crying so hard he was finding it difficult to breath.

Alan pleaded with them all, "I didn't... I thought it wasn't mummy. I would never, ever..."

"She squeezed her eyes shut and tried to yell with all her might, although it was still more of a gravelly hiss. "Get away from me!"

The boys looked at him as if he was an imposter. Simon hugged Jenny and looked back at Alan with a look of absolute horror.

"Boys. It's daddy."

Now both boys shouted at him. "Go away, daddy!"

He wished he was dead.

What else could he do? He grabbed his dressing gown from the back of the door and left the room. For a while he stood on the landing, until it seemed that the sounds from the bedroom had calmed down. Then he opened the door quietly to look in. But the instant they saw him they all started to scream. Jenny stumbled over to the door red-faced and pushed it closed with all her might.

"Get out, you bastard," she growled.

He felt useless and unclean wondering listlessly down the stairs, shame, humiliation and guilt burning him with every step. Wondering into the kitchen he looked around and opened a cupboard door, taking down a ceramic jar, pulling out a tea bag, his hand shaking. He filled a kettle and waited, in the hope that someone would call him back upstairs. The kettle boiled and no one called. He filled the mug and sat down in an old-fashioned armchair. He rested the mug on a side table, then leaned back onto the headrest, hypnotised by the ceiling which throbbed in chromatic aberration, like a film of oil on a deep puddle in the wind. His eyelids became heavier, and the room shifted in and out of focus, pulsing like a beating heart.

He sank into a dreamless sleep, and when he woke, it was still the middle of the night. He had no idea how long he'd slept. The grandfather clock ticked loudly, but it never gave the correct time. Steve warned him about that. He resolved to go and see how things were. Softly, he made his way up the stairs, and along the landing until he came to the boy's bedroom. The door was open. He went in, but there was no one in there. He thought they must have all got into bed with Jenny. He took a deep breath and opened the door to the main bedroom. The bed was empty. Where were they? The only clothes on the chair were his. He became dizzy, pausing to hold onto the doorframe for balance. The entire hallway shifted in and out of phase as his head throbbed.

He stumbled over to the wardrobe to discover that the only clothes in there were his. The same was true of the chest of drawers. He took a slow journey downstairs again and opened the front door. The hire car was gone. There were tyre tracks in the snow. He dropped down onto his knees and sobbed like a baby.

With a massive effort, he managed walk back towards the lounge, unintentionally kicking a large antiques vase over, and breaking it. In his drugged-like consciousness, the scattered pieces of blue and white bone china seemed like alien artefacts, acquiring a deep and impenetrable sense of the esoteric.

Something was acting directly on his nerves, sapping his strength and weakening his will. He hoped it wasn't her. Within a minute of sitting in the armchair again he began to shake uncontrollably, as if he had contracted a fever. He was sinking into a deeper and deeper stupor. The grandfather clock chimed for an hour that had nothing to do with the time, snapping him out of his stupor. Then it struck him – he should call Robert. It may be the middle of the night, but he'd understand. He reached around for the Bakelite phone on the coffee table, grabbed it and sank back into the seat, exhausted.

The phone now rested in his lap. Finally, he lifted the receiver, as if it was a holy relic. He had learnt Robert's number off by heart, for fear of just such a necessity. He dialled and waited. No reply.

He tried to focus again. Who else could he call?

In his confused state he didn't think of Cornelia and Bella. Instead, the idea of Gary proved to be overwhelming. Gary said he had some knowledge of the nature of a succubus and was familiar with Robert's book on the subject. It would be good to talk to him anyway, as a friend. The phone rang for a good while. Eventually a sleepy female voice answered.

"Who is it?"

It was a relief to hear another human being.

"Fiona. Thank God. You're there!"

"Where else would I be? I live here. Is that Alan? Do you know what time it is?"

Alan found it hard to speak properly. His words came out too fast.

He tried to speak again. "Look I'm really, really sorry. Things are bad. I can't explain right now. Please... can I talk to Gary?"

She sighed and there was another long wait.

Alan heard a deep groan through a muffled receiver. It sounded like Gary, "Huh? What?"

"Phone call. For you."

"Now?"

Fiona's was speaking. She sounded angry, but he couldn't make out what she was saying. Then Gary's voice came up, slow and sleepy.

"Alan? What the hell time is it? What are you doing?"

"I'm really sorry, but I'm in serious shit. Really bad - you're the only person who can help me."

"What are you talking about?"

"You read that book, the succubus book, right?"

"Oh, that. Yeah. So?"

"I'm being attacked by one."

"You what?"

"I didn't tell you anything about it, basically because it's all so embarrassing. But I went to see Robert Stringfield about it, and he has been trying to help me exorcise it."

"That's… that's just mad."

"Seriously, I've had this succubus-demon-thing come for me several times. She was here – and I think she'll be back to finish off what she started?"

"But aren't you with Jenny and the kids?"

"I was. Jenny's gone and she's taken the kids with her."

"Fuck."

"I… I did something terrible; I think this demon – or whatever she is – she's fucking with my head, making me do terrible things, I was sort of still half in a dream and… I hurt Jen. Now she's driven off with the kids. I'm on my own, and the weirdness is starting again. This time she'll – she'll finish what she started. You've got to come over here before it's too late."

"So, you're in Cold Spring still, right?"

"Yes."

"Not Brooklyn?"

"No."

"Call a cab. It'll cost a fortune but… get here now. Alan, can you hear me?"

Alan had dropped the receiver with a thud to the floor. The energy began draining out of his body, along with all his will. Now left depleted of all his defences, the strange, entrancing force began to overwhelm him once more, drip-feeding through at first and then gushing forth like a tidal wave. He could only lean back into the chair and submit to it all. His eyes eventually opened a thin slit, and the room began to pulse once more, as a green mist ghosted up from the middle of the room. At first, it flickered and then coalesced slowly to resolve itself, into the demon. She shimmered in the faint light, dissolving a little at the edges, before becoming absolutely in phase with the room. She stepped forward, naked, moving with sinuous grace, her breasts shaking to the rhythm of her motion, filling him with horror and delight. There was no question. This was the girl he spoke to by the pagoda.

Then everything went black and there was a hissing close to his ears. A husky woman's voice was whispering his name. He opened his eyes, and it was her, leaning over him, twisting her upper body so that she brushed his face with each breast. He didn't remember taking off his pyjamas and dressing gown, but he was naked. Her arms clasped him around the neck. His nerves were tingling. A shudder went through him. He couldn't move.

She brushed loose strands of hair from her face, as her smooth skin basked in the warm half-light. He didn't know how, but he sensed her anguish and melancholy. His moment of calm vanished when she stretched out her arms and pushed him down by the shoulders, and her long delicate fingers felt their way towards his crotch. He knew this would mean lifelong impotence. Yet how could he stop himself from climaxing? She faced him, knees bent, her body hovered a little above his crotch, levering herself from her feet, reaching for his prick and lifting it into position, before pushing herself onto it, arching her back in a spasm of ecstasy.

But then something extraordinary happened. She flipped off him, as if he had become an electric fence, landing with a thud on the floor, where she thrashed around and screamed. It was as if she was fighting off an invisible weight pinning her down. She lashed out at one point, clawing at the air. And then she was gone.

It could've been hours before he found he could move. He barely had the energy to lean forward. And then the front door opened, and he heard footsteps approaching.

Chapter 19

The moon was high and partially obscured by thick dark clouds. There was very little street lighting in the residential districts. Gary had been up to Steve's house a few times with Fiona, and even in the daytime they always had a hard time finding the place. When he eventually found the road, he decided to stop outside the only house with no car outside, and with lights on.

As he got out of the car he heard a high pitch scream coming from the house. It was terrifying and bewildering, because it didn't sound human – more like an animal being tortured. Worried, he ran up the pathway and found that the front door was open. He nudged it in and stood in the hallway and shouted:

"Anybody in? Al! Where you at?"

A couple of seconds later there was a cough followed by a groan. It came from the lounge to his left. He entered that room saw the back of Alan's head over the top of an armchair. He walked around to see that the guy didn't have a stitch on. He was gripping the armrests, as if in pain, looking up at Gary with moist and tired eyes, like a helpless old man.

"Gary? Thank fuck you're here," he said, almost in a whisper.

Gary reached down to the floor, picked up a dressing gown and threw it at him.

"Here," said Gary. "What do you think this is, a men's sauna?"

It fell in Alan's lap, where he looked at it as if he'd never seen one before, and then squinting hard at Gary, as if an excessively bright lamp was being shone into his face.

"What time is it?" he asked.

"Time I should be in bed."

"No, really."

"Coming up to four-forty-five in the AM. That clock is wrong," said Gary, pointing to the antique grandfather clock, which said nine-thirty.

"Come on, put that thing on, then we can get out of here. I'll go make some coffee."

Alan started to find the strength to move.

"So, what was that screaming noise just a minute ago?" shouted Gary from the kitchen, while he ran some water into the kettle. Alan didn't answer.

"Was it… you know, *her?* "

He nodded with a completely blank expression. But obviously Gary didn't see that.

"Never mind," he said. "You can tell me all about it on the way home. Get packed so we can get the hell out of here? You're crashing at my joint tonight."

When Gary came back into the lounge, he found Alan wearing a shirt and thick woolly jumper, jeans and Caterpillar boots and carrying a suitcase. He'd skipped the dressing gown stage. Gary was sipping what must have been his third cup of black coffee.

"There's still a bit left," said Gary.

Alan sat at the table and poured out a cup.

"I cleared up the pieces of broken vase. I hoped for your sake it wasn't an expensive one. Steve will go apeshit."

Alan shrugged. "Yeah well… That's the least of my worries. Anyway, I really appreciate you doing all this, Gary. You're a good friend."

"Yeah well," Gary cut him dead, "drink up. I want to get the hell out of here and back to Greenwich Village in time to grab whatever shut eye I can."

Chapter 20

They were driving across the Hudson to Bear Mountain State Park, aiming to pick up the Palisades Interstate Highway. Alan scratched his head and stared ahead vacantly.

"So, what are your plans for tomorrow?"

Alan turned to Gary, raised his eyebrows. "Well, I guess I'll be trying to save my marriage."

When they crossed into Manhattan, Alan felt a sense of relief. But too much had happened in the last couple of days. He needed to take some time out and think. Gary parked across from the apartment on Greenwich Avenue and slapped Alan on the thigh.

"OK buddy. Out you get."

They trudged across the icy road with the bags. Alan saw that, even at this unearthly hour, the deli downstairs had a few customers.

Alan's head was still throbbing when they were walking up the stairs. On the landing Gary opened the apartment door and put his finger to his lips; "Shh."

Gary pulled off his shoes and told Alan to take a seat in the living room as he made a much-needed visit to the bathroom. When he came back, he was carrying a pile of sheets, a duvet and a couple of pillows. Alan was sitting cross-legged on the floor rummaging around in his bag. Gary put the bedding on the sofa and told Alan to help himself to the bathroom.

A few hours later, Alan had a feeling of rising to the surface of a floatation tank. He knew it must be morning, but he didn't know what time. There were little sounds all around him: footsteps, running water, cupboards opening and closing, the kettle boiling, the toaster clicking off. He sneaked open his eyes to see it was still dark outside, then closed them again quickly. Fiona was getting ready for work. There was no way he wanted her to have the opportunity to question him about last night. He knew there moments when she hovered around looking down at him as he lay spread out on the sofa, but he kept his eyes shut throughout. She coughed loudly a couple of times, but he still didn't move. Finally, she gave up and went off to work.

Gary was fully dressed, and wearing his heavy-duty black coat when Alan was awake enough to be sitting up in bed.

"What's happening this morning?' he said.

"How do you mean?" said Gary.

"At work."

"Oh… nothing. I'm working with Jeff on some ideas for Nike. He's a good designer, but not much of a *thinker*."

Alan grinned. "So, does that mean you miss me."

"Fuck off."

He took off his glasses and rubbed the lenses clean using the bottom of his sweater. When he put them back on, he came to sit at the end of the sofa, near Alan's feet.

"Listen. I'm arranging for you to see Robert tonight. I think it's best, considering…"

Alan shrugged.

He lifted his holdall. "There's bacon, beans, juice, bread, whatever. Just don't leave a mess."

And then he was out the door.

Alan decided to call Jenny. He would willingly fall on his knees for her to forgive him. Her phone rang for a long while before switching to answer phone.

"Hi, this is Jenny. Sorry I can't get to the phone right now, but if you leave your name and number and a short message after the beep, I promise I'll get back to you as soon as I can. Thanks. *Bye!"*

Should he say something? He's already waited a few seconds. He took the plunge:

"Hi Jen. It's me. Uh, I just really, just… please will you give me a chance to explain everything. I am so, so sorry. I can't tell you. That wasn't me. I would never do anything to hurt you. When have I ever laid a finger on you before? Something was screwing with my mind. Please believe me. I want you back. I need for us all to be together again. I love you. Call me. Please?"

When he hung up, he sat down and thought about what he'd said, wondering if he could've mentioned anything more. He tried to work out his best strategy from this point, and nothing came to mind. One thing he had decided on was that he didn't belong in Gary's apartment. He called Gary in the office to let him know he was going back to Brooklyn.

The cab was slow going through Chinatown, but Brooklyn Bridge heading east was clear. When then it pulled up outside the entrance to the apartment block, Alan told the driver he didn't need any help with the bags. He couldn't be bothered to check the mailbox and just headed straight on up the narrow stairs. There was no one in the hallway as he fumbled for the keys. When he went in he immediately noticed the blinds were up. Both bedroom doors were open too and there was the unmistakable odour of Jean Paul Gaultier Classique. Jenny must have been there in the last couple of hours.

The chest of drawers had been ransacked in the main bedroom, and just as in Steve's place, only Alan's clothes were left. In the boy's bedroom, the duvets were gone, and there were no clothes, toys or books left, but the mobile he'd bought them was still hanging from the ceiling. He pulled at the draw string hanging from a rocket, so that the planets started wobbling and spinning around it. Alan sat down on Jack's bed and watched the mobile slowly come to a stop, wracking his brains to try to understand why all this was happening to him, and what he should do. After a while, he went back into the lounge and found an envelope on the table with his name on it. It was near the black vase, which was full of black tulips. He opened it up. It was written hurriedly in a thin marker pen, and all it said was:

'Listen to the answerphone messages. Jenny"

How much worse could things get? He reached over and switched on the black machine. Almost immediately her voice came up. She said his name. We've gone, Alan. We've left you. It's not just because of the horrible thing you did to me last night. Things were wrong from the minute we saw you in the airport. Even the boys could see it. Jack never said anything to you, but he was worried. Simon felt something bad was happening that we didn't know about, though he couldn't explain to me why he believed that. But he's always been sensitive. You didn't open up about whatever it is that was troubling you. You gave us any clues. What's obvious is that your mind has been on other things. It's like you weren't really with us. I felt strange, like a substitute when we made love. A part of you was missing. Has there been someone else? It would have been so easy for you to meet someone while we me and the boys were still in

London. You're in advertising for God's sake. You can lie about anything. Maybe you did that, and you thought it wasn't important, and now you realise that perhaps it was. But that's all academic now. We're going home. I can never forgive you for the way you throttled me. Maybe you didn't know what you were doing, and there's some serious psychological shit happening to you, but I'm not about to hang around to find out. You could've *killed* me. I… Anyway, I just don't know what else to say. I've made up my mind. Don't try to call me. You'll be hearing from a lawyer soon."

And that was it.

He didn't have the mental strength to listen to it again. He was just dumbstruck. Did she have a point? Was it possible that the thing with him and Juliette had some effect on the way he behaved with Jenny and the boys? It never even occurred to him for a moment. Then the dam broke as all his uncertainties, repressed awareness and fears burst through and he rested his head in his arms on the table and cried. Time passed, the tears dried up, he lay back and fell asleep. He stayed that way, until he heard the buzzing of the intercom. When he looked up the streetlamp outside was the only thing lighting the apartment.

Reluctantly he got up and walked over to the intercom and pushed the speak button.

"Hello?"

Gary's voice came up. "Took your time. Buzz me up for Christ's sake."

He left the door off the latch and went back in to put some lights on and pull down the blinds. He was halfway through doing that when the door flung open against the wall and Gary came in, in his long trench coat, striding in like a civil war officer after a battle.

"Did you come straight from work?" said Alan.

"What do you think?"

"Shit. Where did the day go?"

"What've you eaten today?"

"Huh?"

"Let me put it another way, have you eaten today?"

"I haven't really thought about it."

233

He leaned heavily to the left, took out a brown bag from his coat pocket and threw it on the table.

"Come on. Eat. We need to get going."

Alan picked up the still warm foil wrap and took out a cheeseburger wrapped in white, waxed paper.

"Going where?"

"Uptown – to Robert Stringfield's place. What are you waiting for?"

Chapter 21

Gary had dropped him off outside the building and then drove off home. He was now at the mercy of Robert and Isobel. The elevator took its time, giving his anxieties a chance to percolate. Isobel seemed distracted when she opened the door for him. The female vocals from *White Rabbit* by Jefferson Airplane were coming from inside the apartment.

"Oh hi, Alan. Go right on in." She ushered him towards the main lounge.

The place had a kind of sick room feeling about it, with the lights very low. Isobel steered him over to the drinks cabinet near the kitchen and poured a generous measure of Napoleon Brandy, dropping in a few lumps of ice, using silver tongs.

"You'll probably notice Robert's not quite himself," she said. "He's just a little fragile. But he's been looking forward to seeing you."

Alan nodded, not knowing for sure if he could believe her.

"Perfect. Well, you'll have to excuse me," she said. "I'm still two paintings short for the show. I do hope you'll be there for the opening."

"Of course. Thanks Isobel."

He found Robert sitting in an armchair to one side facing the large window. His face was in profile against the scene across the park and in soft shadow. Alan thought he might be in a dressing gown and slippers, since he was unwell, but he was smartly attired in black trousers, a green tweed jacket, over a peach-coloured silk shirt and a geometric brown and grey green patterned tie. Alan couldn't help noticing how shiny his face seemed, almost as if he'd been running and forgot to shower. His normally impressive head of white hair seemed lank, and moist. Some of it was stuck to his face. It was as if he was recovering from a fever.

He seemed to be staring dreamily at the thick blanket of snow covering Central Park, and the buildings opposite. To Alan the park seemed like a cemetery without headstones.

Robert's manner was not particularly warm. Without turning to face Alan, he lifted his right arm and waved him regally over to the sofa across from where he sat. Alan found himself looking at Robert through the stems of pussy willow on the coffee table.

"I was sorry to hear about your marriage," said Robert.

His voice seemed as deep and commanding as usual, but much quieter. It would be too simple to say he looked exhausted. But there was an element of self-satisfaction about him, as if from the glow of some imperceptible glory. He was like a swimmer who had gone beyond his physical limits and achieved something nameless and extraordinary.

Alan nodded politely, took a sip of brandy and said, "Thank you, but I don't think it will turn out to be as bad as it sounds. Time heals all wounds, doesn't it?" he said.

"I hope so," said Robert, still looking straight ahead, leaving him in profile to Alan.

"I have to say," continued Robert, "you seem impressively stoic for a man who has been through so much and found his life in complete upheaval."

Alan wiped his lips and let out a little laugh. "Perhaps it's just shell shock," he said.

Alan didn't want to discuss the trials and tribulations of his marriage, and he couldn't help feeling a little patronised at that moment. But he took a deep breath and hid his irritation. He needed Robert's help.

"I suppose Gary told you what happened with the Succubus last night?" he said.

He coughed before he spoke. "He didn't need to tell me."

Alan thought he had misheard. "Sorry?"

Then Robert turned to face him. "I was there."

Alan couldn't help noticing four luminous pink marks on Robert's left cheek. The sight of it gave him the shivers.

At the back of his mind something started to make sense. "Your face!"

"Oh yes, that," he said, touching the strange blemish with the tips of his fingers. "It might not look like much, but it stings like hell." He half smiled and took a sip of his brandy.

"What happened to you?" asked Alan.

"I think you know."

Alan's disbelief gave way to the force of the inevitable truth. He recalled the Succubus thrashing around on the floor, as if she was pinned down by an invisible force, and then he was struck by the sight of her suddenly thrusting out and clawing at something he couldn't see. "Was that you who…"

"Yes, it was," said Robert. "And lucky for you I arrived when I did."

Robert was starting to give him the creeps, and that was despite knowing that he had saved him from a terrible fate. Alan felt as if he was conversing with a vampire.

"I just… Christ. I don't know what to believe any more."

"I'm glad we're beginning to understand one another. Another few seconds and it would have been curtains for your manhood, my boy.

She was close to the point of ecstasy, so I had to drag her off you immediately, which wasn't easy. She is strong, demented and vicious." He pointed to the four claw marks on his face.

By this point Alan was speechless.

"But it's not quite over."

Robert tried to describe how he had projected his transcendental self to the house in Cold Spring, which went over Alan's head. He just recalled the nauseous sensation he was going through at the time, as he shifted in and out of consciousness, unable to determine what was real and what was imaginary.

Robert could see the glazed look in Alan's eyes.

"You're not really following me, are you?"

Alan snapped out of his reverie, feeling instant embarrassment. "I'm sorry Robert. The whole experience… since she first appeared, or before even, has left me unable to think clearly or to focus properly.

"It's not an issue," said Robert, getting up with a bit of a struggle, to change the CD, and then stumbling awkwardly. Alan quickly rushed over to help him, but he held out an arm to make it clear he needed absolutely no assistance.

"It's fine. Just lost my balance there for a second, I'm good. But she really did take it out of me, your girlfriend."

Alan felt the blood rush to his face. "Oh God. Don't call her that," he said.

Robert found the disc he was looking for. The low light of the orange laver lamp, next to the pile of CDs, cast a twisting, organic, orange light over his face, making him look almost demented.

"I hope you like The Dead," he said, taking out another CD from its case."

"Huh?" I was feeling a bit dizzy by now.

"The Grateful Dead. Something called Dark Star. The studio recording was two minutes-forty, which is pathetic. It doesn't allow Jerry and the guys the freedom to express themselves freely, to grow into the rhythm, to find the mystery. This version runs for over twenty minutes."

Alan feigned the requisite enthusiasm.

"Great."

The spacey, eastern-sounding, slow lead guitar came in, building a melody that was so spaced out that Alan thought that he'd dropped a tab of acid. Robert stood where he was, in a kind of semi-sleep. Eventually his eyes blinked open and he walked back cautiously to his armchair, and after a little cough he said,

"You know that Isobel and I took a trip to Brooklyn to check out your apartment. The surprising conclusion we came to was that your apartment wasn't the source of your demonic visitor. It has to be you. You are her incubator, her sustenance. The fact is, you transported her to your home, just like you took her with you to Cold Spring."

"What?"

"You were already infected with her, before you moved in. The only question is, when did you acquire her, and how."

"You've lost me," said Alan.

It was like he hadn't heard.

"That's mad."

"Her essence – her ethereal signature – is new. Very recent. What's more, the dreams you've had featuring those strange, spotted people. I don't believe they are the fruits of your subconscious. They're hers. She's hitched a ride in your soul. You're dreaming her dreams. I know it can't be easy for a guy like you who's living so much in the material world to understand, but she is in a state of symbiosis with your psyche. When she has built up enough spiritual strength, by draining your physical and emotional energies, she acquires the capacity to manifest."

Alan sighed in despair.

Robert smacked the armrest with his right hand. "Look Alan. I don't want you feeling this is all hopeless, because it's not. There is no answer to your problem, and we will find the source of your 'infection', because that's all it is. She is a feeding off your soul, but she's already been weakened."

"Oh." Alan was confused, but he was also clearly somewhat relieved.

Going forward, I need you to tell me anything important that occurs to you in connection with those dreams, especially in connection with those people with red spots, especially that sinister old couple. They're likely to be the key to all this. My feeling is that they will turn out to be disturbingly unsavory characters, if they exist outside of your dreams – which I believe they do."

Alan recalled their leering, spotted faces, and once again it made his skin crawl.

"How will I ever find out what you need to know?"

"Ah! Don't' worry about that. If that information should ever come along, you'll know."

Chapter 22

The events of recent weeks had totally undermined Alan. His understanding of reality no longer fitted with the things happening around him. He was disconnected. Too much mysterious and strangeness had invaded his life for him to ever be able to restore his faith in his ability to distinguish between the imaginary and the real. It wasn't so much that he was in a void. He was that void. Even simple things, like the view out of the window, had changed. The buildings opposite, which were once impressive and grandiose, now seemed oppressive and intimidating. This luminous pale blue sky outside that was untainted by clouds, should have filled him with inspiration, but nothing stirred. And the entropy of the crowded street below, which would have normally stirred him with a vibrancy and urgency, had no effect. Its emanations were not reaching him in the usual way. These things were not happening for him. He had sunk into his own silent, personal world – which had been invaded by an incubating demon.

When Alan had been back at work for just over a week, Gary had to go off for a debriefing on some copy he had written while Alan was away. Unusually, most of the other guys on the creative floor were out, for different reasons. Some were on photo shoots, others were on edits, some were at client presentations, which was why the creative department was unusually calm.

I was precisely at that time that he went to the deli around the corner to pick up a sandwich. On the elevator going down he spotted Sally, his producer on Supermint Gum, chatting with Juliette in the atrium below. After the initial shock, he was filled with an overwhelming desire to talk to her. Seconds later she was heading out of the building. Without even thinking he ran down the last few steps and chased after her, touching her shoulder just as she was about to go through the revolving door. She turned to face him with a look of surprise.

There were a dozen things he wanted to say, but the words just wouldn't come. He was distracted by her delicate, round gold earrings and smooth flowing hair.

"H-h-how are you?" was the best he could do.

She smiled nervously, with an innocent, wide-eyed look about her. He sensed that she held no malice at all; it was written all over her face.

"Uh, fine. You?"

As it was lunchtime, people were having to force themselves around them to get to the door.

"Yeah OK. I guess. Oh, this isn't such a good place to talk," he said. He ushered her gently to one side.

"You got time for coffee?"

She winced and took a step back, tilting her head down while giving him a sheepish look with her watery eyes. For no reason, he had a nightmarish flashback of the terrifying, ravenous expression of he demon, which vanished as quickly as it came. It left him worried.

"I can't," she said.

The disappointment was written all over his face.

"I don't mean I *won't*. "I just can't. I'm meeting my parents for tea this afternoon downtown. They've come down from Groombridge."

He sighed with relief, "Oh, right."

There was an uncomfortable silence, as she waited for him to say something more, though he was all-out of courage by then. She reached out and touched his elbow, and it felt right then as if she was draining away all his worries of the last few weeks.

"But we should be done around six," she said helpfully. "Dad has to get back tonight. Maybe you can come over after you finish work? We'll be at Balthazar, on Spring Street. You know that?"

The shadow that had been hanging over him was gone. "I'll find it, Jules. No problem. See you at six."

However, he had a feeling that he had something pencilled in at work for the end of the day, though he couldn't remember what it was.

"Great," she replied. "I have to get over to Sophie's for 8.30, but we'll still have an hour or two."

When he left her he went back to the office and found himself looking at the photograph of Simon, Jack and Jenny on the desk. He opened the drawer and put the picture away.

Gary came in an hour later moaning about his debrief, which in fact had evolved into a total re-write. Alan was unsympathetic. Instead, he threw a layout pad full of ideas he'd put together for a banking client and said, "Feast your eyes on this lot. The Chemical Bank brief is cracked."

Gary took a sip of coffee and turned over a few pages of the pad slowly.

"Hey. Not bad for a Limey."

"You're very kind," was Alan's ironic response.

After a while Gary picked up a black magic marker and began to add a few tweaks to what Alan had done, here and there. He also drew up a few of his own concepts.

Alan said nothing about bumping into Juliette.

At Spring Street Alan got out of the subway station and walked as fast as he could in the deep snow. A little ahead he spotted a yellow cab pulling up outside the large, modern glass, restaurant frontage of Balthazar. Juliette emerged from it and walked towards the red awning, before turning to rush back and say something to the cab driver. Then she looked up and saw Alan approaching.

So, you finally made it," she said while shaking her head.

"I would've been here twenty minutes ago," he said. "But I got dragged into a departmental meeting at five."

She gave him her little frown. "I forgive you."

He glanced behind her. "So... where are your parents?" he asked.

"Dad wouldn't let me pay, even though I'm a working girl. He's picking up the tab. We almost had a scene over it."

Alan laughed. "Does he know how much you're making?"

She didn't have time to answer, because the restaurant doors swung open again and from Juliette's expression, Alan guessed that it was her parents who were coming through, but he wasn't prepared for what he saw. In fact, the blood drained from his face. Where had he seen these people before? Then it hit him. The man with the leering smile and the woman with the horrible, cackling laugh. This was the sinister old couple from his dream. He was sure of it. The only thing missing were the red spots covering their faces. If he ever needed confirmation that reality was merging with his dreams, this was it.

"So, you must be Alan," said Mr Doyle holding out his hand. "Abe and Molly. We've heard everything about you." He was wearing a long, heavy, expensive looking cashmere coat, and Mrs Doyle was in white fur.

"Hi," Alan said, nervously taking Mr Doyle's hand and shaking it as warmly as he could in the circumstances. However, his heart was beating fast, and his hand was shaking. Mrs Doyle noticed that.

"My, you're a very nervous young man. No need to be anxious in our presence, Alan. Juliette thinks the world of you, and if she's come to that conclusion, I'm sure we will too."

Alan didn't believe for one minute that Juliette would have mentioned anything about the fact that he had a wife and kids. Mrs Doyle came closer to give him a look of concern.

"Are you feeling OK,' she said. "Maybe you should go inside and get a glass of water."

"Uh… no need," said Alan. "I'll be fine."

Juliette tried to make light of the situation: "See the effect I have on men, mom?"

"Oh, Juliette!" said Mrs Doyle, as she nudged her daughter playfully

"I'm sorry," said Alan. "I've been recovering from a virus."

"Poor you, said Mrs Doyle. You shouldn't be out if you're not well, especially in this cold. You should be at home in the warm."

"I wish I could be," he replied. "But there's just too much to be getting on with at work."

"Those corporate slave drivers in the advertising industry need a good dressing down."

"But the pay's good," he replied.

They all laughed. Then Mr Doyle slapped the sides of his heavy coat, bringing the chat to an abrupt end.

"You'll have to excuse us Alan," he said. "It's been a pleasure meeting you, but we need to get to the station pronto. I have a Rotary Club meeting tonight, and I'm the chair. It wouldn't look too good if I didn't show up."

"No problem," said Alan.

When Mr and Mrs Doyle were comfortably seated in the back of the cab Mr Doyle lowered the window of the cab. "Do you play golf?" he said, looking over at Alan.

"I'm afraid not," said Alan, rather ashamedly.

"Never mind. You should come over sometime."

"Sure. Sounds great."

"Juliette, fix it up, will you?"

Juliet nodded. "Sure dad. If Alan has the time."

"He'd better! Bye."

When the cab sped away Juliette turned to Alan and sighed, as if she was relieved, they'd gone.

It wasn't easy shaking off the state of mind he was in. Dreams are supposed to be the distorted reflections of waking life, aren't they? That's how Alan saw it. So how did he manage to dream of people he never saw before in his life? And why should such a very ordinary looking, seventy-something, wholesome, all-American couple come across in such a hideous and terrifying way in his dreams? Nothing made sense to him anymore.

Just then, Juliette interrupted his reflections. "Are you feeling well enough for a glass of vino, Mr White?"

They touched glasses. After they'd taken a sip, he felt compelled to spill it all out. He took a deep breath.

"Juliette. I have to tell you. My wife has left me and taken the kids."

She raised her eyebrows and stayed open mouthed. "Oh."

With his hand, he gently turned her face towards him and tears welled up in her eyes. "You were a mean, selfish bastard," she said almost in a whisper.

"You're not the only one who thinks that" he said.

She opened her mouth to speak and then thought better of it.

"Don't be afraid," he said. "Say what you need to say."

Now she became angry. "What do you want me to say?"

"I'm not expecting you to say anything." he shrugged. "I just don't want you to hold back. I deserve your anger. I know that. I've fucked up my life up, and everyone else's that I love."

People in the wine bar were looking at them, almost as if they were watching TV. Juliette wiped her eyes.

After a moment she said, "That was really strange back then."

Alan fell back into his seat. "What was?"

244

"The way you fell to pieces in front of mom and dad. And don't give me all that bullshit about being ill. You have this schoolboy-type tendency to look up quickly before telling a fib, like you're reading from an autocue above your head."

"Am I that much of an open book?"

"Sadly."

She had him cornered. He considered telling her how since they had split up, he had lost control of his life, but he knew that didn't explain his shakiness earlier. What was the point of lying?

"I've seen them before," he said.

Juliette gave him a look that suggested she was worried about his sanity. "What?"

"It's true. I've seen your parents before - in my dreams."

She shook her head. "What are you talking about?"

He scratched his head in shame. "I know. It sounds crazy. You don't have to believe me. Look, you know normally how cynical and sceptical I am about anything remotely esoteric, or mind, body and spirit, or whatever you want to call it. Remember my views on astrology?"

"How could I forget?" She squinted, looked at her watch, stood up and said, "Shit, I have to get going. But you know what? Against my better judgement, I'll go this far... I believe that you believe you're telling the truth. Listen, I'm running late. Sophie is cooking a meal for me and..."

"OK. But... will I see you again?"

She lowered her head and took on the most enigmatic expression he'd ever seen in his life. "Bye Al."

Alan stayed behind to finish the wine, of which there was still had two-thirds of a bottle left. He also ordered a Salad Nicoise. His appetite had returned a little, since being with Juliette. But the discovery that her parents were the nightmarish couple from his dreams had left him feeling disorientated and afraid. What did it all mean? They couldn't have been any warmer in welcoming of him. And yet the power of his dream, and the memory of it, left him disgusted to be around them. It was like treading on dog shit in bare feet.

He left there after an hour and went through a horribly restless night. The images of Mr and Mrs Doyle plagued him. Jules had always said nothing but good things about them. They were, apparently, loving parents, and true pillars of their community, helping many charitable causes. How did that idea correspond to the evil, leering characters in his dream? There was only one person who might be able to make any sense of all this, and that was Robert Stringfield.

Alan's natural inclination was towards scepticism, and he wished it still was. That was despite a few little happenings in the past almost tempting him to reconsider. Now, however hard he tried, he couldn't discount the almost inexplicable irrationality and coincidence of the dream alongside the unfolding of reality. His rationalism had been shaken to its foundations, first by the appearance of the demon. But now he was going through a mental revolution he couldn't ignore. He thought about phoning Cornelia and Bella, to ask their opinion about coming across these nightmare characters in real life. But they had already emphasised that he should trust Robert Stringfield in anything connected to the demon problem. Unfortunately, Stringfield made him nervous, perhaps because of his military and intelligence background. Those kinds of people are never easy to work out, and their motives are inevitably other than they appear to be.

Despite all that, the next day, when Gary left the office for a meeting with a photographer, Alan took the opportunity to call Robert, who answered in his usual calm, business-like voice.

Alan explained the events of the previous evening, coming across Juliette's parents, who happened to be the strange, leery couple in his dreams. Robert became instantly alert.

"Wait. Stop right there. Let me get this straight. Her parents are those two people in your dreams – the strange couple?"

"That's right."

"And who are they?"

"They're Juliette's parents – the girl I had the relationship with."

"I remember now. Juliette."

"What are their names?"

"Sorry?"

"Her parents. What are their names?"

"Oh yes, Abe and Molly Doyle."

"What do you know about them?"

"Not much. They're in their sixties, and they live in a place called Groombridge, Connecticut."

"Groombridge. Yes. I know it. OK, I'll take it from here."

"Uh… so, what are you going to do."

"You don't need to know."

Chapter 23

"So, what's your plan?" said Isobel. "Will you do some RV, I mean, to find out if this freaky couple are connected to the succubus somehow?"

"I need a lot more information to do that. Like where these people lived for the last twenty-five years, their backgrounds, if they have any criminal records, their connections – stuff like that, so I can build a picture. The main thing is to locate a place – and of course a time."

Isobel brought over a glass of brandy with ice.

"That could take a while and a ton of digging around in public records offices and reference libraries."

"Yes. It would normally. But I'm calling Mitch."

She looked at Robert in disbelief. "What? You can't go asking for favours from Langley. You do that enough times and they'll draw you back in."

He coughed. "Listen Izzy. This kind of request is small beer. And anyway, after what I went through for the flag, they owe me."

Chapter 24

Alan started to feel marginalized at work, and to add to his troubles, things with Jenny were getting worse. But even if she really wanted to go the whole hog, with separation and divorce and everything, he wanted to resolve things amicably, just between themselves. It would have been great just to get some common sense from her. If for no other reason than so that he could talk to the boys. But it was useless. She had made herself uncontactable. She never replied to his calls or messages. She only communicated through her lawyer, most recently with a date for a court hearing and a whole lot of miserable demands. He would have to get himself a lawyer too, sooner rather than later. More than once he found himself sobbing in the apartment at night.

He called Barry Tonks, a copywriter friend of his working in the London office of GGP. Barry thought Alan wanted to discuss some campaign ideas. But they didn't talk about advertising for long, because Alan needed advice about other things. Barry had been through it all with his wife kicking him out of the house a few years back, and after a lot of shit, he had now come out the other end. Barry told him straight, if there was any way to fix his marriage he should give it his best shot, because he wouldn't wish this crap on his worst enemy. "She hurts you, you hurt her, and the kids get hurt for the rest of their lives."

Alan listened with trepidation, but said he wasn't hopeful of any reconciliation. By the end of the call, Barry gave Alan the contact details for his solicitor.

Alan had the number in front of him when he picked up the phone again, but then he changed his mind and dialed another number. He honestly thought Juliette would tell him to get lost when he asked if she would like to join him to an opening night in a gallery downtown. After a long silence, she said it happened to be her night off from the play. She was only going to stay in and watch TV.

She'd been standing outside her front door in her grey three-quarter length coat freezing. As soon as she saw him look out of the taxi window, she trotted down the steps of her brownstone. Her hair was a slightly redder shade of auburn now and she'd tied it up in a loose bun. When she was in the back of the cab, she held up her cheek for him to kiss, which he did sheepishly, after which she smiled and buckled up. He had an urge to take her in his arms and carry her back up those stairs and into the bedroom.

Traffic was moving at a snail's pace, so they got out at Broadway and Lafayette and walked the rest of the way, though it was snowing heavily. The conversation between them was not exactly flowing freely, so it was a relief when they arrived. The Sylvia Lake Gallery was sandwiched between two clothing boutiques on Greene. Its white marble entrance was made up of neo-classical columns, framing four windows. There was a large grey-green granite statue of the god Shiva at the front.

The crowd was already pretty healthy. Chamber music was coming through the speakers. Amazingly, some people were even looking at the artwork. Alan and Juliette declined to hand in their bags and coats. However, they did accept a glass of wine each, and made their way through a crowd of people into a space where they could appreciate Isobel's paintings. They were mostly early evening or nighttime scenes of New York. People didn't feature in them much, and when they did, they seemed very much alone, and unconnected to one another. Alan wondered if Isobel was an existentialist.

Alan steered Juliette towards one of the walls where some of the smaller paintings were hung, and from the corner of his eye, he noticed Isobel, in a tight fitting, sky-blue, silk brocade dress with short sleeves, and silver high heels. She was talking to some people at the back of the room: a big balding, Middle Eastern looking man, in a blue suit, and a thin woman, with her hair in a sharp bob. There was also a forty-something couple there, both dressed in black. All these people appeared to be hanging onto every word Isobel said. Nearby was the obviously disinterested and lonely figure of Robert Stringfield, in a single-breasted grey mohair suit. When he caught sight of Alan, his face came to life, and he hurried over to him, his voice resonating as he approached.

"Alan! Well, aren't you going to introduce me to your lovely friend?"

Juliette seemed somewhat awed by this huge man who exuded such power and self-assurance. She looked at Alan and reddened.

"Of course. This is Juliette. We... uh work together occasionally. Jules, this is Robert."

'Oh," said Juliette.

Robert knew exactly who Juliette was. He shook her hand and showed her his pure white, toothy grin.

"Charmed!" said Robert. "So, Juliette... tell me, are you enjoying the show? You can be completely open with me, because it's not my work, it's my wife's."

Juliette and Alan both laughed.

"Oh, well... I'm no expert," said Juliette, "but the paintings I've seen are really beautiful."

Robert rubbed his hands together while leaning forward slightly, as if inviting Juliette into a confidence. "Well don't tell Isobel. Her ego's swollen enough as it is."

"Oh, I'm sure she..."

Juliette was interrupted by the voice of Isobel, who had just come over at that moment. "Excuse me, I heard that."

Robert pulled a fake look of terror.

"Ah. About time you broke away from those boring people."

"Shush Robert, or the reviews tomorrow will be less than flattering."

He put his arm around her and left it there. "Sorry sweetheart."

Alan then leaned forward to kiss her on the cheek. "Hello Alan."

"Hey Isobel," said Alan, pointing all around. "What can I say? Gorgeous work."

"Oh you, naughty flatterer. Stop right there. But speaking of gorgeous... who is this delightful creature at your side this evening?"

Alan hadn't expected Isobel and Robert to be so welcoming to Juliette and was secretly delighted. "I'll let her introduce herself," he said.

She held out her hand. "Juliette Doyle. Pleasure to meet you."

Isobel then took it "Likewise..."

As Isobel held Juliette's hand Alan noticed that she threw the briefest look of astonishment to Robert, but she quickly composed herself. She let go of Juliette's hand and pointed to a large painting on the wall beside where we stood.

"So, what do you think of this one, Alan?"

Alan turned to his left and stepped a little more towards the painting.

"Ah. Now let me think," he replied, "It has a kind of Edward Hopper flavour, and maybe also a touch of Frank Brangwyn too, if you don't mind me saying."

"Clever boy. I love both those painters."

Robert shook his head in mock despair and took Julia by the elbow.

"Why don't we leave these two to go through their memorized list of Who's Who in Fine Art, and go meet some interesting people?"

And they went off, to enter deep discussion for quite a while. Alan wondered what they were talking about.

Meanwhile he moved a fraction closer to the painting Isobel pointed out. It was a strange picture, because it took for its subject matter the entrance to a tunnel. A shadowy modern block type building took up much of the picture, with a steel-ribbed structure that seemed to be stretched over the mouth of the tunnel. The sky was painted in a rich blue-violet, and the cars at the bottom of the picture moving towards the entrance were like phantoms.

"Is it the Holland Tunnel?" Alan asked.

She laughed. "Got it in one. You've obviously travelled to New Jersey a few times?"

"Actually no," he said. "I'm familiar with it only because it's just around the corner from the hotel I stayed at before I found the apartment."

"Ah."

"So, what inspired you to paint this scene?" he asked.

"Are you just being polite?"

"No. Really. Please."

"Well... I did it years ago. Just a few weeks before I was due to go for an operation to remove a tumour. I didn't know if I would come out the other end, if you know what I mean, and a dark ominous tunnel seemed about right..."

"Oh, I see the..."

Just then Alan felt a strong tap on his shoulder, and as he turned around, he felt an almighty slap in his face. He was shocked and bewildered. His right cheek throbbed as he realized, the culprit was Gary's wife, Fiona. She faced him with a stare of intense malice. From behind her people were staring at open mouthed. He hated the attention and simply wanted to be anywhere but here. Fiona was struggling to find words to express her venom. Eventually she found some:

"Is that how you get your kicks, Alan White? Beating on your wife? Do your friends know about you? Huh? Do they?"

Thoughts were popping on and off in his brain like so many cheap firecrackers, and none of them fitted. He felt too dirty and unworthy, and couldn't bring himself to respond in any way, particularly with anger, even though Fiona was making a complete spectacle of him – and herself. Ironically, he had always been very fond of her, having imagined she was sociable and warm, as well as great fun to be around. But the depressing thing was, everything she was saying was right. Fortunately, Gary, stepped into the fray to drag her away.

"Come on Fi. This is no good, honey."

He looked at Alan and his face said, "Sorry."

But she wriggled free from him and yelled, "Let go of me!"

Two over-sized security people in black suits and electronic earpieces came over, but Isobel stepped in to assure them everything was under control. Reluctantly they moved away. Isobel then approached Fiona and spoke calmly.

"I know you mean well, Fiona... but Alan was not responsible for his actions the other night. He meant no harm to Jenny at all."

"Really? Well, he sure went about it the wrong way. I spoke to Jenny this afternoon - and she can still barely talk. She sounds like she has a bad case of laryngitis. Aside from the bruising that goes all the way round her neck, she has bleeding and swelling *inside*. She's also suffering from blurred vision and ringing in her ears. She can't sleep and she's a nervous wreck. Happy with your night's work Mr. White?"

Alan was taken aback, because he had no way knowing any of that. Her lawyers hadn't mentioned those issues, but he guessed that they were saving it for the courts. Before he could say anything, Robert stepped in:

"Fiona, please. I know you mean well, but Jenny is not aware of the terrible stress Alan was going through. Like Isobel said, he was not himself at the time and…"

Gary was now looking more embarrassed than Alan had ever seen him before. Fiona had her face in her hands while weeping. Gary put his arm around her again, trying to lead her away. "We'd better go, love."

Fiona turned to him and spat out, "Oh piss off!"

Then she shook herself free to walk briskly towards the exit of her own accord. Gary shrugged and followed.

Juliette, who had been watching all this from a distance, came over with Robert.

"What the hell was all that about?" she asked.

"Let's get out of here, and I'll tell you everything."

Isobel decided it was best for her to be gone, so wandered off to be the hostess again. When Alan and Juliette were leaving together Robert called out, "Hey, Alan. Wait a second."

They stopped and turned around and saw him holding two wine glasses for them.

"Where are you guys going? I got you these."

"I'm sorry, Robert," said Alan. "We really have to get going."

Robert seemed anxious about something.

"Are you sure?"

Juliette stood in and said, "I have a bit of a headache and…"

"Sure. I get it. I've never seen Fiona going off like that before."

"What can I say?"

He bit his lower lip and then said, "Alan, I wanted to tell you…" He flicked a glance at Juliette and then back to Alan, as if to say that he really didn't want anyone else to hear what he was trying to tell him. "Uh, how can I put this?"

He waited for Alan to show some sign to confirm that I knew what Robert was referring to.

"Uh-huh?"

"It's my belief that the problem you were asking me to look at for you is over."

"Really?"

Robert nodded, "Call me later."

The snow was falling heavily as Juliette and Alan left the gallery. They walked towards Houston when Juliette stopped dead, and the flakes started to settle on her hair.

"Alan. What the fuck is going on? Did you really beat on your wife? I mean... Gary's wife said you tried to strangle her and... is she crazy, or what?"

"No, I...."

"No, what?"

"No, she's not crazy."

"So, it's true?"

"It's complicated, that's what it is."

"Fuck!"

"Please give me a chance to explain..."

"Well?"

He scratched his head, then hailed a cab which pulled over. But Juliette would not get in until he answered her.

"Right. It's not what you think, and I promise I will tell you everything - but not here."

"Then where?"

"Let's just get in and we'll talk."

"Where to?"

"I don't know... what about if we go to my place and order a Chinese?"

She licked her lip and seemed unable to decide, but by this time the cab driver was getting irritated, so they both got in.

When they were on their way Alan asked, "So how did you get on with Robert?"

"Oh him. Jesus. Is he for real?"

"What was he talking to you about?"

"He was like, you know... really interrogating me about my *parents*. He must've asked me maybe *dozen* questions about them. Don't you think that's kind of weird? What is it with my parents?"

Alan didn't say a thing.

Chapter 25

The next morning Robert was a little hung over. He dragged himself out of bed at around ten and opened the apartment door to find the New York Times on the doormat, as usual, but there were also a few letters. He put it all on the kitchen counter and made a pot of coffee. As he filled the kettle he shouted out to Isobel, "You want some coffee!"

There was no reply, although he thought he heard a groan or two.

He poured the water into the cafetiere and took it to the table, along with his cup, and started opening the mail. The first letter was a bill from the phone company. The next was a statement on his military pension. The third came from Virginia. He opened it up enthusiastically. It was from Mitch.

Hey Rob!

I knew you would only get around to writing when you had some kind of ulterior motive. Still, it's good to hear from you. Send my congrats to Isobel for the success of her new show. Always knew that girl had talent (other than the one she used here, I mean).

You two did the right thing getting out when you did. I'm tearing my hair out. You won't believe what's going down. They've brought this bozo over, General (Clamforth), to muscle in on the project, and he wants to change things around a bit, and he's started by trying to break our links with Stanford Research Institute. The word is Washington wants to cut the cord with us "time-wasting, overpaid mumbo-jumbo psychics". They're threatening to wind the whole project up, or maybe they'll set up a paired down operation out of Fort Mead. So, if things ever kick off, the military will be as ready as they were at Pearl Harbour. Right now, I'm sitting here doing nothing but watching the reports pile up. Which is why I had plenty of time to do some rooting around for you.

So here it comes...

That couple from Connecticut you wanted me to check out: you crazy? The Agency is strictly verboten to gather intelligence on US citizens. OK, from time to time, out of extreme necessity, we might bend the rules. But, lucky for you, over at the Bureau, when they investigate specific domestic crimes, they can provide other law enforcement agencies (like us) with cooperative services. They also have a huge database on just about everyone in the US of A. So, I gave my friend there a call, and he did some digging.

You might find this interesting:

Abraham Leonard Doyle and Margaret Elisabeth Philomena Doyle (affectionately known as 'Molly") are pillars of their community in Groombridge, a small town out on the edge of Cockaponset State Forest, Connecticut. It's an unusually wealthy place: population of under four thousand, 96.5% of which are white. And virtually none of the families are below the poverty line. Abe is a successful, self-made businessman, who has gone on to very big things and she is a respected judge, doting wife and mother, ceaseless charity worker, and chair of the town's women's institute. In 1962, he formed his own construction company that became highly successful within four years and is well known for the quality of its public building projects throughout Middlesex County. In 1966 Abe served as a member of the Connecticut Constitutional Convention, becoming President and C.E.O. of GD Bank, and served as a member of the Board of Directors of the Federal Home Loan Bank of Groombridge, and Chairman of the National Council of Savings Organisations. Apart from that he is also on the board of directors of the William Walters Technical College, and the local Groombridge Town Advisory Board, as well as an active supporter of the Middlesex Community Foundation, and founding member of the Blackheath Golfing Association. He is now Chair of the Groombridge Symposium, which takes up a lot of his time these days. His wife's too.

You referred to her as 'Molly' Doyle, but in her professional life she is better known as Margaret Doyle, or rather Justice Margaret Doyle. Apart from being a mom and a district judge, Margaret Doyle is active in an array of community, charitable and business activities; that includes running various businesses from her home and becoming the President of the Groombridge Chapter of the Women's Institute. She graduated from Fairfield University (which is where she met Abe) and the University of Connecticut School of Law with High Honors, before she joined the law firm of Waterhouse & Barnett, where she specialised in bankruptcy and financial restructuring. Accusations have been expressed as to her integrity, in respect to the possible misuse of public funds. It's interesting to point out here that the Connecticut Judicial Review member committee has fielded hundreds of complaints filed by citizens against judges in Groombridge, and Judge Doyle's name came up in several recent State legislative hearings, in which hundreds of Connecticut families claimed to have been victimised by corrupt public officials working within the State's courts and the Department of Children and Families. So far, any charges against Judge Margaret Doyle and other public officials in Groombridge have not stuck, for lack of evidence – (or obstructions which appear to have been put in the way by certain people in high places). However, U.S. Attorney Elizabeth Goring is working to set up a Connecticut Public Corruption Task Force in a joint initiative with the FBI, Internal Revenue Service, and the Inspector General's Offices of the United States Department of Health and Human Services, to investigate further. But don't hold your breath.

Now, like I said, Goombridge is mostly a town of white-collar types with plenty of disposable income and too much leisure time. Maybe that explains all the wife-swapping that goes on there, of which Abe and Molly are keen practitioners, as are a lot of their friends and associates in the Groombridge Symposium – a local business association.

In 1978 Abe's firm, Premier Construction, lost out on a massive $9 million restoration project in Hartford, in a bid. The winners were, Kean & Butler, a local rival. Lucky for him almost the same week the internal revenue did an audit on Kean & Butler's business operation, following a detailed tip off from an unknown source. They raided their offices and took away several folders that resulted in charges against Kean & Butler of unlawful accounting and tax evasion. It led to a bill for back taxes of $5,678,104, and ultimately the suicide of Simon Kean, the lead partner in the firm. The company then filed for bankruptcy, meaning they were unable to carry out the major public works project and consequently Abe's company, coming second in the bid like they did, was awarded the project. Now you can read what you like into this, but soon after that Victor Martinelli, the former chief accountant of Kean & Butler, was recruited by Abe into a senior position in his firm. If you were a gambling man, would you bet against Mr. Martinelli being the Internal Revenue's 'unknown source'?

Another story that could be of interest is in 1979 Abe fell out with his business partner, Hank Partridge, over a dispute relating to profit shares. Precise details are not known, but just before the case was due to be heard in court Hank's car careered into a tree on Route 8. Within fifteen minutes he was taken by ambulance to a hospital in Hartford but died soon after arrival from severe internal injuries. After that his family didn't pursue the dispute with Doyle, because Abe settled with them out of court – probably for a tiny fraction of the figure in question. So, it seems like Abe has a fairy godmother, or someone up there (or maybe down there), watching over him. Don't you think?

Moving on: you specifically asked for any details that were available about the death of Abe and Molly's daughter. As you know, she was one of twins – both girls - Vanessa Maria Agatha Doyle, and Juliette Eva Alexandra Doyle: born June 21st, 1967, at the Banbury Medical Centre in Connecticut. Records state that it was at the same hospital at 2.05am on July 23rd, just four weeks after she was born, that Vanessa died. Cause of death is sited as pulmonary embolus (which I gather is some kind of clot to the lung). But the coroner's report is a little too succinct for my friend's liking. The medic assigned was a Dr. Richard Fenwick, friend of Abraham Doyle and long-term member of Groombridge Symposium. The coroner was Professor Stephanie du Cann, wife of Richard Fenwick and member of Groombridge Symposium. The judge at the Coroner's Court was Justice Peter Marson, a good friend of Margaret (or Mollie) Doyle, and a member of the Groombridge Symposium. It's also worth noting that the cremation was done in a real hurry too. Oh, and the funeral director at the burial was James Clarkson, also a member of the Groombridge Symposium. Can you see a pattern building here?

I asked Matt, my friend at the bureau, to give me whatever he could on the Groombridge Symposium. I thought it might be like some kind of Rotary Club, dishing out support to children's groups and third world charities and the like. And it does do some of that. But it seems to be hard to pin down what the real point of this organisation is. If anything, it's closer to Freemasonry than Rotary, though it has many women members. My friend at the Bureau said *there is evidence of an esoteric side to this organization, but he didn't have much time to dig up any more on that, though he may be able to at a later date.*

I have to say, I'm kind of curious. In all the years I've known you, you never showed a propensity for detective work, building up character profiles, or hunting people down, other by means of RV, of course. So, what's all this about?

Anyway, don't be a stranger. Call me up if you're ever in these parts.

Ciao.

Mitch

As soon as he'd read it, he rushed off to the bedroom and nudged Isobel awake.

She turned around, sat up to rub her eyes and then glared at him. "What the hell time is it?"

"Mitch wrote back. I'm going to need your help, Izzy. We need to do a session."

Chapter 26

It was snowing heavily as Gary followed Fiona out of the gallery, when she stormed out hugging her elbows and tensing her shoulders, trampling along the sidewalk in shoes that were totally inappropriate for the conditions. What a waste of an evening. There was still over an hour and a half on the meter when he found her waiting for him by the car. She didn't look at him as he unlocked the door to let her in. She leaned her head against the side window, wiping her eyes and sniffing theatrically. He got in and sat down by the wheel, trying to think of something to say. "You want to pick up a Chinese?" was eh best he could do.

She gave him a look of disgust, so he just started the engine. They were home in less than ten minutes, neither of them having said another word. After parking up, they walked across Greenwich Avenue. He felt sorry for the long line of people outside the jazz club. Some of them were stomping up and down on the spot to keep warm, and others were brushing snow off their shoulders. Whoever's playing there tonight must be really good, concluded Gary.

Upstairs Gary unlocked the door and Fiona blew past him like a gust of wind, heading straight for the bedroom, and slamming the door behind her. It needed a braver man than Gary to follow her. So, he sat down to watch the Giants and the Dallas Cowboys over a couple of beers. Just when it was getting tense (in the last quarter) she decided to come out and sit on the armrest near him. He realised this was his cue to switch off the game.

"Do you think I'm going a bit crazy?" she said.

He cleared his throat and tried hard to think of an appropriate reply. The best he could do was: "Oh, you're upset, is all. Jenny is your friend, and understandably... the way you see things, Alan was, you know..."

She opened her eyes wide and furrowed her brow.

"I know what?" she said.

"You, uh, responded in a way which you thought appropriate when you saw him just now."

"Hm. And you're saying I went a bit overboard?"

Gary took a sip of his drink, and there was a moment there when they were both waiting for each other to react. Finally, Gary found he couldn't stop himself spraying out a mouthful of beer and laughing like a hyena. It was the best thing he could've done, because she started to giggle too, before reaching over to hug him around the neck. She lifted his arm around her shoulder and rested her head there.

She had a sullen look when she asked, "Do you still think Alan is an OK guy?"

From her reversion to baby talk, Gary realised she was giving him an opportunity to make a case for Alan. He gave it his best shot.

"It's not as simple as that," he said. "What he did to Jenny was totally, totally wrong. I know that. But the important thing to remember here is that he didn't know it was Jenny. It was like a waking nightmare. And when he realised what he'd just done, well he was, uh, you know… absolutely distraught."

She moved out of his arms and sat up straight to face him. Her already dark complexion erupted into an even darker shade whenever she was angry.

"Oh, I see. He thought it was some other woman?"

"No, no, no! That's not what I'm saying. Jesus. Look. He was having some kind of episode. He had this terrible dream, he believed he had this hideous, half-dead thing next to him on the bed, so he lunged for it. But… it was Jenny."

Fiona shook her head.

"He told me a while back that he occasionally gets these kinds of a flashbacks. He dropped a tab when he was an art student, and he had a bad trip. It totally freaked him out: his thoughts went all kind of sinister, focusing on death… depression, bad suff."

"So, he was a dopehead."

"No, no, no. He was a student. He was just experimenting. It's just that, well… his constitution was not suited to psychedelics. And you know, it's a medically accepted fact that lysergic acid, can cause flashbacks years after the event."

"Oh." She nodded a few times, "That's very reassuring. So basically, what you're saying is... he could do something like this again?"

"What? No. You're not listening to me…"

"Pf. All this crap about him not being responsible for his actions, I bet that's what every wife-beater comes out with when they're pushed into a corner. Well, I won't fall for it. I still can't believe Jenny doesn't want to press criminal charges. I want him completely out of our lives. Do you understand me, Gary Cummins?"

She stood up, hands on hips, and gave him her intense, schoolmistress stare, and repeated very slowly: "I-said-do-you-understand-me?"

Fiona's intensity was not to be challenged. Yes, he had to work with Alan every day. He was his partner – and friend. Creative teams that don't have the kind of camaraderie going on are missing something. And Fiona was demanding that he put the kibosh on it all. Bang! He thought for a moment about telling her the truth about what Alan was really going through, referring to Robert Stringfield's book. But he knew very well that she would never have the patience to listen to that kind of reasoning, especially when the supernatural was involved. Like the novocaine that blocks patient's ability to feel pain, her scepticism bars any sensory data that doesn't fit with her well-ensconced worldview. Gary was sure that if Liz ever saw a ghost at the end of the bed, she'd find a way to deny it, because to do otherwise would be to blow away her worldview. He considered that maybe someday the piecing together of disconnected facts will reveal such a terrifying picture of reality, and the insignificance of our place in the universe, that even extreme sceptics like Fiona will either go mad or flee from the terrifying light of disclosure into the false safety of unknowing in a new dark age. But her attitude to the supernatural was deeply entrenched. So now he had to split from the best art director he ever had. Nevertheless, he needed her. She was his little Fi. There was no choice: what she was saying was: 'It's either him or me'.

The next morning at work was a bit awkward. Alan came in way after Gary did (as usual). He looked sheepish as he took off his coat, so to break the ice Gary said he was just going off to get some coffee, did he want anything?

Alan nodded. "Sure. Strong black, one sugar."

Ten minutes later, while he was checking his email, Gary pushed the door open with his backside and carefully placed his paper cup on top of a copy of Advertising Age that was lying in front of

Alan. After that, he sat down, chin in his hands, staring at Alan, who was looking at the steaming coffee as if it was a thing of wonder.

"Drink it," he said. "You look like you need it."

Alan took the tiniest sip and said, "I've decided not to fight Jenny's demands."

"You what?" said Gary in surprise, causing coffee to dribble down his chin. He wiped it on his sweater. "What about the fucking exclusion order? If you don't do anything about that, you won't even see your kids."

Alan took off his watch and started fiddling with the winder.

"This watch is useless... "

"Never mind the fucking watch."

But Alan just kept on winding. Then he looked at Gary and said, "Last night… I don't blame Fiona for saying what she did."

Alan's downheartedness was worrying Gary.

"Look bud, you don't have to be so magnanimous, really. I should be apologising. She was.... You know, out of order. Emotional."

"She was right."

"That's bullshit. I love her to bits - but her mind is about as open as Fort Knox. Anyway, she's got this regular phone call thing going with Jenny right now and - well, you don't need me to tell you…"

"Gary, listen. Fiona is one of the loveliest, most genuine people I know. She wears her heart on her sleeve, that's all. I just hope that one day all of this, settles down, and things can get back to how they were."

Gary leaned back into his seat and breathed in deeply. Alan frowned.

"You don't seem too hopeful."

"No. I'm thinking… well, it's kind of related."

"What?"

"Look, there's no easy way for me to say this, because you're not just my art-director, you're a buddy."

"And?"

He leaned forward, chin still in his palms, elbows on the table and rubbed his eyes with his fingertips. "I am going to ask Steve to team me up with Jack," he said. "Sarah is going on maternity leave, and the likelihood is she's not coming back anytime in the next three years. Her husband is a Wall Street trader, so there's no pressure to earn a buck or anything. So, Jack needs a writer."

Alan said nothing. He didn't even show any kind of response. Gary expected him to at least put up some kind of argument. Maybe they would even get into a shouting match, or something. But there was none of that. Alan simply pouted, then furrowed his brow, as if he was answering a trick question in a pub quiz. Then he nodded and said, "OK."

It didn't seem right.

Next morning Gary got into work early, as usual, and after sitting down to go through his messages he found there was an email from Alan saying he wasn't feeling too good, and he had a sore throat. But he might come in later.

He didn't.

Gary was furious. There was a ton of stuff to get through. He tried to call him at home several times throughout the morning, but he didn't pick up. By lunchtime he gave up and started working on the initial pitch ideas for Cheerios on his own. In the afternoon he decided to call Juliette. Surely, she would know where to find him. But she didn't pick up either. He then left a message for her at Juilliard. At one point Steve popped his head in the office and asked where Alan was. Gary just said he'd picked up some kind of virus.

Steve took a deep breath then said, "What the fuck?"

This was not good for Alan, or Gary.

Working on his own, Gary somehow managed to come up with some semi-decent ideas for the pitch. The trouble was they all needed more thinking, and the only way that would happen is if he could bounce things around with someone else, whether that was with Alan - or whoever. Just as he was packing away to go home, he got a call back from Juliette. She sounded a bit out of breath and apologised for getting back to him so late in the day, but she'd been at rehearsals. He asked if Alan was staying with her. She said no. He wanted to stay at his place the night before. But she did say she would go around there to check out if he was OK. (She had a key).

Back at their apartment in West Village, Fiona and Gary were sitting down to their supper, while watching TV when the phone rang. They thought about ignoring it, but Gary had a feeling it was important. It was Juliette. She sounded concerned. She said Alan was not home, and his bed had not been slept in. Did he think Alan may have flipped and got a flight back to London maybe?

Gary felt a wave of pins and needles pass through him. He didn't know what to think. He wasn't hungry anymore. Fiona asked what was going on. He told her Alan may have taken a flight home, and she just snarled and said if he went anywhere near Jenny he would be arrested and locked up. Gary needed some space to think, so he used the bedroom phone to ring round the airports: JFK, Newark – even La Guardia, just in case Alan was getting an internal flight somewhere (God knows where). They all came back to say that there was no Alan White registered for any flights yesterday or today, or tomorrow. Gary knew he had a good friend in LA, so maybe he took a train there, or maybe he even hired a car.

Alan didn't show up to work the next day either, but Gary was ready for that. He had arranged to hook up with Brian, another art-director, and they got down to working up the pitch ideas Gary did the day before. By lunchtime they had four solid routes to explore.

In the afternoon Gary had a meeting about some work for an existing client, with

The account team, Brendan, Elaine and Christine, in one of the smaller meeting rooms, which was interrupted by Steve's PA, Jackie, knocking on the door.

"Phone call from your wife. She says it's urgent."

He took the call in his office.

"Hi Fi. I'm in a meeting." He could tell she was snivelling. "What's up, honey?"

"Oh God."

"What the hell is it?"

"I got a call from Jenny just now."

"Is she OK?"

"She's fine, given… given the circumstances."

"What circumstances?"

"She just got a call from NYPD. Alan's body was fished out of the East River this morning."

Chapter 27

Robert sat in the leather armchair, dreamily checking out the lights of the West Side across the white blanket of the park. An antique copy of *Saducismus Triumphatus* opened in his lap, but he had enough of reading and was weighing up the idea of rolling up a special cigarette. That was when Isobel breezed into the lounge in her messed-up dungarees, wiping paint off her fingers and making noises like she was in pain:

"Argh! I hate doing portraits of rich people who refuse to sit and then don't even let you take a proper photograph for reference."

"Turn the job down."

"I can't. She's my biggest patron."

"Who?" he said twisting around to face her.

"Philomena Steinberg. Who else? Heiress to the du Pont billions, if she lives long enough to inherit."

Isobel came closer to him and bent over his shoulder to get a look an illustration in his book of a bat-like demon summoned by witches.

"Jesus, What the hell is that?" she said pointing.

"You wouldn't understand," he said.

She gave him a look of contempt and threw the rag onto the coffee table.

"So anyhow, I'm ready now. You still want to do this thing?"

He slammed the book shut. "Let's go."

They had everything set up in his office, as before. The EEG monitor was fine-tuned, Isobel set the lighting on low. Robert sat in his usual chair.

"Right," he said. "Thanks to Mitch we know where Abe and Molly Doyle were living at the time. We also know that their girls, the twins, Vanessa and Juliette Doyle, were born on June 21, 1976, and that one of them died four weeks later."

"So, what does that mean?"

Robert looked up at the ceiling in disappointment.

"The first full moon after they were born was Sunday July 11, 1967," he said. "So that's my target. I'm going to check in just before midnight that day."

She bit the bent knuckle of her forefinger. Then she spoke while wincing, as if she was pained or embarrassed by what she was about to express.

"Robert, I'm only going to say it once, but I have a really bad feeling about this."

"About what?"

"I don't know. That weird couple, the one's in Alan's dream - your obsessiveness, everything."

"C'mon, how many times have we done this? Two hundred? Three?"

She shook her head, with a look of sadness and confusion.

"My sensitivities are not as finely tuned as yours, but my radar is up. And that's the truth."

He went over to kiss her on the forehead.

"I'd say you're tired from the work you put into your show. You need to slow down Izzy. After this maybe we should spend a few days on the coast."

She looked up at him with watery eyes and said, "That would be nice."

While Isobel set the dials on the electroencephal-ogram (EEG monitor), Robert dimmed the lights further and sat down facing the empty chair. She left the room to get changed while he relaxed through the various mental states. By the time she came back, in her French fisherman's striped sweater and a smart black skirt, he was sinking into a calm, warm and velvety beta state. As usual, she sat opposite him and picked up the target folder, taking out a piece of paper and holding it out to him. He looked at it and noticed that Isobel's short hair appeared to glow, because of the soft light behind her, making her look like a religious icon. Slowly his head dropped, as he reached the theta stage. He was now in the zone.

She put a pencil in front of him, which he picked it up dreamily, along with a pad of paper that was clipped to a board. Isobel then started reading out the coordinates.

"Seven, three, two, seven, one, nine... four, one, one, seven, five, eight."

As he listened he sank deeper and deeper into his theta state. She took the pad from him to get a good look at it. He'd drawn a circle made up of much smaller circles with a small rectangle inside it, near the top.

"Is it a sort of clock that's stopped," she asked.

"I don't know'" he replied, as if in a dream.

"Well, there are thirteen circles going around, so maybe it's not a clock."

"No."

"So, what is it?"

He looked back at the drawing and his left eye started to water, as he dropped the pencil and grew more and more limp. A part of him was loosening up. The room seemed to be dissolving. Somewhere there was an intense tingling going on. He was aware of a dual consciousness that was out of synch with everything around him. There was a body there, but he was only loosely connected to it. For Robert Stringfield, the room was made up of pulsing semi-transparent squares. Nothing seemed fixed. Everything was fading at the edges. It stayed that way for a while before things began to settle down and he was able to focus on looking into those squares, to go in... deeper and deeper, until he lost track of his original perspective. He was a completely disembodied consciousness. Complex, kaleidoscopic patterns shifted around chaotically, disorientating him. He closed his eyes, but it made no difference, because it wasn't his eyes that were seeing – it was his mind. Soon several green dots appeared from nowhere. They were aligning themselves into an endless series of squares over a violet background. His thinking had become more focused, as he relaxed even further, floating between the complex arrangements of squares. Eventually the saturated colour drained away leaving behind a nighttime scene of rooftops, roads, driveways and countryside. He was falling gently now, like a feather in a breeze. A tingling sensation ran through him as he was floating in a swirling blue-grey mist. A woman's voice came from somewhere.

"Relax Robert. Get a sense of where you are. Let yourself find it. Focus on the coordinates."

It was a relief to know she was there.

"What can you see?" she asked.

He had to concentrate. Communication was not easy in this state.

"A big moon low in the sky and some dim stars between ominous clouds. I've... I've got a visual of a rooftop... a grey one. Hold on..."

He was shifting involuntarily around the target and had to summon all his will to make his position more stable.

"OK now?" said Izzy.

"Mm."

"Good. What are you seeing?"

I had to think hard. "I... I...I'm now at street level outside this large, white, colonial house... A gust of wind is bringing in the fresh, faint smell of the sea..."

"Good. What else?"

"There's a classical portico and a large lawn with a white picket fence on the street and a row of healthy-looking red roses behind it. Huge elm trees all around... and I'm getting a strong whiff of freshly mown grass.

"OK..."

He paused for a moment to re-connect to his innate syntactical abilities so he could describe what he was seeing, while he adjusted his movements in this phantom state.

"Parked outside the front lawn at the end of the gravel path, behind me, there's a big blue car, a Pontiac, I think. I'm looking round now. Wait... a thin man in his forties wearing a fitted leather jacket and Wyatt Earp moustache is leaning against the driver's door of the car, picking his fingernails with the nails of his other hand. Someone is calling him. Let me look back. Yes. A slightly shorter, but overweight guy in a lightweight and heavily crumpled suit is walking towards him from the house... waving aggressively to him to get into the car. Then the big set guy is going back to the porch – looks like he's waiting there, like a nervous best man at a wedding. The house door is opening and... yes. It's them. Abe and Mollie Doyle are stepping out of the house. They look much younger than the photo of them Mitch sent us. She is blonde and fair skinned, about 38. Abe is a little older, with a slightly receding head of medium length brown hair. They're each carrying a white bundle in their

270

arms. There's a baby inside each bundle. The big guy in the crumpled suit is closing the front door and follows, catching up hurriedly to open the car doors and let them each in at the back; first Mollie, on the near side and then Abe at the far side. Now Fatso's getting in at the front."

"Get in with them."

"Me?"

"Yes, you."

"OK. I'm in the back of the car behind Abe and Molly Doyle. The baby Molly is holding is crying and it's woken up the other one who is just starting to do the same. Mollie's taken out two dummies from a small bag, and... she's put one in each baby's mouth. It does the trick. They're quiet now. Suck, suck, suck."

"That's enough with the sound effects."

"Looking at the road now... the town is thinning away. We've passed two large industrial warehouses, and there are hardly any streetlights. Beyond the suburbs... approaching the outskirts, moving along country lanes. Dark, thick woodland either side of us. The babies are looking back my way – obviously not at me... they can't see me, but they're watching the furry dice hanging at the back. The atmosphere is quite solemn. The fat guy's asking, 'We nearly there yet?'

The driver is throwing him a quick glance and nodding, like he's too cool to speak."

For a moment Robert lifted off the chair and then jerked back again.

"What was that?" asked Isobel.

"Sorry. A bump. The road just dipped a bit. OK now. In the headlights I can see the tops of bushes and tall trees jutting out of a sort of mist in front of us. The higher branches to my left are showing up black against the starry sky - even more so in front of the low, swollen moon. Abe Doyle has just said something. He's asked the guys in the front to put on some music. The fat guy is clicking the radio on, a Country Music station. The DJ is announcing a song, by Hank Williams - Long Black Limousine.

There's a long line of mourners driving down our little street
Their fancy cars are such a sight to see

They're all of your rich friends who you knew in the city
And now they finally brought you back home to me
And…"

Robert was suddenly startled. "FUCK!"

"What is it?" said Isobel.

"The view in front of me, including the back of Abe and Molly, as well as the two guys sitting in front, was swinging in and out of focus because a huge, monstrous yellow truck pulled up out of nowhere. Its headlights were blinding.

We steered away and were inches from smashing into a huge oak tree over to our left. Hold on… Abe is shouting something. The driver's saying it wasn't his fault. The argument has cooled down now. He straightened up and we're continuing, turning left into a narrow road where the branches of the tall trees are leaning over us either side, and meeting up over our heads, making an arboreal archway. There's another bump. The driver is swinging left onto a muddy verge.

"They're all getting out of the car now. The driver's grabbed a pile of stuff from the boot. Looks like sacks. No. No… It's clothing of some sort. Abe and Mollie have given the babies to the driver and the fat man while they put these, sort of, monk's habits on."

"Can you fast forward a little," asked Isobel.

"OK. Abe and Mollie are fully changed into their monastic robes, hood up. Now the other guys are handing the babies back and putting their outfits on. They're locking the car and setting off into the woods."

"Robert. Now slow down into real time again."

"Right… OK. They're walking silently along the soft, dewy grass. Both the babies are asleep. Occasionally, a small frog croaks. Weaving through the trees in single file. The guy who was driving the car is leading the way. I think his name is Russ. At least that's what it sounded like when the big guy called him. It's dark, but I can see a faint glow among the trees in front of me.

We've stepped into a sort of clearing. In the distance, I can see a bobbing lantern. The person carrying it has approached from the direction we're heading. He is talking to Russ and the big guy, but I can't hear what they're saying. OK. Now we're on the move, following the lantern carrier. The air is oppressive and warm. There's drizzle. Surprisingly both babies are quiet as our mini procession continues. We're back among the trees, which are reaching an imposing height and the ground either side of us seems to be rising into banks, as if we're walking along a dried-up riverbed. They've started to move a bit faster ahead and Abe and Molly are struggling to keep up. The trees are thinning out. I'm looking up at the big fat, dark clouds – but the moon is still in a clear area of sky. We're over the ridge. There are more points of light glowing in a hollow ahead of us. Lanterns. A few closely packed trees now, and then... we're coming into a clearing now. Like a meadow. Shadows and silhouettes caused by all the lanterns. It's still hard to make out exactly what's happening; there are quite a few other people dressed up in monk's gear – with hoods up... Hold on. I'm getting chromatic aberration now. Like there's some kind of weird interference going on... having trouble keeping it together."

Isobel touched his knee. "That's just transitional noise. Pay no attention to it. Just focus on the target. Breathe slow. Relax."

He took a deep breath and continued.

"Some of the people's faces are catching the lamp light. They're like actors readying themselves for something. This must be what my ideogram, my drawing, was pointing to. It's this circle of people: thirteen of them, with one lantern in front of each – and the square 'font' (that's just a flat-topped piece of granite) in front of a slightly raised plinth. This clearing is a natural amphitheatre. I feel a terrible coldness, not from the weather – it's a warm night. What am I anticipating?

There's quiet conversation and mumbling going on. Reverential. Like in church, a congregation preparing for mass. The whispering just stopped, as if someone flicked an off switch.

Abe is passing the baby he was carrying to one of the other people. I think it's a woman. Now he's standing at the font, like a priest about to perform a baptism. He's raised up his arms to make a 'V', in a gesture of power and shouting 'In the name of the Holy Master!'

At this point, from Isobel's point of view, it seemed as if Robert was trying to fight off being sick, like he was swallowing bile. He coughed and spluttered.

Isobel looked worried. "You OK?"

"Queasy. Not sure why."

"OK. Take it easy. Breathe slow. What's happening now?"

"Someone just rang a bell. Abe Doyle is speaking in a low tone, building up towards some sort of invocation. Saying something about the four corners and the elements and… now he's almost entering a euphoric state – kind of self-hypnotising. He's invoking Lucifer, I think, and mentioning the names of what sound like demons, Yog-Sothoth, Dagon and Azathoth, conducting the emotions of the congregation like one of those slick Bible-belt preachers. The whole circle of the congregation seems to be entering a kind of trance-like state now. They're like stems of barley in the wind."

"Can you tell me exactly what he's saying?"

"I'll try…"

'Lord of Darkness… I Beseech You that… You shall receive and accept this which I offer to You, I, upon whom You have set Your mark, I ask for thy unfailing guidance, to be purged of all conditioned ignorance… that has been forced upon me!'"

He stopped talking again. Isobel prompted him. "Yes?"

"One of the babies…"

"Yes, go on." What is happening to the child?"

"Mollie has handed her baby to someone, and she's now approached the font. The other baby… someone gave it to Abe. He's taken off its wrapping and laid it down gently on the font."

"Yes? Robert. Robert!"

"Horrible… horrible."

To Isobel it seemed that Robert had become completely numbed by whatever it was he was seeing. His voice became high, as if he was being strangled. It was horror mixed with anguish.

"I can't go on," he said.

Isobel tutted. "C'mon, you're a fucking war hero. Grow up. Of course you can go on. What would be the point of stopping now? Man-up and tell me what you see!"

"I-I-I see them…"

"See who?"

"Mollie and someone else are holding the baby down…"

He didn't tell Isobel that he could hear a prayer to Lucifer, which he knew was a literal translation of one that had been used by various covens in the eighteenth century, in and around Lyons in France:

"Deliver us, Lucifer, Lord of Light, bringer of Enlightenment,
from all past error and delusion,
with the Fires of Hell purify the void of my mind.
For we walk upon the Left Hand Path and have vowed to ever serve you.
We travel through Boundless Darkness illuminated by the Black Flame,
the breath of divinity at the very core of my being,
the Light of Lucifer infused."

Then Abe chanted alone:

"O Dark Lord, I am Thy Faithful Child,
I do trust in your boundless power and might.
It is through You that gifts come to us, knowledge,
power, wealth is yours to bestow upon Thy Spawn.
I renounce the spiritual paradise of the decadent and weak,
for I place my trust in myself and in You,
God of the Flesh, God of the Living.

In the darkened office, Robert was gritting his teeth and tightening his fists so hard that his knuckles became white.

The initiates were writhing around feverishly, while still forming the circle. Their movements becoming more vigorous and jerkier, and somewhere else in time and space Robert's pulse was beating faster. He was too shaken to describe what he was seeing. He heard a woman speaking softly… it seemed full of love. Was it his mother? Or a nurse?

No, he remembered. It was Isobel. Her voice echoed, as if coming from inside a deep, cave.

"What are they doing now?" she asked. "Say something, Robert."

He took a second or two to unravel his thoughts.

Dassos Petrou

"I can't look," he yelled. "This place reeks of horror, perversion and death. I saw some terrible things in Nam, but nothing as sick as what these fucks are doing…"

He was almost sobbing now.

"Robert. Relax, slowly. Breath slow. That's it. Good… good. Excellent. Now *look*. Tell me what is going on there.*"

He could feel her gently wiping away the tears from his cheeks. He was trembling now.

"Someone has just handed a long knife to Abe."

Isobel now took a deep breath. "Oh Christ. Go on…"

"He's taking it and… and twisting back round to face the font again… gripping the handle with both hands. Everyone is chanting and… oh God."

"What?"

"He's… he's lifted up the blade high above his head, and it's pointing over the baby and… No."

"What?"

He let out a terrible scream. A wave of misery and pain swept through him.

Now he was shouting hysterically.

"He's plunged the blade into the baby's stomach. The baby made a horrible, ear-piercing shriek and blood spurted out like a fountain into his face and Molly's. Their faces are covered with little red spots."

Isobel put her hands to her mouth. She was speechless.

"The baby is making horrible gargling noises… arms flailing. Then they drop. Now it's just making a sort of dry rasping sound. It's over. M-M-Molly is taking a metal goblet and she's holding it underneath the edge of the font… She's collecting the blood."

Isobel was now standing up and moving away from Robert.

"It's half full now… and the person holding the other twin has stepped forward. Ugh. Molly is making the other baby swallow the blood."

"Sick fucks." Said Isobel.

"The baby is coughing, can't take that much liquid, but Molly doesn't care. She has a smiling, leering face. Sadistic. She is enjoying the baby's horror and discomfort, forcing it to drink more."

He could hear Isobel crying in another place – far from here.

"Now Mollie Doyle is drinking the blood, the crazy bitch. Callously wiping her upper lip with her tongue while passing the goblet to Abe. He drinks, smiles and passes the cup on. When they are done passing the goblet around Abe becomes master of ceremonies again."

Robert was crying so much that he couldn't repeat what they were chanting then:

Hail Lucifer, and Hail all the Gods of Liberation, by whose assistance we are liberated in conscience and in heart! Hail Thyself!
And so, it is done!

"The woman wearing glasses is ringing the bell again," he said. "The ceremony has ended."

Robert's phantom body dropped to its knees, while his physical body slumped sideways, falling onto the floor with a thud. Isobel helped him up, back onto the chair again.

"Robert? Robert. Listen, I want you to come back. Let everything go now and come back."

Her voice was like a cool summer breeze, brushing softly past his ear. He felt a brief sense of release, and his eyes flickered open. Small beads of sweat had formed on his forehead. He looked up and saw Isobel in soft focus, sitting in front of him again, tears running down her cheeks. He rubbed his eyes. he was exhausted.

"They can't be allowed to get away with it," he said.

"What can we do? You read that report from Mitch. They have so many friends in high places, politicians, law enforcers, police and the media. No charges have ever stuck against these two. They're untouchable."

Robert took the glass of water Isobel offered him and drank, soiling some down his chin and shirt.

"Oh no they're not," he said.

Chapter 28

Robert couldn't shut out the memory of the evil grimace on that depraved woman's face as she drank the blood of her own daughter. He fell against the back of the chair, exhausted, bewildered and almost feverish. Another wave of nausea was welling up inside him. The odour of corruption, and sickening images of the demented and perverse ceremonial he had just witnessed were choking him with grief. Isobel gave him time to rebuild his composure. Slowly he began to recover to the point where she felt he could converse.

"What are you going to do?" she asked.

"I'm going back," he said, with calm authority.

Isobel was stunned. "What?"

His expression hardened. His gritted his teeth and his cheek muscles rippled. His eyes had the look of death. His steely resolve horrified her. She knew there was no dissuading him. He had become a warrior again.

She stood up shaking her head and frowning in disbelief. "You're crazy. You don't know what you're saying. Here, drink this."

She handed him a glass of water. He took a sip and handed it back to her, saying nothing. The sentient part of her was terrified. She smacked her hand on the table and glared at him, with such anger and frustration that he had to lean back and squint.

"Who the devil do you think you are? What can you hope to achieve by going back? You'd only end up watching passively as the whole thing unfolds all over again, and suffer the whole experience all over, for what? You're tired. You need a break. It's pointless to even think of going back."

She stood up. "I'm hungry," she said. "Splash some water on your face and let's go get a pizza. We haven't seen Gino for ages."

He shook his head slowly. "Later maybe. Got to do this thing now."

She sat back down and sucked in her lips. He could see she was getting a handle on where he was going with all this, because she was looking distressed.

"Robert. You're not thinking of pulling off what those disgusting black-ops guys used to get up to in StarChild – the ones who wouldn't even speak to us, because they thought we were beneath them – is that what you're thinking?"

He shrugged. "I'm going to do what's necessary, Izzy. That's all. I need to go back in."

"You're way out of line. You have no idea where to start. We are not schooled in that type of thing. Forget about it."

"How do you expect me to forget about what I just saw? We can't let that shit go. These people are evil."

"It happened twenty-one years ago, Robert. Leave it alone."

"Time is not linear, Izzy. You know better than anyone."

She closed her eyes, leaned her head back and sighed. He stood up and walked over to the coat stand and came back with a packet of Camels and lit one up with a silver Ronson.

Neither of them spoke. He lit another one for her and put it on her lips. Her hand was shaking as she took it out of her mouth.

"Are you going to help me or am I doing this thing on my own?" he said.

She blew a thick plume of smoke in his face. "You are one stubborn son-of-a-bitch."

He was thinking about how he would make this up to her as she was setting up the monitor again. Maybe he could take her to Mexico for a couple of weeks, to escape the winter. She came back and stood over him to make sure he was properly wired-up and then sat down again.

"Let's get this over with," she muttered under her breath.

Robert put his hand on her shoulder.

"What is it?" she said. "I thought you wanted to get on with this."

"Yeah but... Izzy. This is going to be a little bit different."

"What are you getting at?" she said.

He put the side of his fist to his mouth and coughed. "I want to do this without questions and answers."

She leaned her head back. "Huh?"

"Stick with me on this," he said. "It's not a big deal, really. I will do the viewing then come back. It'll be quick, I promise you."

"But..."

"Trust me."

She sunk back into her chair. "Whatever."

It didn't take long for him to reach the alpha wave state again, and then he drifted quickly into Theta. At first there was a restless kaleidoscopic blur. He was becoming dizzy, experiencing a kind of vertigo, leading to a feeling of drifting through a wind chute, while flashing, coloured lights flicker on and off all around him. He felt as if he was being sucked down into a spiral for what seemed like an age, before jerking to a sudden stop. The scene ahead of him was a complete blur, but it eventually came into focus, at first seeming to be a stained-glass window version of where he was before, when he was in the car driving to the woodland clearing with Abe and Molly, Russ (the guy with the Wyatt Earp moustache) and the Big Guy sitting in the car in front. Eventually the saturated colour drained away leaving the stark reality and the shadows. This was the moment where the car was leaving the outskirts of the town, on the way to the ceremony in the woods. One of the babies was making cooing noises and looking through Robert at the furry dice. He was sure the child could see him in his transcendental state. This was something new. In the past, he had always been an inert observer. He never became involved in the events unfolding in the viewing. His group were taught that interference was impossible. But that was a lie. Somewhere there was a quiet echo that sounded remarkably like Isobel, and he heard it saying, "No. You can't do a one-eight-seven, not in a viewing Robert. No! We don't do that!" It kept repeating, and then it faded, like a gust of wind in the fall.

He knew what he had to do. It was something he was never trained for, but he had heard what was possible from a guy in the Manta Ray section. He needed to merge with the driver's mind, to become an invading floating consciousness. He ghosted into the guy's head, seeking dominance, forcing out the seedy thoughts he encountered in the driver's head, crushing them, forcing them into oblivion, like an unfair battle between a turbocharged group of deadly wasps against a hopelessly unprepared gathering of somnambulant bees. Robert's consciousness began vaporizing the other's memories, his intentions, and his instinctive attempt to defend his brain, but with less and less capacity for resistance. Soon the Robert's thoughts were the only ones left. The hands on the steering wheel were his now. And as he took control, he was instantly shocked by a gigantic yellow truck pulling out of a sharp bend and turning precisely into his path, on a collision course. The driver's heart rate shot up, but it wasn't Robert's heart, so he drove head on into the yellow truck. Then blackness. There was an enormous pounding. Everything shook. Robert pulled his consciousness away, out of the driver's mind, through the roof of the car, into the air. The impact sent the car spinning over, into the verge. It was now a twisted wreck.

The moon was still low behind the dark woods to Roberts left. The horrified truck driver screeched to a halt and jumped out of the cabin. Only the front headlamps of the truck lit the scene. The upturned Pontiac rocked for a bit and then became still. Robert waited, hovering nearby, until he could hear crying: two babies crying.

Then everything was sucked into blackness. Robert's breathing became heavy – and there was a glaring flash, searingly painful in its intensity. Slowly it faded into glowing blobs floating in front of him. When they finally dissolved away, he could see he was in a shadowy room. He sat in darkness for a while, waiting for his breathing to slow down to normal as he began to pull out of the theta state, moving away from preconsciousness to wakefulness. For a while he didn't have the strength to get up out of the chair, and he dropped back down at the first attempt. The adrenalin was still rushing through him, but he was exhausted, emotionally and physically. His thoughts were cloudy, but as the fogginess dissipated, he realised that things didn't look right. The furniture was repositioned and there was a sense of untidiness that Isobel would never have tolerated. And where was Isobel? She would never leave him during a viewing. He called out her name and waited. Nothing. Again, he tried to get up. On this attempt he was able to stumble forward towards the door to his office. He wondered along the hallway awkwardly, almost as if he was sleepwalking and went into her studio. He leaned against the frame of the door, waiting for his sense of balance to come back. It was dark in there, so he reached for the pull-string. But there was no pull-string. There was only a wall switch.

"When did that happen?" he wondered.

What he saw in there left him in shock. Instead of her easel and canvases there were piles of dusty cardboard boxes and bags. This was now no more than a storeroom. This was all so wrong. Then an idea struck him, and he went over to the cabinet in the lounge to pull out his photo album and sat by the coffee table flicking through the pages with photographs of himself and Isobel at Langley with Mitch, Jerry, Stella and the guys. There were also some pictures of their vacation in Sweden, as well as the log cabin in Concorde… but after that he didn't recognise any of the pictures at all. This was crazy. And then he came across a spread of himself and the guys at a funeral. Brett and Stephanie are there, and so is Mitch and almost everyone who had been part of Starchild. But not Isobel. When he turned the page, he came across a picture of a headstone:

Isabel Greene 1941-1989
She made the mundane beautiful

Being so weak, he could barely move. He ended up taking a few steps and standing still again, wondering, fearing and doubting. The silence in the apartment was endless, and the stillness was unbearable. he could only whisper her name, and then he collapsed.

ADDENDUM

Robert discovered that Isobel Greene died, following unsuccessful treatment for cancer in 1989. She had her operation at a different hospital, and by a different doctor to the one who succeeded in removing Isobel's aggressive tumour in the previous reality. Robert visited her grave in Green-Wood Cemetery, Brooklyn several days in succession that winter.

His journal entries become considerably shorter and sporadic after this point. The bulk of them can best be described as incomplete and irregularly composed, loose jottings.

He succeeded in tracking down Gary Cummins to a public high school in the Bronx, where he had been teaching English for several years. Gary is married to fellow schoolteacher Mary-Anne Tracey, with whom he has three children. They live in a small brownstone within walking distance of the school.

The following week Stringfield tried to make contact with his former line chief at Langley, Michael Craig (affectionately known as 'Mitch'). He was hoping this would help him get some things in place with regard to the changes that were now existent. But he failed to make contact*.

Stringfield then traveled to England, making his base at the comfortable and discreet Brown's Hotel in central London. From here he set about tracking down Alan White. After searching public records for a couple of days his investigations led him to an address in Canonbury, North London. He found that Alan lived there and worked as a (not very successful) sculptor. Stringfield took a bus there from Piccadilly the following week. He had prepared a cover story about having an interest in moving into the area, and he wondered if this particular property was for sale. When he found the house, Alan White opened the door but did not encourage conversation. However, when Stringfield feigned interest in the sculptures on display in the hallway he was invited in. Eventually Stringfield commissioned a bust from Alan, which he agreed to sit for over two days. Alan's wife, Melanie Elisabeth Leech, is a wealthy city banker. She was away on business in Zurich at the time. They have no children.

Stringfield spent an additional three weeks in London in an attempt to track down Jenny White, but not knowing her maiden name, or even her date of birth the quest proved fruitless.

On returning to New York, Robert used the information he remembered from the hospital records of the birth of Vanessa and Juliette Doyle. He discovered that a local court handed custody of the children after the crash to a half-sister of Molly Doyle, who lived in Montreal, Canada. Christine Devereux was not on speaking terms with her sister, but she accepted the responsibility. Christine and her husband Trevor had no children of their own, and they were clearly devoted to the girls. Vanessa and Juliette took on the surname of their aunt and uncle and were educated in a convent on the outskirts of the city. Trevor was an insurance salesman at the time. Stringfield learned that Vanessa and Juliette Devereux had graduated from McGill University recently. Juliette majored in Film and Vanessa achieved a First in Art History. They now live in a small apartment above a vintage magazine shop in 8th St. Juliette works as a junior assistant to the editor of a magazine. Vanessa was a waitress in a bar in Greenwich Village when Stringfield went there and sat down to order a coffee. Vanessa was the girl he had fought so desperately with on the floor of the house in Cold Spring in another reality, the girl who had been transformed to a demon by her evil parents, existing in limbo – unless she was made manifest by sexual contact with a victim. He was totally struck by her gentle nature and her beauty. She had a mole high up on her left cheek, which was very becoming.

At this point he becomes a little more informative in his journal:

"On a dull, warm afternoon, I wondered downtown to the café in Greenwich Village. It was one of those oak panelled places, with a huge chandelier and wooden floor. I recognised her instantly. She wore a white blouse and newly pressed black skirt. Her long black hair was tied in a ponytail, and her eyes were violet. She had a definite shyness about her. I managed to start up a conversation after making my order, by asking if a facsimile painting on display was by Rubens. Her accent had a Canadian flavour. She said 'aboot' instead of 'about'. I learned that this would be her last week as a waitress, as she recently had a successful interview to become a photographer's

284

assistant. She stopped talking to give me a look of concern. 'Mister,"
she said. "Are you OK? Why are you crying?"

MATTHEW BLACKWOOD and LAWRENCE DE FRIES
Atlantean Research Group,
Vancouver, August 22, 2007

*Through the efforts of several members of our group we have
discovered that 'Mitch' now works for the office of Naval
Intelligence.

Dassos Petrou

LAST ONE IN

It was a dull October Monday morning, and the sun was struggling to break through a blanket of thick white cloud (and failing – as usual). Dan made his way through the crowds emerging onto street level from the northeast exit of Tottenham Court Road Station. Reaching the grey, concrete monstrosity of the YMCA, he turned into a tree-lined street that led directly to his current place of work in Bloomsbury, leaving the bulk of the crowd behind him. Opposite the modernist Trade Union Building, he stopped at a little Italian café for his usual cappuccino and two slices of buttered toast. Soon after he left there, he couldn't resist studying some sable brushes that had caught his eye at a fabulous art equipment store just a few shops along, before looking at his watch and realising he was a quarter of an hour late.

He was really chuffed to be working at Pepper. It was a prestigious little production company, so he would be careful not to take too many liberties. The director, Paul Asher, and producer, George Locke, had built up a solid reputation internationally for producing quality animated films. Pepper Films was based in a large building, from the first floor up, at the end of an elegant Georgian terrace. He was just across from it when he charged over the zebra crossing outside the hotel and stopped in front of a black wooden door at the far left-hand side of a shop that occupied the whole ground floor, which specialised in Scottish highland clothing, including tartan scarves, coats, mohair jumpers, and even kilts. Most of its customers were European tourists. It wouldn't be open for business for another forty-five minutes. Its huge window displays extended around the corner into Great Russell Street, leading to the British Museum. Dan pressed the button and waited, eventually speaking his name into the intercom and getting buzzed in, probably by Marion.

He trudged up the three flights of hessian-carpeted stairs to the equally hessian-carpeted layout department studio, which was staffed by just himself and Dino. He reached the third-floor offices and, as usual, Dino was already at his desk, sipping a dry cappuccino from a pale blue cardboard cup, and biting into a ham and cheese croissant, while studying the drawing of a farmyard scene he was about to get stuck into.

Hearing Dan dump his heavy bag behind him, Dino turned around and blinked a kind of hello through his black-framed specs, which Dan immediately understood. Dino was a few years older than Dan and was instrumental in bringing him into the animation business, away from the advertising visualising wilderness, first by recommending him to the producer of an animated feature of Swan Lake the previous year (which led to seven months of work), and now as his partner on this current project, *Bertie Badger Goes South*. Everyone involved in the production was helpful and encouraging to him, from the director right down to the in-betweeners and colourists, so he had settled in very quickly and was doing some good stuff. Dan was grateful to Dino, and Dino was really pleased to have Dan working alongside him. This job offered them both great possibilities because the director, Paul, and producer, George had given them a huge amount of creative freedom in the way they design and style the production, so they were pulling out all the stops to do their best work.

"Hey, Dan. Good weekend?"

Dan started unbuttoning his coat and then he froze for a moment, before bending his torso and laughing at the floor.

Dino shook his head. "Was it something I said?"

"Look, I can't explain it yet. But something happened that I can't work out. I mean it. Let me just explain everything that happened, all the little bits... because, I think I'm going nuts, I need you to tell me what the fuck *you* think was going on, because... to tell you the truth, it's a little bit disturbing."

"Disturbing?"

"Yeah. I'm not kidding. Just hear me out, and you'll see what I mean."

"Is this a wind-up?"

"Will you just *listen*?"

"OK. OK. Go on then."

"Right. So, after you went to the dentist on Friday, I was hunched over my desk working on that fucking thing," he pointed to the five feet long, unfinished drawing of cartoon badgers running away from an angry farmer, in a luscious country scene, which was stretched out on his desk, which was surrounded by various pencils of all lengths and colours, an electric sharpener, two scalpels, a putty rubber and a metal ruler.

"My nose was maybe three inches from the paper, so I was totally zoned out. I must have been like that for a while before I couldn't focus any more, and I had to lean right back into my chair and stretch my arms out. Then I was rubbing my eyes for a bit, and I looked out the window. It was getting dark. The lights were on in the offices at the back opposite. I looked at my watch and it was only twenty past six. I got up and looked to see if anyone was in the room next door. Dead as a doornail in there. Then it hit me. There was no music coming from downstairs."

"Marion must've gone home."

"Or her ghetto blaster was broken."

"I wish. No more Phil Collins and Bruce Springsteen every day."

"No such luck.

At that moment George stepped out of his office hurrying through into Paul's office, uttering, "Morning chaps," and flashing them a less than gracious stare. They took it as a signal to begin work, but it didn't stop them from carrying on their conversation unabated.

"I've never been the last one in the building before," said Dan. "It made me feel, you know… uncomfortable. I had a lot more stuff I wanted to draw, but I just wanted to get out of there. I thought, fuck it and I grabbed my coat and bag and shot out of here. On the way down I saw the light was on in paint and trace. I got curious and checked to see if there was anyone in there. Their white gloves were chucked on the lightboxes and freshly painted cells of Bertie Badger were hanging up to dry. Oh, and Marian's ghetto blaster was left on, with a Bruce Springsteen CD left in its open pocket."

Dino laughed. "No one's going to nick that."

"In the back room some clown had plonked a potted plant on the glass screen of the Grant enlarger," said Dan. "But there was no one in there. Even Christine and Syd were gone."

"That's not like them. Missing out on overtime."

"On the next floor, I went into the background department. It was like a morgue in there."

Dino laughed. "Ha! It's like that even when they're in there."

Dan turned to face Dino with a sneer.

"That's a bit harsh."

Dan was about to respond when a girl with long dark hair, and a hippy-ish style of dressing breezed in from the hallway with a whiff of patchouli oil. She was carrying a pile of green cardboard folders in both arms, which the boys knew were dope sheets that the animators needed to time out their scenes.

Dan interrupted his narrative. "Hi, Nicola.

They both respected Nicola, even though they thought she was a bit eccentric, and because she was such a brilliant animator.

"Hi, guys! Nice weekend?"

Dino looked up at her, smiled and shrugged. "It was too short."

Nicola paused for a moment, pursed her lips and nodded in agreement.

Dan waited for her to go through to Paul's office before continuing.

"When I saw there was no one in backgrounds I really felt strange. I had this urge to get out of there as soon as possible, and I don't know why. It wasn't like I had anything to be afraid of."

Dino shook his head and turned back to his drawing.

"This is when it starts to get weird. I couldn't get out."

Dino stopped drawing again and twisted around. "Huh?"

"It's true. When I got down to the ground floor, I turned the handle on the Yale lock, only the door wouldn't open. Someone had gone and double locked."

"The Chubb lock?"

"Yeah."

"Shit. What did you do then?"

Well at first, I lost it. I kicked the fucking door and stood there staring at it and yelling, like I was daring it to hit me."

Dino was back drawing again and chuckling to himself.

"Ha. What were you yelling?"

"Can't remember." He wasn't entirely open about how he felt at the time. He didn't want to discuss how the silence of the empty building was starting to get to him.

At this stage, Dino stopped drawing and turned round to face Dan directly.

"I thought about calling Marian to get her to come over and to let me out, but I don't have her number. Anyway, I don't know how to get an outside line on the phones."

Dino concurred. "Mm. Come to think of it, I don't either. I always go through Eileen on switchboard."

Just at that instant, George stepped out of his office in his ankle-length grey coat, carrying his satchel over his shoulder, followed by his editor (and much younger) French girlfriend, Murielle in a mink jacket, with her long black hair tied in a ponytail. George reminded Dino of General Custer, with his shoulder length and wild ginger hair, goatee beard and a long moustache hanging down the side of the lips. George stopped to look at what the boys were working on, and Murielle went on out to the hallway, not realising.

"Is this the first part of the chase scene?" asked George.

"Yep," said Dino. "Long way to go."

"Did you chaps have a good weekend?"

"I did," says Dino, "but Dan nearly didn't. He was locked in here on Friday night."

"What?"

Dan. "Long story."

George put his hand on his hips and gazed at Dan in mock disappointment.

Murielle interrupted.

"George, we have to be at Portland House in ten minutes."

"Oh yes. See you soon, boys."

After George and Murielle had gone, Dan asked, "Where are the going?"

"BBC. They're trying to get the next lot of funding early. So, what happened next? How did you finally get out?"

Dan sucked in his cheeks and looked up at the ceiling for a moment. He was considering what Dino had just said, which concerned him a bit, because it could mean the budget is being burned up too fast and they could be laid off. But he was also thinking that he wouldn't reveal how he had to struggle to pull himself together when he realised, he was trapped, and how he had to pull himself together to shake off these weird negative vibes he was feeling, that he knew were unrelated to him being locked in.

"The only thing I could think of was maybe getting out through one of the windows onto the roofs and ledges upstairs, he said." So, I turned to go back up and there was a slither of light coming from the back of the hallway."

"What was that?"

"It was coming from the right, under the stairs. I went around there, to the back of the hallway, and saw this white wooden door. It was open a crack, and that's where the light was coming from. I opened it a bit more and saw stone steps going down. There was a sort of slurping sound followed by a rattle coming from somewhere down there."

"Weird."

"I thought there could maybe be a door down there, leading into a courtyard or something, so I started walking down."

"Weren't you a bit worried?"

"I just wanted to get out."

Dan was lying. He felt a shudder up his spine at that moment, and he felt it get colder with every step.

"After a few steps I was looking down on this old man wearing a flat cap."

"Really. What was he doing there?"

"He was busy sucking the meat out of a stack of oyster shells from a dirty metal plate and then throwing the empty shells into a fireplace grate. I think he was meant to be decorating the basement, but he must've been on his break. Quite a big guy, with a white moustache and beard. He was sitting on a paint-splattered bench, wearing paint splattered overalls under a dark, paint splattered suit jacket. He didn't look bothered about me being there at all."

"That sounds weird."

"Who owns that room?"

"I guess it's the landlord of our building, or maybe the shop downstairs. Anyway, he

didn't speak, and the only thing I could think to say was, 'Working late?'"

Dino stopped drawing and looked baffled.

"Are you winding me up?"

"No way. I'm telling you; this is how it went down. He had a small stepladder beside him. There were brushes in glass pots and tools on the floor all around him. He looked up and saw me and chucked another empty oyster shell into the grating. It clattered into a whole pile of other empty oyster shells."

"But how could a painter and decorator afford to eat oysters? I mean, they're not cheap, are they? I've forgotten what the price is for a plate of them in Wheelers. Not that I like them. The one time I tried one, I nearly vomited."

"Well, Wheelers is a restaurant. He wouldn't want to pay those kinds of prices. He must've got them from a fishmonger."

"What fishmonger? There isn't one within miles of Bloomsbury."

"How the fuck do I know. I'm not an expert on fishmongers."

"So, what happened when you got down there?"

He just said, 'Evening lad', in a gravelly voice, then let out a huge burp, and put his fist to his mouth."

"Very pleasant."

"Then he stood up, wiped his nose with his jacket sleeve and pulled out a packet of cigarettes from his pocket. He put one it in his mouth and pointed the packet towards me, with a blank face, not unfriendly, just… kind of expressionless, or maybe it was serious. I felt he was saying, "These are really good, and we're both fellow sufferers in this world, so I'm sharing one with you.' He looked like an old seadog, the kind you see in some of those black-and-white films.

Is that what he said?

No. That's what I imagined he said.

So, what did he say?

"Smoke?"

That was it?

"Yeah. The fag packet was green. Brand I've never seen before: Woodbines? You smoke now and again. You ever heard of them?"

Dino was intrigued. He stopped drawing, and had turned around in his swivel chair to face Dan.

"Yeah," said Dino. "I've heard of Woodbines. Do they still sell them?"

"Well, *he* had some. And I noticed there were quite a few empty packs in the fireplace too, mixed in with the pile of empty oyster shells he'd thrown over there."

"Weird. So did you take one?"

"Why would I? I don't smoke."

"Just to be polite."

"I suppose I should have… anyway, I didn't. I just asked him if he had a key to the front door. I told him that I worked upstairs for Pepper Films, and that everyone had gone and left me locked inside without a key. He had a think about that, and sat back down again, and took a box of Swan Vestas matches that was lying on the bench beside him and lit his fag. Then he spoke with the cigarette still in his mouth.

"I ain't got one," he said. "Me gaffer's got one, but he's nipped out. He'll be back after he's knocked back a couple of bevvies."

Dino chuffed at that. "Sounds like a bit of a retard."

"No… I'd say the opposite. I thought he was deceptively clever and shifty."

Dino, who was still facing Dan, was now quite entranced by all this strangeness in the basement. He scratched his nose and said, "What made you come to that conclusion?"

"To be honest, I can't say. It's just a feeling I got while I was there… that he wasn't to be trusted. There was something not right about him. I don't know if it was his eyes, his lack of expression, or that I might've felt he was lying about not having the keys.

So, I asked him if I could wait until his mate came back. He took a long drag on his cigarette and breathed out a couple of smoke rings. It all seemed a bit arrogant and nonchalant to me. I didn't like it.

"Couldn't tell you, son," he said. "Might not be back till the pubs close – know what I mean? He does like his drink."

Dino shook his head. "What a wanker."

Dan shook his head. "Yeah. That's what I thought. He seemed a bit devious, to be honest. But I was too stressed out to think about that too much because I saw there was a small window near the ceiling that I might be able to squeeze through.

"Does that open up," I said, pointing to it.

"No idea," he shrugged. "Never tried it."

Dino laughed. "Helpful sort of chap. A bit 'Right Said Fred."

"You could say that. Anyway, he didn't object to me moving the ladder over a bit to see if I could get it to open. Trouble is, I kicked a jar of dirty turps with a paintbrush in it onto the stone floor. That got him animated. He started to get up, but sat back down again after his arse hovered over the bench precariously a moment.

"Oi! Steady on, lad," he said, thumping himself back down again.

"I was going to pick up a rag to give the milky spillage a wipe, but he told me not to bother. So, I stood up and dragged the steps over to get up to that window. I could only get up about five steps before my head hit the ceiling. I then managed to lean forward to look through the dirty glass of the rectangular, tea tray size window into a small, narrow paved courtyard, bordered on three sides by tall Georgian, dark-bricked buildings. I wiped away some of the dust, and to the right I could make out a black, wooden gate about seven feet high. I thought it wouldn't be that hard to clamber over, if I could get through this goddamn window. It had a little lever lock, which I lifted up, and then I took a step down, so I could stretch my arms right out to get more strength into it, and pushed with all my strength at the window, which was hinged at the top and designed to open outward. I pushed with everything I had, you know I can lift a couple of hundred pounds in the gym, but it was completely stuck. I couldn't shift it a single millimetre."

Dino was vaguely interested in all this, but he turned back to his desk, being conscious of the fact that his drawing needed to be done by the end of the day, as the animator, was starting work on this scene the next day.

"What did you do, smash it?"

"Bollocks, did I. My idea was, if I could scrape away some of that thick paint that had sealed the joint, I could maybe prise it open. I turned around to ask the old geezer, "Hey mate, you got a screwdriver so I…""

But he was gone. The bench was empty, and so was the room.

"What? He must've gone to the loo or something."

"No. He was gone. That was it. I climbed back down the ladder and ran up the back stairs to the hallway to find him. There was no one there. I tried the front door again, but if he had gone out, he locked up behind him again. I guessed he must've been lying about his mate having the key. I thought he must have always had the key, and he just let himself out."

"Maybe he just went upstairs"

"No. I went back up. I never found him. Anyway, he didn't have any business being up here. George and Paul never mentioned anything about having decorators in."

Dan and Dino suddenly became alert, when they could hear stomping coming up the stairs, but it was just Marion. She came in carrying another pile of dope sheets in their green cardboard folders. She stopped abruptly, on her way through to Paul's office, to look at the boys' drawings, on her way to Paul.

"He-y-y-y. Nice work, guys."

They replied in unison, "Cheers Marion."

She turned to address Dan directly, with an expression of pain.

"Oh gosh, I'm so sorry. I hear I locked you in on Friday. Honestly, I know it's stupid, but I thought everyone had gone home. And I was in a terrible hurry to meet Amanda – we were going to see Aladdin. I didn't realise the time, and when I looked, I was running late. I didn't have time to do the usual check, and I just went halfway up the stairs and yelled out, 'Anyone there' and of course, I got no reply. I thought it was empty up here."

Dan shrugged. "Oh well…"

Dino laughed and said, "I bet he had his headphones on listening to Prince at maximum volume, Marion."

"It wasn't Prince. It was the Commodores… probably Nightshift," said Dan. "I listened to it about ten times on Friday. Love that tune."

"And that's why you were locked in here, doing the Nightshift," snapped Dino.

Marion just looked mournful, and Dan wasn't impressed.

Just as she was about to ask Dan how he managed to get out, Paul's voice bellowed from the other room: "Marion!"

She looked at Dan and then Dino, her eyes wide with fear and with her left lower lip twisted low, revealing her teeth gritted. Then she hunched her shoulders and hurried sheepishly away.

Dan and Dino waited for her to go, before snickering quietly. They both turned back to their work. They carried on working that way without speaking for a while. Eventually Dino felt satisfied with himself, arched himself right back and yawned.

Dan looked over and laughed. "What's the matter? Didn't you get any sleep last night?"

"Not much. Sally and me were watching Godfather Part II till God knows what time. Then we entertained ourselves for a while, if you know what I mean… So anyway, what happened after you found out the old man wasn't there."

Dino swivelled around on his chair to face Dan to find a combination of fear and laughter written on Dan's face.

"Shit. By then I was mad, you know – steaming. I just wanted to get the fuck out of this place, and that whole fucking basement incident was like a horrible joke. I don't know what it was all about, but the old geezer was a timewaster, wherever he was now. I'd had enough. I didn't have a plan or anything. I just ran straight back up to the first floor again, because I couldn't think what else to do. I went into the background studio and groped around in there to switch on the lights. The two windows in there had locks on them; you know, the ones behind Alan and Fiona's desk. No chance of shifting them and I looked in all the drawers and I couldn't find any keys in to open them up. I tried the next floor, in animation and then in production. Same thing there. Those fucking steel, oval window locks are a bitch. I tried every window on every floor. It was useless. By then I was going bonkers. The adrenaline was starting to pump now, I was shaking, and I think that's why I knocked over the statue of the Badger, you know, the main model the animators use for reference. A bit of the ear broke off. It was on Nicola's desk when I squeezed around to try the window in there."

"You idiot. They'll go mad if they find out. That cost George a fortune to commission from that sculptor from Madame Tussaud's."

"Who gives a shit?"

Dino laughed, but Dan's mind was wandering. They worked quietly for a minute, and then Dino decided to break the silence.

"You still haven't told me how you eventually got out."

"Oh yeah. Well, after backgrounds, I came up to this floor and went through to Paul's main studio. You know there's that door that leads to the flat roof at the back, where we sat and had drinks and snacks in the summer a couple of times when we celebrated finishing a sequence."

"Oh yeah. Is that how you got out?"

"No. It was locked."

"But I suddenly remembered that little cubby hole that Paul works in. No one else is supposed to go in there. It's in the very corner, up a little narrow set of stairs at the back. When he was in the pub with George, Jean, took me in there once to show me the new storyboard he was working on."

"Yeah, I've been up there a couple of times. It's tiny. It must have been the servant's quarters in the days when this building was a house."

"Probably was."

"I remember I hit my head on the low-sloping ceiling. All there is in there is a chair, a single wooden desk, an Anglepoise lamp, a telephone... and a poster from that film he made in the sixties."

"*The Pepper Pot Man.*"

"That's the one. Have you seen it?"

"No. Anyway, I went in there to have a look. There's a single tiny window in there. It's nothing like the other windows – kind of square. More like an original window. Not updated like all the other windows. It didn't feel like a window that you would bother securing. I dragged Paul's chair over and tried to stop it swivelling. Carefully poised, I tried the sash window to see if it lifted, and miracle of miracles, it did!"

"You lucky bastard."

"After that, I managed to lift myself up on the sill and squeeze through. It was quite a squeeze I can tell you. Not much bigger than a tea tray. I went through headfirst, sort of flapping through like a seal and cushioned my fall onto the flat roof with my hands. Meanwhile, the window I came out of dropped shut behind me. I stood up and I went over to see if I could prise it open again, just in case I needed to get back in, because I didn't want to be stuck on the flat roof, four floors up all night. And I couldn't. So that was that. Still, the cool breeze felt good. I brushed myself down and looked around, to see if I could work out a way forward. I looked at all the buildings, all around, you know the upper floors are mostly offices, and I saw there was one window that was still lit. The rest had the lights off, so I guess in there everyone had locked up and gone home. This one window was my only chance. If there was someone in there I could ask for help. Trouble was it was about three flat rooftops further along, and I'd have to climb over a few low walls to get there – and, of course, I'd be trespassing. But what else could I do?"

"So, you were doing a Spiderman."

"Not quite. Anyway, I got over there, it was about fifty yards from our building, The wall that this window was in butted right up to the flat roof I was on, so the flat roof I was standing on must have belonged to the same building. I manoeuvred myself into a position where I could look directly into those windows, set in the black brick wall of a tall Georgian building. I stood to one side of the window because I wanted to be hidden at first. I didn't want to frighten anyone. What I could see was there were two girls in there, sitting at a long desk: probably young graduates, that sort of age. Casual, jeans and jumpers. They were putting these little objects, that I couldn't make out, into little, brown, square cardboard boxes, and writing something on the lid. I could see there were shelves full of these boxes filling two walls. I thought, fuck it, it's now or never, and I went close and knocked hard on the glass. They looked up at me straight, and it was obvious I scared the shit out of them. I pointed to our building, which was behind me then, and shrugged – trying to express the fact that he was not a burglar – or anything. I waved frantically and shouted a bit, but they couldn't hear through the double glazing. They watched me for a bit. One of them was more confused than scared, and she went off, out the room, leaving her friend a bit nervous, still watching me, the strange black man standing outside knocking on their window. Soon the other girl came back with this guy in uniform. An old fella, a bit bald, dark hair, glasses. He looked at me for a bit, and then he opened the window and held it up, inviting me to crawl through. The guy took one look at me, shook his head, and told me to follow him, as the girls just stared in disbelief. I wanted to laugh, but I thought if I did, he might call the police or tell me to get back out there. He told me to go out and followed me down a few flights of stairs. We came out on the left side of the courtyard of the British Museum. There were these huge black wooden double gates ahead of me, that I guess would be opened to let lorries through. He opened one up, and I came out onto Great Russell Street. "

"Fuck me, you were so lucky. He could've easily called the police and kept you in there."

At twelve-thirty, Dan and Dino decided to take their lunch break, and as they came down onto the ground floor hallway and were about to open the front door, a small girl in her early twenties, with beautifully long black hair, and wearing a green, tartan skirt, black polo neck, black tights and ballet shoes, while carrying a pile of jumpers, in their celluloid packaging, rushed past them both and through to the back of the hallway. Dino stopped Dan from stepping out into the street by grabbing his shoulder.

"Hold on Dan. That girl works for the clothes shop. She's taking those boxes to the basement. Let's see if your old geezer is still down there, working on decorating the basement.

Dan looked a bit baffled.

"You can't just ask to go down there…"

"Just watch me."

Dino rushed over to her, with Dan nervously following in his wake.

"Excuse me," said Dino. "Sorry to interrupt, my name's Dino and this is my colleague Dan. We work upstairs for Pepper Pot Films. The thing is, my friend here, he got locked in on Friday, and he says he ended up speaking to that guy you've got decorating down there."

The girl looked at them both, slightly perplexed. "What guy?"

Now Dan answered. "There was a guy decorating down there on Friday. Well, he said he had a mate who was out, for some reason. He was on his own when I found him, having a break from his painting and decorating."

The girl looked at Dan and leaned back as if she'd just eaten something odd tasting."

"You must be imagining things. There's no one decorating for us down there. That's our stockroom, and it was locked up all weekend. I'm the only one who's been in there since Friday.

"What? No – that can't be."

Dino felt he should step in to resolve the confusion here.

"Look, sorry love. What's your name?

"Sarah."

"Sarah. Is there any chance that we can just take a quick look at the room, just to put my mate's mind at rest? I'm beginning to think he was dreaming the whole incident."

Dan protested. "I was not."

Dino ignored him. "Can we?"

The girl thought for a few seconds and seemed to conclude that they were harmless enough.

"Take these". She gave Dan the pile of sweaters to hold on to and then took out a set of keys from her skirt pocket and opened using two different keys. She then pushed the door in, switched on a light inside, and took the pile of sweaters back from Dino.

"Right. Follow me."

Dino and Dan entered, and Dan stood frozen, halfway down the carpeted stairs. He could not believe his eyes. There was no stone floor – just wall-to-wall carpet. The entire room was filled with boxes, neatly stacked. There were also a few clothes rails, with items of clothing on hangers squeezed in on each rail, including sweaters, coats, and jackets. There was hardly any room to move down there.

"B-but what happened... how is this possible? All this stuff... who moved it back in here?"

"What are you talking about?"

"All this room was empty apart from a step ladder a bench and some pots of paints on Friday. How..."

The girl was getting agitated now.

"Sorry guys, but I must lock up and get back into the shop. It gets busy at lunchtime, and I've left my friend on her own in there."

A thick blanket of cloud loomed overhead as they walked towards their usual restaurant in Covent Garden. Dan was in a daze as they negotiated the obstacle course that was the crossing of New Oxford Street, on Shaftesbury Avenue. On the other side, Dan broke his silence.

"I don't get it. I mean, what happened to me on Friday in that fucking basement? Who was that old man?"

Dino just laughed. "Dan, I have no idea, but I tell you now – I believe you. I don't know what it was, but I know you well enough to know you're not lying. Sometimes, the laws of reality crumble. They sort of just stop operating for a short time, nothing seems right. Reality is relegated. There's no explanation for it – it just happens, not for long. Before long, everything just goes back to normal. I've experienced it myself."

"You have?"

"Yeah."

"What happened?"

Dino pursed his lips and seemed anxious. Then he overrode his concerns and gave a sigh of relief.

"Christ, I haven't spoken about this for years, but when I was a kid, I had a conversation with a tramp.' He looked down as he walked, then shook his head and continued. "I was about seven years old, I think. This tramp, his trousers were knotted at the knee like sausages, because he had no lower legs. I was with a school friend my age, David White. We heard this voice calling us as we were walking to the school gate and we looked down to see this bearded, filthy tramp sitting on the pavement, leaning his back against a brick wall. He looked up and kept firing questions at us, and we felt compelled to answer them because it would have been rude for us to walk away. We had it rammed into our heads in those days by all our teachers, that we must never be rude to adults – ever. But this tramp was making us feel nervous with his questions. We just wanted to walk on… I felt I had to think of something to break the spell because that's what it felt like – a spell. And then I got this idea that I would ask *him* a question. I did that, and it had an effect."

"How?"

"He suddenly stopped talking, just for a moment. I must have surprised him with what I said. I must confess, I felt really pleased with myself, thinking how clever and mature I was, to come up with something like that."

"Weird."

"Yeah, well it got even weirder, because suddenly he let loose this horrible cackling laugh, and vanished."

"What do you mean?"

"Poof! He was gone. He wasn't there anymore."

"What?"

"We were just left looking at the pavement he was sitting on and a bit of the wall he'd been leaning against. We were completely stunned. My friend wouldn't talk about it ever again. When I tried to bring it up a bit later he got so angry, we had a fight over it."

"That's mad. So, what question did you ask the tramp?"

"I just said, 'Where do you live?'"

301

"Is that it?"

"That's it."

"Shit."

"Yeah. That's what I thought."

The sun came out as they strolled past Freud's wine bar before turning into Neal Street. It changed the atmosphere completely. People all around had an extra spring to their step and at that moment Dan suddenly realised how hungry he was.

Soho in the Dark

SOHO IN THE DARK

They went out of the square towards Dean Street, passing through the throng outside the Guinness bar, and every step they took Alan could see that Jason was becoming visibly more and more lethargic. They carried on, along the narrow alleyway where Private Eye Magazine was based, which was just around the corner from one of their favourite lunchtime venues, the faithful old Star Café. But this was no time to think of food. Turning into the road with the Old Hat Factory, they headed towards Wardour Street. It was getting dark now, even though it wasn't that late. Confused, Alan looked up to see a massive cloud spreading itself across the sky, a black duvet moving in slow motion.

Reviews from the 2nd Edition

Watkins Bookshop
Leading Esoteric Bookshop in central London
A fine addition to our London Mysteries section – stories that are full of local esoteric atmospheres that haunt the West End around Soho and beyond.

Atlantis Books
Historic Esoteric Bookshop, Bloomsbury, London
Well written short stories are rather more interesting when the author knows the landscapes – urban or otherwise they are describing. Dassos Petrou has worked in London's Soho and Los Angeles for years and his comfortable familiarity with them and the people who exhibit their 'creature' side when under pressure, especially when it is their damaging, fun for only them, creature, he records in 'horrible' and clever ways. He has seen Soho loose it's tatty image by day, becoming a Boho office space for a few years and now the globally corporate anonymous place of today. But the sex and sordidness that once only came out at night to satisfy punters has grown into a very strong egregore that they still feed. Most enjoyable.

ISBN 978-1-78695-912-6

90000

9 781786 959126